CONTENTS

INTRODUCTION

When I was young, I often woke up screaming in the middle of the night, but it didn't bother me too much as long as I woke up on my bed as opposed to hovering near the ceiling, which could sometimes happen. On those occasions, I usually hit the floor the moment I woke, which was at least as painful as it was embarrassing. Still, as I reflect upon those turbulent years, I must conclude that sleep-hovering was probably the least of my problems.

Before going any further, I should warn you that the story you have in your hands is not a happy one. This may seem pretty obvious, but it is not fun to be lost, scared or injured, and it is never entertaining when someone you love dies. Nor is this a story about courage and noble deeds, for this is the real-life account of many things that I wish had never happened.

If this were a fairytale, it would involve a prince or great warrior. Or perhaps someone who starts off as a nobody but rises to greatness through heroic deeds. In real life, you start off as nobody and usually you end that way too. You do what you can, and what you have to, but no one is destined to live or die, and your fate is determined not so much by courage or brains as it is by sheer dumb luck—or lack thereof.

For the record, there are no ghosts, goblins, witches or vampires in our world, but that doesn't mean there are no real monsters out there. I sometimes wonder if people make up fantastical demons to avoid having to face the real ones living among us every day. There is no great battle between good and evil either. Good is whichever side you think you are on, and evil is whichever side you are fighting, or running from. I am not, nor have I ever met, a true hero.

My experiences have taught me much that I would have lived happier being wholly ignorant of, but nevertheless I have chosen to share my past with you in the firm belief that you would be better off in the know.

Because it could happen to you too.

However, if you would rather dream about wish-granting fairies, noble dragon slayers and other such nonsense, now is the time to put this book back on its shelf.

Still reading? In that case, let me introduce myself.

My name is Adrian. For your own safety as much as for mine, I'm not going to tell you my real full name. I will completely change many of the other names. Let's say that my name is Adrian Howell. I was named Adrian by a distant, part-Italian relative, and the reason behind that is a story in itself that has absolutely nothing to do with this one, so I'm not going to go into it. And no, I won't tell you why I chose "Howell" as my family name for this story. Otherwise, it would be too easy to find me.

I am older and arguably wiser than I was when I lived the events you are about to read. I had a family once, and was young and naive enough to believe that things would always be the way they were. Take this from someone who has been there: Your whole life can change in the blink of an eye, and change again in the next blink. Even end.

And speaking of change...

I don't want to alter many parts of my story because that feels too much like lying. Instead, often I'll just leave certain information out. Not just people's names, but places too. I know that can be annoying to you, but if it were entirely up to me, I would tell you every little detail. Unfortunately, truth is dangerous. There are just too many people who could get hurt, including you.

Anyway, here is most of my story from the start...

1. A SUMMER SECRET

In the early lukewarm spring near the end of my sixth-grade year, our class went on a three-day camping trip up in the mountains, a four-hour bus ride from our comparatively quiet and peaceful little town. We went hiking on a narrow woodland path, fished in a small pond, and slept in sturdy log cabins set in a circle around a grassy field where, at night, we sat around a campfire roasting marshmallows and telling stupid ghost stories. It was the last school trip I ever went on.

On the second night, after the teachers had gone to sleep, some of the bolder girls snuck out of their cabins and into the boys', and some twelve or thirteen of us resumed our storytelling in the dark. I didn't know any really scary stories back then, but when my turn came, I tried my best to impress.

Then something bizarre happened. This was what started the chain of events that would change my life forever. Just as I was getting to the climax of my story (about a bloody ghost that lived in a toilet), a picture frame fell from the wall, its old glass cover shattering into tiny shards.

That the picture fell wasn't what was strange, at least to me. I actually expected that to happen, so I didn't jump in fright. But boy did everyone else! I looked around at my classmates, worried that we might have woken the teachers sleeping in the next-door cabin.

"What is it with you all?" I whispered anxiously. "Couldn't you tell?"

"Tell what?!" one of the girls demanded in a much-too-loud whisper, her voice shaking. The boys didn't look at all better off.

"That the picture was about to fall, of course," I answered, still baffled

3

by their overreaction.

How very, so very wrong I was.

It never occurred to me that it was at all unusual for things to suddenly fall off of walls, shelves and tables. For me, that was just a part of daily life.

Usually there was some pattern of events, and it would go like this: I would be sitting, calmly watching TV, reading, or doing homework when, in the corner of my eye, something would seem to move, and I would look up at it. It was usually a card or a book, or perhaps one of my mother's many ridiculous house ornaments such as a green glass penguin. I would glance at it for a split second, just to make sure that nothing was amiss, though by then, I usually sensed what was about to happen. When I turned my attention back to my reading or whatever, I would hear the crash or soft thud as the item I had just looked at fell to the floor. It always seemed to happen the moment my attention was removed from the object.

When the picture frame fell from the cabin wall, I had sensed that too, and though I didn't actually look up at it while telling my ghost story, my attention did wander to it for a brief moment. It wasn't like I was the one who made it fall. I didn't do anything directly to it. I just knew that it was going to fall. That's really all it was, or so I thought at the time.

What surprised me more was that none of my classmates agreed that it was commonplace for things to suddenly fall off of shelves. After all, it happened once or twice a week in my house, and sometimes at school too, or at least wherever I went. I told them as much.

"That's weird!" said one of the boys, and the others nodded in agreement. "That's a really scary story. Forget about ghosts!"

I was dumbfounded.

After we returned from camp, very few of my classmates made any great deal about what I had told them. Most of them probably thought I had made it all up anyway. But sometimes, when a poster fell off a wall near me (and of course, I knew a split second before that it was about to, as I usually do), my friends looked at me, but I just shrugged and kept my mouth shut. "Weird!" That was not how I wanted to be thought of as at school.

Still, I won't deny losing some sleep over it, for what I once thought was ordinary was now extraordinary, and I knew that I was somehow different. But in what way? Was this power that I had simply the ability to see into the future of soon-to-fall items on shelves? Part of me—the sensible part—hoped so. But another part of me wondered if perhaps I was, in fact, causing the objects to fall. Could it be that I was mildly telekinetic? I had heard stories about telekinetic powers, but I was also old enough not to believe in magic and spells. Nevertheless, here I was, wondering if it was possible to somehow take control of this ability, if, that is, I really had it. The two parts of me, the sensible and the hopeful, feared and wondered, *What if?*

The hopeful won.

One day after school, I spent well over two hours shut away in my room, willing things to move. I stood an eraser up on its end and stared at it with more concentration than I ever knew I was capable of. In my mind, I repeatedly told the eraser to move. It didn't. I tried picturing in my mind that the eraser was moving. It didn't move. I even talked to it. The eraser didn't budge.

Every time I failed to move the eraser, I felt like a fool, but then I would snap back into hopefulness. If I really had this power, what fun it would be to use it at school to disrupt a boring history class! I imagined myself sitting in the classroom and controlling a piece of chalk to draw on the blackboard while my teacher and classmates looked on in amazement. Naturally, I would pretend to be amazed, too. "Weird." I realized that I didn't mind being just that, as long as no one knew. But of course, it was all in my head. The eraser didn't move. It just lay there on its side and did nothing.

One morning, about two weeks later, I was hit by a minivan while running for the school bus.

Actually, I have no memory of the accident, which is probably a good thing because it must have really hurt. Instead, I remember the morning before it. I remember vividly that Mom made pancakes which were a bit soggy on the inside while Dad complained about the cost of getting a new oven. Our current one was nearly baked out. It was a warm and sunny spring morning, and the sunlight hit the table at just the right angle to make me squint and sneeze.

"Cat, stop playing with your food," said Mom.

Cat, at least according to Mom, was not a house pet. Cat is what we called Catherine, who was my sister. She was two years younger than me, and she could be annoying at times. Actually, most of the time. Looking back, I often wonder how different her life would have been too if none of this had happened, but I'm getting ahead of myself.

That morning, Cat was cutting her pancakes into tiny squares and stacking them up on her plate, which even I thought was a bit childish for a ten-year-old.

"Quite a tower you got there, Cat," Dad said amiably as he sat down with the newspaper.

Mom shot him a stern look. "Richard!"

"Oh, right," chuckled Dad. "Cat, eat your breakfast."

"Yeah, Cat, we're gonna be late for the bus!" I said loudly. Cat's elementary school and my middle school were side by side, so we still had to ride the same bus, which was a royal pain in the neck.

I used a butter knife to knock over Cat's leaning tower of pancakes. Cat elbowed me hard, and I pushed back, a bit stronger than I intended, shoving her off of her chair.

Mom's frown jumped from Dad to me. "Addy! Let your sister eat."

"I wish you'd stop calling me that, Mom," I said, grabbing Cat by the shirtsleeve and hauling her back into her chair.

Addy was the baby name I used to be called when I was much younger, and only Mom still used it. Cat liked taunting me with it, but only with a running start.

"Oh, Addy, you know old habits die hard," said Mom as Cat smirked at me.

"At least Dad knows my name," I grumbled, and finished my orange juice in one long swig. "Hurry up, Cat, or I'm going without you and you can come jogging after the bus."

"Adrian, wait for your sister," Dad said without taking his eyes off his paper.

"If you like, I'll go trade her for a new oven?" I asked hopefully.

Dad laughed, but Mom glared. "Addy!"

"Bye, Mom. Come on, Cat, let's go!"

The brain is kind of strange that way. I don't even remember what I had for breakfast this very morning, but that day's breakfast is burned into my memory for life.

The next memory I have is of waking up on a hospital bed with plastic tubes stuck up places you wouldn't believe. I had been unconscious for two days. The minivan that hit me hadn't been going much faster than I usually cycle, but even so, I ended up with a couple of broken ribs, broken right arm, lower left leg, two fingers on my left hand and, of course, a complimentary cracked skull. In short, I was dressed for the pyramids and cursed with a dull throbbing pain that lasted weeks. If it had only been an arm or a leg, rather than both, I might have been able to return home in a few days wearing a cast hard enough to hit Cat with, but as it was, my parents both worked and my home environment wasn't suitable for my recovery, or so the doctors said.

I was moved to and spent nearly two months in the hospital's long-term recovery ward. There, I met a kind nurse I came to know as Miss Julia who sometimes took me outside in a wheelchair, and Cat often came to visit after school along with some of my friends and a bag full of homework from my teachers. It's very painful to laugh with broken ribs, but nevertheless my friends and I were so rowdy that, after repeated reprimands to which we never listened, I was moved to a private room.

And it was in that room that I learned how to do my homework without touching my pencil.

At first, it was just a daydream pastime. If you have ever been hospitalized, or been forced to stay indoors for a few days with nothing to do, then you will know exactly what I'm talking about. Television can be really boring in the mornings and early afternoons, and when you're stuck on a bed, there's not much else to keep you occupied. You can only sleep so much at a time. I whiled away the dead hours staring at the clock and hoping time would go faster so that I could see my friends. They didn't come over every single afternoon, but even Cat's company would be better than none at all.

Sometimes I would concentrate on a picture on the wall, or the get-well cards on my bedside table, seeing if I could make something happen. Nothing ever happened, so I went back to willing the clock to go faster as I slowly fell into a half-sleep in which I dreamt of flying erasers and spinning clock hands.

When I woke, it was nearly six in the evening. No one had visited. I lay there groggy and dejected, wishing I hadn't woken up. Dinner was always at six, but that day Miss Julia did not come with the tray. Although I wasn't really hungry yet, I was beginning to worry that I had been forgotten. I was just about to push the "call" button when in walked Cat.

"Homework, Addy," she said, using my baby name on purpose. If I had been able to get up and do something about it, she wouldn't have dared. At least not at this distance.

I frowned. "Don't call me Addy."

Cat started singing, "Addy-baby! Addy-baby!"

"I'm warning you, Cat!" I growled.

Cat just laughed. "What are you going to do, sneeze at me?"

"You just wait till I get better!"

"Okay, okay. But until then, *Addy-baby,* here's your homework," said Cat, plopping the books and papers onto my bedside table.

"Why didn't you stop by on your way back from school?" I demanded, remembering my original annoyance at her lateness.

Cat rolled her eyes. "That's what I'm doing, dummy!"

"It's 6:30, Cat."

"No, it's not. It's 3:30 like always!" said Cat, and then looked at the wall clock and laughed. "Your clock is fast. Look out the window."

She was right: It was just a bit too bright outside. Cat showed me her wristwatch. I must have only been asleep for an hour and a half. Time had not sped up for me—but the clock had!

The slow pace of life at the hospital was what set me on my path. I discovered that my telekinetic power existed in a small space between consciousness and unconsciousness, that is, between being awake and being asleep. I slowly learned to find that spot, and once I did, I could, with days of trial and error, bring it closer to the conscious side. Or perhaps my consciousness was just becoming more aware of that tricky space. Whichever way it was, less than two weeks later, I could make small objects move. I could make a pencil start to roll across the floor. I could make it stop, and roll back. Eventually, I could even make it stand on end for short periods of time. I also found that erasers and get-well cards were much easier to move than pencils. Paperclips were more difficult, though I didn't discover why until much later.

As excited as I was about my new power, I was careful not to let anyone see me using it. I agreed with that boy at camp: This really was weird. I wanted to understand it far better before I even considered showing it to anyone. As I'm sure you already know, secrets are incredibly hard to keep alone, but for the time being, I kept my mouth shut. Not even Cat suspected, I think.

Once I thought I had gotten the hang of rolling and standing up pencils, I tried drawing a simple smiley face on my notebook. This, I discovered, was much harder. I could get the pencil to stand up on the paper, but making it press down at just the right pressure while moving it in the direction I wanted? Well, it would have been easier doing it with my left hand minus two broken fingers. Sometimes the pressure on the paper was too weak to draw good lines, and sometimes the pressure was too much and I broke the pencil tip. Once, my pencil slipped off the notebook and stabbed me in my right thigh. Ouch! I had to call Miss Julia to help me clean and bandage the wound, and I didn't want to tell her the truth, so she must have thought I was a real klutz to stab myself like that.

Even so, just three days after stabbing myself in the thigh, I was "willing" my pencil to do my homework, slowly writing book reports and doing math worksheets. I had lots of reading homework too, and it was fun to turn the pages without touching them. Useless, really, but fun.

But that wasn't all. By now, I could also lift small objects into the air, which was difficult but far more exciting than turning book pages. Levitation was no different from sliding things across the floor. It just required more concentration. Increasingly tired of being trapped on the hospital bed, I even tried levitating myself, but I wasn't able to do that... yet.

One day in mid-June, I was flying a paper airplane around and around my hospital room. It didn't have to be in the shape of an airplane, of course. It could have just as easily been any small object. But it was more fun this way, and besides, when I briefly lost my concentration, the paper airplane would just glide along until I reconnected with it. It was fortunate too, because that day, Miss Julia suddenly opened the door, and the airplane collided with her forehead. Miss Julia complimented my "aviation skills," thinking that I must have folded and thrown the plane using only my left hand and still it sailed right across the room, landing a bull's-eye. I was left thanking my lucky stars that it wasn't something that looked less aerodynamic, like my toothbrush.

I admit I was sorely tempted to show Miss Julia what I had actually been doing, but I knew, deep down, that this was not the kind of thing you just told anyone about. It wasn't just weird. It was dangerous. What if that airplane had been another sharpened pencil?

It was already a week into summer vacation when I got out of the hospital. There was a welcome-home party with lots of ice cream and cake. Cat spilled orange juice all over herself and the living-room sofa, which I would have found funnier if my mind wasn't elsewhere at the time. My power, while not all too alarming (it wasn't like I was making things explode), was growing too quickly, and I was having trouble getting used to it. All my school friends had come over too, and I had to be careful during the party not to enjoy myself too much because if I got carried away with some game, I might do something I'd have a hard time explaining.

Finally, the last of my casts were taken off, and I was told to get "safe exercise" in the form of non-aggressive sports. When I wasn't commuting to the rehab center, I went cycling and swimming, often with my friends, but sometimes even with Cat. The last two months had brought us a bit closer together than we had been before the accident. Feeling the continuing strain of solo secret-keeping, I seriously thought about showing Cat my newfound powers, but I couldn't trust her not to go blabbing about it to everyone she saw.

Besides, at the time, it seemed as if my telekinetic power was disappearing. After returning home, I found it much more difficult to focus on the things I was trying to move. There were times, especially during the daytime, that I couldn't even make a tissue paper twitch. The distractions of daily life were taking their toll. That's what I thought was happening, anyway, and it didn't bother me very much because the sensible part of me insisted that I was better off being normal. Looking back, I guess my power wasn't fading at all, but growing despite my lack of focus.

And by now, focus was not only what made my power work, but also what kept it in check.

On the hottest day of the summer, four of my friends and I, as well as Cat and three of her friends, were at our local water-slide pool. After a few runs down the slides, the five of us (that's us minus Cat & Co.) were playing water tag. It wasn't easy swimming in a pool full of little waves made by people smacking into the water as they came down the slides. Besides, though my bones had mended well and weren't causing me too much pain anymore, my muscles hadn't fully recovered from the weeks spent in bed, so I ended up being "it" much more often than I would have liked.

My sister wasn't about to make it any easier for me. She and her friends had been watching us for a few minutes, treading water near the shallow end of the pool, when she called out to me, "Adrian, can we play too?"

I almost answered yes. Cat was ten, and would be easier to catch, as would be her friends. But they were *girls.* No, I couldn't live with that.

"No, Cat," I said. "Go back to your slides."

"Aw, come on, Adrian!" whined Cat.

"No! It wouldn't be fair. You girls would be too easy to catch. Start your own game if you want."

"Bet you can't catch me!" Cat smirked, swimming a little closer.

"I don't want you to get hurt," I said. "You can't play with us."

"Addy-baby!"

"Cat!"

"Addy-baby! Addy-baby! Bet you can't catch me!"

That was it! Nobody calls me "Addy-baby" in front of my friends and gets away with it.

I swam toward her, but she knew I was coming. Cat was a fairly good swimmer, but even so, I should have been able to catch her easily. However, she was right: In my current condition, plus the fact that I was already a bit tired from playing, I wasn't about to get near her anytime soon. Cat managed to stay well ahead as she laughed at me, saying, "See?! Girls can swim too! Addy-baby!"

That was when it happened. Cat was near the edge of the pool when she was lifted clean out of the water and thrown onto the poolside concrete. She let out a yelp of pain, having twisted her right ankle landing. I knew perfectly well that it was my doing, but I swear I wasn't trying anything of the sort. At worst, I was just going to grab her and push her under the water for a second or two. I never wanted to actually hurt her.

"Cat, are you okay?" I panted, pulling myself out of the pool.

"I think so," said Cat, sitting up on the concrete. "I hurt my leg. What happened?"

"I don't know," I answered, which was, in part, honest.

By now our whole group was crowding around, and the lifeguard had come over too. He checked Cat's ankle, making sure she could limp well enough, and suggested that we take her home and let our parents decide whether or not to take her to a hospital for an X-ray.

"Did you see that?!" exclaimed one of Cat's friends as we left the lobby of the water slide.

"It was like she was ejected from a fighter plane," said one of mine.

"It looked like something grabbed her and threw her out," said another.

I kept silent, hoping that my camping trip story wouldn't resurface here, but sure enough...

"Hey, Adrian, did you do that?"

"Do what?!" I asked, trying to cover my fear with an annoyed tone.

"You know, like you said at camp. That things sometimes move when you look at them?"

"It was a story, okay?" I said, my voice rising higher. "How can you compare that to what just happened?! I didn't do anything!"

"Okay, okay! Don't have a fit, Adrian. Just asking, you know."

Nothing can bring out emotions better than the truth. And the truth was that I did do something that day. Something I had inwardly feared ever since I realized that I had this power: I had hurt someone with it. It wasn't fair to Cat that she didn't know what had happened to her.

Near bedtime that day, after taking my bath and changing, I knocked on Cat's room door. "Cat, can I come in?"

A moment later I heard Cat answer, "Yeah, okay."

My sister's room was next to mine on the second floor. I used to just barge in whenever I needed to, but Cat was ten and a half now and I would be thirteen in October, and we respected each other's privacy.

I opened the door and stepped through, glancing around her room. I hadn't been in here in a while, and some of the posters had changed a bit. Sitting at her desk, Cat was in her pajamas too, having taken her bath right after dinner.

"What are you doing?" I asked, trying to keep my tone casual.

"Just reading." Cat held up a magazine and looked at me apprehensively. Did she already know what I had done? Maybe she thought I was going to throw her again.

"Can we talk?" I asked cautiously.

"Oh, come on, Adrian! It was just a little joke! I promise I won't do it again, okay?"

"Do what?" I asked, wondering what I had missed.

"You know..." said Cat, and silently mouthed, "Addy-baby." I was so caught off guard that I actually stared at her for a moment, my mouth hanging open.

"Cat, I—I don't care about that!" I sputtered. "Call me whatever you want. That's not what I want to talk to you about."

Cat gave me a surprised frown. "Oh. Well, what do you want to talk about?"

"Um, yeah... Well, hey, Cat, is your ankle okay? I mean, does it still hurt?"

Cat blinked twice, and then said, "I'm fine. You know that. I was okay at dinner, wasn't I? You know, you're acting really strange."

"Really strange?" I repeated. "No, I'm just getting warmed up."

After swearing her to absolute secrecy, I told my sister everything that had been happening these last few months. I even gave her a demonstration, first by making an eraser fly around her room, bouncing it off the walls and ceiling, and then by making one of her dolls move through her doll house. I couldn't actually make the doll walk properly, but Cat got the idea.

"So you threw me out of the pool?" she asked.

"I swear I didn't mean to," I said. "It was an accident. I just lost control."

Cat narrowed her eyes. "You lost control?"

"Yeah. I mean, I wasn't even trying to use my power on you at all, to catch you or anything. It just, sort of... happened," I said uneasily. "I'm really sorry, Cat."

Suddenly Cat grinned widely. "Can you do it again?"

"What?" I asked, incredulous.

"Can you lift me up?" Cat asked excitedly. "Can you make me fly? Like you did with the eraser?"

"Of course I can't," I said. "That's just an eraser. You're much bigger."

"But you did it at the pool, didn't you?"

"I wasn't trying to, Cat," I said, shaking my head. "Like I said, it just happened."

"Come on, Adrian. Can't you at least try?"

"Cat!"

Cat looked at me imploringly. "I want to fly! Please?"

"So far, I've only moved things that aren't alive, like pencils and cups," I protested. "I don't know how it would work on a person. It might really hurt you."

"You didn't hurt me at the pool," said Cat. "I hurt myself when I landed."

"But it might not be the same this time."

"Please-please-please! Come on, Adrian! I promise I'll never call you Addy-baby again."

I sighed heavily. "You already promised that a moment ago, not to mention like a hundred times this year."

I knew well enough by now that I was going to lose this argument. If Cat was nothing else, she was persistent. That was probably why my sister so often got her own way in my family.

"Oh, Adrian, you came in to apologize, right?"

"Well, yeah..."

Cat grinned. "Then you can do this for me instead."

"That makes no sense at all," I said, scratching the back of my head. "Alright. But don't say I didn't warn you!"

Cat jumped up and gave me a big bear hug. My ribs still hurt a bit.

Disentangling myself, I gave her a stern look. "Cat, since you obviously can't land like one, I want you to go stand on your bed. No, actually, sit down on your bed so there's more space between you and the ceiling. And take your pillow and hold it over your head."

Cat did as I told her to, sitting cross-legged on her bed with her giant yellow psychedelic flower-patterned pillow held firmly over her head. She looked like a mushroom.

"Ready for takeoff, Captain!" Cat giggled nervously.

"This probably won't work, you know."

Cat gave me an impatient scowl. "Just try!"

At that moment, it occurred to me that the sensible thing to do would be to pretend I tried and failed. I ignored that thought and focused on levitating Cat.

I soon discovered that size did matter. It was like learning my power all over again. The focus had to be just right, evenly spread all over Cat and her crazy pillow. Then it had to be powerful. Just like weightlifting. Minutes went by as I concentrated all of my consciousness on lifting my sister into the air.

"My arms are getting tired holding this pillow," whined Cat. "Can I just balance it on my head?"

"No," I breathed through clenched teeth, "and shut up!"

"Adrian! I think it's working!"

She was right.

Cat was now hovering a few inches off of her mattress. She was still cross-legged, though her feet were sagging down a bit and her toes were lightly touching her bed. I lifted her higher, halfway between her bed and the ceiling.

"Wow!" shrieked Cat. "I'm flying! I'm really flying!"

"Be quiet, Cat!"

I was no longer clenching my teeth, and I realized that I had gotten a little used to her weight.

"But this is so great!" cried Cat.

"Mom and Dad will hear you," I hissed. "Be quiet!"

Sure enough, there were two rapid knocks on the door and I heard Dad's voice say, "Cat, what are you doing in there?"

Cat panicked, pulling her pillow off her head, and I panicked, losing control.

Crack! Cat hit her head hard on the plaster ceiling before falling straight back down onto her mattress.

Dad opened the door just as she landed.

"Cat? Adrian?" he said. "What are you two up to in here?"

Cat got off her bed, wincing painfully, her right hand pressed firmly over what was sure to become a towering bump on her head.

"We were, um... just talking," I said, trying to look innocent.

"Doesn't look like it," said Dad. "What were you talking about?"

"Flying," Cat said casually.

I froze. Was Cat about to spill the beans on me?

"Flying, huh?" repeated Dad, eyeing Cat's hand on her head. "You mean you were talking about flying or you really were flying?"

Cat laughed. "Just talking, Dad. You know I can't really fly."

Dad gave her a slight frown. "Aren't you getting a little too big to be jumping up and down on your bed?"

"Sorry," said Cat. "But Adrian said I'd feel weightlessness if I was falling.

Just like an astronaut!"

"Adrian!" said Dad, shaking his head.

"Well, it's true," I said lamely. I had, in fact, said that to her once, not too long ago.

"Is your head okay?" asked Dad.

"I read it in my science textbook at the hospital!" I answered defensively.

"I was asking Cat," Dad said dryly before turning to my sister. "Do you need any ice?"

"No, it's not that bad, Dad," said Cat, removing her hand from the bump.

"Okay. Just don't break the mattress. Or the ceiling," said Dad, chuckling as he left the room.

Cat and I looked at each other for a moment, and then Cat smiled broadly and whispered, "Ouch."

We burst out laughing. When we finally stopped, Cat looked at me and said in an awestruck tone, "That was *amazing*, Adrian."

"Yeah, amazing you didn't break your neck," I said, getting up to leave. "We're not doing that again."

"Well, not indoors anyway."

"Nowhere, Cat!" I said firmly. "I mean it! Not until I can control it better."

Cat smiled playfully. "So you'll do it again when you can control it better?"

"No promises."

"Okay, Adrian. But I really had fun. Even at the pool. Hurt my leg and bumped my head, but it was still fun. Really!"

"Glad you enjoyed it," I said. "You won't tell anyone?"

"Did I tell Dad just now? Don't worry. I won't tell."

"Okay. Well, goodnight, then, I guess," I said, walking to the door.

Cat grinned. "Goodnight, Addy-baby."

"Yeah, whatever. Goodnight, Cat."

Cat had been my first experiment with the living. In the days that followed, I learned that there wasn't that much difference in the essence of what I did between living and non-living when it came to moving or lifting them. However, not only did size and weight matter, but the complexity of the object was also important. A table is heavy, but it's basically a big lump of wood, which is a single material. A person, on the other hand, was much more complex, with skin and bones, muscles and organs, solid and liquid.

There was something else, too. Metal was harder to move than any other material. I first thought that this was because metal was heavier than other materials, but after a few experiments in and around the house, I found that it was easier to levitate a stack of glass plates, a brick, or even a small tree branch than it was to move a handful of coins. Between metals, aluminum was much easier than steel.

And here's the killer part: My telekinetic power was greatly affected by how much metal was near me. If metal was actually touching my skin, it weakened my power so much that I couldn't move a single strand of hair. Back at the hospital, I had lived in a cloth gown, and what I thought was a dip in my power after I came home was actually caused by things like the zipper on my jeans, my belt buckle and, worst of all, the stainless steel back of the wristwatch I wore during the day. No wonder I had the strength to throw Cat out of the pool when I was floating in water wearing only swimming trunks, and how I managed to lift her in her room when we were just in our pajamas.

This weakness to metal contact was my first real breakthrough in keeping my power under control. I took a short length of copper wire from Dad's toolbox and wrapped it around my right ankle, hidden under my sock. The wire completely negated my power, and I was normal again. I was sure that there would be no more accidents like the one at the pool.

Of course, knowing how to limit my power only made me bolder. After all, as long as I was careful to wear the wire when I was with my friends, I could keep practicing when I was alone, or, as often was the case now, with Cat, who stuck around me more than ever. It was easier sharing this secret with someone, even if it was with my little sister. I still occasionally worried that she might tell her friends, but Cat turned out to be a better secret-keeper than I gave her credit for.

One of the few ways in which our parents were really cool was that, ever since I turned eleven, they stopped hiring a babysitter for Cat and me when they left us at home. They weren't trying to be cheap or anything. After all, they did pay who-knew-how-much for my private hospital room. They just believed in giving us some room to grow, and that philosophy didn't change even after my car accident. Mom might go ballistic over a broken vase or stained rug from time to time, but provided we didn't burn down the house, it was ours to do with as we pleased. It was the ideal training ground for secretly developing my powers.

It was now mid-August, and Cat and I were enjoying the last few weeks of summer vacation.

"Higher, Adrian!" cried Cat.

"No! Someone will see you."

In the fading afternoon light, Cat was zooming around our backyard on my telekinetic roller-coaster ride. I could keep her afloat for nearly two minutes at a time before having to rest and catch my breath. I was exhausted after half an hour of this and I knew that I was losing my concentration, so I set her back down on the lawn as gently as I could. We lay on the grass for a few minutes, breathing heavily. For me, it was more tiring than exciting, but I was happy too. I felt that I had mastered my power at last. I had, in fact, done nothing of the sort, but at the time, I believed that things were going to get better and better. I was actually looking forward to going back to school and attending my next history class, or rather what I was going to do to it.

Suddenly Mom's voice rang out from inside the house. "Addy! Cat! Dinner!"

My heart missed a beat. I had thought Mom was going to be out until much later. I hadn't heard her enter the house or cook dinner. I shuddered to think what would have happened if Mom had walked into the backyard mid-Cat-flight.

Cat might think this was just a fun new game, but I was sure Mom would want to have me checked at a hospital. It was all just too unnatural, and I was afraid that if any adults found out what I could do, being called "weird" at school might be the least of my problems.

Cat, apparently unconcerned, skipped up to the path leading around the side of our house, stopped, and smiled mischievously.

"Come on, Addy-baby!" she taunted. "Mom says dinner!"

She took off as soon as I stood up. Knowing perfectly well she expected just that, I sprinted after her. I almost knocked over the TV as I tore through the house trying to catch her, but Cat had a knack for timing, and she was safely seated at the dining table under the watchful protection of Mom by the time I caught up.

As soon as Mom's back was turned, Cat stuck her tongue out at me. I made a green pea jump up from her plate and hit her nose.

We both laughed.

2. THE BERSERKER

After Mom and Dad had gone to sleep that night, I was standing in the middle of my room making a book fly around me, flapping its covers like a bird. I thought I heard a strangely rough and deep voice off in the distance. I let my book fall to the floor and wondered where the voice had come from.

An instant later, it felt as if someone was stabbing my forehead with a burning hot knife. The headache had come so suddenly that I first thought I was being physically attacked, but I was alone in my room. The stinging pain was unbearable even at the start, but then it got worse. I fell to my knees, clutching my head and trying not to scream.

And suddenly, just when I was about to cry out, the pain vanished as if it had never been there. I looked up, but everything was blurry.

I heard loud knocking on my door and Cat's worried voice. "Adrian, can I come in? I'm coming in, okay?"

I wiped my eyes and tried to steady my breathing as Cat entered, looking anxious.

"I heard you yell. Are you okay?" asked Cat.

"Yeah, Cat," I breathed. "I'm okay." So I guess I did cry out.

"What happened?"

I gingerly touched my forehead with my fingertips. "I don't know. Did Mom and Dad hear?"

"I don't think so," said Cat. "What do you mean, you don't know what happened?"

"I mean I don't know!" I bellowed back, really angry with Cat. I felt that something was seriously wrong with me, but I didn't care. Suddenly, I wanted to hit her. I wanted to hurt her. I wanted to hear her scream.

Cat stared. "Adrian, you look white. Are you really okay?"

"Just get out!" I raged at her. "Leave me alone! Leave me alone, Cat!" If I had to be with Cat any longer, I knew I'd hurt her.

"Okay, okay. I'm going."

"Shut up, Cat! Get out!"

Cat looked at me really frightened and backed out of my room, hastily shutting the door behind her.

I was furious. How dare Cat come into my room like that?! How dare she talk to me?! How dare she even exist?! I could kill her for that!

With the last shred of sanity left to me, I forced myself to look away from the door and out the window. The windowpane exploded outwards into tiny fragments that rained into the backyard.

I breathed easier. I was still angry, but calm enough to know where I was, and what I had just done. I grabbed the copper wire which I kept under my bed, and instantly my energy drained away along with my anger. I slowly wrapped the wire around my left wrist. I felt really drowsy and worn out, but it was comforting after what had just happened.

I walked to my door and whispered, "Cat?"

"Adrian, are you okay?" Cat asked through the door. Somehow I knew that Cat wouldn't have gone very far.

"Yeah. I think so," I said.

"Is it safe to come in?"

I opened the door and smiled at her weakly. She returned a hesitant smile, and then entered.

"Cat..." I started, but I didn't know how to say it in a way to give it justice.

"Don't say it, Adrian. I know you're sorry. But that wasn't even you. You were all white, and... and..." Cat's voice trailed off. We looked at each other, and Cat finished in a hushed voice, "For a moment, I thought you were going to kill me."

I replied quietly, "For a moment, so did I."

"I think maybe you should tell Mom and Dad about this."

Cat had voiced exactly what I knew was right but was afraid to do, so I protested, "Cat, I really don't know what happened. It was like I was pumped with anger. It wasn't mine at first, but then it was. What if I'm going crazy? What if they take me away? I'll have to live in some hospital for the rest of my life!"

"No!" Cat looked at me, her eyes a bit too watery for comfort. "I don't want that."

I shook my head. "No, Cat, you're right. I should tell someone."

"I take it back!" Cat said hastily. "Please, Adrian. What if they do take you away?"

"Look at the window, Cat."

"I know. I saw it. I heard it break."

"Cat, I almost tried to kill you."

"But you didn't! And let me have that." Cat pulled the wire off of my wrist and said gently, "See? You're okay now. You're okay."

She gave me a quick hug, and I said quietly, "Yeah, I'm okay."

"So," said Cat, cheerful again, "here's what happened. You were bouncing this"—she picked up my tennis ball and held it under my nose—"against that wall, and… Oops!" she cried in mock-alarm as she threw it out into the yard.

I had to laugh.

Then I looked at her seriously and said, "If it ever happens again…"

Cat nodded. "I know, Adrian. We'll both tell."

"I just can't believe Mom and Dad didn't hear all that."

"They sleep like rocks!" said Cat, giggling. "You should too. And, oh, keep the wire." Cat threw the copper wire back to me and stepped out of my room.

The next day, Mom threw a typical fit about my window while Dad did his best to look angry. I knew I should have felt sorrier about it, but I was just glad the truth didn't come out that morning. Mom and Dad really did sleep like rocks.

I quickly learned something which, when I thought back, I wondered why I hadn't figured out much earlier: whatever had possessed me that night, breaking the window was not directly connected to it.

I could use my power to hit things just as easily as I could to move them.

Blasting, which is what I came to call it, required a different kind of focus, not surrounding the object, but against it. Anger, even make-believe anger, helped that focus, but it wasn't really needed, just like you don't really need to be angry at something to hit it with your fist. It was more like semi-controlled aggression. Instead of surrounding something with carefully focused energy, I could throw my energy directly against things, hitting them with the force of a good punch even from across a room.

The blast energy was usually invisible and silent, just like with levitation. But if I pumped enough power into the shot, I could hear a slight whooshing sound and just make out a faint shimmering silvery line in the air along its path. Also, unlike moving or levitating things, blasting didn't need nearly as much control. I could do it without much thinking or focus. But this also meant that it was more dangerous because I could end up blasting something (or someone) by accident. In fact, now that I thought about it, I wondered if perhaps it was a combination of blasting and levitating that had ejected Cat from the pool.

Once I got the hang of blasting, which, surprisingly, took only one day, I demonstrated it to Cat. I lined up four soda cans on the picnic table in our backyard. Standing ten paces away, I knocked the first can over by just looking at it and focusing. It rolled off the table as if I had slapped it with the palm of my hand. For the second shot, I stretched my right arm out toward the cans. I had learned that extending my hand in the direction of the target helped focus my power. Two cans went flying off the table, being thrown about three yards, bent like they had been punched. Finally, I pointed just my right index finger at the last can, concentrating really hard for nearly a full minute on making a small, focused shot through my finger, just like a bullet from a gun. It hit the can dead center, and the soda sprayed out of the hole I had made. The blast didn't go clean through the can, but the other side did lump out a bit. The cans were made of aluminum, but that didn't matter with this kind of energy. I could hit anything with equal force, and the closer I was, the more powerful the blast. I showed Cat an old red brick that I had managed to split in half using several focused finger shots at point-blank range.

"That's amazing!" said Cat, but I caught a slight hint of tension in her voice. Perhaps she was regretting her decision to talk me out of telling our parents.

"I'll tell Mom and Dad if you think I should, Cat."

Cat shook her head. "No, Adrian. You can control it, right?"

"Yeah."

"Then it's okay. Really!"

It really wasn't. But that wasn't Cat's fault. It was mine. I shouldn't have listened to her. She didn't have this power and couldn't know what it felt like. I should have listened to that small part of my mind back in the hospital: the part that was trying to warn me that when your life is changed, it's changed forever. There is no going back.

Three nights later, I didn't wrap the wire around my ankle when I went to bed, and I woke up hovering. When I opened my eyes, my nose was so close to the ceiling that I first thought I was lying facedown on the floor. Then gravity came back and winded me as I hit the real floor, hard. Unlike Cat, I wasn't lucky enough to land on my mattress.

Though that was the first time I did it in my sleep, it wasn't the first time I had hovered. I had managed to levitate myself soon after I gave Cat her bump on the head. However, I couldn't keep myself airborne for more than a minute. I was larger than Cat, and the same rules applied to lifting myself as with anything else. I had no way to know how long I had been sleep-hovering, but I figured that I must have woken up just after I lifted off from my bed. The greater question was how I had used my power in my sleep in the first place, but again, I didn't know.

"Now, that's weird!" said Cat the next day when I told her. Our parents were out playing golf, of all things, and we were, as usual, left at home by ourselves. Cat was sitting on the living-room sofa across from where I was standing and looking at me like she hadn't really seen me before.

"All of this is weird, Cat," I said, annoyed. My sister's opinion of this had finally gone from "amazing" to "weird," and I felt a little betrayed.

"I know, Adrian. But you said you could control it."

"I can," I said. "I mean, with the wire."

Cat frowned. "Yeah, but it's like you're getting stronger and stronger. What if someday the wire doesn't work anymore?"

"It works fine, Cat."

But that was a tad and a half on the dishonest side. Oh, the wire worked alright, but it actually worked too well. Recently, when I was wearing it, I felt really weak and tired. It was like my body could no longer support itself without my power free. I wondered if perhaps my telekinetic power was eating up my physical strength. I had no real answers. All I knew for certain was that the copper wire didn't make me normal at all. It weakened me. That certainly made going to sleep easier, but sometimes I was afraid I wouldn't wake up. That's why I had skipped wearing it the night before.

And school was starting in only a few more days. If I wore the wire, I wouldn't have the energy to play any sports, or perhaps even commute, but if I didn't wear it, I might do something that… well, something…

"Are you sure the wire works?" asked Cat, carefully studying my unconfident expression.

"Listen, Cat, I know this is weird. But I think I'm going to be okay. Just—"

But I couldn't finish the sentence.

"I am coming."

I heard the deep, growling voice inside my head, and it sounded more like an animal than a man. Once again, the headache followed an instant later. It felt like my head would explode, or be crushed, or both at the same time. I realized that the voice I had heard was actually a "thought." A vile thought. It hit me so hard I couldn't tell up from down. One moment I was on my knees, grabbing my hair, the next, I was on my side, thrashing about. It felt like a blender churning up my brains. It pounded me from the inside, and this time I knew I cried in pain. Loudly. Whatever was doing this to me, it was much closer than before.

And then, just as suddenly as the last time, the pain was gone.

"Adrian? Adrian!"

Cat was crying. My whole body was shaking. I couldn't think straight. Everything seemed to be in slow motion.

I felt… fear. That was mine. Anger. No, that wasn't mine. Not yet. But it would be.

"Cat! Get out!" I yelled. "Get out of the house, Cat!"

"Adrian? Oh please, what's happening? Are you okay?"

"Something's really wrong! Please, Cat, run!"

It wasn't just anger. It was pure, unfiltered rage and hate. I picked myself up and roared at the ceiling. Cat was gone. It didn't matter. I would find her. And kill her. And everyone. I would kill everyone. And everything. I would

WITHDRAWN
5555 S. 7th St.
Ralston, NE 68127

destroy everything.

I sensed something move behind me.

I turned around and snarled. "Cat!"

Cat jumped on me, hitting my face with a frying pan that she had gotten from the kitchen. The moment the metal surface made contact, I fell to the floor, my nose bleeding. My emotions, my power... my very being was fading away.

"I'm sorry, Adrian, I had to," Cat sobbed hysterically.

"Cat... oh, Cat... What is happening to me?"

I could barely see her for the tears in my own eyes. She gripped me tightly and pushed the frying pan into my hands. I held on to it as if it were a lifesaver in a thrashing sea, feeling the comfort of the nothingness it gave me. Here, there was no pain, no energy, and no emotion. The cold, black metal tuned out the whole world. I vaguely heard Cat saying that she was going to get my copper wire, and when she stood up, I passed out.

Steel was one of the most draining of metals. I don't know if Cat knew that, but the frying pan saved her life. Probably mine too.

When I woke, my nose had stopped bleeding, and it didn't seem broken. Cat had removed the frying pan from my hands while I was asleep, and only after I woke did she hand me the wire.

"I was afraid if I put it on you, you might not wake up," said Cat.

"Maybe I shouldn't have," I replied wretchedly, wrapping the copper around my wrist.

"Don't say that, Adrian! Come on, you're all bloody."

Wearing the wire wasn't so bad since I had just slept. I felt dazed, and my legs were a bit wobbly, but otherwise I could walk. I wiped my face and changed my shirt. When I came back to the living room, Cat was waiting for me. She looked pleadingly into my eyes and opened her mouth to speak, but I already knew exactly what she was going to say.

"I know, Cat," I said. "I will."

"Today, Adrian."

"I will. Today. I promise."

Mom and Dad wouldn't be back until past six. Cat sat beside me on the sofa, staring up at the ceiling. Neither of us said anything for a while. We just sat there trying to restore some normalcy to our day.

Cat broke the silence first. "Adrian, what are you going to say to them?"

"What do you mean?" I asked.

"Well, are you going to tell them everything, or..."

"Wouldn't be much point telling them at all if I didn't tell them everything, don't you think?"

"I guess so. But Adrian, there's just so much we don't know."

I gaped at her. "You're telling me!"

Cat laughed, and suddenly so did I, though rather nervously. What exactly was I going to say to our parents? I had no idea. But it was just good to sit there and laugh a bit. For all the annoyances a little sister can often be, that was the one thing I really loved about Cat: She always had a smile tucked away somewhere. Even when her big brother had almost tried to kill her... again.

After dinner that evening, we were all watching TV together. Actually, Dad might have been the only one watching. Dad, Cat and I were on the sofa while Mom sat in the easy chair knitting something purplish. Cat, who was in her usual spot between Dad and me, had curled up into a ball and was resting her head on Dad's arm. She kept throwing me furtive looks. I still had no idea how to go about this, but I had promised.

"Dad," I said hesitantly, "can I ask you a question?"

Dad looked over at me, a little surprised. Usually, when I ask a question, I just ask it, so he probably knew it was something serious.

"Sure, what is it?" he asked.

"Can you... I mean, do you think it's possible... I mean, there's something different about me, and..." my voice faltered.

Dad gave me an understanding smile and said, "Adrian, you're going on thirteen soon, and a lot of things are going to change in your life."

"Yeah, no kidding," I deadpanned. For a crazy instant, I thought he was going to say that he knew about my power and that every adult had it.

"If there's something worrying you, it's okay, you can tell me. But maybe you want to talk about this privately?" asked Dad, nodding toward Cat. Mom stopped her knitting to listen in as well.

"It's okay," I said. "Cat knows."

"She does?" Dad looked surprised, but then he calmly asked again, "What is it, Adrian? If you told Cat, you can certainly tell me."

"It's just... Well, I was wondering..."

"Yes?"

"Can you make things move without touching them?" I blurted out, and I knew it sounded utterly lame.

Dad stared at me curiously for a moment, and then grinned, saying, "Why sure I can! Hey, Kitty, you want to be tickled?"

Dad waggled his fingers near Cat's neck. My sister jumped up out of the sofa, shrieking. Dad got up too and chased Cat around the living room until she took refuge behind Mom's easy chair.

"Nothing to it!" laughed Dad, sitting back down beside me. "I didn't touch her even once, see?"

I laughed too, but then I said, "Come on, Dad, you know that's not what I mean."

"Well, what do you mean?" asked Dad, still chuckling. "Moving things without touching them... What, like magic?"

"Well," I said, knowing there really was no good way to explain it, "not exactly magic, but kind of like this."

I focused on a flowerpot, raising it up near the ceiling. I flew it once around the room before setting it down at Dad's feet.

This time, it was Dad's turn to jump up from the sofa.

"What the... How in... What?!" he sputtered.

Mom was speechless. Her knitting needles fell silently from her hands.

"There's more," I said quietly.

I had to take them out to the backyard to show them the blasting thing. This time I demonstrated it on Dad's beer cans. Even I was surprised at how easy blasting was, considering how little experience I had with it. In the dark backyard, we could clearly see the shimmering streaks of light as they hit the cans, knocking them over and rupturing them, pouring beer all over the picnic table. Cat couldn't stop laughing, watching our parents' eyes widen with surprise, amazement, fright, what have you.

But if it weren't for Cat, I couldn't have put on my show. Her support was the only thing that gave me the courage to tell Mom and Dad the next part of my story: the part about the headaches, and the rage. It was a lot for them to take in, but they handled it well.

"So it's happened twice?" asked Dad.

"Yeah," I said quietly, "and it was a lot worse the second time."

Dad picked up one of the ruptured beer cans and examined the hole in its side. "This—this power of yours is what's causing it?"

"No! It wasn't me!"

"How can you be so sure, Addy?" asked Mom.

"Because I am! It was from outside. I just know!"

My voice must have had more than a touch of panic in it. But they had to understand, whatever I was, I wasn't that monster.

Dad put a reassuring hand on my shoulder. "It's okay, Adrian," he said. "We'll believe you. Just give us time. We've never seen anything like this before, you know. Maybe nobody has. When you said you had a question, I thought we were going to talk about girls."

Cat giggled.

"Addy," Mom said in a concerned tone, "your father and I don't know exactly what's going on, but we're on your side. You know that, don't you, dear?"

"Yes," I answered glumly. I knew Mom was trying to cheer me up, but I couldn't shake the feeling that something in my life was about to be lost, or had already been lost, forever.

"And we're going to find out, Adrian," said Dad, smiling encouragingly. "Tomorrow. We'll take you to the hospital. Don't worry. They're not going to lock you up. I won't let them. They'll just take a look at you, okay?"

"Okay," I mumbled.

"Cheer up! You'll probably be famous!" said Dad. "They'll find a way to take care of the headaches. I'm sure of it."

That was the last real conversation I ever had with my parents.

Later, past midnight, I lay awake on my bed in the dark, staring up at the ceiling. Mom and Dad must have either been asleep or pretending. Either way, the house was silent. Tomorrow, I was going to the hospital. Despite what Dad had said, I felt deep down that I wasn't coming back home.

This might be my last night here, I thought.

I didn't even notice my door open, and I nearly jumped out of my skin when I heard Cat whisper, "Adrian?"

"Cat?!" I said, rounding on her. "Don't do that! What if I hurt you again?"

"You didn't hurt me, Adrian," said Cat. "And you won't. I'm not afraid."

"What are you doing in here, Cat?" I asked, annoyed.

"Same as you. Staying awake because I can't sleep."

"Go do it in your own room!"

Cat looked at me defiantly. "Addy-baby."

"Go away! I'm in no mood to chase you around."

"Feeling sorry for yourself?" asked Cat.

"Wondering if I'll ever be normal again."

I got up and turned on the light. Cat sat on my bed, and I slumped down in my desk chair. I looked at Cat, who sat expressionless and silent, staring back at me.

Maybe she was right. Maybe I was feeling a little sorry for myself. But more than that, I was scared. I was scared of so many things now that it was difficult just keeping them organized. What if my powers overwhelmed me? What if I hurt my family or my friends? What if I had another headache? What if the doctors locked me up? What if I never saw Mom or Dad or Cat ever again?

"Adrian, what do you think is going to happen tomorrow?" asked Cat.

I shrugged. "Dad said they'll probably do some tests." I forced a smile and added, "Then maybe they'll put me in a big frying pan for the rest of my life."

Cat didn't laugh.

"How do you think it's going to end?" I asked.

"I don't know..." Cat paused, and then she looked at me and smiled. "How about, 'And they all lived happily ever after'?"

"I'd like that, Cat," I said quietly. "That'd be great."

Cat reached down the front of her shirt and pulled out her pendant. It was a cut and polished amethyst on a delicate silver chain, and had been a birthday gift from our uncle who was a rare-stones dealer. The amethyst was Cat's birthstone, and she wore it almost every day, calling it her lucky pendant.

But Cat didn't usually wear her pendant inside her clothes or at night. I wondered why she had it now, but I soon found out. Reaching behind her neck and unlocking the chain, Cat took the pendant off and held it out to me.

"I want you to have this," she said. "For luck."

"Cat, I can't."

"Please, Adrian. If they take you away... If I never see you again..."

"You know I can't wear that," I said. "The chain is silver."

"Oh yeah," said Cat, and slid the chain out of the hole in the stone. She placed the amethyst in my hand, saying, "Just keep the stone, then."

I slowly closed my hand around it. "Thanks, Cat. When things get back to normal, I'll give it back, okay?"

Cat smiled. "Deal!"

I pocketed the stone, and we gazed at each other in silence for a minute.

"Adrian..." Cat's voice was barely audible.

"Yeah, Cat?"

"I love you."

I looked at her, startled. In all our years together, I don't think either of us ever said those three words to the other. And suddenly I knew what Cat had meant when she accused me of feeling sorry for myself. She was just as scared as I was. Mom and Dad too, no doubt.

"I love you too," I mumbled awkwardly.

"I am here."

The deep growling thought hit my head like a gong, reverberating through my skull. This time, I was ready.

Grabbing the copper wire, I shouted to Cat, "It's happening again! Get out, Cat! Get out of here now!"

The ceiling lights flickered a few times, and then the room was plunged into darkness. The windowpane, replaced only three days ago, exploded inwards, showering us with glass fragments. A powerful gust of wind swept around the room, making papers and bits of trash fly around.

Weakened by my contact with the wire, I could hardly stand up in the whirlwind that my room had become. Cat started to scream. I heard a loud crashing noise from what I thought was the living room.

Someone was in the house!

I dropped the wire. The headache wasn't coming. This was different.

"Cat! Addy!" Over the sound of the wind, I could just barely hear Mom frantically calling to us from somewhere in the house.

Then I heard screaming. It was Dad. It lasted a few seconds, and then stopped. The wind had stopped too, and for a brief moment, the house was dead silent.

"Richard! Are you okay?" cried Mom's distant voice, full of fear.

I had to stop Dad. I dashed out of my room and down the corridor. The wind started to pick up again. Soon it was whipping through the house, rattling windows and knocking over houseplants and even bookshelves. I was almost to my parents' bedroom when I heard Mom scream.

I opened the door and saw them.

I'm not going to tell you how my mother died. If you really want to know, you can go dig up the newspaper articles on them about what the police found the next day. There are records of all of this, but I'm not going to point you to them. In short, Dad killed her.

Then he came after me.

I tripped backwards over something soft, and realized that Cat had followed me. I grabbed her arm and pulled her back into my room. I could hear Dad roaring in fury. Like a rampaging bull, he came bearing down on my room door as I was trying to shut it.

The door clicked in place a moment before Dad crashed into it with a loud thud. There wasn't a lock. All Dad had to do was turn the knob. But by the sound of it, he was clawing at the door like a wild animal. Even so, I felt it was only a matter of seconds before he either opened it or broke it down.

I turned to Cat and shouted, "Out the window!"

Cat shook her head, her eyes wide with fright.

"Jump, Cat!" I said again. "I'll break the fall."

Cat still didn't budge. I grabbed her and threw her out, doing my best to telekinetically slow her down before she hit the ground. It wasn't easy because I was panicking and couldn't concentrate, but Cat quickly stood and looked up at me, so I guessed she was okay.

I called down to her from the window, "Run, Cat! I'll hold him off!"

Cat finally seemed to come out of whatever trance she was in. She sprinted out of the yard, into the semi-dark street and out of sight.

Meanwhile, I heard Dad roar again, but the clawing noise had stopped. Dad had turned around and gone after someone else. Instinct told me to jump out of my window and follow Cat, but something stopped me. I was sure that whoever had done this to us was still in the house. Maybe Dad had gone after that someone. I had to help Dad. Besides, after all that had happened, I couldn't just run away without any answers.

Or maybe I just wanted to see the monster.

The wind was still whipping up a storm of papers and torn leaves, so there was no way anyone could hear me, but nevertheless I crept as quietly as I could down the hall to the stairs. I peered over the banister and looked down into the living room.

There was glass everywhere. All the windows had shattered. The curtains had been torn off their rails. In the little moonlight that was shining through the living-room window, I saw him. He was a big, wide-shouldered man, though I couldn't tell in the darkness whether he was fat or muscular. I could also make out the shape of my father's body lying on the floor nearby, his arms and neck bent strangely. He wasn't moving.

The big man slowly turned his head and looked up at me. And he grinned, but his eyes were cold and fierce. Then he looked away, turning slowly on the spot as he searched the room for something else. I could only see the scene from above. What was he looking for?

A blink later, his whole body twitched once, and I saw a glint of silver near his neck. Then I saw the metal shaft. An arrow had been shot through his throat. Clutching his neck, the man fell to his knees, and then flat on his face.

"Come on out," said a wheezy voice from below. "I'm not going to hurt you."

I realized that the house was silent again. The wind had stopped.

"Who are you?" I called down. My voice was almost steady.

"I'm a friend," said the voice, coughing lightly once. "Come on out! He's dead now. We don't have a lot of time."

At the bottom of the stairs, I was met by an old man who, in the dim light, looked a bit like a scarecrow. He was holding a heavy wooden crossbow in his hands. Weathered and gangly, he fidgeted constantly, shifting his weight from one foot to the other as he examined my face.

"Adrian Havel?" he asked.

"Howell," I corrected. "Adrian Howell. Who are you?"

"Of course... Adrian Howell," the old man muttered to himself. Then he smiled and said, "I'm Ralph. So we meet at last, Adrian Howell."

"How did you know my name?" I asked suspiciously.

Ralph looked into my eyes and said calmingly, "I'm a friend. Where is your sister, Adrian Howell? Where is Catherine?"

"I don't know," I replied. "She's outside somewhere, probably far away by now."

Ralph scowled for an instant as if he was conflicted over something, but then he said, "No matter. We need to get going."

"Who are you?" I asked again. I wasn't afraid of him. I didn't know why, but if anything I felt calm and at ease.

"I'm the man that's rescuing you, lad," Ralph replied matter-of-factly. "Come with me."

I looked back at my father's lifeless body on the floor. "My parents... I can't just leave them."

"Yes you can," Ralph said hurriedly. "You have to, anyway. There's nothing you can do about your parents now. That's a berserker I just killed for you, and there's no guarantee he's the only one after you. We have to go right now. I know you want answers, and I promise you'll get them, but if you want to live, you're going to have to trust me and come with me now. You can trust me, lad. I promise you that."

Things had gone from "weird" into a nightmare. My parents were lying dead in the house. Cat was gone. And I was standing in a room with an old, crossbow-wielding stranger telling me that he had just saved me from a "berserker," and that I had to go with him to get my answers.

I quickly followed him out of the house. Ralph had a car parked nearby. It was a small blue convertible, streamlined like a sports car, but in the light of the full moon, I could easily see that it was rusty and old. The top was up.

Oh yeah, never get into a car with a stranger. That's the rule you follow when your parents are alive, your sister is annoying as opposed to missing, and there isn't a big dead man on your living-room floor with a crossbow bolt through his neck. Somehow I knew that going with Ralph, however strange a man he might be, wasn't about to make my situation worse. In fact, I felt that, despite his bizarre appearance and manner, I could trust him more than anyone.

Once again, I was wrong.

3. ESCAPE FROM ESCAPE

We drove all night. I asked questions, and Ralph answered them in his wheezing voice. He looked really old, at least sixty or so, with pale, leathery skin and beady, sunken eyes that were nearly hidden by his unkempt, curly white hair.

"Where are you taking me?" That was my first question.

"Away from here," said Ralph as we sped out of town.

"I have to find my sister, Ralph. She ran off."

"Out of the question, lad. Your sister will be okay. She's better off without you anyway. It's you that they're after. Your sister wouldn't be in any danger if you weren't about."

"But she's lost!" I insisted. "It's the middle of the night and she could be anywhere."

"I'm not much of a finder, lad," said Ralph. "I can find most power alright, but a child like that... no, I can't sense her. But she'll be okay. The police will pick her up and she can go live with your relatives."

"But Ralph..."

Ralph glanced at me, keeping one eye on the road. "You can't help her, lad! You just can't. Heck, you can barely help yourself, can you? But don't you worry. You're in good hands with old Ralph. Saved you from that berserker, didn't I?"

"What's a berserker?" I asked.

Ralph smirked. "He's the one that was messing with your father's mind.

He's a controller. The worst kind."

"A controller?"

"That's right, lad. A controller is a dangerous enemy to make. Some of us can hide, and some can fight, but the real scary ones are them controllers. Especially berserkers. They can make you go psycho, lad. Did it to your father, didn't he? And look what your father did."

I had been looking out the window when he said that, beginning to wonder why I had been so willing to get in this man's car. I turned to him and shouted furiously, "Shut up about my father!"

Ralph turned his head to look into my eyes again and said kindly, "Easy there, lad. I'm not disrespecting your father. But if I hadn't rescued you, you'd be dead too now. That berserker was sent by the Angels."

"Angels?" I was having a lot of trouble keeping up with the conversation, and Ralph's raspy, accented voice wasn't helping things.

"They don't need you, lad," said Ralph. "That's why they sent a berserker to kill you. If they wanted you to join them, they would have sent someone nicer, like me, eh?"

Ralph chuckled at his own joke, but I was even more lost. Every question answered was making things harder to understand.

"The Angels, see," Ralph continued in his near-breathless voice, "they've got enough destroyers, so they won't bother with a kid like you. But we don't want you dead. We want you on our side, to fight the Angels. You aren't much of a destroyer, but you're still a destroyer, so maybe you'll make good cannon fodder."

Ralph chuckled again. I wasn't sure what Ralph meant when he called me a "destroyer," but I did know what cannon fodder was. Like pawns in a chess game, they were the weakest soldiers that nobody cared about. I didn't like his joke at all. I glared at him, but he just smiled back.

"Who knows, lad," he said lightly, "you might even make a good destroyer someday."

I felt a little calmer and said, "Okay. What's a destroyer?"

"Why, you're a destroyer!" laughed Ralph. "You're a telekinetic. You can break things and you can fight. You can't heal, you can't hide, you can't mess with minds. You're a destroyer, pure and simple. Maybe you got some other tricks up your sleeves, but the Angels know you're a destroyer."

"That's why they want me dead?"

Ralph nodded grimly. "The Angels don't need you, lad. They've got enough better fighters. But they don't want you joining us either because then someday they're going to have to fight you. And if they're going to have to fight you someday, they might as well fight you today, before you get stronger, see?"

Ralph coughed loudly once, cleared his throat and continued, "Right now they can kill you easy, and if they could kill me too while I was bringing you in, it'd be a bonus. But ha! I killed him, so that's one less Angel, one less controller, eh?"

I asked, "So the Angels are the bad guys?"

Ralph shook his head. "There are no bad guys in this war, lad, because there aren't any good guys either. It's just survival, see? For you, it's just who wants you dead—that's the Angels—and who wants you alive—that's us."

"Who is 'us'?"

"We're the Guardians," said Ralph.

"And you're at war with the Angels?" I felt I was finally getting somewhere.

"Well, sure we are. Angels, Wolves, Slayers—you name them, we kill them."

"You mean there are people like us everywhere?"

"People like who, lad?"

"Like us!" I cried. "People with strange powers!"

"What? You mean psionics? But of course there are!" said Ralph, chuckling. "What, you thought you were the only one, did you? You thought you were some freak of nature or something? There've been people like us since before history was written, lad. How do you think Jesus walked on water?"

"Jesus was like us?" I asked, incredulous.

"Well, there's no proof that Jesus was a psionic," said Ralph, grinning, "but light-foots can walk on water." I stared at Ralph disbelievingly as he continued, "Come to think of it, I bet you could sort of walk on water too, you know, by hovering just over it. You're a right powerful telekinetic, after all."

Only a minute ago, Ralph had called me cannon fodder, and now he was saying that I was powerful. I was beginning to wonder if anything he said could be trusted, but then I caught Ralph's eye and relaxed again, thinking that he probably just complimented me to make me feel better.

"Well, I guess I could hover over water," I answered. "But do you mean that people with powers... um, psionics, have always been around?"

Ralph nodded. "Welcome to the world, lad."

"But then how come people don't know?"

"What do you mean, people don't know? Of course they know! Governments know. Churches of course know. Everyone that matters knows. Ordinary humans just stopped believing in us these days because we know how to hide ourselves. We know how to blend in, see?"

"Yeah..." I said slowly. I didn't see at all how this man managed to blend in, but I didn't want to get on his wrong side either. He did, after all, kill the berserker with his crossbow. He saved my life.

Ralph glanced at me again. "Enough questions for one night. You have to get yourself rested. Sleep now, lad. Sleep."

As he said that, I felt the weight of the night bearing down upon me as if I had been touched by steel again, and a moment later, the darkness closed in.

When I woke, I was alone in the car, which was parked in a small lot. The outside world was covered in thick fog, but by the dim sunlight shining through it, I guessed it was late morning. Where had Ralph gone? I couldn't see far through the mist, but I guessed I might be in some small town up in the mountains. I could hear the chirping of birds in the distance and the occasional sound of an engine as a car sped past somewhere nearby. I sat there confused, trying to make sense of what had happened.

Dad had killed Mom. He was hit by the berserker's anger, and he killed Mom, and he almost killed Cat and me. Then he went after the berserker, who must have killed him.

My parents were dead.

It was like I was discovering this for the first time. I didn't cry. It felt like a dull, heavy weight in my gut. They were gone, and there was nothing I could do. I wasn't sure exactly how I felt, but it was more emptiness than grief, and try as I might, I couldn't even picture their faces.

And Cat... Where was she? Why wasn't she in the car?

Then I remembered: Cat was lost. I had left her and gotten into Ralph's car. I hadn't even tried to look for her! What had I done?!

I had to get back home and talk to the police. I had to find Cat. I pulled the handle on the car door and started to open it, but suddenly it got pushed back closed again. I saw Ralph's beady eyes peering in through the window.

"Whoa, lad, where do you think you're going?" he said. "You can't go out like that—in nothing but them night things and all! I bet you're hungry, too."

Ralph walked around to the driver's side and got in, plopping two paper bags onto my lap. "Those are your day clothes and your breakfast."

"Hamburger and fries for breakfast?" I asked, peering into the smaller bag.

"Well, I'm no delver. I don't know what you want." Ralph turned the ignition, and raised his voice over the sound of the engine sputtering to life as he said, "We still have a long ways to go, but we'll be there by night."

It turned out that I was right about where we were. Ralph's rusty blue convertible sped on up a winding mountain road cutting through a sweet-scented pine forest. We were already near the top of the mountain range, and we soon started our descent.

I felt a little better after eating, and somehow, without leaving my seat, I managed to change into the clothes Ralph had bought. There was a light brown T-shirt and a pair of gray sweatpants that were a bit too long for me. Ralph had also gotten me a jacket, but it turned out to be too small. It didn't matter. I didn't feel very cold in the car, even up in the mountains.

As I was rolling up my pajamas in order to stuff them into the paper bag, I felt something hard in the pants pocket. Pulling it out, I discovered it was the amethyst Cat had given to me moments before the attack.

"Ralph! I have to go back," I said, suddenly panicked. "I have to find my sister!"

Ralph looked over at me. "No, no, no, and no! I already said, now, didn't I? Your sister will be okay. She'll be found by the police and she'll be okay."

"But..."

"No buts, lad, no buts. She'll be okay, you'll see."

Again, a strangely dull but relaxing sensation washed over me. Why was I so worried about my sister? Ralph was right: Cat would be okay. I was the one in trouble, though I still hadn't realized how much.

Just past noon, Ralph stopped to buy us lunch at another sleepy little mountain town, but he insisted that I stay in the car. He said it was for my own safety and that I shouldn't be seen outside. I didn't care. I had a feeling he was right, and I didn't want to leave the car anyway. He brought back turkey sandwiches, and on we went. I continued my questioning.

"Ralph, how did you kill that berserker?"

Ralph grinned as he said, "I shot him with my crossbow. I thought you saw that."

"No, I mean why couldn't the berserker find you and hurt you?"

"What do you mean?"

"When I move things, I have to see them," I explained. "But the berserker could sense me from miles off, and he got to my father right through the walls. He never even saw either of us before he used his power on us."

Ralph shrugged. "Everyone's power is a little different, lad."

"But how come he couldn't get to you, standing in the same room?" I asked.

"Because I know how to block his mind. I can block his bad thoughts, so he can't attack me."

"I wish I could have blocked him," I said unhappily.

"But you can! Someday I'll teach you how. All in good time, lad."

"I can learn?"

Ralph nodded. "Anyone can learn, alright. It takes practice, mind you. It takes lots of practice to block powerful thoughts. Controllers are dangerous. But it's not impossible. I'll teach you someday, lad."

"Thanks," I said. "What else can you do?"

"Oh, this and that, lad. This and that," Ralph said airily. "Mostly I play with the wind. That's good for hiding me because I'm no good at real hiding. I can block thoughts but I can't hide. I made that powerful wind as a distraction so the berserker couldn't find me in your house."

Ralph chuckled and looked at me. "Can't teach you that, though, you know? Every psionic's power is different. You're a telekinetic anyways, so you've got no need for wind. A proper destroyer beats a windmaster any day."

"Where are you taking me, Ralph?"

"Patience. You'll see. We're going to the big city. We're going to the ocean, and to our friends."

I was really starting to like Ralph. Despite his constant fidgeting and his strange way of talking, despite everything about him, I knew I could trust him. When he talked to me, my worries seemed a little more distant, and I felt that I was going to be okay.

By late afternoon, through fleeting glimpses over the edges of some of the sharper curves in the road, I could already see the glittering of the ocean and the hazy shroud of city smog blanketing our destination. We were soon out of the mountains and the forest, speeding through one small town after another.

We stopped at a small hotel just inside the city's edge. I was hoping to smell the salty ocean air, but we were still too far from the coast. I was getting a bit tired of Ralph's overprotectiveness, but I didn't argue when he told me to stay in the car while he checked us in.

Ralph led me in through the hotel's back door, up two flights of stairs, and down a short concrete corridor. He unlocked our door and we entered.

Inside was a gloomy room with an old TV, a small dining table and two hard wooden chairs. There were also two simple, single beds, each with a tiny bedside table atop which sat identical, cheap and dusty shaded lamps. It was a dismal place.

Ralph turned to me and said, "Our gathering isn't for another two days, so we have to lay low for a while. Now I'm going to go do us some shopping, lad, and I don't want you wandering off. You might get scared, but you need to stay put, you understand?"

"Yes, Ralph, I understand," I said dully.

"That's a good lad. You trust me, don't you?" said Ralph, looking deep into my eyes for nearly half a minute.

"Yes, Ralph," I repeated. "I trust you."

"Good. I'll be back soon. You stay put."

Ralph stepped out of the room, and I heard his footsteps fade away.

I wandered around the dingy hotel room, carelessly sliding my fingertips over one of the bedposts. It turned out to be made of metal. Feeling drained, I quickly removed my hand.

As my head cleared, I noticed how bright and clean the light blue curtains looked. The TV also looked shiny, like it was brand new. The beds looked large and comfortable. In fact, the whole room was beautiful.

41

Surprised at my discovery, I looked around again. This time, the room didn't look all that nice, but it was still much better than my first impression.

Like the room, my whole existence was becoming clearer, glowing a bit before returning to normal. I was surprised at how sharp my senses were becoming, at how I could smell the air drifting in from the vents and feel the texture of the cold plaster walls. But what did it mean? I hadn't even realized what I was missing until I got it back.

And what about Ralph? Did I really trust him? At first I was surprised at my own question. Of course I trusted Ralph.

But then a small voice in my head said, *No.*

No, I didn't trust him. I had no good reason to. Ralph didn't help me find Cat.

Ralph didn't care about my sister. He didn't care about my parents. My parents were dead... All the silenced emotions from last night were rushing back to me. I couldn't see well through my tears, but even so, it was like I was waking from a deep sleep. I could feel again. This pain inside me made my life real, and I was myself for the first time since leaving home.

I thought about Ralph once more. How far had he gone? When would he be back? I thought about running away. It scared me because I didn't know where I would go. And I still wasn't exactly sure what was going on between me and Ralph. I racked my brains trying to remember our conversation in the car. Last night and this morning, every time Ralph looked at me, I felt calm and relaxed, and then everything became dull. *Everyone's power is different.* That was what Ralph had said about the berserker.

I was lying face up on the window-side bed when Ralph returned. I could tell by the noise he made entering that he was carrying large paper grocery bags.

I heard Ralph say, "Come here, lad. Help me with these."

I didn't get up. I didn't even turn toward him. Through the corner of my left eye, I saw Ralph set the bags down on the floor and sit on the other bed. Still looking up at the ceiling, I asked, "Ralph, how did you know my name? How did you know my sister's name?"

"I told you, lad, I'm a friend."

"Whose friend?" I asked evenly. "I don't know you."

"Here, look at me, lad."

I still didn't turn to him. Instead, I turned my head the other way and looked out the window to the darkened sky and city lights. I could vaguely see Ralph's reflection in the glass. He was fidgeting even more than usual.

"You're not my friend, Ralph," I said, keeping my head turned away from him. "You made me follow you here. You're a controller. Not a very powerful one. Not like that berserker, but you're a controller too."

I heard Ralph snicker, and then he said, "I'm a man of many talents, lad. They wouldn't have sent me alone if I couldn't take care of myself."

My head was still clear. Ralph needed to look into my eyes in order to work his power on me.

"Why did you try to control me?" I asked.

"I needed you on my side," said Ralph. "I needed to take you in quietly. I didn't want you worrying about your sister when we had to get moving. I'm not like that berserker, lad. I wanted you alive."

"I need to find my sister, Ralph. I need to know she's okay!" I sat up on the bed, keeping my eyes on the window, steeling myself for what I was about to do. "And Ralph?" I said, steadying my breathing.

"What is it, lad?"

"I'm not going to fight in your stupid war."

I turned swiftly, just enough to get a quick glimpse of about where Ralph was sitting. But even as I extended my arm out toward him, I already felt a wave of calm creeping over me. I heard my bedside lamp shatter as the room was suddenly alive with churning air, and the blankets whipped up around me. Still, I was ready, and I released my blast a moment later. I heard Ralph grunt in pain, and my calm vanished. The wind was weaker too, but I knew Ralph wasn't badly hurt. I had only knocked him off his bed and onto the floor, and in a moment he would pick himself up.

I stretched my other arm toward the window and blasted it out. Ralph would just have to get over his disappointment.

I jumped out, hoping to make a telekinetically controlled descent to the street below, but suddenly a powerful rush of air pushed me right back into the room! I hit the floor hard, barely able to keep my eyes open because of the wind, which was stronger than ever. I groped around the floor until my right hand found the small, broken lamp. Squinting, I could see Ralph standing over me, and I tried to throw the lamp at him, but my arm stopped mid-swing.

I couldn't do it. He was just an innocent old man.

"Oh, you're a tough one, my little destroyer," said Ralph, smirking. "You almost got away. But you aren't going to do that again, are you?"

"No, Ralph, I won't," I answered. And I meant it too. I felt really ashamed of what I had done. How could I have thought of running away when Ralph needed me so much?

Ralph gently pulled me to my feet, saying, "No you won't, lad. Not till you learn to block it, anyway."

We went downstairs and apologized to the hotel management. Ralph, pretending to be my grandfather, told them that I had accidentally knocked the lamp over and that it had hit the window. They gave us another room after Ralph agreed to pay for the damages.

That night, Ralph told me that he was going to tie me to the bed. He said it was for my own safety. Though I didn't know what danger I was in that required me to be tied down, nevertheless I was sure Ralph knew best. I removed my shoes and socks, but didn't bother going back to the car for my pajamas, preferring to sleep in the clothes Ralph had bought for me.

Ralph took a sturdy iron chain he had brought from his car and secured one end to the headboard of the bed. Then he wrapped the other end around my neck once, pulling it tight enough so that it wouldn't come off over my head, and locked it in place with a small padlock through the links. I was basically a dog on a leash, but I didn't mind it at all because I knew Ralph was my friend. I did feel a touch of fear when he put the chain on me, but soon I felt calm again. The chain drained my strength and made me drowsy.

I lay there staring up at the ceiling until I could hear Ralph's quiet snores from the other bed. I still felt extremely weak because of the chain, but my mind was much clearer now. It was easier to return to my real self this time, knowing what it was supposed to feel like. I kicked myself for not running away when I could, before Ralph had come back. I had wanted to confront him and make sure he really was a controller. I realized that even when he wasn't directly controlling me, he had manipulated my actions through my fears and my curiosity. It was stupid of me. My escape plan had been foolhardy at best. Ralph wasn't just some crazy old man. He was a powerful psionic. He had killed the berserker. He was a fighter.

I tugged at the chain, but it was futile. Drained of my powers, I was not even as strong as a normal twelve-year-old boy. The chain felt increasingly heavy around my neck.

Ralph had said that the "gathering" was in two days, so we would probably be staying another night here. When Ralph woke up, I would be put back under his control, which meant I wouldn't try to escape even if I had the chance. Ralph had done enough shopping already. He wouldn't leave me alone again.

Ralph's power as a controller wasn't at all like the berserker's. The berserker could cause pain and make people angry. Ralph did the opposite. He made me calm and trusting, and made the world seem peaceful and dull. How could I fight that?

I'd have to learn to block it. That's what Ralph had said. He said anyone could block controllers, but that it took time and practice. I already knew I could block Ralph by not looking into his eyes, but that was just the nature of Ralph's power. He could block the berserker completely. How did he do it? The obvious answer was to simply stay focused. But how?

I didn't know how to block it, nor could I hope to learn in one night, but there was another way that was much simpler. And I already knew the answer because it was around my neck! The difference between Ralph's control and the berserker's didn't matter at all. It was how they were similar. Metal drained my powers, but it also drained my emotions, which, just like my physical strength, were tied to my powers now. Draining broke the connection. Ralph's control over me had weakened when he put the chain on me. The only reason his control didn't break then and there was because Ralph was still looking into my eyes. As soon as Ralph lay on his bed and well before he fell asleep, the metal had drained my emotions and the control was broken.

When Ralph talked to me, that is, when he looked at me, he was using his power to suppress my feelings, but he didn't do it continuously. He just did it often enough so that I wouldn't come back to being myself. If I could drain myself when he wasn't looking, I'd snap out of his control, and then... Well, I'd have to think of that later.

I was getting very sleepy now. The chain felt heavier than ever.

I looked at the bedside table and saw what I wanted: a cheap plastic ballpoint hotel pen lying next to the lamp. The metal tip would be too small to affect me very much, but maybe, just maybe, it would keep me sane. I reached over and picked it up, feeling nauseous from even such little movement. Slowly pulling the cap off, I slipped the pen deep into my sweatpants pocket with the tip pointing outwards.

Unable to keep my eyes open any longer, I desperately prayed that I wouldn't die in my sleep. A moment later, I woke up.

Ralph was leaning over me, unlocking the chain. The sunlight streaming in through the curtains was horribly cold, but I felt my strength return and looked up at Ralph, who peered into my eyes and smiled.

"Did you have a good night's sleep, lad?" he asked pleasantly.

"Actually, I think I had a strange dream," I told him.

"I'll make us some breakfast. You go wash up now."

"Okay," I said, going into the bathroom and closing the door.

The faucet handle was made of metal. Not wanting to be drained, I wrapped it in toilet paper before turning on the water. After splashing some cold water onto my face, I looked at my reflection in the mirror. I could hear Ralph humming to himself outside and thought, under the circumstances, how fortunate I was to have him taking care of me. Ralph was a good guy, always on my side. He would keep me safe.

I was about to go back into the bedroom when I noticed that there was something in my pocket. What was it? I reached in. Suddenly I felt a little dizzy. I pulled out a ballpoint pen and wondered how it had gotten there.

Slowly, my memories from last night were coming back to me. It hadn't been a dream after all. I had put the pen in my pocket to trick myself into touching it. But why would I do such a thing? Why did I want to drain myself? Why had I thought that Ralph was a bad guy? Why did I want to run away from him?

It didn't make any sense. I certainly had no desire to run from Ralph. Ralph was my friend. He needed me, and he was one of the good guys.

No, said that small voice again.

No what? I thought.

Just... no.

Not even sure exactly why I was doing it, I touched the tip of the pen again, and a minute later, my mind cleared.

All of my previous questions answered, now I was faced with the one question that I had failed to answer last night: What next? I was trapped in a bathroom. The moment I stepped out, I would be put right back under Ralph's control.

I turned the faucet to hot water only and touched the stream with one finger. It was scalding. After filling a plastic drinking cup with the steaming water, I stepped back into the bedroom.

"What's that you got there, lad?" asked Ralph.

I didn't answer, and I made sure not to look into his eyes. There'd be no building up to this fight. I couldn't let him see it coming. I threw the water at him and, before he could even scream, I blasted him backwards with both arms stretched out. He fell flat on his back, winded by the impact and blinded by the water that had, miraculously, splashed onto his face.

The wind was beginning to pick up. My first instinct was to run, but I knew Ralph would catch me. I grabbed one of the wooden dining chairs by its back and brought it down on him as hard as I could. I didn't actually want to kill him, but I didn't not want to either. I didn't care at all. All I cared about was stopping him. One of the chair legs hit his head, and the wind stopped. I didn't know if Ralph was alive or dead, but I wasn't about to find out.

I grabbed Ralph's black leather wallet, which was sitting on the little dining table, and ran from the room. When my feet touched the cold concrete of the outside corridor, I realized that I wasn't even wearing socks, but I didn't stop. I jumped both flights of stairs, hardly bothering to soften my impact at the bottom of either. Bursting through the back door of the hotel into the early-morning light, I just kept on running.

4. NIGHT HEIGHTS

I didn't care where I was going. I just had to go as fast and as far as I could. I sprinted down the sidewalk, past little shuttered shops and cheap-looking apartment buildings, and dipped into an alleyway where a squawking murder of crows had to take evasive maneuvers to keep from being trampled on as I darted through them. I came out the other side to another wide road where I saw a group of people, mostly dark-suited businessmen with leather briefcases, filing onto a commuter bus. They stared as I rushed aboard at the last second, barefoot, out of breath and clutching a stitch in my side, but I didn't care.

I had to pay my fare in coins taken from Ralph's wallet, but I didn't want to touch the metal money. This drew even more awkward looks from the passengers because I asked the bus driver to pick out the correct amount directly from the coin pocket. The driver must have thought I was crazy, but he didn't comment as he took the coins.

I kept looking back as the bus started to move, expecting Ralph to come running after me at any moment, maybe sending a tornado at me. The bus crawled along its morning route altogether oblivious to my impatience. At every stop, I was torn between the need to get farther away from the hotel and a panicked desire to get off the bus and find a place to hide. In the end, I rode the bus to the end of its line, which turned out to be a large city square surrounded by a shopping center, some tall office buildings, and a giant train station.

I first ran into the shopping center, which had just opened its doors for the day. I bought a new pair of shoes, socks, and thin gloves. Then I headed to the train station where I got a ticket to a neighboring city.

At the time, it didn't matter to me where I went, as long as it was far away. Ralph had said he wasn't much of a "finder," but that he could find power. Whose power? Mine or the berserker's? Ralph had shown up a moment after the berserker. Perhaps Ralph couldn't find me. Perhaps he had been following the berserker, and that's how he found me. As my train pulled out of the station, I didn't quite breathe a sigh of relief, but I felt that, for the moment, I was probably safe.

Nevertheless, when I got off the train a little before noon, I immediately started looking for a way to get even farther away. I was inwardly hoping that a chair to the head would have convinced Ralph that he really didn't want me in his group, especially since Ralph himself had said that I wasn't much more than cannon fodder anyway. But I didn't want to take any chances. I guessed that Ralph's "gathering" would include many other people with powers that could find me from a great distance away. I had to keep moving.

After a fast-food lunch, I took a two-hour bus ride to yet another city. Even though I was calmer and dressed properly this time, some of the passengers still looked at me curiously. An elderly woman who had the seat next to mine asked me where my parents were, so I told her that I had been visiting my relatives and I was going home before school started. I had always been a little small for my age, and the woman didn't seem to believe me when I told her that I was twelve years old.

As I got off the bus in the early afternoon, I discovered that Ralph's wallet was already running on empty. Now I was faced with questions of survival. I'd be thirteen in another month and a half, but that was a long way off from being an adult. I knew I couldn't find work, and it was only a matter of time before I got picked up by the police. As soon as the new school year started, which I realized was now only two days away, I would look out of place on the streets in the daytime. Even if I had the money, I couldn't just check into a hotel, either. The world simply wasn't designed to accommodate children on the run.

For the rest of the day, I wandered the streets alone, resting on park benches from time to time. At night, finding nowhere better to go, I snuck under some bushes in a public park. The night air was chilly, and I hugged myself to keep warm.

My parents had been killed just two days ago, and here I was shivering under a bush with nowhere to turn and, for all I knew, being hunted by people who had powers I couldn't even begin to imagine. It was a while before I realized that I was crying.

I wondered if perhaps I should just turn myself in to the police and explain, or at least try to explain, what was going on. But I remembered what Ralph had said to me on our first night in the car: "Governments know." What did that mean? How would they treat me? Somehow, I felt that I didn't want to find out.

I was still very worried about Cat, but even if I had the money for the return journey, which I didn't, I was deathly afraid that there might be a trap waiting for me back home. I managed to convince myself that Ralph was probably right about my sister. The police would have found her by now and perhaps sent her to my uncle's place. I wanted to call my uncle and check, but I didn't know his phone number or exact street address. I forced myself to push aside my fears about Cat. I had to concentrate on taking care of myself.

The next morning, tired and stiff from my night in the park, I made my way to a nearby supermarket. There were still a handful of coins left to me, and I was hungry. But when that food was gone, I would have to choose my next move. I remembered my PE teacher's favorite saying: "Either you get up and face your problems, or you wait around until your problems are facing you." That day, I chose the latter.

At night, after another full day's aimless wandering, I was once again sitting under the bush in the park. Not having eaten any lunch or dinner, I felt weak and even colder than the night before. There was nothing for it: I would eventually have to steal something, either tonight or the next day when I was even hungrier than I was now. To be perfectly honest, I wasn't all too bothered by the moral side of that. I was merely trying to survive. If someone was going to give me a job, or any "right" way to make it out here, I'd take it. I knew that was true, and so I felt it wasn't a real crime to steal when there weren't any other options. The real question was how to do it.

I got up and walked toward the downtown area. It was about 11pm, and many of the shops and office buildings were closed. But there were still plenty of cars on the streets, and people were strolling or just milling about on the sidewalks. As I trudged along, I realized that I had no idea where to start. All I knew was that crime was best committed at night, when it was dark. For adults, anyway.

"Hey, kid, where are you going?" a young woman in a sparkly green dress called out to me from across the street. I ignored her and kept my pace, bringing my head down a notch. A child alone on the streets at this time of night drew too much attention. This wasn't going to be easy.

I ducked into a narrow alleyway between two buildings. The alley was dimly lit, with only two neon tube lights attached to the sides of the buildings. One of them was buzzing and flickering feebly. This was exactly the kind of place your gut warns you about, saying, *Stay away from there. That's where bad things happen.* But I had been through a good deal of fear these last few days and I knew that there were much scarier things in the world than dark alleyways.

I looked up at the fire escape on one of the buildings. The rusty iron staircase extended from the top of the building down to the second floor, where it stopped. There was a ladder that could be extended from there down to the ground, but of course it was lifted up so that burglars couldn't climb it.

No matter. I stood there and calmed myself for a few seconds, gathering my focus before levitating myself up onto the stairs. Once I landed on the staircase, I felt my power drain just a little from being surrounded by all the metal, but it was no big deal. My new shoes kept me from touching the fire escape directly. Though I was wearing my gloves, I didn't use the railing as I quietly climbed the steps.

The problem was that at each floor, there was a locked steel door, but no windows to look in from. I couldn't tell what kind of building this was, whether it was an apartment or an office or a hospital or what. I climbed to the top and stood on the flat, asphalt roof. I hadn't been counting, but I must have been about ten stories up.

I looked at the other buildings around me. Many of them were about the same height. Peering over the edge of the roof, I saw the people far below me walking this way and that, minding their own business. I looked up at the night sky. A thick layer of dark clouds slowly slid over the waning moon, and suddenly, my hunger temporarily forgotten, I was seized with a reckless desire… to fly!

I lifted myself up a few yards and hovered for a moment, and then rose higher, and higher. Once I was sufficiently above the roof of the building, I tried swooping back down toward it. I lost my concentration for an instant and almost crashed into the roof, but I quickly changed course and instead went down over the side. For a second or two, I was in freefall between the building and the one next to it, but I checked myself and rose back up as fast as I could go. I felt the wind whipping past my face as I flew up into the sky. I didn't know exactly how fast I was going, but it must have been faster than pedaling my bicycle at top speed.

I flew higher. This was amazing! I had never so much as hovered more than a few feet over the ground, but now I was soaring through the sky like an eagle!

And higher!

A sea of lights spread out below me. The cars looked like miniature toys. I cut my ascent and went back into freefall, enjoying the weightlessness for a couple of seconds before kick-stopping in midair. I realized I had complete control over my motion. I was standing on air! My heart pounding, I let out a howl of delight. This was really fantastic!

But I had been flying now for nearly two minutes, and I was really beginning to tire. It felt like I was carrying someone else that weighed as much as me, and I knew I was approaching my limits. I cut down on my power and drifted back down as if on a parachute, landing lightly on a different building roof. I couldn't find the one I had taken off from. I must have drifted off course with the wind.

My mind and heart were still racing from the experience. I took a few calming breaths and looked over the side of the building. This building was only about five stories tall, and as I looked down at the people walking below, I had an idea. Not one of my best ideas, for sure, but an idea nevertheless.

A lot of people were carrying shoulder bags, especially the women. I noticed that some of them were left open, and though I couldn't see into them at this distance or lighting, I could pretty much guess what was inside. If I could levitate a purse out of one, either from above or behind, I'd at least have enough cash to eat for a day or two. To do this, however, I would have to get considerably closer.

I levitated from rooftop to rooftop until I found what I was looking for: a single-story 24-hour drive-thru fast-food restaurant with a flat roof. Landing on it, I peered cautiously over the edge. It was getting late, probably past midnight, and fewer people were on the streets.

Excellent, I thought, and waited.

A few minutes went by. I saw a pair of women exit the restaurant, chatting, and one of them had an open shoulder bag. I could even make out what looked like a purse inside. I stretched my right arm toward it, hoping that it would help my focus. This was still a bit farther than I was used to, and the two women were getting farther away with every step. It was either now or another customer, so I bent my consciousness upon lifting the woman's purse out of her bag.

Here's my observation on women's purses: They are packed with lots of junk, making them almost as complex as a person's body. They are also filled with coins. As in metal. Heavy. Very, very heavy at this distance. I did manage to lift the purse out of the bag, but promptly dropped it onto the sidewalk. I ducked out of sight as the woman turned around to pick it up.

Like I said, it wasn't my best idea. I needed to be closer, and hopefully get at the paper stuff. Lacking a better plan, however, I decided to try again.

A few minutes later, I spotted another likely target. A group of two men and two women were coming down the sidewalk toward the restaurant. They all seemed to be very drunk, talking loudly and swaying from side to side. As the foursome came alongside the restaurant, the light from the windows illuminated a small rectangular bulge in one of the men's right jacket pocket. A billfold! I waited for them to pass so that their backs were to me before I focused on pulling it out.

It was a bit heavier than I had hoped, but I was closer than the last attempt, and the billfold slipped smoothly out of the man's pocket. The moment it did, however, one of the women swore loudly, and I jumped in surprise, almost losing my concentration completely. I stopped the billfold just a split second before it hit the sidewalk, and breathed my relief when I saw that no one in the group had looked back. I levitated the billfold up toward me and caught it in my right hand. It was only then that I realized how fast my heart was pounding. I might have just flown to the moon.

I found a small pack of bills and a few coins, which I transferred to

Ralph's wallet. There was also a driver's license and some bank and credit cards. I didn't need those, so I threw the billfold back over the side. I was hoping someone would find it and deliver it to the man.

After calming myself down, I flew up to the top of a taller building nearby and spent the rest of the night on the roof. It was stingingly chilly, but at least I was safer than in the park.

The early-morning light woke me, and for a brief moment I panicked. How was I going to get down without anyone seeing me? I couldn't just fly in the daylight. Fortunately, there was a fire escape here too, and I walked down it, jumping off where it ended at the second floor. I only cushioned my landing slightly, just in case someone was watching.

I breakfasted on snacks from a convenience store and then went shopping for clothes at a nearby mall. My shirt and sweatpants were getting really dirty, and besides, I didn't want to spend another cold night. I picked up a dark green long-sleeve shirt, a pair of jeans, two pairs of socks, and a black denim jacket. The jeans and jacket had metal zippers, but I wouldn't have to touch them as long as I wore my gloves.

"Aren't you supposed to be in school, boy?" the man at the cash register said gruffly as he looked at my grimy attire.

Oops! I had completely forgotten that today was the start of the school year. I paid the cashier without answering and hurriedly left the mall. He was right: There wasn't a single kid on the streets today. I jogged to another deserted alleyway, levitated onto the fire escape of yet another building, and found refuge on the roof until late afternoon.

For nearly three weeks, that's how I lived. During school hours, I hid on rooftops, safely out of sight from the busy city. Just once, someone came up the fire escape, but I heard him first and jumped over the side, trying to hover behind the wall until he left. He stayed on the roof for a few minutes too long and I was getting tired, so I made an emergency landing in the alley below, where, I couldn't be sure, but I think an old homeless man saw me.

I did my grocery shopping in the early evenings, sometimes also buying soap and bottled water to wash myself after it got dark. The water felt freezing in the chilly night air, but I knew that if I didn't keep clean, I'd be too noticeable as a runaway and people might start calling the police.

I also bought a few comics and magazines in order to pass the time on the roofs. But I wanted to be careful with my money, so I ended up spending a lot of time just lying on my back and watching the clouds drift by, or gazing at Cat's amethyst, which I miraculously still had. The stone was my one and only physical link that remained of my past life. It glistened as the sunlight shone through it, and I sat for hours playing with it in my hands. Eventually, because I was afraid it might fall out of my pocket while I was flying, I bought a leather cord and wore the stone around my neck.

Every time I ran out of money, it was back to the restaurant. There were some risky moments when I was almost seen, and one very close call where a man nearly saw his wallet flying up into the air. But I was getting the hang of this, and a few coins in a wallet or purse didn't keep me from my prize.

The only really horrible part of stealing was that sometimes my loot would contain a family photo, or pictures of kids. I hated seeing their happy faces smiling up at me. Was I bitter? Envious? Embarrassed? I wasn't sure, but it just irked me.

I also knew, of course, that eventually someone was going to catch me lifting wallets into the air. I couldn't keep this up forever. And even if I could, how much longer would it be before Ralph or some berserker or someone else found me? Face the problem, or wait till it faces you. I still hadn't learned, and so the days drifted by.

Nighttimes were not only for stealing money. The darkness gave me my one true pleasure: flight. Zipping through the air with the wind on my face, I could, if only for a brief moment, forget the nightmare my life had turned into, and all the fears I had of what might come. I was getting good at flying too, staying up for more than three minutes at a time.

Then, one night, I was flying high into the sky, higher than ever before. I wanted to know where my limit was. I had decided that once I got too tired to continue my ascent, I was going to go into freefall until I was close to the tops of the buildings, and only then slow myself down. That way, I wouldn't need much energy for the return flight. The new moon had come and gone, and the nights were getting brighter, but I still felt comfortable concealed in the quiet blanket of darkness which had become my only true refuge. This night was nearly cloudless and I felt like I was swimming in a sea of lights, the stars above and the city below. Higher and higher I went.

My heart was screaming in protest as I pushed myself to keep on going.

The howling wind was getting colder, but the wind wasn't the only thing I could feel. I noticed that the air around me was vibrating like a rhythmic drumbeat. I briefly wondered what it might be, but I wanted to go higher.

Just a little higher...

Suddenly I was blinded by a brilliant white light brighter than the sun itself. The pain forced me to shut my eyes tightly and my concentration was instantly broken. I felt my upward motion slow. For a split second, I was frozen in midair like some crazy cartoon character, and then I began to fall. I opened my eyes and saw the dark silhouette of a helicopter above me. It shined its spotlight on me again. I turned away from the glare, redirecting my body so that I was diving headfirst toward the ground, which I realized was still some distance away.

The light was still chasing me and I knew I couldn't land on a rooftop, so I veered left and dipped in between two buildings. A moment before I hit the concrete surface of the alley, I turned myself upright and tried to kick-stop. But I was going too fast, and although I considerably slowed my descent, I still slammed feet-first onto the pavement, painfully spraining my left ankle.

I could still hear the helicopter thumping somewhere above me, so I didn't dare climb back up to the roof to get my stuff. Instead, I limped away as quickly as I could, braving the open streets for a few blocks before hiding in another dark alley, which I found, thankfully, deserted.

5. THE HIDER AND FINDER

I woke at daybreak and realized that I was back to square one, having lost all my money, extra clothes, everything. I touched Cat's pendant to make sure it was still around my neck. There was no question of retrieving my other belongings from the rooftop. Instead, I used the hours I had before school started to put more distance between myself and the scene of my sighting. The only positive thing about that morning was that my sprained left ankle had miraculously healed overnight. There was no pain there, and I could walk briskly. I once again hid on top of a building, hungry, thirsty and dejected, waiting for night to fall so that I could go wallet hunting.

The days were beginning to get noticeably shorter, but it was still a long wait till sundown. I didn't even have anything to drink, and I crept between two large water tanks to shield myself from the biting wind that was blowing over the roof. Once the agonizingly uneventful day had darkened, I was about to go rooftop-hopping for another suitable location to steal money, but then I heard a quiet female voice in the darkness.

"Hey there," it said.

It had come from the fire escape. I was still sitting in my hiding place between the tanks, and if the voice hadn't taken me so completely by surprise, I might have just run to the edge of the building and jumped over.

"It's okay. I'm not going to hurt you." The voice was soft and gentle. I remained silent, and she continued, "You're the freefall person, aren't you? There was an article about you on this morning's newspaper. Something about

57

a mystery skydiver whose parachute didn't open. Don't worry. They didn't catch you on camera, but I think the police were looking for your body all day."

I still kept as quiet as I could, but my heart was thumping so loudly I was sure it would give my location away.

"I'm not going to hurt you," the voice said slowly. "I just want to talk. Is that okay?"

"Yeah," I breathed, not even sure if she could hear me. "It's okay."

"That's a start. My name's Cynthia Gifford. You can call me Cindy. What's your name?"

I didn't answer, and a moment later she said, "Come on, I told you mine, didn't I? I know you're scared, but I wish I could at least know who I'm talking with."

"I'm Adrian," I whispered. "Adrian Howell."

"That's better. Adrian Howell, it's a pleasure to... Well, I haven't exactly made your acquaintance yet. Do you want to come out, or do I have to keep talking to the water tanks?"

I tittered nervously. Everything about this woman's voice helped me to trust it, but I still hadn't gotten over Ralph.

"I heard that," she said. "That was a laugh. Come on, Adrian. I promise I won't hurt you."

I warily stepped out from between the tanks and looked toward the fire escape. There wasn't enough light to see her very well, but the owner of the voice was a slender woman with long silvery hair that seemed to glow faintly in the moonlight. She was sitting on the raised edge of the building with her feet on the asphalt roof, her hands folded neatly on her lap. Even in the darkness, I could see she was smiling serenely at me. She looked like she was in her early forties, quiet and, for lack of a better word, motherly. I smiled back, but I didn't go any closer.

"Are you a psionic?" I asked, remembering the word Ralph had used in the car.

The woman nodded slightly. "Yes, Adrian. Just like you."

"What do you want from me?"

"Actually, I was wondering if you might want something from me."

"Like what?"

"Food, clothes, a place to sleep, perhaps?"

"How can I trust you?"

"You can't," she answered, still smiling peacefully. "Not if you don't. But you're not going to survive long out here by yourself. Surely you know that by now. Your powers are incomplete, and you are still a child."

"I'm not a child!" I said angrily. "I have control of my power."

"Control?" said the woman, chuckling. "Adrian, pardon me for saying this, but you don't know the meaning of the word. Controlling your power includes knowing better than to go flying around the city and stealing people's money. And letting them see you! Not just last night. I saw the tabloid headline about the man whose wallet flew off into the sky."

Now *that* was news to me! I had been pretty sure he hadn't seen anything.

"Adrian Howell," the woman continued in a tone that sounded more concerned than critical, "do you have any idea how long a show-off like you would survive out here? It's lucky I found you when I did. Even the Slayers will be looking for you by now."

"Slayers?" I asked.

"I'll tell you about them later," she said. "Listen to me, Adrian. I don't have a whole lot of time. If you really want to stay up here by yourself, that's okay. I'm not going to force you to come with me. But if you want, you can come. If you change your mind, you can leave at any time, I promise you."

"Alright," I said, stepping a little closer to her. "I'll go with you if you want."

"No, Adrian," said the woman, getting to her feet. "You'll come with me if *you* want. Do you want to come?"

"Yes—yes, please," I answered, taken aback. She was very different from Ralph.

"That's better. In fact, it's probably the best decision you've made in a long time," she said warmly, walking up to me and holding out her hand.

Slowly, I reached out and shook it.

"It's a pleasure to make your acquaintance, Adrian Howell," she said.

"Um…"

"Please call me Cindy."

Cindy, as I knew her from then on, had parked her dark green compact

SUV right under the fire escape, which was how she had managed to climb up onto it. She opened the car door, and I got in beside her.

I felt dizzy as I handled the seatbelt buckle, having accidentally touched the steel part. Cindy gave me a concerned look.

"It's the metal," I explained weakly, leaning back in the seat to rest my head.

"Oh, of course," she said, and started the engine

Once again, I was in for an overnight drive. As soon as Cindy heard my stomach growl, which couldn't have been more than five minutes into our trip, she pulled into the very same drive-thru restaurant that I had been using as my base of operations until yesterday. When I told her, she laughed and told me not to worry, placing a steaming hot bag onto my lap.

"I don't like fast food much, but since we're on the run…" she said, driving up the ramp to the highway. We were leaving the city.

I ate ravenously, nearly choking on my burger and downing my soda in large gulps.

"So," said Cindy once I had finished the last of my onion rings, "tell me your story."

"My story?" I asked.

"Yes. Your story. How did you end up in the middle of the city nicking wallets from drunks and doing aerobatic stunts for helicopters?"

"Well, I—I just don't really know if…"

My voice trailed off, but Cindy picked it up in an overly innocent tone, saying, "…if you can trust me?"

"Yes… I mean no! It's just that I…"

"Look, Adrian, I can't read your mind. If there's something you don't want me to know, I'm not going to find out, okay?" Cindy breathed deeply once and continued gently, "But Adrian, I found you, and I didn't have to do that. And you came with me, and you didn't have to do that either. I was kind of hoping that might be the start of a friendship. Friends have to trust each other."

"Okay," I said, looking at her apologetically.

"I'll understand if you're not ready to talk about it."

"No, I'm ready," I answered, and I was.

I told her everything. Everything I've told you and then some. The words just gushed out of me like a dam had burst. Sometimes I choked up, but Cindy patiently waited for me. At times, I must have been almost incoherent. I was jumping all around the story, adding bits here and there. I told her about losing Cat, and about Ralph and the berserker, and my escape from the hotel. When I finished, the dashboard clock read one o'clock in the morning. We were well beyond the city limits, driving down a dark, backcountry road past farmhouses and pastures that smelled of cow manure.

"That's quite a story, Adrian," said Cindy. "Not the worst I've ever heard, but still quite a story. I wonder how it'll end."

I gave her a weak smile. "Cat once suggested, 'And they all lived happily ever after.'"

Cindy grinned. "Smart cat."

"She was," I said quietly, touching my sister's pendant.

Cindy gave me a sympathetic look, saying, "It must have been hard for you, gaining your power so early. You're a wild-born, like me."

"What's a wild-born?" I asked.

"Psionic powers run in families," explained Cindy. "In the thickest of bloodlines, almost everyone has some degree of psionic power, but with the lesser bloodlines, some people have it and some don't. Then there are some psionic bloodlines that are entirely dormant. 'Dormant' means sleeping or inactive."

"I know what 'dormant' means," I said, feeling somewhat insulted. "But how does a bloodline become dormant?"

"Usually through intermarriage with non-psionics. When a bloodline gets too thin, it can no longer develop psionic powers, and generations can go by without a single psionic being born. Wild-borns are people who don't have any psionics in their families to help them adjust to their new powers. You don't know anyone in your family who could defy any natural laws, do you?"

I shook my head, and Cindy said, "Well, believe me, it was a shock for me too, when I first discovered what I could do. Wild-borns are considered to be a threat by established psionic factions. Threat and opportunity, actually."

I gave Cindy a blank stare, and she explained, "Most psionics don't want normal people to become too aware of their existence. The problem with wild-borns is that they are more likely to do something that'll compromise our secrecy."

"You mean like flying around a big city?" I asked meekly.

"Exactly," Cindy said with a smile. "But a wild-born also presents the opportunity to bring new blood into a faction. So whenever a solo psionic is discovered, there's a mad rush by the surrounding factions to catch him and bring him into their group." Cindy sighed once and added, "I'm guessing that the Guardians must have wanted you pretty bad if they sent old Ralph after you. That or they really wanted to kill the berserker. Either way, Ralph would be the man."

"You know him?!"

"Ralph P. Henderson. Yes, I know him," Cindy replied quietly. "I haven't seen him in years, though."

The fear must have shown on my face because Cindy slowed the SUV considerably, saying, "Adrian, you're not about to jump out of my car, are you? If you want out, just say so and I'll stop. Ralph and I aren't friends, you know."

Feeling embarrassed, I mumbled an apology. Cindy shifted the car back up.

"Oh, and Adrian," said Cindy, "I'm pretty sure Ralph was lying to you when he said the Angels wanted you dead."

I asked, "Why do you say that?"

"Well, it's true that the Angels outnumber the Guardians now, but they wouldn't have passed up an opportunity to get you to join them. Not with powers like yours."

Surprised, I said, "Ralph told me that my power wasn't strong enough for the Angels to be interested. He said I was cannon fodder."

"Ha! Adrian, very few telekinetics can fly."

"But then why did the berserker try to kill me?"

"He didn't," said Cindy. "He tried to get you to kill your family. That way, it would have been easier to get at you."

I thought about that for a minute. True enough, the first two attacks were on me. But if what Cindy was saying was true, why did the berserker use his power on my father the third time? Dad had tried to kill me and Cat. What had happened that night?

First, I had heard the berserker's voice, and then, just before the main attack came... the wire! I had drained myself before the berserker could hit me

62

full force. The berserker could somehow sense that I was weakened, so he turned his attention to the next strongest person in the house who couldn't block him. By then, I had dropped the wire, but the berserker didn't know. He was perhaps hoping that Dad would turn against Ralph, and didn't expect me to come out of my room.

And Ralph had lied to me about the Angels in order to get me on his side. How many other people were chasing after me?

"Cindy, back on the roof, you said that Slayers were after me. Ralph said something about them too. Who are they?"

"Slayers? Oh yeah, they're the church people," Cindy said grimly. "It's short for God-slayers. They've been trying to exterminate our kind, that's psionics, for centuries."

"Why?"

"Because we're a danger to their beliefs," explained Cindy. "They call us lesser gods or false gods, demons, and often much worse. They claim we're of Satan."

"Ralph said Jesus himself might have been a psionic because he walked on water."

Cindy chuckled a little before saying in a serious tone, "One way or another, Adrian, Jesus had power. But whether Jesus really walked on water or whether he was just a great person with loyal followers and politically unpopular ideas... Who knows, really. One thing's for sure, though: there are plenty of religious-minded people out there who, unlike Jesus, are neither good nor honorable."

I stared at her. I didn't attend church regularly myself, but I had friends who did, and I never thought to criticize religion like Cindy was doing now.

"Don't get me wrong," said Cindy, seeing my expression. "I know many wonderful people who are church-goers. But the sad truth is that there are some very sick people out there who believe that God wants them to destroy anything they don't understand."

"I'm not a church-goer," I said quietly.

"Neither am I," said Cindy, "but have you ever studied the Bible?"

"No."

"Really? That's too bad. There are some good things you can learn from the Bible."

"Maybe."

Cindy smiled. "Tell you what, Adrian, let's just focus on keeping you alive for the time being, and worry about your salvation later."

"Where are you taking me?"

"To my home sweet home, of course. I have a guestroom you can sleep in, and you'll be safe there. No one has ever broken through my defenses. At least, not in the last fifteen years."

"So, um, what are you?" I asked, instantly regretting my choice of words.

"Excuse me?"

"I mean, what are your powers?"

"Oh, well, let's see..." Cindy grinned. "I guess I'm mainly a cook."

"What kind of power is that?" I asked. "Can you breathe fire or something?"

"No, but I can make wicked lasagna!" laughed Cindy, and added, "Adrian, people are not their psionics."

"You're not a controller?"

"Oh, good heavens, no. If you must know, I'm both a hider and a finder. Strange combination, really. And oh yes, I can also breathe fire."

I gaped at her, believing it for just one second before I noticed that her lips were twitching. We both laughed.

Then I asked, "What's a hider?"

"I'm good at protecting myself and others from detection," said Cindy. "You see, most of us can, with a little practice, sense power, but only if it is similar to our own. Power knows power. You are a telekinetic so you'll learn to know when telekinetics and other types of destroyers are around you, but only a true finder can sense and find anyone. Anyone, that is, who isn't a hider. A hider like me can conceal signs of power, making it pretty much impossible for a finder to locate me. That is, me, or anyone or any place I choose to protect."

I asked, "What did you mean when you said other types of destroyers? What's the difference between a telekinetic and a destroyer?" I hadn't been able to fully understand what Ralph had meant when he kept calling me by both names.

Cindy explained, "'Destroyer' is just a general term for psionics who have potentially destructive powers. A telekinetic is only one type of destroyer, just like a berserker is a type of controller. There are others."

I wanted to hear what the others were, but there was something else much more pressing on my mind, now that I had met someone who I thought could help me find Cat.

"And you're a finder too?" I asked.

Cindy nodded. "That's right. Like I said, it's a strange combination, because when you're in my hiding bubble, even I can't sense you unless I'm really close. But as long as you're not psionically hidden, I can locate you from quite a distance away. That's how I found you and... well, you'll see. It wasn't easy, though, finding you. The city has so much metal in it. It's hard to focus a search."

I tried not to let the hopefulness show on my face as I asked her, "Can you find anyone? I mean, can you find my sister?"

"Oh..." she said uneasily. "I'm sorry, Adrian, but finders can only sense psionics. I can't locate people who don't have powers."

"I see."

"I'm really sorry."

Disappointed, I looked down at my knees, but then Cindy said, "Listen, I have some contacts in the police. As soon as we get to my house, I'll call in a favor and see if we can't find your Cat, okay?"

"That'd be great. Thanks, Cindy."

"Can't promise anything, you know. Hopefully, she'll be with your uncle by now, like you said."

"Yeah," I said, stifling a yawn.

Cindy looked at me. "You've had a rough week. Try to get some sleep, little destroyer."

"I'm not little," I said in an annoyed tone, partly because I was, in fact, small for my age, but mainly because I remembered that Ralph had once called me "little destroyer" too.

"Sorry," said Cindy. "But how old are you, anyway? Ten? Eleven?"

"I'll be thirteen in three weeks."

"Oh. Sorry again, Mr. Howell."

"Just call me Adrian, please."

"You don't have a nickname or anything?"

"No," I replied dryly, "I don't."

"Well, then Adrian it is, I guess."

I yawned again. Tilting back my seat, I turned onto my side as best as I could. It wasn't the most comfortable way to sleep, but it certainly beat a concrete roof. And Cindy was right: It had been a rough week. A rough month, really.

I dreamt I was flying madly through the night air while being chased by squadrons of giant helicopters. Then I saw Cat's terrified face as she was lifted into the air by the wind. I tried to follow, but the wind was too strong, and I was pushed backwards into a dark tunnel filled with screaming voices. I could hear Ralph laughing as he said over and over, "I'm your friend, Addy-baby. You can trust me. You can trust old Ralph."

I woke with a start. It was still dark, and the car was still moving. As I closed my eyes again, I fell into a deeper sleep. If I had any other dreams or nightmares, I couldn't remember them the next morning.

The early-dawn light felt cold on my face as I yawned and shook myself awake. Still driving, Cindy looked over at me and smiled.

"Good morning, Addy," she said pleasantly.

I stared at her. "Did you just call me…"

"So that is your nickname, yes?"

"How did you…"

"You talk in your sleep." Cindy winked. "Addy-baby."

I groaned. "Please don't call me that."

"Yeah, I think you said that in your sleep, too," she said, grinning.

"Well, no doubt I meant it in my sleep, too," I said grumpily.

"Okay, if you insist. I just thought it was kind of cute."

"So, I talk in my sleep?" I asked, desperate for a change of topic.

"That's just the tip of the iceberg," replied Cindy. "Good thing your seatbelt was on. You started to levitate out of your seat. It's amazing you never drifted over the edge of those buildings you were sleeping on."

Actually, I nearly had, once. This sleep-hovering was getting a bit worrisome.

I rolled down my door window and felt the chilly but refreshing wind on my face. I remembered having woken up once in the car and wondered if Cindy had stopped at all during the night.

"Aren't you tired, Cindy?" I asked, resting my elbow on the open window.

"Why, yes I am, actually," she replied. "But remember I said I don't have much time?"

"Oh yeah... What did you mean by that?"

"Well, I'm hiding my house. Actually, I'm hiding my whole neighborhood, and that's a lot easier to do when you're in it."

I looked at her questioningly, and she continued, "You see, Adrian, hiding protection is like a bubble. I create it around my house, and then make it bigger and bigger until it covers several blocks. But over time, the bubble shrinks, so I have to keep pumping more power back into it. I've put a hiding bubble around this car too, of course, but it's much smaller, and moves with us."

I pictured in my mind a brightly glowing force field surrounding the SUV. In reality, however, Cindy's hiding bubble was completely invisible, and I couldn't see how far it extended. I hastily pulled my arm back into the car and rolled up the window.

"I have to get back home soon so I can reinforce the protection there," said Cindy, and then muttered to herself, "Besides, Alia will be worried sick by now."

"Alia?" I asked.

"Another guest at my house. I'll introduce you as soon as we get there. I wanted to bring her along, but she's not really the going-out type."

When I gave her another questioning look, she said quietly, "You'll see."

"One mystery after another," I grumbled.

"You'll have plenty of time to solve them all once we get home. Like I said, you can stay as long as you like. I can give you better protection than almost anyone and, if you like, I'll teach you some new tricks too. You can trust me, Adrian."

I huffed. "That's exactly what Ralph said."

"Suit yourself," replied Cindy, stopping the car.

"I'm sorry," I said quickly. "That's not what I meant."

Cindy nudged my shoulder and laughed. "I'm kidding! I just need to stretch a bit. It's still a long road ahead."

6. THE OTHER GUEST

We arrived at Cindy's house at around two o'clock in the afternoon. It was a square-ish white two-story in the middle of a row of similar houses, fairly spaced apart, each with neatly cut lawns and small flower gardens. The town we had come into looked very much like the one I had grown up in, and although I was painfully reminded of what I had lost, it was still nice to be back on familiar ground. Cindy parked her SUV in the garage, and the shutter closed automatically behind us as I followed Cindy through a side door that led into the kitchen.

Cindy called out, "Ali, I'm home!"

I instantly heard the pattering of small footsteps coming from another room. The door on the other side of the kitchen burst open, and a little girl with long walnut-brown hair and unnaturally pale skin stood in the doorway for a brief instant. Then she jumped in fright, letting out a little shriek, and disappeared back into what I could now see was the living room.

Cindy called out, "Oops. Sorry, Ali, I should have warned you. It's okay. He's not going to hurt you. Come into the kitchen."

Then Cindy turned to me and said, "Sorry, Adrian, I probably should have warned you a bit more, too. No sudden movements, okay?"

"Okay…" I said slowly, not understanding what the big deal was.

Cindy called out again, "Alia! Come on now, we're really tired, and I missed you. Were you okay by yourself? Come into the kitchen, honey."

"Maybe we should go into your living room," I suggested.

Cindy shook her head and whispered, "No, let her come to you. This will take some time."

Suddenly Cindy called out toward the living room, "No, Ali, he's not!"

A pause, and then she called again, "I swear, Ali! I wouldn't have brought him here if he was. He's lost, just like you. He needs a home."

Another pause.

Cindy said sternly, "Alia, that is not going to happen! Please come into the kitchen and say hello. His name is Adrian, and he's going to be here for a while."

The little girl's face slowly reappeared from behind the doorway. As she peered timidly into the kitchen, I carefully lifted my right hand and gave her a little wave and a smile. She ducked out of sight.

"Come on, Ali, just say hello," Cindy called again in a slightly exasperated tone. We waited for a moment in silence.

"Hello," I heard her quiet voice say inside my head, and I finally understood what was going on. Alia could speak directly into people's minds!

"She said hello," I whispered to Cindy, and then called out, "Hi there, Alia!"

"That's a little better," called Cindy. "But remember what I said, Alia? You have to speak the words too. With your mouth. And it wouldn't hurt to come into the kitchen and say it directly to him."

"It's okay," I said, unsure why the girl was so afraid of me but not wanting to cause any trouble.

But Cindy shook her head and said, "No, it's not okay. She needs to learn."

I looked toward the doorway again. Alia was standing there, silently looking at me, her face rigid with fear. She looked really small in her oversized cotton shirt and pants, and I guessed she was about four or five years old. I smiled again, trying my best to look harmless. She took one small step forward, then another. Ever so slowly, she crossed the kitchen until she was almost close enough to shake hands with.

"That's right, sweetie," Cindy said softly, "say hello. This is Adrian Howell. Adrian, this is Alia Gifford."

"Hello, Alia," I said as gently as I could.

Alia tensed up, but she didn't back away. I could see her lips quivering slightly.

Then, in a barely audible whisper, she said, "Ha-ow."

"Hi," I said, breathing a sigh of relief.

Cindy stage-whispered to us, "Shake hands!"

I stretched out my right arm, but a little too suddenly. Alia jumped back like a frightened cat. She surveyed me with infinite caution before finally stepping forward again and slowly putting her arm out. As her trembling hand reached mine, I didn't squeeze it or shake it, but just let our fingers touch for a moment.

"Good girl!" said Cindy, crouching down and opening her arms wide. Alia jumped into them, and Cindy gave her a big hug, saying, "That was a pretty good hello, sweetie."

Picking her up, Cindy said to me, "Alia has a lot of trouble speaking with her mouth, so usually she'll just talk into your head, okay?"

"Sure," I said, shrugging. Judging by the way the kid was clinging to Cindy, I seriously doubted she was ever going to speak with me anyway.

Cindy carried Alia into the living room, which was spacious and clean, with a rectangular coffee table and two long sofas. There was also an old-fashioned redbrick fireplace with fake firewood in it. There was no TV, but instead there was a long bookshelf built into one of the walls. A stairway led up to what I assumed were the bedrooms.

Cindy tried to set Alia down onto a sofa, but Alia refused to let go, so Cindy sat down herself, keeping the girl in her lap.

Cindy then closed her eyes, as if in prayer. I watched her, wondering what she was doing, but then I noticed that my staring was making Alia really scared, so I looked away.

After a few minutes, I heard Cindy say, "Listen, Adrian, I'm really beat. My shift starts tomorrow, and I have to get some sleep. Like right now. Let me sleep for a few hours."

I turned to her. "Yeah, okay. What do you want me to do?"

"Just stay put. Don't leave the house. Our protection has gotten smaller. I've reinforced it just a bit now, but it still might not even cover the whole street. I'll restore it completely as soon as I sleep some. Sit here. Read. Do whatever."

"Okay, sure. What about..." I nodded toward Alia, who was still clinging

70

to Cindy for dear life.

"Oh, this little monkey?" Cindy smiled, and then said to Alia, "How about it, Ali? You want to stay here and make friends with Adrian?"

Alia looked up at Cindy and frantically shook her head.

Cindy laughed, saying, "Yeah, didn't think so. But he's going to live here too now, you know. Sooner or later, you'll have to get used to it."

After a quick glance in my direction, Alia buried her face in Cindy's chest.

Cindy stood up and grinned at me. "She says later. She looks like she's ready for a nap anyway. I usually try to get her to sleep in her own bed, but today I think we'll make an exception."

With that, Cindy carried Alia up the stairs and disappeared.

My first order of business was exploring the house. I wasn't going to climb the stairs, accepting that the second floor was a designated Adrian-free-zone until Alia said otherwise, so I took a tour through the rest of the first floor.

There wasn't much, really. The only other large room on the first floor was the dining room, which could be entered from either the living room or kitchen. It contained a heavy oak table, set with an expensive-looking flower vase on a lacy white tablecloth, and surrounded by four sturdy straight-back dining chairs. There was a large calendar hanging on one wall. Seeing it, I realized that I didn't even know what day of the week it was. I'd have to ask Cindy later.

As for the rest of the first floor, there was a hallway that led to the front door, as well as a moderately spacious bathroom and toilet. I noticed that the front door had an additional lock near the top. I could just reach it, but I briefly wondered whether Alia was a guest or a prisoner here.

I looked at myself in the bathroom mirror and was shocked at how grimy I was. I thought I had been washing myself well enough with bottled water these past weeks, but apparently not. I smiled to myself as I remembered how Alia had jumped when she saw me. I would have been a bit scared too!

I hastily undressed and stepped under the shower. Even before using any soap, the steaming water swirling into the drain turned dark gray. I could feel the dirt coming out of my hair, and out from between my toes. It felt wonderful. It made me feel like a normal person again.

After toweling myself dry, having no change of clothes, I had no choice but to put my dirty stuff back on. At least I was clean underneath now.

Then I went back to the living room and looked through Cindy's bookshelf. I was half-expecting to find titles about supernatural powers, strange religious cults and ceremonies, or vampires and the devil, but there was nothing of the sort. There were a few cookbooks, various magazines, quite a few novels including several (ugh!) romances, a big black leather-bound Bible, and a full set of very thick encyclopedias. Cindy had yet to discover the internet. I pulled out a nature magazine with a cover title that read *Paradise Lost* and flipped through it, looking more at the animal pictures than reading. Time passed slowly, but at least I was inside a house as opposed to on top of it.

Cindy came down by herself at about five o'clock.

"Hey, I see you cleaned up," she said, looking me over.

"Yeah," I said, self-consciously fingering my dirt-stained left sleeve.

"I'll get you some new clothes tomorrow."

Cindy's eyes stopped on my hands. I glanced down at my rough and uneven fingernails. During my first week on the run, I had bought and tried using a proper nail cutter, but the steel drained my strength too much for me to hold it to my fingertips. I had been using my teeth ever since.

I gave Cindy a sheepish look. "I'm not a nail-biter, Cindy. I just can't cut them by myself."

Cindy smiled. "I'll trim them for you later. Your toes too."

I almost shook my head. After all, what kind of twelve-year-old would let someone cut their nails for them?! But Cindy obviously understood about metal draining and I felt it impolite to refuse her offer.

"Thank you," I replied, feeling utterly embarrassed.

"It's no problem."

"Just out of curiosity, what day is it?"

Cindy laughed. "Sunday. We're a week from October. You really were out of it, weren't you?"

I ignored the assessment. "You said that your shift was starting tomorrow, Cindy. What does that mean?"

"Oh, I'm a nurse at the general hospital near here. I have to be there for the day shift tomorrow," said Cindy, and then suddenly switched to a really fake game-show-host-like cheerful sing-song tone as she added, "And *that* means *you* get to spend the *whole* day *alone* with Alia tomorrow! Isn't that *nice?*"

I rolled my eyes. "How is she going to survive that?"

Cindy dropped the game-show voice and said grimly, "Oh, you'd be surprised at what Alia has survived. She'll manage."

"I hope so."

Cindy gave me a concerned look. "Alia isn't a controller. You know that, don't you? She's just telepathic. That's all."

"I won't hurt her, if that's what you mean."

"I know you won't. But Adrian, I really would like you to try and be her friend. She needs that right now."

"How old is she?" I asked.

"Seven and a half. I know she's small for her age."

Like me, I thought to myself, but I wasn't about to say that out loud. Instead, I said, "She doesn't look much like you."

"She's not related to me, if that's what you're asking," said Cindy. "She's just borrowing my last name. Not that she's ever needed it."

Cindy picked up the telephone and started dialing, saying to me at the same time, "Sorry I didn't do this earlier, but I wanted to catch him at home."

Guessing what it was about, I got closer to the phone, hoping to listen in if I could. A moment later, I heard a click and then a male voice at the other end probably saying hello, though I couldn't quite make it out. Cindy took on a businesslike tone that I hadn't heard before, but guessed was her work voice at the hospital.

"Hey, Brian, it's me, Cindy... Yeah, great... Listen, I'm calling in a big-time you-owe-me... I need you to do a check on a missing juvenile report. Well, two of them, actually... I know that's public, but I don't want to attract any attention to my interest in this case. You have to do this quickly and quietly... Yeah, I know I'm on the phone! Don't worry so much! Their names are Adrian and, um..."

"Catherine," I mouthed.

"Uh, yeah, Adrian and Catherine Howell. Siblings, twelve and ten, respectively. They went missing a few weeks ago. I just want to know when the reports were filed and whether or not they were found... No, not here.

73

They lived in..."

Cindy relayed to him my hometown address, told him how to spell our names, thanked him and hung up.

Then she turned to me and said, "Well, all we can do now is wait. Brian said he'll get me the information tomorrow, during his break. He'll probably bring it directly to me at the hospital. The police station is right across the street from where I work."

"He's a cop?" I asked.

"That's right."

"So, um, what was the 'big-time you-owe-me'?"

Cindy giggled and said, "Well, among other things, I once helped pull a bullet out of his butt."

I laughed too, and Cindy asked brightly, "Hey, are you hungry?"

"Oh yes!" I answered truthfully.

"We'll remedy that in a moment. Alia's still asleep, though I'm afraid she might not sleep well tonight, the way she's out now. I'm guessing she stayed up really late last night. I'll wake her just before dinner, and then maybe she'll go right back to bed."

I gave Cindy a disbelieving stare, but she shrugged and said, "I'm an optimist."

Then Cindy looked me in the eye and, in a slightly over-serious tone, asked, "Do you want to learn a new power, Adrian?"

"Sure," I said. "Is it possible?"

"Yup. I'm going to teach you how to cook."

We made lasagna together. In truth, I didn't learn much about cooking, blindly following Cindy's directions, but I did make another important discovery.

"Here, hand me the knife," said Cindy, busily mixing something, her back turned to me.

I reached out for the kitchen knife lying on the counter. It had a black wooden handle, and probably because I wasn't expecting it, it took a moment for me to realize that I was being drained. I fumbled the knife, tried to catch it, but instead sliced open my left thumb before dropping the knife back onto the counter. My senses were too dimmed for there to be much pain, but I could feel the blood trickling slowly down my hand. I covered my bleeding thumb with my right hand, putting pressure on the wound.

Looking carefully at the knife, I could just make out the dark little circles on the wooden handle, which were the ends of metal bolts running through it and connecting to the blade. Those were what had drained me. My head was still swimming, and I leaned against the counter for support.

"Adrian? What's the matter?" said Cindy, turning around. She didn't know I had cut my thumb, but saw me steadying myself against the counter and asked, "What did you get drained on?"

"The knife handle," I answered, still tightly holding my injured thumb.

"I had a feeling about you when you had trouble with the seatbelt," said Cindy, "but I didn't think it was this bad."

I didn't understand why, but my head wouldn't clear. It was like I was still being drained. I slumped down on the kitchen floor.

Cindy looked at me anxiously. "Hey, hey, hey, are you going to be alright?"

"It'll pass," I answered weakly.

"Honestly, Adrian! Even Alia doesn't get nearly this bad."

"Oh, thanks a lot," I said sarcastically as I forced myself to stand up straight.

A drop of blood hit the floor, and Cindy stared at me, horrorstruck. "You're bleeding!"

"It's nothing," I told her. "It's not deep. I just need a Band-Aid."

I didn't care about my thumb. Something else was much more wrong. Why couldn't I recover my strength after dropping the knife? I wasn't touching metal anymore, was I?

"You need to wipe the blood off," said Cindy.

She grabbed my arm and dragged me to the sink, where she showered the blood off of my hands. I instantly felt better, my head clear again, but the pain from the cut came back to me in full force. Cindy popped out of the kitchen for a moment and returned with a small first-aid kit. Opening it, she pulled out a bottle of antiseptic and a box of Band-Aids.

"You have to be careful about bleeding, Adrian," she said, cleaning my cut. "You know that there is iron in your blood, right? It doesn't drain you because it's inside your body. But if you start bleeding, the iron coming out of your body will drain you, like it did just now."

"I had a nosebleed once, a few weeks ago," I said, remembering Cat and her frying pan, "and it didn't affect me very much."

"Well, that was weeks ago, right? Your power has grown since then, and your body has become more sensitive to draining. A little blood is usually not as bad as touching a bigger piece of metal, but, well, you know how it feels now."

I wrapped the Band-Aid around my thumb as Cindy picked up the kitchen knife, holding it delicately by the blade to examine the metal bolts in the handle. Looking closer at the blade's edge, I noticed that it had only the slightest trace of my blood on it. The knife must have been razor-sharp, and I was lucky that I hadn't cut my thumb off. Cindy was a serious cook.

"I have knives with plastic handles too, but please be careful with them," said Cindy as she deftly flipped the knife in the air and caught it by the handle.

"Cindy, why does the metal affect me like this?" I asked.

"Oh, it affects all of us in the same way, though to different degrees," said Cindy. "I'm actually very sensitive to metals. Even a little contact can drain me completely."

"But you don't…"

"Fall down when I touch it?" Cindy smiled. "That's because I have my power properly balanced."

"And what does that mean?" I asked, irritated at how easy Cindy looked holding the knife in her hand. I also remembered how Ralph didn't seem to have any trouble handling the chain that he put around my neck.

"It means I know how to keep my power from taking over my physical body," said Cindy.

My continued lack of understanding must have shown on my face because Cindy crouched down in front of me and said slowly in a concerned voice, "Adrian, I want you to listen to me very closely now, because this is important. I'm not worried about the metal draining your psionic power, as long as it's just that, and not your whole body. You are being physically overrun by your power. This can happen to people when their power comes too early or too suddenly, which in your case is both, and they haven't had time to learn how to separate it. If you don't learn balance, you will lose yourself in your power."

"Lose myself?" I asked.

"Your power has already started to support your bodily functions. You've let your body rely on your power too much. That's why you get dizzy when your power is drained. Do you understand?"

I nodded.

Cindy continued, "Once you learn how to balance your power and keep it from supporting or replacing your physical strength, you'll be able to freely touch any metal without feeling dizzy or tired, even if you can't fly or telekinetically knock things over."

I thought back to the berserker attacks. If I hadn't been physically and emotionally drained by touching metal, I might have seriously hurt or killed Cat even without my power. And what about Ralph? Could I have escaped him without draining my emotions on the pen tip? I realized that I might not be alive now if I didn't have this weakness. Still, Cindy had a point: I couldn't go on feeling faint every time I touched a piece of metal, especially if there was metal in my own blood. I was lucky not to have been injured until now.

"And you can teach me how to balance my power?" I asked.

"Even Alia could probably teach you a thing or two," Cindy said with a chuckle, and I scowled at her.

I decided to shift the topic, asking, "Can you also learn to resist metal? I mean, so that your power doesn't get drained at all?"

"As far as I know, that is impossible."

"And what if I can't learn to separate my power from my body?" I asked, needing to hear the worst.

Cindy looked at me for a moment, perhaps contemplating how, or how much, to tell me, before answering, "Well, the sad truth is that some people never learn balance, and their bodies slowly decay. Like a degenerative disease, your muscles will deteriorate and you will age faster. It can turn into a vicious cycle, with your body needing more and more support from your powers as your muscles and organs get weaker. And if you were drained in that condition..."

"I could die," I said quietly.

"Yes, Adrian. You could."

Finally, I understood. Cindy was right: I definitely needed to learn how to separate my psionic power from my body.

"So, how do I learn to balance it?"

"All in good time," said Cindy, passing me the plastic bowl and a large wooden spoon. "For now, mix."

Alia came down by herself as we were about to set the table. She looked a bit groggy, and didn't make as much fuss about me as she did earlier. However, she still kept her distance, preferring to cling to Cindy's leg or nervously study me from behind a chair.

Once the table was set, complete with plastic forks and knives, Cindy sat on one side with Alia next to her, and I sat across from Cindy. Dinner was a bit of a comical affair, with Alia speaking telepathically to Cindy, who, of course, replied out loud.

"Adrian," said Cindy.

"Yes?" I asked, looking up from my plate.

"No, not you," said Cindy. "I'm teaching Alia your name again." She turned to Alia, saying, "It's Adrian. Try saying it out loud, honey."

Alia refused to try until Cindy had asked five more times. I could tell that Cindy was quite used to Alia's refusal to speak aloud.

"Adrian, honey," Cindy repeated to her patiently. "Just try."

Alia finally uttered hoarsely, "A-en."

"Adrian?" Cindy said again.

"Me?" I asked.

"Yeah, you. Would it be okay if she called you Addy? I think Adrian might be a bit hard for her."

"Practice makes perfect?" I asked hopefully.

"Adrian! Addy is your nickname, isn't it?"

"It's not my nickname, Cindy," I said. "It's my *baby* name."

Cindy grinned. "I still like Addy better."

Alia glanced at me once and then turned to Cindy, who laughed loudly. "She says she likes Addy better too."

I groaned, but Cindy looked pleadingly at me.

"Okay, okay," I sighed. "She can call me whatever she wants."

"Great!" Cindy smiled broadly and chirped, "Addy and Ali! That sounds like quite a pair, don't you think?"

"Cindy?" I said, narrowing my eyes.

"Yes, Addy?"

"You call me Adrian, please."

"As you wish, Addy."

I made a face, and Cindy giggled. For the first time, I saw a slight hint of a smile on Alia's lips too.

After dinner, the three of us sat together in the living room where Cindy read a fairytale to Alia. Although Alia still preferred to sit as close to Cindy as possible without occupying the same space, at least she no longer jumped whenever I moved. Cindy seemed relieved that the ice had broken a bit before her day shift started, but I still felt very uncomfortable about the prospect of being left in the house with Alia.

Cindy put Alia to bed at around nine. Then, asking me to remain silent while she worked her power, Cindy sat down cross-legged on the living-room floor, closing her eyes in quiet concentration. I couldn't feel anything different, but nearly half an hour later, Cindy opened her eyes and stood up.

"That'll hold for a while," said Cindy. "Still, I'd prefer it if you didn't go out... just yet. You are still officially missing, and if you're found by the police, you'll be taken away from my protection."

I asked hesitantly, "Cindy, um, how long does 'just yet' last?"

Cindy looked at me for a moment, and then threw her hands into the air, saying, "Alright! I lied. You can't go out at all, Adrian. Ever. As long as you're staying with me, you're trapped in this house, just like Alia. If people see you, they'll ask questions. If they ask questions, you'll be found."

It took a moment before I felt the full weight of her words. At the same time, I was, and wasn't, a prisoner here. I could leave Cindy's protection whenever I wanted to, but then I would risk being caught or killed. That Cindy's hiding bubble covered the whole neighborhood made no difference at all. I would be safe only as long as I stayed inside her house. I felt like I was back in the hospital after my accident. I had to force myself hard to consider that my situation was still better than it had been yesterday.

"So Alia has been here... how long?" I asked, not entirely sure I wanted to know.

Cindy's eyes met mine for an instant, and then she looked away. She took a deep breath and answered, "Three years."

"Three years?!"

"There was no other way, Adrian! You've seen what she's like. I've been taking care of her here ever since I brought her back from the..." Cindy's voice trailed off.

"Back from where?" I asked.

Cindy looked at me, her eyes starting to swim with tears.

"Back from where, Cindy?"

"From the forest," she whispered, her voice quivering slightly. "From the forest, Adrian."

"Tell me about her, Cindy. Please. Tell me her story."

"Well, I guess you ought to know," said Cindy, wiping her eyes. "You see, most people don't turn psionic until they are adults, or at least very close to adults. Sometimes, they don't gain their true power until they're really old. Babies and very small children can have a touch of ESP, but that's not real power. You, Adrian, are a rarity. I called you 'little destroyer' in the car because it's almost unheard of for someone your age to be able to do what you can do. But Alia..."

"She had her power from birth?" I guessed.

"That's right," said Cindy. "She was probably a full telepath from the day she was born. She didn't know that people communicate using their mouths. Her parents thought she was a mute—until she started talking directly into their minds. Her parents..." Cindy paused, sighing deeply once before saying, "They were religious fanatics. You know the kind... the devil this, the devil that."

I didn't exactly, but nodded anyway.

Cindy continued, "They thought Alia was possessed. They must have tried to exorcise her many times. And they beat her, and cut her. They poured boiling water down her throat. They tortured her, Adrian. They tried to torture the devil out of her. When she was four years old, they finally decided that they couldn't save her soul, so they took her into the mountains, tied her to a tree and left her to die."

Cindy stopped talking for a moment and closed her eyes. I stared at her, horrified and speechless, and Cindy resumed her story.

"Alia had somehow broken free of the rope tying her to the tree," explained Cindy, her eyes still shut. "Days later, I found her wandering through the forest, half-dead, naked, with a piece of rope tied around her ankle. Her whole body was covered in mud and leeches."

Cindy slowly opened her eyes and wiped them with her fingers. "I brought Alia home and nursed her back to health, but her physical injuries were nothing compared to how hurt she was on the inside. For the first year, Alia didn't say a single word to me, even telepathically. She doesn't trust people, Adrian. She doesn't trust the world, and you can hardly blame her."

I looked down at my hands, not knowing what to say.

"So now you understand," I heard Cindy say softly, "why I said that your story wasn't the worst I've ever heard."

"Yes," I answered dully. Thinking of what Alia must have gone through made me feel as drained as if I had been lying on a metal bed. Under the circumstances, I decided, if anyone deserved to live happily ever after, it was Alia.

"You'll take care of her?" Cindy asked hopefully. "You'll watch out for her?"

I nodded silently, and Cindy said, "Alia is a healer."

I looked up. Cindy smiled a little and explained, "Telepathy isn't such a big deal in terms of psionics, unless you're a pair of devil-obsessed psychopaths, but healing is. Healers are rare, Adrian. Even rarer than controllers. Alia can close wounds and mend bones."

I glanced at my Band-Aided left thumb.

Cindy nodded and said, "I'm sorry I didn't ask her to take care of that during dinner, but I didn't want to pressure her."

"It's okay. It doesn't hurt anymore."

Cindy looked grimly at me, saying, "What do you think your pal Ralph would do if he learned that there was a healer here? What would any Angel or Guardian do? Despite her age, Alia's power as a healer is already as refined as any adult's, and I'm guessing she may become very, very powerful someday. What would happen, do you think, if the existence of a powerful healer became known among the psionic factions?"

It was a rhetorical question so I just blinked back at her, and Cindy said, "Please don't get me wrong, Adrian. I wanted to help you too. I do want to help you. But I was also hoping you could help me as well, with Alia. You're right. Three years is a long time. She's getting older, and I know it's wrong to keep her shut away in my house. But I'm afraid for her."

"You don't have anyone here to help you with her?" I asked. "Family?

Or friends?"

Cindy shook her head. "Not at the moment. At least, no one I can really trust."

"No husband or anything?"

"Oh, well, I was married for a while, but…" Cindy's voice trailed off.

I felt awkward asking these personal questions, but I pressed her, saying, "Cindy, I told you my story. You told me Alia's. What about yours?"

"I'll tell you my story, Adrian. I promise I will. But can it at least wait till tomorrow? I'm still pretty tired, and you'll be here in the morning, won't you?"

"My parents are dead, Cindy," I replied quietly. "Where am I going to go? If only I could be sure that my sister is okay, I'd stay and help you all you need."

"Thank you, Adrian. I'll show you to your room, okay?"

Cindy led me up the stairs. There were four rooms along a narrow corridor. Cindy briefly opened the door to her own bedroom just to show me where it was, and then opened another door that led into a dusty storage room with some old furniture and many cardboard boxes. After I had taken a quick peek in to satisfy my curiosity, Cindy closed that door and led me farther down the corridor toward the last two.

"This one here is Alia's room, which we won't open because she'll wake up. And here is yours," said Cindy, opening the last door. "Sorry it's so Spartan. I didn't have a lot of time to prepare it, and besides, I wasn't entirely sure I'd find you before someone else did."

"I was wondering about that," I said as I stepped into the tiny room, which was furnished with a small bed, an old oak cabinet, and a black antique writing desk with a cushion-less wooden chair. There was just one small square window over the bed. The room wasn't much, but to someone who had spent the last three weeks outdoors, it was a five-star hotel. I decided that Spartans had it easy.

"Wondering about what?" asked Cindy.

"Oh," I said, sitting down on the bed and looking up at Cindy, "I was wondering why no one else had found me sooner. I was always afraid that the Angels might send someone else to kill me, or that Ralph was still chasing after me."

Cindy smiled. "Even after you hit him with a chair?"

We laughed, and Cindy said, "He's never going to hear the end of that. Clobbered by a little... well, clobbered by a soon-to-be-thirteen-year-old. Still, I'm sure that sooner or later, you would have been found by someone. Wild-borns never stay wild very long. And it's not just psionics that try to find us, either."

"You mean the church people?" I asked. "The God-slayers?"

Cindy nodded grimly. "On their holy crusade to kill all gods but the one god. But as for the Angels and Guardians, I'm sure they were already closing in on you. Both factions would want you on their side, and no one likes a lone wolf, Adrian."

"A lone wolf," I repeated, raising my eyebrows, "like you?"

"Like I said, I'm good at hiding," said Cindy.

"I'm not good at hiding."

"Locating a child, even with powers like yours... Well, very few finders are up to the task. Besides, it's hard to sense anyone in the city with all that metal. That's why the Guardians' gathering that Ralph was taking you to was being held in the city. They almost always are."

I looked at her, urging her with my eyes to say more.

Cindy laughed, saying, "I can see there's no end to your curiosity, Adrian. It was a mistake to mention the Guardians again. We'll be up all night if I talk about them."

"Oh please, Cindy," I begged. "At least tell me what a gathering is."

"Okay, that won't be too hard," she said, sitting down next to me on the bed. "You know that the Angels and the Guardians are fighting, right?"

"Ralph said it was a war."

"Ralph is old and senile. He's exaggerating. It's more like a feud. Do you know what that is?"

Obviously Cindy still thought I was ten years old.

I answered mechanically, "A feud is a series of small clashes between two families that lasts through many generations."

"Exactly," said Cindy, nodding. "It's not an all-out war. If it was, it'd be all over the news, I guarantee it. But both sides know that, and neither wants to be discovered by common people. We may have power, Adrian, but not in numbers."

"And the gathering?" I asked.

"Well, even in a large psionic faction like the Guardians, the members don't all live in one place, but rather in small clusters all over the country," explained Cindy. "A gathering can be called for any of a number of reasons. It could simply be for entertainment or exchanging news. Occasionally, they might pool their forces for an offensive against another faction. Gatherings are often held underground, where it's even harder for enemy finders to locate."

"And how many gather?"

"Oh, a fair few, usually. The Guardians are slowly dying out, but still, there'd be, ah... possibly fifty or sixty."

"That's it?" I asked. I had been imagining a stadium-size location jam-packed with all kinds of people with wild abilities.

"Well, they don't all gather at once," said Cindy. "Besides, it could have been just for the leaders, in which case, only a handful. I don't know. I'm not a Guardian anymore."

I stared at her. "Cindy!"

"Oops!" laughed Cindy, putting her hand to her mouth. "Did I just say that?"

"Yeah, I heard it," I said, narrowing my eyes. "Loud and clear."

"Look, Adrian, that is a really complicated story, and long too. Do you really need to hear it right this instant? I promise I'm not with them."

"Okay, Cindy," I said. "It can wait."

Cindy smiled warmly and got to her feet. "If you want to stay up, it's okay, but it's bedtime for me."

"Cindy?" I said as she reached the door.

Cindy turned around. "Yes?"

I smiled. "I'm glad you found me."

"I'm glad I found you too, Adrian. Goodnight."

Cindy closed the door behind her. I sat on the bed for a while, thinking of all the things I had learned that day. About power, and the people who have it. Only twenty-four hours ago, I was alone on a building roof with nowhere to turn to, in constant danger of being found by Ralph or someone like him. I realized that I had been extremely lucky to be found by Cindy. I touched the pendant around my neck, feeling the smooth, polished stone between my fingers. For a brief moment, it felt like Cat was sitting right there beside me, and I was home.

After turning out the light, I stood up on the bed and looked out from the small window. I was hoping to catch a glimpse of the moon before I went to sleep, but I guess it was on the other side of the house.

7. LIFE IN HIDING

I wasn't woken until half past eight the next morning when, of all things, I heard Alia's small voice in my head calling, *"Addy? Addy, Cindy says wake up."*

I quickly got out of bed and rushed downstairs. In the dining room, Alia was just finishing her bacon and eggs. She jumped a bit when I ran in, and I apologized for scaring her. As I wolfed down my breakfast, Cindy asked me about my clothing size.

"I'll do some shopping for you on my way home. Please don't hate what I get. I'm late! I'm late!" she panted, grabbing her handbag as she headed for the front door, Alia and me following in her wake. Apparently, Cindy didn't drive to work.

At the door, she gave Alia a quick hug and said, "That's right, Ali. Addy is going to watch over you while I'm away. You can play with him. I'll be back for dinner. You be a good girl, okay?"

Alia nodded smilingly, and Cindy turned to me. "Adrian?"

"Yeah, yeah, good boy, play with Alia, stay in the house, no problem," I mumbled.

Cindy patted my shoulder, smiled once more at Alia and me, and exited the house.

As soon as the door closed, Alia sprinted back down the hall, through the living room and up the stairs. It seemed that Alia was still very afraid of me, and I didn't know what to do. Through the little window on the front door, I could see Cindy getting on her bicycle, which had been standing just outside. I wondered if I should call Cindy back, but while I was debating this course of action, she rode off and out of sight.

Cindy wanted me to be nice to Alia, but it seemed that the only way to be Alia's friend was to stay far away. I walked back into the living room and sat on the couch, feeling slightly dejected. I wondered if Alia would get hungry enough around lunchtime to brave my presence. Perhaps the best thing for me to do was to go hide in the garage so that the poor little girl could have the run of her house again.

Then I heard a voice in my head say, *"Addy, let's play."*

Surprised, I turned my head toward the stairs, and suddenly I found myself face to face with Alia, who was standing so close to me that our noses were almost touching! I hadn't heard her come down the stairs at all, so naturally I gasped and jumped up. Alia also jumped back a step, and then looked at me, letting out one quiet giggle before darting back up the stairs.

"Come on, I'll show you my room," said her telepathic voice.

I cautiously followed her upstairs.

I hadn't yet seen Alia's bedroom, and when I entered, I was met with a kaleidoscope of colors. It was a miniature toy shop in here, the floor and shelves overflowing with dolls and stuffed animals, the bright pink wallpaper covered with even more brightly colored posters and pictures of panda bears and ponies and all sorts of cute stuff. Whatever I thought about Cindy's decision to keep Alia locked up in a house for three years, there was no denying that Cindy was spoiling her rotten when it came to presents. Looking around, I suddenly understood: This wasn't a kid's room at all. It was a nursery! Cindy was letting Alia relive her baby years here.

But it seemed that Alia had outgrown many of her more babyish toys, preferring the Legos and wooden blocks to the giant stuffed unicorn which stood leaning against her bed.

I sat with Alia all morning, actually enjoying myself as I helped her build a castle with the blocks and played a few board games with her. She still seemed to be keeping a very slight distance from me, and was often silent for minutes at a time. Perhaps I was just more used to Cat's lively personality, but I didn't mind Alia's quiet ways at all. During the last few years before my car accident, I hadn't spent much time even with Cat, naturally preferring to play with friends my own age, so I never imagined I'd enjoy sitting around with a little girl. But after nearly a month on the streets, it felt good just being in somebody's company for a change.

Completely used to being left alone in the house, that day Alia was the one who fixed our lunch of peanut butter and jelly sandwiches, which we ate along with some salad that Cindy had left in the refrigerator for us.

After lunch, I carefully peeled the Band-Aid off of my thumb to check if yesterday's cut had healed. There was still a very thin line left on my skin, but when Alia came over and put her right hand near it, the line disappeared instantly.

"Thanks, Alia," I said, almost patting her on the head before thinking better of it.

Alia took a short nap on the living-room sofa in the afternoon, and I was left to my darker thoughts. True enough, Alia was nothing like Cat, but being with her reminded me of my sister, who I hadn't seen since I sent her running off into the night. I put my hand to Cat's amethyst pendant, which had become a bit of a habit for me, and hoped my fears about my sister were unfounded. Surely, Cat would have long since been picked up by the police and be comfortably adjusting to life with my uncle.

"Addy?" Alia had woken up and was looking at me.

"What's the matter?" I asked.

"My back is itchy."

It still felt a little strange to hear her voice without the accompanying mouth movements, but I was getting used to it.

"Um, okay, come here," I said carefully, apprehensive as to whether she would jump again if I actually touched her. However, she unhesitatingly came up to me and turned around, so I went ahead and scratched her back for her, running my fingernails over the back of her T-shirt.

Even as I did so, I could tell something was wrong. The skin under her shirt just didn't feel right. I ran my fingertips softly along her back, and realized how scarred it was, with lines crisscrossing this way and that, as if her back had been repeatedly cut up. I shuddered. Cindy telling me the story last night was one thing, but actually feeling it on Alia's skin was quite another.

"That tickles!" Alia cried into my head, giggling loudly at the same time and pulling away. Hearing her laughter, I realized that her voice was actually quite normal. She just didn't speak words.

After a sip of apple juice, we were back up in Alia's room playing with her set of wooden ABC blocks. Actually, I was flying the blocks around and over Alia's head as she jumped up and down trying to grab them. When she finally managed to get one of the blocks, Alia turned to me and asked, *"Addy, can you make me fly?"*

"Well, I can, but I don't know if I should," I said, remembering how I had once bashed Cat against her bedroom ceiling.

"Please, Addy?"

I thought about what Cindy had said on the rooftop: "Control? You don't know the meaning of the word."

Well, Cindy, I thought to myself, *someday you'll teach me, I'm sure, but until then…*

I levitated Alia up into the air. She let out a loud shriek, and, mistaking it for fear, I quickly put her back down.

"Again!"

That's how Cindy found us when she came home later that evening: me sitting on the living-room sofa, and Alia laughing and screeching in delight as I flew her around and around the room. Actually, I was just setting Alia down on the floor to take another quick break when Cindy opened the front door, which was fortunate because if I was caught off guard, I might have thrown Alia against a wall or something.

"Adrian!" Cindy cried anxiously. "The neighbors will hear her!"

I grinned. "Tell them you left your TV on."

"I don't have a TV, Adrian."

"Oh, so you did know that?" I said sarcastically.

Cindy laughed loudly herself at that one. Then she held up two large shopping bags that she had brought home. How she had managed to carry them on her bicycle is a mystery I never solved.

"Your new clothes," announced Cindy. "I do hope they fit. But no complaining about my choices, okay?"

As I stood up to take the bags, I felt a dull pain in my left ankle. It wasn't much, but I still wondered why it was there. Hadn't I sprained that ankle a couple of days ago crash-landing after being spotted by a helicopter? Why hadn't I felt the pain before? I wasn't sure exactly why, but I felt it was important, and decided to ask Cindy about it later. Right now, I had a more pressing question.

"Cindy, did you get…"

"…the reports?" Cindy finished for me. "Yes, I did."

"And?"

"Um, Adrian…" Cindy looked at me uneasily.

"She hasn't been found, has she?"

Cindy looked away and said quietly, "I'm sorry."

It was like being plunged into icy water. Somehow, despite all of my fears, I had convinced myself that there was no way Cat wouldn't have been found by the morning after the berserker attack. Hearing Cindy's words brought me back to the real world, where people die and are lost and do not live happily ever after at all.

"Cindy, I need to find her… I need to go home."

Even as I said that, I questioned the wisdom of it. If the police couldn't find her in three weeks, what would be my chances? And yet I felt I had to do something. At the very least, I could poke around in my house, where she might possibly have returned to later that morning. I could visit her favorite park and other places she liked to go. I could talk to her friends…

"Listen, Adrian," Cindy said in a concerned tone, "I understand you want to go looking for your sister. I'll help you in any way I can, but I can't go with you right now. And I honestly don't think you'll have much luck wandering around without any clues."

I was barely listening to her. I looked out the window.

Cindy crouched down in front of me and grasped my hands. "I know I can't stop you from leaving. If you want, I'll give you some money and some hiding protection for the road, but it'll wear off, and then it would only be a matter of time before you're taken by another finder… if the police don't pick you up first."

Looking back at her, I felt a dull surprise as I realized that Cindy was actually offering to help me get back home and search for Cat. Cindy was the first person to offer me any real help since the berserker attack, but I felt even more confused. Clearly Cindy believed, as the small sensible part of me did, that my search would be in vain.

"I should never have let her go off by herself," I mumbled hollowly, pulling away from Cindy and walking to the stairs. "Excuse me."

I went up to my room and closed the door.

How could I have let this happen? If only I had gone with her that night, if only I had been more concerned for Cat's safety than about finding some monster...

I sat down heavily on the bed, trying to gather my thoughts, hoping that they might smother my emotions. So much had happened since I first realized my power. So many things had gone wrong, and so many questions were still left unanswered.

Even with Cindy's aid, I could do little more than go wander around my old neighborhood. And Cindy was right: How long would I last before I was hunted down and captured or killed? But then again, how could I live with myself if I didn't even try? I held Cat's pendant tightly in my hand, desperately hoping I could hear her voice and ask her what I should do. But of course, no answer came.

I heard a soft knock on the door, and Cindy's voice from behind it. "Adrian, maybe you're not hungry, but dinner is almost ready. Can I come in?"

I didn't answer, but Cindy quietly slipped in a moment later.

"Hey," she said hesitantly, and I forced myself to give her a weak smile.

"I know you feel guilty about your sister," Cindy said slowly, "but what happened isn't your fault."

"If I could find her, I wouldn't have to worry about fault," I replied wearily. "Where do you think she is, Cindy?"

"I don't know," Cindy said with a small sigh. "Please don't take this the wrong way, but people go missing all the time. Sometimes they turn up miles away, sometimes years later."

"What should I do?"

Cindy shook her head. "I can't tell you what to do."

"What would you do?"

"Adrian..."

"Just suppose—"

"No!" said Cindy, and I was surprised by the sharpness of her tone. But then she said more gently, "No, Adrian, she's *your* sister. Don't ask me to come between you and her."

Cindy crouched down and looked into my eyes, saying, "I want you to stay. I want you to be safe. But you have to figure this out for yourself. If you want to go looking for her, I already said I'll help you, but you have to decide."

I asked quietly, "What do you think my chances are?"

Cindy looked at me in a pained way, and I said, "That bad, huh?"

I let my back fall onto the bed and stared up at the ceiling.

Ralph wasn't here this time, looking into my eyes and telling me that everything would be okay. Nor could I lean on the excuse of being alone and frightened in an unfamiliar city. No one was telling me what to think, or how to feel about it. However slim, there was still a chance that Cat was alive in my hometown, somewhere. There was a chance to find her. This time, the decision would have to be mine. Completely mine, as would be the responsibility for the consequences.

I closed my eyes, praying that Cat would forgive me as I said quietly, "Cindy, I'll stay."

"Okay, Adrian," Cindy said softly.

I wasn't hungry at all, but I followed Cindy down to the dinner table and ate just enough to keep her happy. Cindy repeatedly praised my "maturity," saying how it was a "difficult choice" I had made and that she hoped it would be the right one.

My decision not to search for Cat had left something empty inside me, as if, by my betrayal, I had gutted my own soul. With my parents gone, Cat was the only family I had left, and I had given up on her, cowering in Cindy's house. It was a horrible pain in my chest.

And yet, strangely enough, I also felt that I was doing the right thing. The police were still looking for Cat. Right now, I needed to focus on myself, so that if Cat really was still alive somewhere, I would also still be alive to see her. Anyway, that's how I justified it in my mind. Over and over.

After tucking Alia into bed that night, Cindy finally showed me the clothes she had bought, and I really did do my best to pretend that I liked them. They were awful! Everything from flower-patterned, pastel-colored sweatpants to shirts and jackets with little cartoon characters on them. There was even a bright pink sweatshirt with a big teddy bear on the front. My new wardrobe was just a larger version of Alia's. It was almost a blessing that I was required to remain out of sight. I wondered if perhaps this was a deliberate ploy on Cindy's part to make me look cuddlier for Alia. The only good thing that could be said about them was that Cindy had taken great care to choose clothes with no zippers and only plastic buttons. I had to endure Cindy's oohing and ahhing after I changed, but at least I was clean.

In addition to my new clothes, Cindy had purchased a thin, light green rope with a plastic clip attached to it.

"What's that for?" I asked when she showed it to me just before bedtime. At first glance, the rope looked a bit like a dog leash.

"This," Cindy said with a smile, "is to keep you in bed at night. You can tie it to your bed and clip the other end to your pajamas. That way you won't drift away in your sleep."

It *was* a dog leash.

I shook my head. "No thanks, Cindy."

"It won't be forever, Adrian," said Cindy. "Just till you're older. Child psionics often accidentally use their powers in their sleep. I'm sure you'll grow out of it in a few years."

"Absolutely not," I said more forcefully.

Cindy laughed. "Alia's no different, you know. She often telepathically talks to me in her sleep. Or mumbles, more like."

"Yeah, but you don't tie her to her bed," I pointed out.

"Well, I won't force you to use it, but I'm afraid you're going to seriously injure yourself someday."

"I'll take the chance," I said. Cindy looked like she was about to argue further, but I deflected her by saying, "Can I ask you a strange question about Alia?"

"Sure."

"What's with all the unicorns in her room?"

It wasn't just the big fluffy one leaning against her bed. Closer examination of Alia's room today had revealed no fewer than twenty unicorns. There were small plastic unicorn toys, tiny glass unicorn ornaments, unicorn-themed picture books and coloring books, and even a board game about unicorns.

Cindy smiled. "She just likes them. She used to sleep hugging the big one. Actually, she still does from time to time."

"She sleeps with that thing?" I asked incredulously.

"Sure." Cindy shrugged. "Why? Didn't you ever have a security blanket when you were little? Fluffy bunny? Teddy bear?"

I shook my head. "I was more of a triceratops kind of person."

"So, about this tether, Adrian..."

"Goodnight, Cindy."

The next three days passed much like the first. While Cindy was at her hospital, I spent most of my time just playing with Alia. Cindy had hinted that she wanted me to continue my school studies at her house, and also tutor Alia as best I could. But since Cindy hadn't yet managed to get any of the school supplies, Alia and I were still on holiday. I wanted to pester Cindy for more information about the psionic world, but for two days, she was very busy at work, coming home just in time to tuck Alia into bed, do her meditating-hiding thing, take a bath and disappear into her bedroom.

On the third evening, Cindy came home early enough to have dinner with us. She even taught me how to make Chinese noodles. Well, at least she tried.

"She sure loves attention," I commented after dinner as I watched Alia crawling all over Cindy in the living room. Alia had been doing that to me for two days now, and I found it difficult to imagine how she could ever have been so timid at our first meeting.

Gently forcing Alia into her lap, Cindy replied, "She does like attention. But only from someone she can trust."

Cindy nodded toward me and I smiled embarrassedly.

"But it's not easy finding people I can introduce her to," continued Cindy, and then raised her voice in mock-frustration, "because she won't talk! All she does is giggle!"

Alia laughed hysterically for a while as Cindy tickled her all over. Finally breaking free of Cindy's fingers, Alia ran and hid behind me.

Cindy chuckled. "So, you found yourself a bodyguard, huh, Ali? Are you talking with Addy like I told you to?"

Alia looked at Cindy and said something, but I couldn't hear what. That was the frustrating thing about Alia: she could only speak to one person at a time.

Cindy turned to me. "Adrian, are you talking with Alia while I'm away from home?"

I looked at Cindy uneasily. "Well, I'm talking to her..."

"Addy—I mean Adrian—she needs to learn to talk with her mouth," said

Cindy. "She only started using her mouth this year, and she still finds it very difficult. It's like a completely different language for her, and she needs to be taught. Alia is already comfortable being with you. You're practically family. I'll get your school stuff as soon as I can, and I'll also start teaching you how to balance your power from this weekend, but in the meantime, work with her."

Despite her selection of horrendously cutesy clothes for my wardrobe and the fact that she sometimes called me "Addy" in front of Alia, Cindy generally treated me like a mature adult, which I appreciated, so I tried to live up to her expectations. Starting the next day, I did my best to get Alia to talk using her mouth.

Cindy wasn't exaggerating when she said that mouth-speaking was a different language for Alia. While Alia could pretty much manage short vowel sounds, any word that required her tongue to move was beyond her. Whatever Cindy had been thinking when she asked me to let Alia use my baby name, "Addy" turned out to be just as hard for her as "Adrian." Perhaps even harder, because Alia couldn't pronounce her Ds at all. With her best efforts, she could just about manage to say "A-yi." "Water" for Alia was "wawa," and "hungry" was "howie," and "Cindy" was "In-ie." It was like the babblings of a one-year-old, except that Alia could speak normally with her telepathy so she simply didn't understand why she should use her mouth in the first place.

Whenever Alia telepathically asked me for something, such as levitating her around the house, my standard reply became, "Say the words, Ali." It rarely worked. Upon relentless demand, she might try to say a word or two, but her attempts were as feeble as they were frustrating for the both of us. I even wondered if Alia's tongue was somehow handicapped, possibly malformed. Cindy assured me that it wasn't, saying, "She just needs practice."

But Alia didn't want practice. I tried being nice, firm, patient, but nothing really worked. I even bullied her a few times, refusing to let her have what she wanted until she asked for it out loud, but that always ended in tears.

Cindy had to work all day Saturday too. When I asked her about it, she told me that she was making up the time because she had taken a few extra days off from work that month. She didn't tell me why, but I knew it had been to go searching for me.

On the morning of the last Sunday of September, I found myself staring out the window and longing to go out and enjoy the sunny day I knew it was going to become. It would probably be one of the last really warm days of the year. After nearly a month outdoors in the city, I had gratefully welcomed a roof over my head as opposed to under it. But a week was a long time to be trapped inside a house, especially with the knowledge that I couldn't freely leave without risking not only myself, but Cindy and Alia as well, since I knew where they lived.

After breakfast, Cindy sat Alia and me down in the living room and showed us two stacks of books that she had brought home the day before. For Alia, there were first-grade math and writing workbooks, as well as some beginner reading books and even a few coloring books. Since Alia was seven going on eight this school year, I thought she would be given second-grade stuff, but considering Alia's past, I didn't question Cindy's choices. My stack of textbooks included seventh-grade math, history, science, you name it. There was a home-study curriculum guidebook as well.

"I can't be checking everything that you do," Cindy said to me as I glanced through the textbooks, "but I expect you to study those just like you would at school, and I will probably be giving you a test or two before the end of the year."

I peered up into Cindy's eyes, hoping that she was only kidding about testing me on this stuff, but Cindy looked entirely serious.

"These here," she continued lightly, ignoring my frown and handing me some easy storybooks, "are for Alia. They're still a bit above her reading level, but once she's through her first readers, I want you to read these to her and then gradually get her to read along with you."

"Read along with me?" I repeated apprehensively, raising my eyebrows. "You mean with her mouth?"

"Aloud," confirmed Cindy. "Or at least somewhat audibly for starters."

"How?" I asked.

"Experiment. Do whatever works. And in return, I'll teach you how to balance your power."

"Starting now?"

Cindy nodded. "Right now."

"Great!"

"Don't get too excited, Adrian. It's not something you learn in a day."

"I'll try my best."

"I know you will," said Cindy, smiling. "Do you have any questions before we start?"

Actually, I had loads. For starters, I still hadn't heard Cindy's story and what her connection with the Guardians was. But I knew this wasn't the time for questions like that. I asked two others instead, starting with, "You once said Alia has better power balance than I do."

"And she does," said Cindy. "She sometimes gets a little dizzy when she touches metal, but she isn't nearly as bad as you."

"Yeah, but why? If she had her power from birth, how did she learn? You couldn't have started teaching her until you found her, so how did she survive as a baby?"

Cindy paused for a moment before replying, "That's actually a very good question, Adrian, because as far as I know, on the rare occasions that a person is psionic from birth, they are usually destroyed by their powers. But in Alia's case, I think she had some instinctive balance from the start. Some people don't need to be taught how to separate their power from their bodies. They just know."

"How about you?" I asked.

"Oh, I had to learn it. But that's fortunate, because it means I can teach you. Any other questions?"

"Just one more," I said, and explained about how I had sprained my left ankle the night before Cindy found me, and how the pain didn't bother me until the evening of my first day at her house. I asked her why that was so.

"Now that's an even better question," said Cindy, "because it leads right into what I'm going to start teaching you. The short answer is that you had separated your power temporarily. If I remember correctly, you were flying Alia around this room when I got home. You had focused your power away from yourself so much and for so long that your body had to take care of itself."

"But the pain in my ankle went away again soon after that," I said. "Does that mean my power went back to supporting my body?"

"Bingo! So you know that it's possible for you to balance your power, because you already did it once then."

I said excitedly, "So I have to use my power on other things to separate it from my body!"

"No," Cindy said flatly.

"No?"

"You need to learn where your power starts, and where it ends. You need to learn the difference between your psionic power and your actual strength. Only then can you balance the two."

"How?"

"Like this," said Cindy, sitting cross-legged on the floor and folding her hands in her lap.

Sitting across from her, I mimicked. I noticed that Alia had crossed her legs too, watching us. We sat silently for almost a full minute before I asked, "Then what?"

"That's it?!" Cindy cried incredulously. "One lousy minute?"

I stared at her, taken aback, and she said, "I just wanted to see what the natural limit of your patience was. I can see this is going to take some work."

I frowned at the floor, feeling foolish. Giggling, Alia gathered up her coloring books and went upstairs.

For the next hour, Cindy led me through meditation and breathing exercises. Inhale, exhale, inhale, exhale. Focus on your fingertips. Focus on your stomach. All kinds of weird stuff. I promised myself not to interrupt her again, but I was getting more and more frustrated because I couldn't understand what Cindy was getting at. How did this help me know the difference between my power and my body?

"That's enough for the morning," said Cindy, getting up and stretching.

I immediately jumped to my feet, glad that it was finally over.

Watching me, Cindy said, "Your legs should feel numb after sitting like that for so long."

"They don't," I told her.

"I know," said Cindy, grinning. "I just said they *should*."

After lunch, we meditated again for two hours, and yet again after dinner. It was going nowhere for me. Meditation was as tedious as the time spent back on the rooftops, with the added bonus of not being able to see the sky or read a magazine. I think I might even have fallen asleep once during the afternoon session.

"What am I supposed to be looking for?" I asked irritably after Cindy had tucked Alia into bed that night.

"It'll find you," she answered simply, and I was left even more confused.

Cindy then said, "Meditation isn't the only way to learn how to separate and balance your power, but it's the best way I know. It worked for me. I know you're disappointed, but promise me you'll keep doing it while I'm at work, okay?"

I did. Even at seven and a half years old, Alia usually took a nap in the early afternoons, and I used that time to meditate. Sometimes I felt foolish sitting there waiting for something to happen, but it wasn't like there was much else to do. My mornings were spent studying my schoolbooks—yes, I did do that too, though not with any enthusiasm. It felt kind of pointless, seeing as I'd probably never go back to school. I started to work with Alia on her school stuff as well, checking her workbooks and occasionally daring to sit down with her and try making her read her books aloud.

Cindy was now regularly coming home by dinnertime, and we sat at the table talking about our days as if we were a normal family instead of a gathering of outcasts in hiding. Cindy would often lead me through more meditation after dinner. I became better at sitting still, though I still didn't feel any different. I hadn't forgotten about asking Cindy for her story, but I was no longer as bothered with it as I had been before. I trusted Cindy, and didn't feel like imposing on her privacy. The Angels and the Guardians felt a long way off, and just part of a bad dream. Bullet-in-the-Butt Brian had promised to keep Cindy updated on Cat's case, though we heard nothing.

Another week passed.

"So what do you want for your birthday, Adrian?" Cindy asked me at breakfast one morning. My thirteenth birthday, October 12th, was only five days away.

"I don't really know," I answered semi-truthfully.

In fact, I had given very little thought to my birthday. Before all of this had happened, there were a number of things I might have asked my parents to get, but none of that mattered now. I had little use for computer games or the new bike I had wanted since last year. A TV might have been nice, but Cindy had once said that she didn't want to have unnecessary metal things in her house, and in the weeks since I left home, I too had gotten pretty used to not watching any television. I didn't want to sound ungrateful and complain about my girly clothes, either. If there was one thing I really wanted, it was to go outside, but I knew that was impossible.

"Well, if you think of something, just ask," said Cindy. "We'll at least have a little party."

Cindy came home earlier than usual on my birthday. She baked the cake herself, and prepared some delicious stir-fried chicken. I was really starting to admire Cindy's "other power," and promised myself that I would pay more attention to her cooking lessons.

Alia gave me a hug and a birthday card she had made by herself, where she had drawn the three of us holding hands. She had also written some words in every crayon color known to mankind, but I couldn't read any of it.

Cindy handed me a brown paper shopping bag, saying, "Sorry, I didn't have time to wrap it. I just got it today. I couldn't decide what to get you, so I thought this might be best."

"You really didn't have to get me anything, Cindy," I said, taking the bag.

It felt light in my hands and I could tell it was more clothes, so I secretly hoped I would find something a touch more masculine than her previous choices.

"Open it," said Cindy, grinning mischievously, and I could tell by her giggly expression that something was up.

I warily pried open the bag and pulled out something long, soft and light blue. It had *frills*.

"A dress?!" I asked, holding it at arm's length as if it might suddenly explode.

"A dress," confirmed Cindy, smiling even more broadly. She switched to her game-show-host tone, saying, "And here's your wig."

I caught the semi-long ball of dark brown hair in my other hand.

"What am I supposed to do with these?" I demanded crossly, not at all sharing her humor in the situation.

"I thought you might like to go outside," said Cindy.

I stared for a moment at the dress and wig, torn between a desire to laugh and rage. I had been shut up in this house now for three weeks, and my skin was starting to become pale like Alia's. Dressing up like a girl suddenly didn't seem such a terrible price to pay to get out for a while.

"I have a cute straw hat for you too, and you'll look like a nice country girl, Adrianna," said Cindy.

"Adrianna?" I repeated in disgust. "I think I'd still prefer Addy."

Cindy laughed. "Suits me fine, Addy!"

The dress actually fit well, though I had a lot of trouble walking in it at first. It flapped around my legs and I was constantly afraid I'd step on it. Seeing me in it for the first time, Alia couldn't stop laughing, which reminded me of Cat, and I wondered what my sister would say if she could see me now.

"So, how about a quick drive?" asked Cindy.

"Great!" I said enthusiastically, though I was admittedly still quite uncomfortable about going out dressed like this.

Cindy looked over my shoulder at Alia. "We'll be back before bedtime, okay?"

"You're not taking her?" I asked.

"Well, she doesn't like going out," Cindy said matter-of-factly. "Right, Ali?"

Alia said something to Cindy, who looked surprised and replied, "Really? There's a break from tradition. Are you sure, sweetie?"

Alia nodded, and then came up to me and tugged hard on my hand.

"What does that mean?" I asked.

Cindy smiled. "It means she wants to go out."

It was only six o'clock in the evening, but the sky was already pretty dark. Cindy drove us to a nearby shopping mall. Located only three blocks from her house, the large mall was well within Cindy's hiding bubble. Cindy told me that this was where she usually did her shopping on her way back from work. It was probably also where she got my dress. As we got out of the car, Cindy told me again that if I found something I wanted, all I had to do was ask.

The inside of the mall was brightly lit, and there were lots of people walking around. I hesitated at the gate, afraid that my disguise wouldn't fool anyone. Even after I had gathered enough courage to enter, I felt very silly walking through the mall in a dress and a wig. But nobody seemed to be taking any notice, and I gradually felt a little more at ease.

Alia, on the other hand, seemed to regret her decision to come with us almost immediately after we pulled into the parking lot. We dragged her into the mall, but she firmly latched herself onto Cindy and, though I couldn't hear her, I knew she was pleading to be taken home.

"It's okay, Cindy, we can come another time," I said.

Picking Alia up in her arms, Cindy said to me, "Well, if you like, Addy, I'll take Alia home now and come back later."

So I was left alone in the mall to wander around at my leisure. I played with some of the computer games on display at the toy shop, but I found that I didn't enjoy them as much as I used to. I strolled through a bookstore and a music store before stopping to look at some clothes, wondering if I might politely convince Cindy to get me something normal after all. Then I suddenly realized how out of place I looked: a girl in the boys' clothing section. I hurried out.

My wig hair felt heavy and was overheating my neck so much that I was actually sweating a little. I never knew how much trouble long hair could be. Did girls feel like this all the time? I stepped out of the mall into the cool night air and sat on a concrete bench overlooking the parking lot.

"Hey there, young lady."

It took me a moment to realize that the deep male voice was directed at me. I turned my head and saw a uniformed security guard standing at the entrance.

"We're closing in about fifteen minutes," he said. "Are your parents around?"

I didn't answer, afraid that my voice would give me away. I must have looked really nervous because the security guard came up even closer and peered into my eyes.

He frowned slightly, saying, "You look familiar."

I just shook my head, stood up and ran down to the parking lot, where I could see the headlights of Cindy's SUV as it pulled into the lot. I nearly tripped over my dress as I sprinted up to the side of the car.

"Adrian, what's the matter?" asked Cindy, opening the door for me.

I jumped in, panting, "Just go!"

As we pulled out of the parking lot, I caught a glimpse of the security guard walking back into the mall. On the drive home, I explained to Cindy what had happened.

"Well, I don't remember seeing your picture in the paper, but that doesn't guarantee your face isn't known," Cindy said to me after we got back. I was still shaken by the close call, and spent the rest of the evening feeling grateful for the invention of walls. All things considered, it wasn't one of my best birthdays.

But it wasn't until the next morning that I realized how much harder a time it had been for Alia.

I was usually woken in the mornings by Alia's telepathic wake-up calls, but that day, it was Cindy knocking on my door and saying that breakfast was already on the table. By the time I got dressed and made my way down to the dining room, Cindy and Alia were already seated.

"Good morning, sleepyhead," said Cindy as I sat in my usual chair across from Alia.

"Good morning," I yawned.

I noticed that Alia looked about as dazed as I felt. She was silently staring down at her plate of ham and eggs. She hadn't even looked up when I sat at the table, which was strange because, these days, she usually started chattering into my head the moment she saw me.

"Good morning, Alia," I said again.

Alia still didn't move, so I telekinetically rattled her plate a little. "Hey, what's the matter?"

Alia finally looked up at me, gave me a distracted smile, and telepathically mumbled into my head, *"Hi, Addy."*

Then she looked down again and resumed staring at her plate.

"It's alright," Cindy said to me as she gently rubbed Alia's back. "Alia's a little out of it this morning. She had a rough night. Bad dreams."

I had no doubt that her rough night had been triggered by her trip to the mall yesterday. I hadn't fully appreciated how frightened Alia was of strangers until now.

"We shouldn't have gone out," I said apologetically.

"Don't worry, Adrian," said Cindy. "She'll come around."

Cindy gently coaxed Alia into taking a few bites of scrambled egg, but Alia left the rest of her breakfast untouched and, without helping clear the table, quietly slipped up to her room.

Though it was a Saturday, Cindy had to leave for work right after breakfast. At the front door, I asked her if Alia was really okay.

Cindy assured me that she was. Apparently, Alia used to act this way much more frequently when she was younger, so Cindy was used to it. "Alia

103

can be pretty moody when she's feeling upset or insecure, Adrian, but it always passes."

"But is that normal?" I asked worriedly.

Cindy smiled. "It's normal for Alia. When she's like that, it's best to just give her some time. Sit with her if you like, but let her come back on her own. You might want to give her a break from her mouth-speaking practice today."

I was only too happy to. Once Cindy left, I made my way upstairs to check up on Alia. She had pulled her big unicorn up onto her bed and was sitting with her arms wrapped tightly around its neck.

"Are you alright, Alia?" I asked from the door.

Alia didn't reply, silently staring off into space with unfocused eyes.

"Alia?" I asked again.

She slowly turned to me and, though she still didn't say anything, she gave me a sad little wave.

"I'll be downstairs if you need me," I said awkwardly.

Studying my schoolbooks in the living room, my mind kept wandering up to Alia, wondering what was going through her head as she sat alone in her room. Alia was often a bit on the quiet side, but this was different. She had looked so... hollow. I couldn't stop thinking about the story Cindy had told me of Alia's past, and about the horrible scars across her back. Where had Alia gone in her dreams last night?

Back when I was on the run, sleeping on the rooftops of buildings, I had often relived the night my parents died. I saw my father killing my mother, I saw the berserker's terrifying grin, and sometimes I woke up screaming. My nights hadn't been nearly as bad since arriving at Cindy's house, but I still had my fair share of nightmares, so I understood how crummy a morning could be after a rough night. Still, you wouldn't find me staring off into space like a zombie. I really hoped Alia was okay.

Alia stayed in her room for most of the morning. I was about to go check on her again when she came down by herself and said that she was hungry. After eating an early lunch, she recovered enough of her spirit to want to play a few quiet games, and by the time Cindy returned from work, Alia was back to her old self.

"See?" said Cindy when I told her about Alia's day. "It's just her way of recharging her batteries."

"And I thought I was weird!" I laughed.

"No more crowded places for Alia until she's older," said Cindy. "And none for you either, Adrian. Even with your disguise, it might still be a bit dangerous."

We never returned to the shopping mall, but Cindy adjusted her work schedule again, allowing us to get out of the house every few days to a more secluded spot.

Cindy knew of a beautiful little pond in the countryside. It was only about eighty yards across, half-surrounded by evergreens and, most conveniently, located on a large piece of private property that was owned by a friend of hers who lived overseas. I had to wear my girl clothes until we left the edge of town, and change back into them before heading home, but while I was there, I could move freely and without the long wig. The pond water was too cold to swim in, and we couldn't catch any fish large enough to eat, but Cindy consented to let me do some flying over the surface.

The first several trips were just Cindy and me because Alia adamantly refused to leave the house. However, after much coaxing and repeated assurances that there wouldn't be any people there, Alia started coming with us too. Sometimes we spent the whole day picnicking in a little clearing by the pond. Having recently read a Peter Pan picture book, Alia asked me to fly her over the water like Tinker Bell. I did, though I accidentally dropped her into the icy water when I heard the distant sound of an airplane engine. Alia had never learned to swim. She came up sputtering, cried for a while, and once she had dried off, asked me to do it again.

"Control, Adrian," Cindy said reprovingly.

We didn't go out on Halloween. I felt I was getting a bit old for trick-or-treating, and Alia certainly wasn't up to the challenge. Even so, with each passing day, I felt better about my new life. True enough, I still hadn't heard any news about Cat, which caused me pangs of guilt every time I felt the amethyst around my neck. Nor was I making any progress on my power balance—something Cindy frequently gave me worried looks over. Nevertheless, life with Cindy and Alia had become as normal as it could be. I stopped worrying about people like Ralph completely.

"How's Alia's mouth-speaking coming?" Cindy once asked me over dinner.

That was another thing that wasn't making much headway. In addition to demanding that Alia "say the words," I was now regularly working with her on her storybooks. But while I could sometimes get her to mumble a few of the words aloud, Alia usually just moved her lips silently. I was no lip reader, but I was pretty sure she was just moving them randomly to keep me satisfied. Occasionally, Alia did say a few easy words and phrases almost loud enough to make out her real voice, but she still couldn't manage any sounds that required tongue movement. "Pea may me fai, A-yi," was Alia-speak for "Please make me fly, Addy," and that was the longest sentence I ever managed to get her to say in one go.

"Keep at it," said Cindy. "There's not much point in having Alia use your nickname if she's not going to say it aloud."

"Hey," I said, throwing my hands up in defense, "I agree, Cindy. But Alia just doesn't speak with her mouth."

"She needs to learn."

"And I'm trying to teach her!" I said exasperatedly.

"I know you are. Keep at it," said Cindy, and I did.

The first snow fell in late November, and we had a furious snowball fight by the pond, which was starting to freeze over. I would have had the advantage, of course, since my snowballs would never miss, but to be fair, I deliberately kept my telekinesis out of the battle. Even Alia got a few good hits on me.

Suddenly, Cindy held up her arms and exclaimed, "Stop! Adrian, come here."

Cindy didn't seem panicked, but rather excited as she got me to sit down and close my eyes.

"Can you feel it?" she asked.

"Feel what?" The only thing I could feel was the snow under my legs.

"There's a destroyer nearby," Cindy said quietly.

I opened my eyes in surprise, but Cindy put her right hand on my shoulder and said, "Relax. He can't sense you. I have us hidden. He's not the first psionic to come near us since you came to my house, you know. But this one is a destroyer, so I thought you might be able to feel his presence. Remember, power knows power."

I closed my eyes again, trying to calm myself. Where was the destroyer?

I did feel something different. It was like one tiny instrument in a giant orchestra. Concentrating, you could just hear it when you knew it was there, but the symphony didn't lose much when it was silent.

"I feel it," I said. "I can't tell the direction, though."

"Direction can be difficult if you're not a finder," explained Cindy. "For now, just learn to feel the power."

"It's still really far away."

"Not as far as you may think. Once you are better at tuning into it, you'll be able to gauge the distance fairly accurately, even if you can't tell the direction."

I opened my eyes. "What is he doing?"

"Probably just passing through."

"He's not a telekinetic, though, is he?" I asked.

"Very good, Adrian," said Cindy. "That's right. He, or she, is a pyroid and a light-foot, and may even be a delver, though not too powerful."

"What are those?"

"A pyroid can control fire. It is the power of a destroyer, and that's what you are sensing. Light-foots can lessen their own weight, and delvers can read your thoughts."

I looked sharply at Cindy. "Control them?"

"No, only read them."

Alia must have been upset by the sudden tension in my voice because she asked to go home early that day. It was getting colder, and neither Cindy nor I objected. It was our last visit to the pond that year.

That evening, I asked Cindy to tell me more about what kind of powers psionics had. She explained that everyone was a little different, but there were enough similarities that most psionic powers could be grouped into basic categories. I had already heard that "destroyer" was just a broad term for people with combat-oriented powers. Telekinetics, pyroids and sparks were the most common of destroyers. Sparks could manipulate electricity, and some of them could even create miniature lightning bolts like the thunder god Thor. A "controller," I also knew, meant anyone who could influence your thoughts and emotions, and aside from delvers, berserkers and peacemakers (like Ralph), I learned that there were dreamweavers who could control dreams and induce nightmares, and mind-writers who could implant, modify, or remove memories. And there were many powers that didn't fall into either category. Phantoms could turn themselves invisible. Some light-foots could lessen their weight so much that they could walk on water, while the most powerful of gravitons could drastically increase the weight of things, including people, making it nearly impossible to move. Telekinetics like me were among the few psionics who could defy gravity completely (even if only for a short time), though a powerful windmaster like Ralph could ride his own gale when he wasn't tearing apart houses with tornados. The list went on and on, and there were even some psionics who had powers so unique that they didn't have names. I still had a lot to learn.

"Cindy, there's something else I want to practice," I said one evening during the first week of December, after yet another fruitless meditation session. I wasn't giving up on learning to balance my power, but after two solid months of this, you can imagine how tired I was waiting for a breakthrough.

"One subject at a time, Adrian," said Cindy.

I raised my eyebrows. "Does that mean I don't have to study my school stuff anymore?"

"What do you want to learn?" she asked resignedly.

"How to block people," I replied. "You know, with your mind."

"How to block controllers? That's difficult, Adrian. I'm really no good at blocking, myself. I never learned how to do it properly."

"But you said it's possible."

"And it is," said Cindy. "But it takes practice. Lots of practice. And you'll need a controller who can help teach you to resist."

"Oh," I said, disappointed.

"Besides," said Cindy, "I think you're still a little too young to learn blocking."

I frowned. Nothing riles a kid more than being told he's "too young" to do something, but that didn't change the fact that, without a controller to teach me, I couldn't learn blocking regardless of my age. I wasn't about to give up that easily, though.

"What about Alia?" I suggested. "I know she's not a controller, but wouldn't it be the same thing if I can learn to block her telepathy?"

Cindy pondered that for a moment, and then said carefully, "Not exactly the same, but yes, I suppose it could work." She turned to Alia, who was lazily crayoning a pink and green unicorn in her drawing book. "Ali dear, do you want to help teach Addy some new skills?"

Alia jumped up from her drawing and came over to us. Cindy explained what she wanted us to do. It was actually quite straightforward: Alia would talk to me, and I would try to tune her out. That was the theory, anyway. Alia couldn't wait to get started.

"Can you hear me, Addy?"

"Yes, Alia, I can hear you just fine," I replied, not sure how to even begin blocking her voice. Unlike Ralph, Alia could work her telepathy without eye contact. She could even send her thoughts through walls, as she often did when she woke me in the mornings.

"Addy."

"I can hear you, Ali."

"Addy."

"Yes, Alia."

"Addy."

"Yes..."

"Addy-Addy-Addy-Addy!"

"Yes, I can hear you, Ali!"

It turned into a battle of willpower. A one-sided battle, really, since try as I might, I could find no way to tune her voice out of my head. Alia had decided that this was a fun new game to play, and often just went about repeatedly calling my name and laughing at my reactions. Cindy had it wrong: Telepathy *was* a type of control. Alia was driving me up the wall! And this battle of wills was not unlike my other one to get Alia mouth-speaking and reading her books aloud. I was losing on both fronts.

I found myself doing less and less schoolwork, instead focusing more and more on my "true studies," as I came to call them, my frustration only fuelling my determination to make some kind of progress in either balance or blocking before the end of the year. Cindy grumbled about my lack of commitment to the textbooks from time to time, but didn't press the matter much. At least Alia was still doing her schoolwork, and I was gradually becoming a better cook.

I could tell you about all the fun we had during the holiday season, but I doubt you are all that interested. If you are as fortunate as I hope you are, you will already know what it feels like to enjoy a peaceful and happy time with a family, which is, no doubt, what I had there. I did miss both of my arbitrary deadlines, still having no clue how to keep my body from relying on my telekinetic power, and entirely unable to tune out Alia's constant name-calling. However, at the time, it didn't bother me very much. As Cindy had once said, I still had plenty of time to learn.

8. THE WINDMASTER

Near the end of January, we went back to the pond, this time taking ice skates. In addition to the skates, Cindy had bought me a new snowsuit for Christmas, and once again I was appalled at her fashion sense. The matching jacket and pants were a truly horrific combination of pink, violet and yellow, undoubtedly designed for girls. Still, I couldn't bring myself to complain about a present. At least it was plenty warm and waterproof, and besides, who was going to see me wearing it aside from Cindy and Alia?

The pond was frozen solid, and I spent some time telekinetically moving the snow off a section of the ice to make it skate-able. The result wasn't nearly as large, smooth or level as a proper ice skating rink, but good enough to have some fun. I had learned to skate when I was six, and I easily glided over the uneven ice, weaving between Cindy and Alia as Cindy tried to teach Alia how to keep from falling over.

"*Addy, stop it!*" Alia cried into my head as I zipped past her at top speed.

"Say the words, Ali!" I called back, laughing at her, and the next thing I knew, I was off the ice and painfully sprawled on the pebbles that surrounded the pond.

I quickly checked myself for cuts, but I knew I was okay because I wasn't being drained. I could hear Cindy and Alia having a nice little laugh at me. Although my steel skate blades weighted me down a lot, I managed to levitate myself a yard up off the ground and flew back toward the two.

I had just touched back down on the ice when I heard the crack of a gunshot off in the distance. Blood spattered on the ice. Alia screamed.

I couldn't tell at first which of them had been shot, but I grabbed their hands and started to pull. The skates weren't helping matters at all. I heard another shot, and then a third. I looked down and saw a thin trail of blood on the ice.

Suddenly I was the one being pulled as Cindy grabbed Alia and me and dragged us off the pond. The three of us scrambled into the cover of the trees at the pond's edge as yet another shot rang out. Alia finally stopped screaming, but her eyes were wide with fright. I could hear some men shouting in the distance.

Cindy was clutching her upper left arm, trying to stop the bleeding. "I'm okay," she said, breathing rapidly. "It just nicked me. We have to get to the car."

Cindy's SUV was parked a little farther away, and we'd have to run in the open, through patches of snow and over uneven ground, to get to it. I wished I could fly us there, but I couldn't even lift Alia and myself at the same time, to say nothing of Cindy. On foot, we would be too slow even if we had our regular shoes, which had been left on the other side of the pond.

"Someone will have heard the shots," I panted.

"We can't wait around to be rescued, though," said Cindy. "We'll have to run."

"Wait! Give me the key. I'll fly to the car and bring it down here."

I wasn't sure why I even said that. I had never driven a car before. Cindy stared at me, looking as uncertain as I felt, but there was no time—the men could be here at any moment.

"Cindy, the key!" I shouted.

"Are you sure about this?" asked Cindy, reaching into her pocket.

"Just give it to me. And stay with Alia."

I was wearing gloves, which was fortunate because I didn't bother worrying about being drained as I grabbed Cindy's key ring. Cindy helped me pull off my skates. I didn't want to be slowed down by the metal blades.

Kicking hard off the ground, I lifted myself about seven feet into the air before heading full speed toward the car. I heard another shot as I landed, and the door mirror shattered, spraying me with silvery fragments. Fortunately, Cindy had left the door unlocked, and I got in quickly.

Keeping my head down as low as possible, I turned the ignition. The engine immediately roared to life, and I clumsily drove the SUV down toward Cindy and Alia, nearly running them over.

Having been practically thrown onto the back seat by Cindy, Alia started wailing again as Cindy pushed me aside and took the wheel. As we sped away, I was expecting to be shot at again at any moment, but no more rounds were fired.

"Amateurs…" Cindy muttered under her breath, pulling onto the expressway.

"Who were they?" I asked.

Cindy kept her eyes on the road. "Probably Slayers. Otherwise, they would have wanted us alive. I just wish I knew how they found us."

"Where are we going?"

"First, we're going home," said Cindy. "I can't hide us out here right now. My blood is draining me. We have to get back into my hiding bubble around the house."

"Can't Alia heal you?"

"Does it look like she can?!" Cindy snapped back.

Used to the calm and collected Cindy, I was shocked by the harshness of her tone, but she had a point: Alia was still bawling her eyes out on the back seat.

"It's okay," Cindy said in a steadier voice. "I think the bleeding has pretty much stopped already. I just need to wipe the blood off."

I looked at her anxiously. "What if more of them are waiting at home?"

"If they knew where we lived, they would have attacked us at home during the night," replied Cindy. "We'll have to be quick, though. We can't stay there."

It was nearly dark when we pulled into Cindy's garage. Inside the house, Cindy told me to start packing my clothes so that I could put them in the car. Then she went to the bathroom to clean up her wounded arm. Alia was still sobbing in the living room, but I left her to it and ran upstairs to do as Cindy asked.

I was about to take my gloves off and change out of my snowsuit, but then an all-too-familiar wind started to swirl through the house.

The windows began to rattle, and I heard a loud crashing noise from downstairs. I crept back to the top of the stairs, and as I looked down into the living room, my worst fears were confirmed.

There was glass all over the floor where the living-room window had shattered. Alia had stopped crying. She was standing amidst the glass fragments, looking up at the face of a man I had hoped to never meet again: a tall and skinny old man with curly white hair. Ralph was pointing his heavy wooden crossbow directly at Alia's chest.

"Well, well, what do we have here?" Ralph said in his raspy voice. "A little healer! What's your name, child?"

Alia gazed into his eyes, and a moment later, Ralph said, "Ah, yes. So you're little Alia. I've wanted to meet you. So you're a healer too, eh? No wonder Cindy wanted to keep you secret."

The wind had stopped.

"Ali!" I heard Cindy's voice calling frantically, probably from the bathroom.

Ralph grinned at Alia and said, "You be nice and quiet now, child, okay?"

Alia nodded silently, smiling back up at Ralph. I watched from my hiding place, sickened by what I was seeing. A moment later, Cindy came in, jumped in fright, and suddenly became quiet as Ralph took control of her too.

"Cindy!" said Ralph. "It's very good to see you again."

Cindy smiled pleasantly and said, "Hello, Ralph, it's been too long. How did you find us?"

"Pure, blind luck," said Ralph, grinning. "I was tracking a team of Slayers and they led me right to you."

"Oh, so it was you that saved us?"

Ralph nodded. "I knew the Slayers were after somebody, though I didn't know who, so I followed them to find out. I figured if they were after our enemies, I'd give them a hand before I killed them too. But it was you they were after, and I wasn't about to let them kill the great Cynthia Gifford, now was I? Bullets don't fly straight in a wind."

"Are you still killing everyone who gets in your way?" asked Cindy, her voice as calm as if she was talking about the weather.

"You're not upset about me saving your life, are you?"

"Of course not, Ralph. I do appreciate what you did. But I don't like it when we hurt people."

"Ha! You always were a soft one for humans. But there's never need to show mercy to people who don't know the meaning of the word."

Cindy nodded slowly. "I guess you're right."

"Of course I'm right!" laughed Ralph, and then said so quietly that I could barely hear him from my hiding place, "Don't think I don't know what you did to this girl's parents, Cindy. You're not so different from me."

I noticed that as Ralph was talking, Alia was coming out of her trance. She shuddered once and looked up at Ralph, her face rigid with fright.

Cindy smiled down at her. "It's okay, Ali. This is Ralph. He's a friend."

Alia shook her head and ran to Cindy, grabbing her legs and trying to pull her away.

"Hey, what's the matter, honey?" asked Cindy. "It's okay. Ralph won't hurt you. He's just visiting. Come on, I want you to say hello."

Cindy tried to push Alia toward Ralph, but Alia started crying again, desperately tugging on Cindy's legs.

"We've already met, though no thanks to you," Ralph said accusingly. "After all I did for you, hunting down her parents and all, you never even told me she's a healer."

Cindy ignored Alia's crying. "Oh, I'm so sorry about that. I was meaning to introduce you someday."

"You should never have left us, Cindy. You know that, don't you?"

"Yes, Ralph. I am sorry."

Ralph chuckled quietly. "I must admit, I never expected to see you in this town again. It was smart, but your vacation is over now."

I watched all of this from the stairs, trying to make sense of it. I knew that Cindy was under Ralph's control, but something was missing from the picture. Alia was still bawling and trying to pull Cindy away from Ralph. Watching her, I wondered why Ralph didn't use his peacemaking power on Alia again. Was it possible that he could only control one person at a time?

But that didn't make sense either. Ralph didn't need to constantly keep his power focused on his target. Why was he still focusing on Cindy when she was already under his control?

Then I remembered how Ralph had done the same with me back at the hotel just before leaving me there alone. Ralph was reinforcing his control on Cindy to make it last longer! Now was my one—and perhaps only—chance to act.

I didn't want to try blasting Ralph from the top of the stairs, fearing that even if I didn't miss, I was too far away to hit him hard enough to knock him down. However, if I could sneak up on him while his attention was on Cindy, I might be able to overpower him. All I needed was something to drain him with. Then Ralph would just be an old man with a wheezy voice.

"Addy! Addy, help!" I heard Alia yell into my head.

I almost shouted back to her, but stopped myself at the last instant. Alia was looking up toward me, and Ralph was bound to notice at any moment.

"You know I was never much of a finder, Cindy," Ralph said slowly. "Not like you, anyway. Still, when I was following your car, I could have sworn there was one more with you. And now that I'm close enough, I can feel him in the house too, even with you hiding this place good and proper. A telekinetic... Perhaps another child? It's hard to track a child. Who's the other guest?"

"Oh, you mean Adrian?" asked Cindy. "I think he's upstairs. I'll call him down, okay?"

There was no time to think. Levitating slightly, I kicked off from the top stair and launched myself straight at Ralph, shutting my eyes tightly just before he turned his head toward me. I felt a sharp pain in my left leg as it made contact with the side of Ralph's crossbow, and also felt a dull thud in my right shoulder and arm as I hit Ralph squarely in the chest, sending us both sprawling.

I had to open my eyes to get my bearings. I was on the floor, for the moment in better shape than Ralph, who I had used to cushion my semi-controlled fall. I struggled to my feet and looked around for something heavy to hit Ralph with, but the furniture here was not as easy to handle as the chair back at the hotel.

"Adrian, no," said Cindy, though without any urgency in her voice. "What are you doing? Please don't hurt Ralph."

Cindy clumsily stepped forward and tried to grab me, but she was clearly very dazed and I easily sidestepped her. A moment later, Ralph had stood up and our eyes met.

"Adrian!" Ralph grinned, picking up his crossbow. "Well, well, well, well! Small world, isn't it, lad? You did me in good at that hotel. Smart lad you are! I was mighty impressed! You don't know yet what your power's worth, but you've got spirit, lad. Oh yes, you've got spirit."

Looking into his eyes, I knew I was under his control. I was furious that he had done it to me again. I glared at him, hating that calm old smiling face that took me from my house last year. Ralph, who always knew what was best for me. Ralph, who tied me to a bed and nearly drained me to death with a chain around my neck. Ralph, who refused to help me look for Cat when it still could have made a difference...

"What's the matter, lad?" he asked, looking deeper into my eyes. "Don't you remember your old pal Ralph?"

I smiled back at him. As Ralph continued to gaze into my eyes, I could feel a slight touch of calm spreading through my body, but that was it. Ralph had no real control over me! Just like with Alia, it was a battle of willpower, but this time I had won!

"Yes, Ralph, I remember you," I answered calmly, still smiling as it dawned on me that Ralph didn't know that he wasn't controlling my feelings. Ralph was still holding the crossbow, though loosely in his hands. Hopefully, it would only be a matter of minutes before Cindy was back to normal, and then it would be two against one.

But then I sensed Ralph's calm even deeper in my heart, and I knew I had let my guard down. I focused my anger at him, willing myself not to give in to his influence.

It must have shown on my face, because suddenly Ralph was no longer smiling. He pointed his crossbow at me and took a few steps back. The wind started to pick up again.

"Well, well," Ralph said quietly, "you really are something special, aren't you, lad? You've learned to block it."

"Yes," I breathed furiously, glaring back at him, "I've learned to block it."

"Block this, lad," he sneered.

Cindy had once called Ralph "old and senile," but I'd add "overconfident" to the list. If Ralph hadn't taunted me, I wouldn't have been expecting it, and if I hadn't been expecting it, I might have died then and there. By the time Ralph pulled the trigger, I had thrust my right arm forward, releasing a telekinetic blast. I had intended to blast the crossbow out of Ralph's hands, but instead I ended up blasting the arrow itself as it shot toward me. I didn't quite stop it, but I did slow it enough so that when it hit me, it bounced harmlessly off my thick snow jacket and fell to the floor.

Picking the steel arrow up in my gloved right hand, I ran at Ralph, screaming at the top of my lungs with fear and rage. But before I could stab him, I was hit by a powerful gust of wind that knocked me back. I heard Ralph laugh loudly.

Suddenly I found myself standing in a mini-tornado that had materialized in the living room. It picked me up, and the next thing I knew, my back was pressed hard against the ceiling, the wind pounding my body from below so that I couldn't move. I could barely keep my eyes open. Squinting, I saw Ralph's indistinct shape walk closer to me. He was looking up at me and saying something, but I couldn't hear him because of the howling of the wind around my ears.

I felt my chest contract. The air was being sucked out of my lungs! I closed my lips tightly, but it was no use. The air was leaving my body through my nose. I couldn't breathe. My vision, already blurry because I was squinting, started to fade.

As suddenly as it started, the wind stopped, and I fell back onto the floor, barely able to move. Something had stopped Ralph. My whole body throbbing from the fall, I weakly turned my head to the side, but my eyes couldn't focus well. I could vaguely see Ralph facing Cindy, looking into her eyes. Something metallic slipped from Cindy's hand and fell to the floor.

My eyes were beginning to refocus now, and I could hear Ralph wheezing angrily at Cindy.

"Naughty, that was, Cindy," he said. "It's not nice to drain people when they're having fun."

"I'm sorry, Ralph," Cindy said in a hollow voice. "I didn't mean to."

I could see straight again. I felt the crossbow bolt still clutched in my right glove. This was where lack of psionic balance was an advantage. My power was taking care of my body, and I no longer felt much pain. Lightly jumping to my feet, I lunged at Ralph. I was closer to him this time, and his back was turned.

This time, I'd kill him.

Ralph turned upon me one moment too late. Our eyes met for a split second, and then I plowed into him, thrusting the arrow toward his neck. Ralph stumbled backwards and hit the wall behind him. I followed through, and a moment later I had him pinned against the wall, the steel arrowhead pressed against his neck.

"Are you going to kill me, lad?!" Ralph laughed manically, his fierce eyes daring me to cut his throat open.

"I should!" I breathed savagely through clenched teeth. I even wondered why I hadn't already. What had stopped my hand? Ralph smirked, and I knew that in the brief moment that our eyes had met, Ralph had taken control, preventing me from cutting him open. But now Ralph was being drained of his power, and I was in complete control of my actions. I pressed the crossbow bolt harder against his skin.

"Adrian, don't!" shouted Cindy, but I ignored her. I was sure she hadn't recovered yet.

"Come on, lad," Ralph hissed at me. "Let's see what you got!"

"Please don't," said Cindy. "He's not worth it."

"He tried to kill me, Cindy!" I shouted, my voice shaking. "He tried to kill us all!"

"Adrian, look at him!" Cindy cried desperately. "He's bleeding."

And I instantly knew that this was the real Cindy speaking.

I looked down. Blood was trickling along the edge of the crossbow bolt and onto my glove. More had dripped down Ralph's shirt. I lessened the pressure on Ralph's neck, being careful to keep the arrowhead touching the skin. I wasn't sure if this was enough metal contact to drain Ralph's power completely, but if he tried anything...

"Get some rope, Cindy," I said.

Cindy returned from the garage a minute later with a length of rope. We quickly marched Ralph into the dining room where Cindy tied him to one of the chairs, but not before shoving a pot lid up the back of his shirt to keep him drained.

Leaving Ralph there, I went back to the living room. I didn't want to be in the same room as Ralph at the moment. Cindy followed me and I turned to her.

"Why did you ask me to spare him, Cindy?" I demanded.

"I didn't want you to become a killer," Cindy answered softly. "Not for him."

I wasn't sure that was all. Cindy knew Ralph from her Guardian days, and she knew him a lot better than I had originally thought. I regretted not pressing her sooner for her story. But once again, this was not the time for it. I steadied my breathing and looked around the living room. When my eyes met Cindy's again, we asked each other at the same time, "Where's Alia?"

At some point during the confrontation, Alia had fled to her room. We found her sitting on her bed with her arms wrapped around her knees. Her eyes were closed as she gently rocked herself back and forth.

"Hey, Ali," whispered Cindy.

Alia slowly opened her eyes, but they were dazed and out of focus.

"It's okay, Ralph is gone," Cindy said soothingly. "But we have to leave soon too, honey."

Alia just stared blankly at her. I don't think she said anything.

Cindy turned to me, saying, "Adrian, I'm going to go finish packing. Stay here with Alia."

Cindy left us there. I had never felt so awkward in my life. Gingerly sitting down on the corner of Alia's bed, I just watched her for a moment. I could hear Cindy rushing about downstairs, but that just made the silence in Alia's room all the more unbearable. I looked around at the toys and dolls.

"Addy," said Alia's faint voice in my head.

"Ali," I whispered back, giving her a smile.

"Addy, Ralph is a bad man. He does tricks."

"I know," I said as calmingly as I could. "The bad man is gone."

I held my hand out to her, but she kept her arms tightly around her legs. I gently touched her knees, and was relieved that she didn't pull away.

"You saved me, Ali," I said quietly. "Did you know that? You helped me beat him."

"I'm scared, Addy."

"I know," I said, but stopped myself before I blurted out the truth: that I was scared too. Instead I said, "Don't be scared, Alia. I'll take care of you."

Alia finally looked up at me. *"Promise?"*

"I promise," I whispered. "I'll protect you. No matter what."

Alia slowly lifted her hand to mine, and I squeezed it gently. She squeezed back, and then wiped some of her tears with her other hand.

Cindy came back in. "How are we doing?"

"We're okay," I answered.

"Finish your packing, Adrian. I'll help Alia."

Back in my room, I quickly changed out of my snowsuit and into some regular clothes. I even put on the teddy-bear sweatshirt, hoping it might make Alia feel calmer. I stuffed the rest of my wardrobe into a duffle bag, placing the birthday card Alia had given me on top. I zipped the bag shut and heaved it onto my shoulder. I didn't have any other important possessions except for the pendant around my neck, which I stroked again for good luck. I had a feeling that luck would be in short supply in the near future.

After tossing my duffle onto the back seat of Cindy's SUV in the garage, I went back into the house through the kitchen and saw Cindy and Alia coming toward me. Cindy was carrying both of their clothing bags, and I felt a twinge of sorrow when I saw Alia dragging her giant stuffed unicorn behind her. She was leaving her nursery, probably forever.

"Where are you going?" Cindy asked me as I passed her.

"I'm going to say goodbye to our friend," I said quietly.

Cindy looked at me uncomfortably, so I added, "Don't worry, Cindy. I won't kill him."

"We'll wait in the car," said Cindy, holding Alia's hand. "Be quick, okay?"

I stepped into the dining room, where Ralph was still sitting, tied to the chair. He hadn't tried to escape. He hadn't even moved.

"Hey, Ralph," I said quietly.

"Adrian," wheezed Ralph. "I always hoped we'd meet again."

"Why's that?"

"You've got the gift, lad. You're as powerful as they come, and you still have no idea how very special you are."

"Save your compliments," I replied coldly. "They don't work without your powers."

Ralph snickered once, and we stared at each other. Cindy had said that she didn't want me to become a killer. I wondered how many people Ralph had killed.

Remembering that Cindy and Alia were waiting in the garage, I broke the silence, saying as calmly as I could, "I have a question."

Ralph shrugged. "I'm not going anywhere, lad."

"How did you know my name?"

"I know a good many things about you, little destroyer. Like I said, you're something special."

I didn't care about being special. "You lied to me when you said the Angels wanted me dead, didn't you? That berserker wanted to recruit me into the Angels just like you wanted me in the Guardians."

"Smart lad, you are," said Ralph, smirking.

"Cindy told me," I said dryly. "But when you took me, you were in a hurry."

"That I was."

"Why?"

"But you already know why, don't you, lad?" Ralph said in a mocking tone.

I did know. The berserker was sent to capture me, but when the Angels found out that Ralph was hunting the berserker...

"There was another Angel," I said quietly.

"That's right."

"Where is my sister?"

Ralph started laughing. "Give it up, lad. You're not going to find her."

"Where is she?!" I bellowed. The flower vase on the dining table shattered.

Ralph didn't even flinch. "She's just another Angel now, and you're not going to find her."

I glared at him, my whole body shaking in fury.

Ralph stared calmly back. "So, lad, aren't you going to kill me now?"

I took a deep meditative breath. "Cindy told me not to."

"Ah, but Cindy isn't a destroyer, is she?"

"That's true," I replied evenly. "A moment ago, you tried to kill me. You knew my sister had been taken by an Angel last year, and you let it happen. You stopped me from going after her so you could save yourself and sell me to your Guardians."

Ralph remained silent, gazing back at me.

I continued quietly, "You're right, Ralph. I am a destroyer. If I let you live, you'll come after us again. You'll tell the Guardians about Alia. You'll tell them that she's a healer."

"That I would. So what are you waiting for?" said Ralph, raising his voice. "Get it over with, lad! Go on, little destroyer!"

I stretched my right arm toward him, taking a step forward and pointing my index finger at his heart. One focused shot, and I could prevent any of that from happening. I looked at the old man's face. I saw the dried blood on his neck and shirt, and I thought again of how Cindy had asked me to spare his life. I could still feel Alia's little hand squeezing mine. I had a feeling now that whatever I did, I would end up regretting it.

"I am a destroyer," I repeated slowly, "and I may only be thirteen..." I lowered my arm and looked deep into his eyes. "But I know better than to fall for your stupid tricks again, Ralph. And I will never, ever, be a killer like you."

I turned on my heel and started to walk back toward the door when I heard Ralph say nastily, "Enjoy your denial while it lasts, little wild-born. You can't run from your destiny forever."

I know I shouldn't have risen to him, but I don't particularly regret it either. I spun on the spot and blasted him hard, knocking him backwards, chair and all. Still tied to the chair, Ralph lay on his back, moaning feebly.

"That's for Cat!" I spat vehemently. "And for Alia, in advance."

I walked to the garage and got into the front of the SUV, slamming the door. Cindy didn't say anything as she started the engine. She pushed the remote control to open the garage shutter, and out we sped, leaving her house, leaving Ralph's rusty blue convertible parked on the curb, and off into the unknown.

9. CINDY AND THE GUARDIANS

Actually, just unknown to me. Cindy seemed to know where we were headed. I sat next to her, silently looking out of the window. Packed between bags of clothes, Alia sat in the back, hugging her unicorn and staring emptily off into space. Cindy kept her eyes on the road. Nobody spoke. I let the silence build until I couldn't stand it any longer.

"I didn't kill him, Cindy," I said stiffly.

Cindy just nodded slightly.

"I did blast him, but I didn't kill him."

Cindy finally looked at me and smiled kindly, saying, "I was hoping that's what happened."

"Did you hear what we talked about?" I asked.

"I heard you talking, but I couldn't make it out," replied Cindy. "I just heard the chair fall over."

I looked at her. "You honestly thought I killed him."

"I hoped you didn't."

"But Cindy, you realize that as soon as Ralph is found, he's going to tell the Guardians about Alia?"

"I know that, Adrian," Cindy answered calmly.

I shook my head in frustration. "She'll be hunted forever. You said so yourself!"

"And I'm sorry that's what's going to happen."

"But Cindy—"

Cindy looked at me sharply. "Adrian?!"

"For the last time, I didn't kill him!" I shouted. A long crack appeared on the dashboard.

"Okay, okay, I believe you," Cindy said hastily. "Lower your voice. You're scaring Alia."

"Are we hidden?" I asked in an annoyed tone, trying to calm myself.

"Of course. And we're together. And we're alive. And you're not a killer. We have lots to be grateful for, Adrian."

Cindy pulled into a drive-thru, buying us some burgers and fries for the road ahead. I thought I wasn't hungry until I took a bite. The last time we had eaten was lunch just before arriving at the frozen pond. Even Alia ate half a burger, which seemed to calm her just a little. Cindy ate while she drove, her prejudice against fast food notwithstanding.

"I'm really sorry, Cindy," I said, gingerly running my fingertips along the broken dashboard.

"It's okay," Cindy said softly. "I'm sorry I didn't believe you."

"I guess I still need to learn control, huh?"

Cindy smiled. "You're getting there."

"Cindy, I know you couldn't sense the God-slayers because they're normal people, but why couldn't you sense Ralph back at the pond?" I asked. "He's no good at hiding, is he?"

"Someone gave him hiding protection," replied Cindy. "Probably because Ralph was hunting the Slayers and knew he might end up near whoever they were hunting, which was us."

"How did the Slayers find us, though?"

"No idea," Cindy said simply.

I had a feeling that Cindy did at least have an idea, but I didn't press the matter. There was something much more important on my mind.

"Ralph told me about my sister," I said as calmly as I could.

"What did he say?" asked Cindy.

"He said an Angel took her."

Cindy closed her eyes for a brief moment, sighing softly before saying, "I was beginning to think that's what happened to her as well."

I stared at her. "Cindy! You never said anything to me!"

"Well, I wasn't sure enough. It was just a hunch, and I didn't want to get you worked up."

"Worked up?!"

Cindy sighed again. "If an Angel did take your sister, Adrian, there was nothing you could do about it then, and there's not much you can do now. She'll have been converted."

I almost didn't want to hear what "converted" meant. But there was another question to ask as well. "The Angels tried to capture me, but they didn't care about my family. Why would they take Cat at all?"

"I have a theory, that's all," said Cindy.

With considerable effort, I forced myself to stop glaring, and Cindy explained, "The Angels sent a berserker after you, right? He was supposed to get you to kill your family and then bring you in. But then Ralph was sent after him. Ralph is strong, Adrian. I know you beat him, but—"

"We beat him," I corrected, remembering that I would have suffocated to death had Cindy not drained Ralph during the fight.

"We beat him," Cindy repeated quietly. "But Ralph is one of the Guardians' best. He was, as you saw, more than a match for the berserker. When the Angels found out that Ralph was after their berserker, they sent another psionic, or maybe even a whole team."

Cindy paused for a moment as if she wasn't sure she should tell me the rest of her theory. I said a little harshly, "Go on."

"Whoever they sent would have had to be powerful enough to take on Ralph. Ralph decided to keep you from falling into their hands by running away. Ralph doesn't usually run, Adrian, but that time, he did."

"Right..." I said slowly, not yet exactly sure what Cindy was getting at.

"Well, that left the Angels in a fix, didn't it? They didn't want to return empty-handed. They might have accidentally come across your sister, who would have looked out of place running through the streets in the middle of the night. Or perhaps they were searching your house when your sister came back on her own. Either way, they got to her."

"But they didn't kill her." I tried to say it matter-of-factly, though I'm sure Cindy caught the hopefulness in my tone.

"No one found her body, so probably not," agreed Cindy.

"Which then brings us back to 'conversion,'" I said, trying hard to keep my voice steady.

"Adrian, this isn't going to be easy for you to hear."

"I'm getting used to hearing things I don't like, Cindy. Just tell me. Please."

Cindy took a deep breath. "Conversion is done by a master controller. It's not like Ralph's control. It doesn't wear off quickly. The convert becomes a loyal slave to the master controller, wanting nothing more than to serve the master's cause, blindly without question. And if it's done at a young age, it's usually permanent."

Cindy looked at me to see how I was taking this. Honestly, I don't remember exactly how I felt when I first heard her words. Confused, lost, betrayed, frustrated, angry... It all just blended together and weighted me down to my seat. Cat had been enslaved by the Angels. It just didn't seem real. And it didn't make any sense. Cat was only ten years old, and she wasn't even psionic.

"What could they possibly want with her?" I asked.

"Do you remember how I told you that a psionic bloodline can become dormant when it gets too thin?"

I nodded.

"No one knows exactly how it works, but through the right combination of parents, a dormant bloodline can suddenly become active and start producing psionics again. That's how you became a wild-born, Adrian. And when a bloodline is reactivated, it's fairly common for the siblings of wild-born psionics to also develop psionic powers."

"You mean Cat's like us?"

"There's no guarantee, but it's very possible. Your telekinetic power is so strong that I would imagine that both of your parents had dormant psionic blood in them. That would increase the chances of your sister becoming psionic by quite a bit. But like I told you before, most people don't gain their powers until they're adults. There's no way to tell whether your sister will really become psionic until she actually does."

I shook my head, asking, "You mean the Angels took her because she might become psionic in the future?"

"The Angels have many slaves, and not all of them are psionic. I think the Angels figured they could convert your sister now, and if, later, she did display any powers, she'd already be loyal to them."

I was having trouble breathing. I pictured Cat living in some dark and filthy room, cooking and cleaning for a monster like the berserker who had killed our parents. I could see her smiling at the monster, like Alia had at Ralph back in Cindy's living room.

"Stop the car!" I shouted.

Cindy hit the brakes, and I jumped out, stumbling to the edge of the road and vomiting onto the grass next to the pavement. My legs gave out, and I slumped down on the concrete, unable to move.

I felt Cindy's hand gently rubbing my back. She crouched next to me and put an arm around my shoulders. "I'm sorry, Adrian," she said. "I'm so sorry."

I couldn't say anything. Cindy sat with me, for how long I don't know. She held me with both arms around me, as if to keep me from being swallowed whole by my pain.

"Addy, are you alright?" Alia's tender voice cleared my head just a little. I saw her squatting on my other side, peering into my eyes. She placed her hands on my left arm, and I tried to give her a smile.

"Adrian, come on," Cindy said softly. "It's cold out here."

She slowly stood me back up and led me to the car, putting me in the back seat with Alia. Alia kept her hands around my arm, and we sat there in silence as Cindy started driving again.

The initial shock of what I had heard was beginning to wear off. I wiped my mouth to get rid of the awful taste, and gave Alia a quick hug to reassure her that I was okay. Then I looked at Cindy's eyes through the rearview mirror.

"Why didn't you tell me about my sister when we first met, Cindy?" I asked accusingly. "You knew all along that Cat might be psionic."

"I'm sorry," said Cindy. "I probably should have told you. But I didn't want to worry you, and I didn't know for sure that the Angels had taken her."

"You still should have told me."

"I know, Adrian. I'm sorry."

I wished that she wouldn't apologize so easily. I so wanted to be mad at her right now. I knew that Cindy had only been trying to shelter me from a painful truth, but she had no right to keep this hidden from me for so long.

Ralph had known about my sister too. That was why he had asked me where she was. He had wanted to take us both. As much as I hated Ralph for his deceptions, at least he had wanted Cat alive from the start. The Angels hadn't cared in the least whether my sister lived or died back when their berserker was using his power on me. And that was the kind of company Cat was in now.

"Is there no way to get her back?" I asked.

"Conversion is powerful psionics, Adrian," Cindy replied carefully. "If your sister had been a grown-up, her conversion could have lasted anywhere from a few years to a few decades. But as a child..."

"It's permanent," I said disgustedly. "I heard you the first time."

"I'm really sorry, Adrian."

"There's got to be a way," I insisted, gripping Cat's pendant. "There just has to!"

Cindy remained silent, but through the rearview mirror, I saw in her eyes that she was holding something back. "There is a way, isn't there?" I asked. "Are you going to keep this from me too?"

Cindy gazed back at me for a moment. Then she sighed once and said, "There is one way, and only one way, to completely break psionic conversion."

"How?"

"The master controller must die. Then, depending on the strength of the conversion, the effects can fade in anywhere from a few weeks to a few months."

So there *was* a way. I had told Ralph that I would never become a killer, but I might bend that vow just once for Cat's psionic master.

"Where are these Angels?" I asked.

"The Angels, like the Guardians, are scattered around the country in small clusters. They don't all live together."

"And which one—"

"Adrian, I don't know. I honestly don't. Even if I knew, I wouldn't tell you. Not until I can be sure you're not going to go off on some foolish suicide mission."

"You once said that you'd help me look for her!" I accused, remembering the night Cindy had come home with the police report. It was easier to be angry with her than to remember my own decision to stay safely hidden in her house. I knew now that it wouldn't have made any difference had I gone back to my hometown three weeks after Cat had been taken, but even so, I hated myself for choosing the easy way out.

Cindy kept her eyes on the road as she said, "It's different now."

"You said you'd help me," I repeated.

"That was when we didn't know what had happened."

I muttered savagely, "Maybe I should have joined the Guardians with Ralph after all."

"You can't mean that, Adrian."

"Then how am I supposed to rescue Cat?"

"I don't know," said Cindy. "But you're not going to be any use to her dead. You should be grateful you know she's still alive."

"Yeah, we sure have lots to be grateful for!" I shot back sarcastically.

Alia gave my arm a little tug, and I lowered my voice, saying, "Cindy, we don't even know if she's still alive, do we? Not for sure, anyway."

"Well, probably still alive," said Cindy. "I'm an optimist, remember?"

I closed my eyes and pictured Cat's face the last time we had talked. I thought back to how worried she was that I was going to be locked up in some hospital, never to come home. Now, she was the one who was locked up. Not in chains, perhaps, but in her heart. In a way, that was even worse.

But, yes, she was still alive. I had just said to Cindy that there was no way to know for sure, but nevertheless, I was sure. It was the only way I could picture it. And that was the very best I could ask for: just that Cat was alive, somewhere. It's never easy to learn a horrible truth. It doesn't get easier with time or practice. But knowing something horrible is better than not knowing. At least when you know it, you also know where you stand.

"Adrian?" said Cindy.

I reopened my eyes and found that Cindy was looking anxiously at me through the rearview mirror.

"I'm okay," I said quietly. "Thanks for telling me."

I gave her a faint smile, and, though I couldn't see her mouth in the mirror, her eyes smiled back.

"So, Adrian, now I have a question," said Cindy.

"Shoot."

"How did you block Ralph?"

"I learned," I answered simply. "I learned how to tune him out."

"I was impressed," said Cindy.

"I had a good teacher," I replied, smiling at Alia, who squeezed my arm.

Cindy laughed. "But you said you couldn't even block Alia."

"I can't," I said with a shrug. "Ralph isn't as strong as she is. At least, not as a peacemaker."

"Huh... Maybe I could learn a thing or two from her. But Adrian, there are other controllers out there who are much stronger."

"I know. I'll keep practicing."

Fighting physically was one thing, but Ralph was right when he described controllers as the most dangerous of psionics. If ever I was going to rescue Cat from what Cindy had called a "master controller," I would need to know how to block mind control much better than I could now.

Alia rested her head on my shoulder. I looked at her and saw that she was falling asleep. It couldn't have been much later than 8pm, but a few minutes later, I closed my eyes, too.

The car was still moving when I woke. I peered over the blanket covering Alia and me (How did that get there?) and read the dashboard clock. I had only slept for about two hours. I pulled the blanket down and stretched my arms a little. Alia's body felt uncomfortably warm against mine, so I gently pushed her away from me, letting her lean on her unicorn. She started to stir a little, but didn't wake as I pulled the blanket up around her shoulders.

I caught Cindy's eyes in the mirror.

"Feeling better?" she asked.

The honest answer would have been, "Not very much," so I didn't reply. I thought back to the time, four months ago, when I told Cindy that I would stay with her and not go looking for Cat. Now that I finally knew what had happened to my sister, I had to ask myself how things had changed.

A small but truthful voice in me answered, *Not at all.*

The Angels were scattered throughout the country, and I knew neither where they were nor which group Cat was with. And I had just barely beaten Ralph, and then only with Cindy's help. Ralph was a Guardian, on the losing side of the war or feud or whatever was going on. In order to rescue Cat, I'd have to break into the winning side.

Four months... Had it really been so long?

"Cindy, where are we going?"

"To a friend's place," said Cindy. "His name is Mark Parnell, and he helped me with Alia for the first year or so after I brought her home. He's not psionic, but he knows about us. He used to babysit when I was away. Alia might even remember him."

"I thought you didn't have any friends you could trust."

"Not in the neighborhood," said Cindy. "We're still another night's drive away."

I leaned forward in my seat. "Are you going to drive all night?"

"Just a few more hours. We'll find a place to hide well before dawn."

"You said we were hidden."

"Psionically, yes," said Cindy. "But that doesn't keep us from being found by the police. Do you want to sit up front?"

I crawled between the seats and sat down beside Cindy, trying to keep her from seeing how carefully I was handling the seatbelt buckle so as not to touch any of the metal. I'm sure she noticed anyway, but she politely chose not to comment. I still had made no progress in the balance department, but at least Cindy had once praised me for not getting any worse.

We were driving down a cross-country freeway. We passed farms and clusters of houses here and there, but the landscape seemed unchanging for a long time. There were very few other cars on the road.

"I'm hungry," I said.

Cindy smiled. "So you are feeling better."

"Yeah, maybe a little."

There were no 24-hour stores in this part of nowhere, but I found some leftovers in the drive-thru bag. The food was cold and dry, but after eating, I did feel somewhat better. Cindy spoke very little while she drove, and I was grateful for the silence as I stared out into the darkness around us.

Eventually, Cindy pulled off of the freeway and onto a narrow gravel road, which we followed for about ten minutes until we came to a small river. I couldn't actually see it, but I could hear the babbling of the water nearby. Cindy cut the engine and the headlamps, and we sat silently for a minute. I guessed Cindy was extending our protection, though probably not very far considering that we were sitting in a metal box.

A moment later, Cindy asked, "Do you want to go fly? No one will see you here, and I can stretch our hiding bubble farther."

I shook my head. "I'm not in the mood."

"Look at the stars," Cindy said in a hushed voice.

I looked up through the windshield. Having grown up in a medium-size town far away from heavy industrial pollution, I could usually see a pretty decent night sky even from home, but this was something different. I could clearly make out the Milky Way spanning the sky above us, and looking up at the spectacular infinity made me feel like I would either be sucked up into it, or perhaps crushed by it. We sat listening to the gurgling water, and for a while just watched the planet slowly turn.

Still gazing upwards, Cindy whispered, "Billions upon billions of stars and planets. Probably even some with life on them. Maybe other planets like Earth, with civilizations of their own. Looking at the stars helps me keep my life in perspective. Kind of makes our problems here feel small and insignificant... No offense, Adrian."

"I like the stars too," I said quietly.

Cindy took a deep breath and turned to me. "So, Adrian."

"So, uh... what?" I asked.

"So ask me."

"Okay, I will. So what's your story, Cindy?"

Finally, I got to hear it.

Cynthia Gifford turned psionic in her early twenties, soon after she had finished nursing school. Her first power was finding, which meant that unlike most wild-born psionics who wait to be discovered by one of the factions, she was the one who went out and found a group of psionics that included...

"...Ralph," said Cindy.

I stared at her. "Ralph?!"

"Keep your voice down, Adrian. You'll wake Alia. Ralph and I lived in the same town. Actually, we still do."

"Ralph was living in the same town as us?" I asked in disbelief. Cindy had never mentioned anything of the sort in the months that I had lived in her house.

"Did you think it was mere coincidence that Ralph was the one hunting those Slayers?" asked Cindy, raising an eyebrow. "Ralph lived across town from my parents' house, where I was living at the time. I found him, and he introduced me to the Guardians."

Introduced would not have been the word I would have chosen. Ralph power-charmed Cindy into coming with him to Guardian headquarters, and the then-leader of the Guardians, a master controller named Diana Granados, converted her into a loyal follower.

"Large psionic factions have always been built around one or more masters, like a bee hive," explained Cindy. "Diana was our queen."

"That's disgusting," I said with a shudder.

"Conversion isn't total mind control, Adrian. You can still think and feel and choose your own life. It just makes you loyal to your group and your master. Some people join by choice, others are converted, and many of the converted ones choose to stay even after the effects have worn off, simply because that's the life they have grown used to."

"But you didn't."

"No, I didn't," she said, and continued her story.

Cindy had married a fellow Guardian. His name was Eric Laude, and he wasn't a psionic at all. Eric was a yoga master who accidentally learned about the Guardians, was converted, and later chose to stay of his own free will. Cindy and Eric, along with the other Guardians, battled the Angels during a time when the two factions were, for the most part, evenly matched. Eric helped Cindy learn to perfectly balance her power through breathing exercises and meditation. Later, when Cindy gained her hiding ability, she became invaluable to the Guardians' protection.

"I don't mean to brag," said Cindy, "but as far as hiders go, I'm probably the best in the world."

"How's that?" I asked.

"Remember how I told you that gatherings are usually held underground in the city? That's because many hiders can only hide themselves. Even really good hiders can't hide much more than a small building."

"But your bubble can hide several blocks."

"That's right," said Cindy, frowning slightly. "Eventually, I was put in charge of protecting Diana."

"The queen bee?"

Cindy nodded. "By then, my conversion had worn off, but they didn't have to do it to me again. The Guardians were my family."

Cindy stayed with the Guardians, but it tortured her to see more and more of her fellow faction members die. And Queen Diana Granados started becoming increasingly aggressive in her tactics.

"We started taking more slaves," said Cindy, looking out the window. "More powerful conversions. It even led to the creation of a small army of non-psionic people. The feud was heating up. Some of our battles were even reported on the news, though very few people knew what was really happening. There were houses catching fire, group suicides, things like that. Normal people explained it away as the result of drug use and religious cults."

That's when Eric killed Diana. The yoga master, who shared Cindy's resentment toward the heavy-handed tactics of the Guardian queen, decided to end it with a knife to her heart. Eric was hunted down and killed, and Cindy fled the Guardians. She returned to her hometown, the one place she felt the Guardians wouldn't think of looking for her, precisely because it was the most obvious of hiding places. Her plan worked.

"And you never met the Guardians again?" I asked.

"They searched for me for a while, but they had other problems now," said Cindy. "You see, master controllers are among the rarest of psionics, and the queen didn't have a successor."

Without their only master controller, the Guardians quickly became disorganized. Lacking central leadership, Guardian settlements and outposts were singled out and destroyed by the Angels one by one. Some of the most powerful Guardian psionics, such as Ralph, worked hard to keep their people united, but the new leaders ended up arguing more than cooperating, and the Guardians gradually lost their strength as a unified group.

"The Guardians today are actually several, semi-independent factions that share the same name," said Cindy, not without a touch of sorrow in her voice.

I asked, "And Ralph is the leader of one of them?"

"Well, Ralph stepped down after a mission he was leading failed horribly, but he's still high up in his group's chain of command."

"And how do you know that if you left the Guardians before they fell apart?"

"You don't miss much, do you?" said Cindy, and it took a moment before I realized that she was complimenting me.

Cindy asked, "Do you remember what Ralph said to me about Alia?"

"Something about him helping you with her?" I said, trying to remember Ralph's exact words.

Cindy nodded. "After I found Alia and brought her home, I wanted to find her parents. Ralph was the one who helped me locate them."

"You mean the crazies?" I asked.

"Yes."

"But you're a better finder than Ralph, and even you can't find normal people."

"Ralph is ex-military," said Cindy. "Special Forces. He's very well connected. Many friends."

"I'll bet!" I said sarcastically, wondering how many of Ralph's "friends" were actually his victims.

"Oh, no, Adrian, you don't understand," said Cindy. "Ralph didn't gain his powers until he had been with the Wolves for several years."

"Wolves?" I repeated, vaguely remembering that Ralph had mentioned Wolves in our very first conversation.

"They're government people," explained Cindy. "Soldiers. They hunt psionics, sometimes to kill, sometimes to capture and study."

"Study?"

"They want to know what makes us tick," said Cindy.

"And Ralph was one of them?" I asked.

"Ironic, isn't it? When Ralph discovered he was psionic himself, he escaped and joined the Guardians. He's one of the few people who knows any details about what the Wolves do."

"Back to Alia, please," I said, not caring to hear what a great asset Ralph was to the Guardians.

"After I brought Alia home, I called Ralph on the phone," said Cindy. "I told him I had found an abused child who was a telepath. I knew he'd help me because he would see it as an opportunity to capture me, and maybe even get Alia in the deal, though he probably didn't care too much about her. You see, I didn't tell him that she was a healer."

"Sounds like a dangerous game you were playing," I said.

"It was. But I had to know what Alia had been put through, so I could help her recover. I wanted to know how she ended up in the forest. I wanted to know what they did to her."

"You wanted revenge," I said, sensing the bitterness in her tone.

Cindy was silent for a moment, and I wondered if I had gone too far, accusing her like that, but then she answered in an almost inaudible whisper, "Yes. Yes, I did." Her voice was shaking, and through the corner of my eye, I saw her put her hand to her face.

I didn't turn my head, but instead concentrated on the stars outside as I said, "You killed them."

"Yes, Adrian. I killed them. It is my deepest regret in life."

"Why?!" I cried, looking at her in disbelief. How could she feel this way, knowing what they had done to Alia?

"Because it's wrong!" Cindy said so forcefully that I almost jumped. She probably would have shouted it if it hadn't been for Alia sleeping in the back.

Cindy looked at me with eyes that were, at the same time, both fierce and hurt. "I'm a nurse, Adrian. My life is dedicated to saving lives. To easing pain. I spent ten years with the Guardians as their finder and hider. I didn't fight, but I helped those who did. I helped them kill each other and I watched them die. I never wanted any of that, for anyone!"

Alia stirred in her sleep, and I heard her murmuring something in my mind.

Cindy turned around in her seat and looked at Alia sadly. "Alia doesn't know her real parents."

"She doesn't remember what happened to her?"

"Oh, she remembers that, alright," Cindy said grimly, sitting back in her seat, "but they weren't her parents. It turned out that Alia was kidnapped by them when she was an infant."

"You ever tell her that?" I asked, actually a bit relieved that Alia wasn't blood-related to her psycho-parents.

"We don't talk about that," Cindy said quietly. "Someday, when she's old enough to understand, I'll tell her. You see, I don't know who her real parents are. Her kidnappers claimed they were saving her from what they called 'her demonic keepers,' which leads me to believe that Alia's real parents were both psionic, though I don't know which faction."

"And Ralph never caught you?" I asked, wanting to hear the rest of her story.

"He hoped to get me during my meeting with Alia's parents, or kidnappers, or whatever you want to call them, but I cornered them away from their house. Ralph never met Alia until just now. He always thought she was only a telepath."

"But now he knows."

Cindy nodded slowly. "Yes, Adrian, now he knows. I'm still glad you didn't kill him."

"Ralph tried to goad me into it," I said. "He sounded like he wanted me to kill him."

"Ralph's a sore loser," said Cindy. "And he's been through a lot in life. I don't think he cares much about people's lives anymore, his own or others'."

I looked down at my knees, thinking about all that Cindy had told me. About her life as a Guardian, and about Ralph and Alia. Alia, who never knew her real parents, and...

"Wait a minute, Cindy. You once said that Alia's birthday is March 24th," I said, remembering hearing that in a conversation we had a few days after my own birthday. "How do you know her birthday if she had been kidnapped as a baby?"

"Oh, well, as to that, it's the day I found her," Cindy said with a slight smile. "I'm pretty sure about her age, though."

"Ah..."

"I know she's small and still acts like a baby sometimes. We just have to give her time, Adrian."

"We?" I asked.

"Yes, we! Come on, Adrian, you can't pretend we're not family now, after all we've been through together."

"You're just saying that to keep me from going after Cat by myself," I said, frowning, though inwardly I was very touched.

Cindy grinned. "Is it working?"

"Don't worry, Cindy. I'll still be here when you wake up."

"Good, because I'm getting very sleepy," Cindy said with a yawn.

"Just one more question," I said.

"Yes?"

"Who turned my sister into an Angel? Who converted her?"

"What makes you think I know?" Cindy asked innocently.

I gave her an exasperated scowl. "You said that large psionic factions are led by master controllers. The Angels must have a master like the Guardians used to."

"If I tell you..."

"I promise I won't do anything stupid, Cindy," I said. "Please just tell me."

After a moment's hesitation, Cindy nodded slightly. "The Angel master's name is Queen Larissa Divine. She is the one who converted your sister."

"Thank you," I said quietly.

I wiped some of the mist from the windshield. Only the brightest stars were left in the sky by now. I found it hard to believe that the last time I had a full night's sleep was before being shot at by the God-slayers. It had been a very long day. We pulled more blankets out from the back, tilted our seats back and shut our eyes, and a moment later...

"Addy, wake up."

I opened my eyes and looked at the dashboard clock. It had only been an hour, and the sun had just begun to creep up. Alia had woken Cindy too, and they were outside the car where Cindy was just finishing helping Alia change her clothes. I smelled something funny.

"She wet herself sleeping?" I asked Cindy as she toweled off the back seat.

Cindy shot me a look that clearly said, *Keep your mouth shut!* and I looked away, embarrassed.

Once Alia was comfortably seated in the back again, though much more awake than Cindy or me, Cindy sighed and said quietly to me, "It's not like I wasn't expecting it. She only stopped doing that last year. Hopefully, it won't go on for a long time."

"Yeah, well, I guess we just have to give her time," I said mildly.

"Glad you agree. I'm going back to sleep," said Cindy, lying back in her tilted seat and pulling a blanket over herself. "You, Adrian, give her time."

"But Cindy—"

"No buts, Adrian," said Cindy, closing her eyes. "I'm the one who has to drive again tonight. You watch Alia. And don't cross the river. That's where the bubble ends."

And with that, she went back to sleep, leaving me yawning in the early-morning sunshine.

Alia asked me to sit in the back with her, so I did, but she wasn't in the mood for talk or games. Instead, leaning her back against my right side, Alia sat silently staring out the window. I asked her twice if she was feeling alright, but she didn't answer. I didn't let that bother me too much. It wasn't the first time Alia had been like this, and I knew it would pass. Sure enough, after about an hour, she quietly turned her head and gave me a smile.

Once the sun had risen higher, I took Alia out of the car. It snowed lightly off and on during the day, and the river was icy cold, though that didn't stop Alia from sticking her hand into it and flicking the water at me. Alia healed my various bruises from the previous night, and I taught her how to make snow angels.

Cindy woke up in the late afternoon. We were out of food, but Cindy didn't want to leave our hiding place until after dark. There was some sugarless gum in the glove compartment, most of which we gave to Alia. If Alia complained about being hungry, she did it exclusively to Cindy as we sat in the SUV waiting for the sun to set. I don't know exactly what time we left the riverside to continue on our journey because by then I was asleep in my seat.

The next dawn found us driving through a quiet university town to the other side, where there were some rolling hills covered by a pinewood forest. According to Cindy, at the top of one of these hills lived her friend, Mark Parnell.

"Father Parnell, actually," explained Cindy.

"He's a priest?" I asked.

"I do hope Alia remembers him. She hasn't seen him in a year and a half."

"A priest?" I repeated, looking past Cindy at the shattered door mirror.

Cindy frowned at me. "Adrian, he's one of the good guys. Not every church person is a Slayer."

"If you say so..."

10. EVERYTHING THAT MATTERS

We had driven for about half an hour up a narrow dirt road from the edge of the university town. There were a few patches of snow here and there. The bottom of the hill was all forest, but the trees tapered out near the top, and I imagined that if the hill was properly covered with snow, it would look like the back of a circus clown's top-bald head. Cindy parked the SUV near the top of the hill, about forty yards away from where a lonely redbrick house sat facing the dirt road. There was a rusty red pickup truck parked in the driveway.

"You two stay in the car," said Cindy as she got out. "Mark's truck is there, so he's probably still home, but I'll go knock on the door and make sure."

"Why can't we all go?" I asked.

"Because I want to introduce you properly," Cindy said simply, which I took to mean that she wasn't sure how Alia was going to react to Father Parnell after not seeing him for so long.

Cindy stepped up onto the porch and knocked. A minute later, the front door opened and Cindy stepped inside. I couldn't see the person who opened the door.

Alia tensed up when Cindy disappeared into the house. I felt a bit nervous too. After all, it was only two days ago that I nearly had my head blown off by a couple of priests or rabbis or monks or whoever they were. I started to wonder whether Cindy's decision to leave us in the car had been prompted by her fears about Alia or about me.

The front door opened again. Cindy came out with a thin, blond man wearing a short beard and round glasses. He looked about the same age as my father. Alia opened her door and got out of the SUV, so I followed her.

"Is that Alia?!" exclaimed the man as he came closer. "My, how you've grown!"

Alia did remember him, probably because there were just so few people in her life. As soon as she recognized him, she sprinted up the road and jumped into his arms. I breathed easier. Anyone Alia treated like that could be trusted.

Carrying Alia in his arms, Father Parnell walked over to me and said, "You must be Adrian. Uh... nice bear."

I glanced down at the teddy bear on my pink sweatshirt and grinned sheepishly.

Father Parnell chuckled and whispered, "Cindy once gave me a strawberry-patterned apron."

I laughed.

"Nice to meet you, Father," I said, shaking his hand.

"Please. This is my home, not my church. Call me Mark."

Father Parnell, or Mark as he insisted on being called, turned out to be a gentle and kind man. He did not pester us with church teachings or quote the Bible to us. His manner was quiet and subtle. Aside from the fact that he was almost as good a cook as Cindy, he reminded me a lot of my own father. When he was at home, he often spent his time reading silently, sometimes from his Bible, sometimes from other books.

There was only one guestroom in his house, which Cindy and Alia bunked together in. Mark offered to sleep in the living room so that I could have his bedroom, but I declined and took the living-room couch myself.

Mark lived alone, but did not seem at all bothered by the sudden intrusion of three unexpected fugitives. He played with Alia and took me around his house, showing me little trinkets he had acquired during his many travels when he was younger. He told me lots of fascinating stories about life in different countries. When he asked me about the pendant I wore, I already trusted him enough to tell him about Cat and how guilty I felt having let her run off by herself. Mark didn't comment, but just listened to me and smiled sympathetically. A few days into our stay, I told him how little he resembled my image of a priest, and he answered, "I try not to preach, if that's what you mean. Jesus led by example. It is the best way."

Alia slept in Cindy's bed every night. More than once, Mark suggested buying a cot for her, but Alia obstinately refused. Our run-in with the Slayers and Ralph had left her very shaken. Back at home, Cindy only let Alia sleep with her when Alia had particularly bad nightmares, but Cindy made no objections at Mark's house, saying, "She can be like this sometimes. I'll coax her out of it once she's calmed down."

Alia wet her (and Cindy's) bed twice just in the first week, and while I felt grateful having the couch to myself, I really felt sorry for Alia. Having gotten used to her playfulness at home, I was painfully reminded of how fragile she was. Alia's telepathic voice was noticeably quieter, and on her worse days, she would sit silently for hours in the guestroom, tightly gripping her stuffed unicorn and staring up through the window at the drifting clouds. Cindy just reaffirmed her "give it time" tactic.

Meanwhile, I wasn't exactly living in Neverland myself. Once the initial shock of all that I had learned wore off, despite having promised Cindy that I wouldn't do anything rash, I often found myself entertaining ideas about how I might go about finding Cat. I couldn't concentrate on my meditation, and with each passing day, I grew ever more restless.

"Cindy, how long are we going to be here?" I asked after dinner one evening.

"I'm working on it," answered Cindy.

Cindy was working on searching for a new place to live in hiding. I wanted to do some finding. And for that, I had another concern.

"Why do I only have one power?" I asked. "Everyone else seems to have at least two, and sometimes more."

"Not everyone has more than one power," answered Cindy. "And besides, psionics develop at different paces. You could easily end up with another in a few years."

"Even Alia has two," I grumbled.

"Feeling jealous?" laughed Cindy. "I always thought that you considered your psionic power a curse."

I did, of course. I wished I had never gained it, because then my family would still be together. But since I knew that there was no going back, I found myself wishing I had more powers, such as the ability to search for other psionics—something Cindy adamantly refused to do for me.

"I'm not going to help you get yourself killed!" was Cindy's furious reply when I first suggested to her a plan that I had been formulating in my distracted mind during our meditation sessions.

My plan was to capture a random psionic. If the Angels were the largest psionic faction, then there was a good chance that whoever we caught would be an Angel. With a fair amount of luck, I might be able to get more information about Cat's whereabouts, and just as importantly, Queen Larissa Divine's. It was a stupid plan, I admit, and I felt embarrassed even mentioning it to Cindy, but it was the only one I could think of. Cindy was entirely unimpressed.

"Besides, I've already told you, Adrian," Cindy said in an irritated tone, "the Angels, like all factions, live in groups that cover each other's weaknesses. You'll never find a psionic living alone."

"But they travel alone sometimes," I pointed out, thinking of Ralph.

"And what about your promise to Alia?" demanded Cindy.

"What promise?" I asked.

"She told me that you promised to protect her."

That telepathic blabbermouth! I had only said that to calm her down after our fight with Ralph.

Cindy asked imploringly, "You did mean it, didn't you?"

"Well, I..."

"Adrian! You know how hard it is for Alia to trust people. Please don't make promises if you're going to break them."

I glared at her. "I didn't say I was breaking any promises, Cindy!"

With a sinking feeling in my gut, I realized that I had just walked into a big bear trap. But now that I thought about it, perhaps I did mean my promise to Alia. I had lived with her for nearly five months, and I certainly didn't want to see her hurt. But Alia didn't really need my protection. After all, she had Cindy. And speaking of promises...

"What about your promise to help me find Cat?" I asked accusingly.

Cindy sighed. "I never made that promise, Adrian."

"You did!"

"I said I'd help you go back to your hometown to look for her. If you still want to do that, fine! I'll even drive us all there."

"That's not fair, Cindy!"

"Maybe not," Cindy replied fiercely, "but that's the way it is!"

I started to protest again, but Cindy cut me off, saying sharply, "Give it up, Adrian! I know I can't stop you from going off and getting yourself killed, but I'm sure as hell not going to help you!"

So I spent the rest of the day sullen and angry with Cindy, who I knew could help me if only she would try to understand how I felt.

The next day, after giving Mark's place enough hiding protection to cover the entire hill and then some, Cindy left in her SUV, telling me that she might have found a place we could move to, and that she'd be gone overnight. I was left to take care of Alia, who clung to me all the way to bedtime. While I flat-out refused to share her bed, I did end up sitting with her until she fell asleep.

I wondered why Cindy didn't take us with her. If forcing me to take care of Alia like this was a ploy to make me feel more needed in her family, well, I can't say it didn't work at all, but it did little to relieve my frustration. Cindy returned just before noon the next day, but told us that we would have to stay at Mark's for a while longer.

After lunch, I tried again to convince her to help me search for the Angels. It turned into another heated argument, and after a good deal of shouting, I spent the afternoon sitting alone and furious outside on the wooden bench in front of Mark's house. It was a clear day, but nevertheless quite chilly outside. I sat there looking down the road that led into the forest below and entertained thoughts of just walking out of Cindy's protection. That way, perhaps an Angel would find me.

I saw Mark's pickup making its way up the dirt road. Mark was back from his church earlier than usual. Parking his truck in the driveway, he asked me what I was doing outside, but I just shrugged and didn't answer. Mark went into his house, and a few minutes later, he came back out holding two steaming mugs of...

"Hot chocolate," announced Mark, handing me one and sitting next to me on the bench.

"Thanks," I mumbled.

"Mind if I speak with you a bit, Adrian?"

"Did Cindy ask you to talk some sense into me?"

Mark grinned. "I'll try not to preach."

"I'd appreciate it," I said as I sipped my drink.

"You may not want to believe this," Mark began gently, "but I do know what you're going through."

"How's that?" I asked in a slightly harsher tone than I intended.

"I lost my twin brother when I was about your age," said Mark. "I think he was kidnapped, but I don't know because I never saw him again." Mark paused for a moment before adding, "We had a fight during school that day, and went home by different roads. But he never came home."

"I'm sorry," I said, staring down into my mug.

"I spent a lot of time feeling guilty about that," Mark continued quietly. "I blamed myself for starting the argument. I wished I could trade places with my brother. I often thought of running away from home so that I could go look for him. Please don't think I don't know how heavy that stone around your neck is."

I looked down at the pendant I had been unconsciously fingering, and quickly pulled my hand away, feeling embarrassed. Watching me, Mark smiled slightly and said, "In the end, Adrian, family is everything. Everything that matters, anyway."

"What about God?" I asked.

"God is family too," Mark answered simply. "But God can take care of himself. It's you that I'm worried about right now. Cindy really cares about you, and while I understand how very frustrating it can be, I hope you'll try to smooth things out with her."

"I just wish she could understand how important this is for me."

"Believe me, she does. But you have to accept that she knows a lot more about the Angels than you do. She knows how much danger you would be in if you went looking for them."

I turned my face away from Mark. I didn't want to hear this, but when I felt Mark's hand on my shoulder, I forced myself to look at him again.

"Cindy understands your pain perfectly, Adrian, because it's exactly how she would feel if she lost Alia," said Mark, looking into my eyes, "or you. You, like Alia, are her family now, and she could no more risk you than you could your sister."

"I care about Cindy too, Mark," I said. "She saved my life. She gave me a home. But she can't ask me to give up Cat. It's not fair."

"I know it's not," said Mark, shaking his head slowly. "I'm sorry if I'm not being much of a help here."

"It's okay," I muttered, sipping some more hot chocolate.

"Will you at least have dinner with us?"

"Sure, Mark."

As Mark stood up, I asked, "What was your brother's name?"

He turned around and smiled at me. "Is, Adrian," he corrected. "My brother's name *is* Jacob. I never really gave up on him."

I actually did feel slightly better after talking with Mark, even if nothing was resolved. I went back into the house and mumbled an apology to Cindy, whose eyes, I noticed with a twinge of guilt, were red from crying.

Mark did his best to cheer us up over dinner, but as I lay on the couch later that night, my frustration crept back upon me. It wasn't like I didn't appreciate the dangers involved in fighting the Angels, even if I didn't understand them as well as Cindy. As much as I didn't want to hurt Cindy, I decided that if ever I had a chance to corner an Angel, I would take it even without Cindy's help. After all, Cindy wasn't the only one who could sense power.

A week later, just past mid-February, what I was hoping for finally happened.

I hadn't had any more serious rows with Cindy since my talk with Mark, but nor had I given up trying to convince her to help me find an Angel. It was the day after Cat's eleventh birthday, and I was meditating with Cindy in the living room after lunch. Alia was upstairs taking her nap, and Mark was at his church.

Sitting on the floor across from Cindy, I wasn't concentrating at all on my meditation, still upset after yet another failed attempt during the morning to convince Cindy to help me. My eyes were not even completely closed, so I saw it when Cindy's shoulders suddenly became tense. What had she noticed? If it was imminent danger, she would have stopped meditating.

I calmed myself, closed my eyes, and felt my way through the orchestra of senses until I found the subtle new note. It was a telekinetic. I couldn't tell the direction, but he was probably right in the town below! I could walk there in a couple of hours. And as far as I could tell, he was alone.

I opened my eyes again, and found that Cindy had already opened hers too, looking at me worriedly.

"You felt it, Adrian?" she asked.

"I did," I answered quietly. "Is he alone?"

Cindy started to open her mouth, but then closed it for a second before saying, "No, he's with some others. They're not destroyers, so you can't sense them, but they're powerful."

"You're lying, Cindy!" I said angrily as I stood up. She gave me a pained look, and I knew I was right.

Stretching my right arm out, I telekinetically snatched my jacket off of the coat rack standing by the door.

"Please, Adrian," said Cindy as she watched me donning my jacket. "I'm sorry I lied. But that doesn't mean no one else is out there. They could be hidden. And this psionic isn't just a telekinetic. He's also a graviton. Telekinesis is his second power, not nearly as strong as yours, but as a graviton he's dangerous."

"You just lied to me! How do I know this isn't a lie, too?" I demanded, but even as I did, I saw in her eyes that she was telling the truth.

I had never met a graviton before. Cindy had told me they could weight things down. Since the graviton was also a telekinetic, he'd sense me as soon as I left Cindy's hiding bubble over the hill, and I'd lose any element of surprise. I hesitated for just one moment, but all the frustration and anger I had been feeling since Ralph told me about my sister and the Angels could not be suppressed.

I opened the front door with much more force than was needed, and strode out. Cindy came running after me.

"I don't need your help to find him," I said defiantly as I walked down the driveway toward the dirt road, not looking back at her. "I can't tell the direction, but I'll know if I'm getting closer."

"Adrian, why?!" Cindy asked frantically. "Why go after him? There's no guarantee that he's an Angel at all!"

"But he could be. And you said he's not a controller."

"That doesn't mean he's not dangerous!"

"I'll be careful."

"Adrian, please!"

"What?!" I shouted, rounding on her. "Stay at home? Be a good boy? Maybe you haven't noticed, Cindy, but I am not Alia!"

"Well, you're certainly acting like a seven-year-old!" Cindy shouted back with equal ferocity. "Maybe you haven't noticed, but you're the only person your sister has left! How do you think she'd feel if you threw your life away?!"

"Don't talk like you know her!"

"If you get killed, who's going to save her?!"

I turned my back to her and started walking again.

"Please, Adrian," Cindy pleaded tearfully. "This is a mistake, and mistakes have consequences. Please don't do this."

"I'm not asking for your help, Cindy. I'll handle this one myself."

"He'll be able to sense you as soon as you leave this hill. Please, just wait, and let me give you some hiding protection."

I stopped. Cindy came up close behind me, and for a moment, I thought she was going to grab me and pull me back toward the house. Instead, she placed her right hand lightly on my chest, and then her left hand on my back. For five minutes or so, we stood together as Cindy worked her power into me. Physically, I didn't feel at all different, but deep down, I was really sorry for making her do this.

Cindy took her hands off of me and said quietly, "The bubble will move with you. You'll be able to get pretty close before he senses you, up to ten yards or less, but only if you can reach him in the next eight hours. It's the best I can do. Please be careful. Even I won't be able to sense you until the protection wears off. Remember, he may not be an Angel."

I turned around and hugged her, trying to keep my voice steady as I said, "I'm sorry if I don't come back."

Cindy held me tightly. "If you're alive, I'll find you again."

Pulling myself away, I turned around and started walking to the road, but Cindy said, "Hold on, Adrian. Wait there for a minute."

"I'm not going to say goodbye to Alia, Cindy," I called to her as she walked back toward the house.

"It's not that."

Cindy returned with a small wad of bills and told me to take Mark's bicycle. Like his pickup truck, it was old and rusted, but nevertheless a sturdy mountain bike that would get me down the dirt road and into town quickly.

"I'll explain to him," she said, and hugged me again.

Thanking Cindy awkwardly for the money, I adjusted the bicycle seat and rode away. I felt as guilty as I could possibly feel, but I didn't look back.

I made my way down the winding forest road, pondering what I was about to do. When I had first felt the psionic's presence, my mounting frustration and annoyance with Cindy had hardened my resolve, but now that I was actually on my way, I was already having second thoughts. Capturing an unknown psionic... I knew that was much easier said than done. And I wasn't in disguise either, which meant I'd be chancing it with the police as well. I regretted my angry words to Cindy, and even thought about going back and telling her that I changed my mind. But then I decided that as long as I was here, I owed it to myself as much as to Cat to see this through.

A short ride from the foot of the hill, the university town looked sleepy and nearly deserted at this time of day. I saw some small schoolchildren walking down the street, laughing and chattering together as they made their way home. For a few minutes, I watched them enviously, realizing that I had almost forgotten what it felt like to be a child.

After Ralph, I really wasn't looking forward to another battle with a psionic. This time, however, I was the hunter. Concealed by the hiding protection that Cindy had given me, surprise was on my side. Even so, I still needed a strategy.

I found a hardware store and bought a pair of leather gloves, a length of thin but sturdy rope, and some copper wire like the one I used to wear back at home. I also bought a cheap radio from which, after I left the store, I removed the extendable antenna. I threw the radio away, pocketing the antenna, which would serve as my drain sword. My plan was to try to blast the graviton from a distance before he could sense me, fly at him, drain him and tie him up. Then I could question him. If he was an Angel (and I sincerely hoped he was), he just might have what I wanted. If he wasn't an Angel, I would have made another enemy, but then, what was one more enemy in a world full of Angels and Guardians, Slayers and Wolves?

As properly armed as I could hope to be, I pedaled toward the downtown area, assuming that this psionic was merely passing through and would probably be staying at a hotel. Once I got within the general area where

I could sense his power fairly close, I realized that getting an exact fix on his location was something only a true finder could do. Or, at least, I wasn't ready for it. I cycled one block at a time, stopping to calm myself enough to feel the telekinetic's song and gauge my distance to it. I often doubled back, thinking I had made a mistake, only to change my mind again. It was painstaking work, and soon it started to get dark. But I knew I was getting closer.

I was standing near a busy intersection, once again calming myself to locate the telekinetic when...

"Adrian?" Mark's sudden voice behind me nearly stopped my heart. I spun around, my concentration broken.

"Mark! What are you doing here?" I asked, trying to steady my breathing. I could no longer sense the psionic anywhere, though I knew he must be very close now.

Mark laughed and said, "No, Adrian, what are *you* doing here?" Then his tone became much more serious as he asked, "Does Cindy know you're in town?"

"Yes," I said uneasily, "she does."

"Won't you be found off the hill?"

"Cindy gave me some protection for the road."

"I see," said Mark, carefully studying my expression. "So she really does know you're out here on my bike?"

"Yeah... I'm sorry I took it without asking."

"No, no, it's quite alright," said Mark. "But what are you doing here?"

Suddenly I felt the telekinetic's presence again. It was much closer.

And getting closer.

I nervously looked around at the street. There were cars, and people on bicycles, and people walking along the sidewalk. Mark was saying something to me, but I was no longer listening. How could I tell which out of all these people the psionic one was, even if he passed right next to me? And that seemed all the more likely as I felt him getting even closer. He must be coming along this road, but from which direction? Cindy had said that ten yards was the limit of my cloak. I started to panic.

"Did you hear what I just said?" asked Mark. "Adrian, are you alright?"

"I'm sorry, Mark. I have to go!"

I jumped back onto Mark's mountain bike, hoping to pedal to the intersection and escape into another street, but suddenly I felt something crash into my side. I was knocked off the bike and onto the sidewalk.

I looked up and saw a young woman, probably in her early twenties, hastily getting off of her single-speed bicycle. She was wearing a navy blue tracksuit and a very surprised expression. Still dazed, I couldn't stand up. And I had lost track of the psionic again.

"Oh, I'm so sorry! I wasn't looking!" squealed the woman as she extended her arm down to me.

I took her hand, and suddenly I felt heavier, as if all of my muscles and internal organs had turned to stone. I couldn't even lift my own weight. I stared up at the woman. Her mouth was smiling, but her eyes were severe, focused on me.

She was the graviton!

My body became light again, and the woman pulled me to my feet. She patted the dust off my clothes, apologizing again and again, but then I discovered that she had another psionic power as I heard her voice inside my head say harshly, *"Ask me for trouble, kid, and I'll give you more than you can handle."*

Aloud, the woman was saying, "I'm really, really sorry. I hope I didn't hurt you."

"I'm okay," I managed to say, though we both knew I was far from okay.

"Your cell phone, ma'am," said Mark, handing her back the phone she had dropped when she crashed into me. Mark was completely oblivious to what was going on.

"Thank you so much," said the woman, getting back on her bicycle. "Well, I must be going."

"Be safe, ma'am!" Mark called after her as she pedaled away, and I was left standing on the sidewalk feeling like the world's greatest fool.

Mark didn't ask me again why I had come to town, but seemed to take it for granted that I was going back home with him. I didn't argue. Dejectedly pulling the bike along, I walked with Mark several blocks to his rusty red pickup, which was parked behind his church. We loaded the bike onto the pickup's cargo bed.

"Do you want to take a quick look inside before we head home?" asked Mark, gesturing toward the church, which was an old but well-built two-story redbrick building not entirely unlike Mark's house on the hill, though somewhat larger.

I was in no hurry to return to Cindy having failed my mission so pathetically, so I gratefully accepted Mark's offer. My uncle had taken me to Mass with him on a number of occasions, but my parents were both agnostics, so it had been a long time since I had been in a church.

We circled back around to the front of the building and entered through the main doors. Inside, I noticed the trace fragrance of recently burned incense, and looked up toward the altar. There was another priest speaking quietly with a nun who, upon seeing us, broke away from him and walked purposefully up to Mark.

Mark greeted her politely and started to introduce me, but the nun cut him off and said, "Father Parnell, excuse me, but there was a call for you a moment ago from a Mrs. Anderson. She asked that you call her back as soon as possible. It sounded quite urgent."

"Yes, of course, thank you," said Mark. "Excuse us, Sister."

Mark quickly led me past the pulpit, through an oak door and into a small office. There was no one else here, and Mark strode up to a wall-mounted telephone set next to an antique lamp.

"Mrs. Anderson is Cindy, Adrian," explained Mark. "I'll tell her you're with me."

I shook my head no, but Mark was already dialing and not looking at me. *Oh well,* I thought miserably, *at least she'll know I'm safe.*

Mark said into the telephone, "Hello, Cindy? It's Mark. Guess who I just met! What? Slow down, Cindy. What are you saying?"

I noticed the tension in Mark's voice and craned my neck to hear Cindy's side of the conversation, but I couldn't make it out. Cindy's voice on the phone sounded frantic.

"No, Cindy, I ran into Adrian," said Mark. "What do you mean? How can she not be there? I know you can't sense her in your own bubble, but that means she's still somewhere in it... Just calm down... Cindy! Cindy, listen to me! Get in your car and start driving toward town. Don't speed on the road or you might run into her in the dark. I'll meet you at the bottom of the hill, okay?"

Mark hung up and turned to me. "Come on, Adrian. Alia is looking for her big brother."

We ran back to the pickup truck, and Mark nearly floored it as we tore out of the parking lot, around the church and onto the main street, heading back toward the hill.

I sat next to Mark experiencing the same gut-wrenching feeling I had when I first learned that Cat hadn't been found. Alia had probably woken from her nap shortly after I left. Cindy wouldn't have told Alia the full truth, but must have told her that I went to town. When did Alia leave the house? How long would it take for her to walk down the hill? Where would she go from there? If Alia had left Mark's house at about the same time that I arrived in the town... It would have been five hours already.

I heard the loud thumping of a helicopter overhead. Looking up through the pickup truck's windshield, I saw the black silhouette of a monstrous military transport in the night sky. I wished I was up there with them, looking for Alia from the air. If only I could fly without being seen! It was already very dark, but I didn't want to risk any more midair run-ins with helicopters.

We were at the foot of the hill in less than ten minutes, but it felt more like ten hours. I saw the road leading up into the dark forest that covered the bottom of the hill, and wondered if Alia was walking beneath those trees right now, or if she had already come through, or if...

I felt Mark grip my shoulder. "Adrian, snap out of it!"

Mark stopped the truck and got out. I got out too, and watched as Mark reached into the cargo bed and unloaded his mountain bike, setting it down in front of me.

"Listen, Adrian, there are only two roads that lead to town from here, and we just came down one of them. This other one," said Mark, pointing to a gravel road that ran alongside the forest, "may still be in Cindy's protective area. You cycle down that road and see if you can't find Alia. I'm going to start driving up the hill and meet Cindy halfway. Once I meet up with Cindy, we'll come after you."

Mark got back into his pickup and drove up into the forest, and I got on his bike and started pedaling as fast as I could over the gravel. The road was empty, with just a barren field on one side and the forest on the other. There were no streetlamps, and by now it was so dark I could hardly see where I was going, but I didn't slow down.

Coming around a gentle curve in the road, I saw a tiny, shadowy shape off in the distance. At first I thought it was a trick of the light, but as I got closer, there was no mistaking her.

Alia heard me coming and turned around. *"Addy!"*

I jumped off the bike as Alia flew into my arms. Alia started crying, her arms wrapped tightly around my neck. I held her until she calmed down a little. Then I forced her off me, shook her shoulders and said furiously, "What were you thinking?! You can't just come down the hill like that! Cindy's worried sick about you!"

Alia started sobbing again. *"Addy, please don't go away!"*

"I'm not going anywhere, Alia."

"But you and Cindy were fighting."

I stared at her in surprise. Alia had been awake. How many of our other arguments had she overheard? Seeing her tear-stained face, I finally realized how much fear and pain I must have been causing her, and what it must have taken for her to walk all this way alone.

"Alia, I'm really sorry," I said. "I promise I won't have any more fights with Cindy. And I'm not going to leave you and Cindy like this again."

"Never?" asked Alia, wiping her eyes.

"I promised I'd take care of you, didn't I? Come on, Ali, let's go home."

I couldn't ride Mark's bike with her, so we'd have to come back for it later. Leaving it leaning against a tree, I took Alia's hand and started to walk with her back the way we came.

All of the fear and tension I had felt during the day had drained away, leaving me utterly spent, and yet strangely at peace with myself. It had been exceptionally stupid of me to suddenly leave the house like I did, and I promised myself that I would apologize to Cindy for putting us all at risk. Everything I had done today was wrong. Cindy was right: I really had acted like a little kid.

But I'd make it up to her. In just a few minutes, we would be reunited, and we would all go back to Mark's house together. In fact, I could already see the shadowy silhouette of Cindy's car coming toward us, and I turned to Alia.

"Look, Ali!" I said happily. "It's Cindy!"

"No, Addy."

I looked at the car shape again. It was an off-road vehicle, but not

Cindy's SUV or Mark's pickup. And its headlights were off.

"Addy..."

Alia inhaled sharply, gripping my hand tighter, and suddenly I was blinded by a spotlight from above. I stumbled, pulling Alia down with me, and when I scrambled to my feet, there were more lights coming from other directions. I could hear the engine of the car in front of us, and the soft thumping of a helicopter above. There was shouting too, but I wasn't listening to it.

I could barely see in the glare of the lights, but somehow I pulled Alia into the forest with me. It was too dark under the trees to see anything, and I stumbled again.

"Stop!" commanded a deep male voice amplified on a megaphone. "Lie on the ground facedown with your hands behind your back! If you try to escape, you will be shot!"

There were men crowding around near the edge of the forest, and they had flashlights, but I was sure we hadn't been seen yet.

I heard another voice say, "They went in here, sir."

My eyes had adjusted slightly to the darkness under the trees. Grabbing Alia's hand, I stood up and started to run.

"Freeze!" someone shouted.

But I didn't. A moment later, I felt a sharp sting in my lower back as if someone had kicked me hard from behind, and I fell forward onto my face. I didn't even hear the gunshot. I was no longer holding Alia's hand.

I painfully rolled over onto my back. I could feel the warm blood spreading over my stomach. The bullet had gone clean through me.

Alia was crouching next to me. *"Addy! Addy, no!"*

"No, Ali," I breathed, trying to push her away. "Run... hide..."

I dimly saw Alia holding her hands over my stomach, and I tried to push her away again, but by now the blood leaving my body was draining me so much I could barely move my fingers. Everything was in slow motion. I heard Alia crying. I heard footsteps rushing up to us. I could hear my own faint breathing as I felt the life draining out of me. Lights were cast everywhere as the men came up and surrounded us.

"Do you want me to take the girl, Major?" The man's voice sounded distant, slowly reverberating through my head like a dull echo.

"No, let her do her thing. I want them both alive."

A moment later, I could no longer see the flashlights.

11. THE WOLF'S LAIR

Even after I opened my eyes, it took some time for my senses to adjust to my new surroundings.

I was lying on a hard hospital bed, dressed only in a thin white gown over my underwear. There was also a pair of heavy bracelets on my wrists. They were made of hard white plastic, each about as wide as a playing card and much thicker than a watch. There were no markings or writing on them. Probably having been designed for adults, the bracelets weren't particularly tight around my wrists, but I couldn't slip them off. I wondered for a moment if they might be some kind of medical monitoring equipment, but my gut told me that they were something more sinister, though I couldn't fathom what.

I carefully touched my stomach, expecting to find some bandages, but there were none. Slipping my right hand under my gown, I felt where the bullet had left my body. Aside from some light scarring, it was completely healed.

The square room my bed was in had dark gray walls, was claustrophobically tiny, and contained no other furniture at all. There was a heavy iron door set in the center of one wall and an intercom next to it. On the ceiling, next to a pair of glaring white fluorescent tubes, a small black security camera was looking down at me. Aside from a tiny vent near the ceiling, the room appeared to be airtight. There were no windows, and even the door fit seamlessly in its frame.

Sitting up on the bed, I reflexively put my hand up to Cat's amethyst, but my fingers grasped air. It was gone.

I thought about Alia. She was a healer, and she had saved my life. How long had I been unconscious, and where was Alia now?

I looked around again, my dread mounting. Obviously, this was no ordinary hospital room. The gray walls, which I had originally thought were painted concrete, gave off a strange sensation that I couldn't quite grasp until I identified the mild draining effect that came from being surrounded by metal. This wasn't even a normal prison cell. It was a vault, perhaps specifically designed to keep psionics in.

I heard a soft whirring noise coming from my bracelets, which vibrated ever so slightly, and suddenly I was being drained. Small metal rods had extended from inside the bracelets, pressing against my skin. I felt dizzy. My whole body weakened, I wanted to lie back down onto the bed, but I forced myself to stay sitting upright. The metal door was opening.

In stepped a middle-aged but muscular man with very short blond hair. He wore a dark green military uniform, and even though I couldn't tell his rank, not knowing how to read the military symbols, I instantly knew what he was. Near the shoulder on his right sleeve was a patch that needed no introduction to someone who had been taught what it symbolized. It was a wolf's head.

The Wolf stepped up to my bed as the metal door automatically closed behind him.

"Stand up," he commanded gruffly.

I carefully got down from the bed. My condition was making it hard to stand straight so I held on to the side of the bed for support. The Wolf lifted my gown and inspected the bullet scars on my stomach and back.

"You have healed well," he said, nodding slightly.

I remained silent.

He let go of my gown and looked into my eyes. "You were brought here yesterday from the forest where you were caught. It is my hope that you will cooperate in our efforts to bring in the others."

"Others?" I asked.

"Cynthia Anderson and Hillary Nash, both believed to still be in the town where we found you. We know Mrs. Anderson has been your keeper after your parents were killed, and if you can help us find her, we would be quite grateful."

Mrs. Anderson... That was the name I heard used in Mark's church. It must have been Cindy's fake identity, which meant the Wolves didn't know her real name. It also meant she hadn't been caught. Hillary Nash might have been the graviton woman I met in town, but I couldn't even be sure of that. Either way, I couldn't simply give this man Mark's address. I looked down at the floor, not knowing what to say.

The Wolf continued in a calm but cold tone, "I don't care about Nash, or, at least, I don't expect you to know where she is. You may have never even met her. But I do care about Anderson. One way or another, you will help me find her."

I didn't dare look up. I wondered if he was going to hit me. The metal rods touching my wrists were numbing out my senses, and I found it increasingly hard to stay standing, even with the bed for support.

The Wolf grabbed my chin and forced me to look up at him.

"The control bands that you are wearing are not merely designed to drain your psionic powers," he said. "They can also be used to induce severe pain, or even kill when necessary. Would you like a demonstration?"

"No," I answered quickly.

"That is good, because if you cooperate with us, there will be no need to hurt you."

"Where is..." my voice trailed off as I wondered if perhaps they didn't know Alia's name as well.

"The healer girl?" asked the Wolf, releasing his grip on my chin. "She is alive and recovering."

I stared at him in horror. "What have you done to her?!"

"You should be more concerned about what is about to happen to you," the Wolf replied evenly.

Gathering my courage, I said defiantly, "I want a phone call." I certainly wasn't planning to call Mark's house, but I figured that demanding to use the phone could not be denied. Anything to get out of this room and away from this man.

"You give me the number and I'll make the call for you," said the Wolf.

I shook my head.

Suddenly the Wolf grabbed my arm and shoved me down onto the floor. I struggled to my feet and, though it must have sounded pretty feeble in my drained condition, I did my best to shout, "Let me out! You can't keep me here! I haven't done anything wrong!"

He merely grinned at me as he pulled a small white remote control from his pocket. I looked down at the white bracelets I was wearing. *Control bands,* he had called them.

"I know my rights!" I shouted as fiercely as I could manage. Actually, I didn't know my rights, but to be perfectly honest, I didn't know what else to say.

"Your rights?" scoffed the Wolf, fingering the remote control. "What rights?"

"My rights as a—"

"Human being?" asked the Wolf, raising his eyebrows. "Is that what you think you are? You will soon be disabused of that notion, psionic."

The man pushed a button on the remote control. I heard a muffled clicking noise from inside my bracelets. Then he pressed another button. A powerful jolt of electricity shot through my arms. I fell to the floor.

The Wolf said coldly, "You do not have human rights, psionic..."

Another shock went through me. I gritted my teeth to keep myself from crying out. Even though my senses were numbed because of the draining, the pain was still excruciating.

"...because you are not human."

Another shock. I let out a gasp of pain as I desperately tried to tear the control bands off of my wrists. They wouldn't budge, and my whole body convulsed violently as the Wolf sent another shock through me.

The Wolf released the remote control button. I relaxed my muscles for a moment. But then the Wolf kicked me in the stomach with his boot, twice. I tasted blood in my mouth.

"Now," said the Wolf, crouching down and looking at me while holding his remote control delicately in one hand, "you will please tell me where I can find Cynthia Anderson."

If I had been thrown into this situation as the sixth grader who thought that telekinesis was a fun way to disrupt a boring school lesson, I probably would have told him on the spot. I would have done anything to keep him from pushing that button again. But so much had happened since then. So many things had changed. Cindy, who had become my mother, my one and only true protector... No, there was just no way...

"Never heard of her," I panted, still nauseous from the draining effect.

"Okay," sighed the Wolf, standing back up. "We'll start with easier questions, and work our way up. What's your name?"

Looking again at the wolf patch on the man's uniform, I spat the blood out of my mouth and recited, "Mary had a little lamb."

Another jolt of electricity. I knew it was coming, but it still rattled me. I closed my eyes.

"Your name?"

"Its fleece was—"

The next shock came much sooner than I expected, and I cried out loudly. I didn't care. He had asked where Cindy was, which meant he didn't know. And every second of his time that I wasted would give Cindy a second more head start to escape.

The Wolf put his right boot onto my chest, pushing me hard against the floor as he said, "I believe the correct answer was Adrian Howell."

"You know my name," I said, gasping for breath.

"That was just practice, psionic," he said, lifting his boot off of me. "Let's try question number two. What's the name of the healer girl?"

"And everywhere that Mary—"

He kicked me again. Then he grabbed me by my hair and, lifting me up, slammed me against the wall.

"You've got spirit, boy, I'll give you that," growled the Wolf.

"Yeah, so I'm told," I coughed feebly, remembering how Ralph had once said the same. Even a reminder of Ralph was a welcome distraction.

"What's her name?" the Wolf asked softly. "You can at least tell me that."

Did he really not know? What had happened to her? Alia might not speak with her mouth, but if they had done to her what they were doing to me, surely she would have said something telepathically to them.

"Bob... uh, Jack... something like that," I mumbled. "Maybe it was Tom."

"Adrian Howell, you are going to die now," said the Wolf, and pushed the shock button again, this time keeping it down.

I screamed. I didn't even know I had enough strength left to scream, but I screamed anyway. The shocks came rapidly, one after another. I could no longer think of anything but the agonizing jolts of electricity pulsing through my body as I writhed on the floor unable to breathe. I wanted to lose consciousness. I wanted to die.

"Alia!" I cried. "Her name's Alia!"

It stopped, and I lay there sobbing with my face on the floor. I realized that I had vomited, and wet myself as well.

"Now that wasn't so hard, was it?" the Wolf said quietly.

I slowly turned my neck and looked up at him, unable to even sit up. My vision was hazy, and I saw double.

The Wolf continued in a cold voice, "Take a deep breath, Adrian, and think of what is going to happen if you miss the next question. Ready? Where is Cynthia Anderson?"

I looked up at him, forcing my vision back into focus. How much could the truth hurt?

"I don't know," I whimpered, preparing for what I knew would be the last moments of my life.

The Wolf crouched down and studied my eyes carefully before saying, "You know what? I almost believe you, Adrian. Almost." He stood up again and continued in an annoyed tone, "The problem is that I do not have a lot of time. Surely you know that, which is why you are wasting it. I can't afford to wait around if you pass out. So let us change the rules of this game a little."

I stared up at him full of dread, wondering what was about to happen now.

The Wolf turned away from me and paused for a moment as if deep in thought. Then, still looking at the wall, he said quietly, "The healer girl... Alia, you said... She refused to speak with me. I doubt very much that a child her age could have managed it, so I can only conclude that she is unable to speak. As a source of information, she is useless to me." The Wolf turned back around and stood over me, his eyes full of malice. "If you do not tell me where Cynthia Anderson is, I will kill Alia."

I believed him. At the time, it was impossible not to. I gave him Mark's address and Cindy's old home address. I even told him Cindy's real name.

"I swear that's all I know," I said, my voice still hoarse from the screaming. I tried not to think of what was going to happen next. Would he kill me now? And Alia as well? Were we "useless" to him, now that he had his information?

"I believe you, Adrian, and you have my thanks," the Wolf replied quietly, and then turned to the intercom, saying, "Open."

The metal door opened, and the Wolf exited, leaving me lying there. Two uniformed soldiers came in. They silently grabbed me by my arms and, forcing me to stand, pushed me out of the room.

I was taken down a narrow and dimly lit concrete corridor. My legs were so weak that the soldiers had to drag me along. We passed several doors and a few turns, and then came to another heavy steel door, which automatically opened when one of the soldiers requested it through a nearby intercom.

I was pushed in through the doorway, and the soldiers left me there, slumped down on the floor. The door sealed itself behind me, and I felt the metal rods in my control bands retract.

I slowly raised my head and looked around at my new surroundings. This room was rectangular and more spacious than the one I had just left, but similarly secure with metal walls, two ceiling mounted security cameras, and no windows. There was some utilitarian furniture here, including a table with wooden benches and a few simple beds. The room was otherwise empty, except for a single occupant sitting on one of the thin mattresses.

"Alia!"

Although I was no longer being drained, I could still barely stand up, and I half-crawled to where she was sitting.

Alia was also dressed in a white hospital gown, though it was much too large for her and had probably been a lot cleaner when she first wore it. She wasn't wearing control bands, most likely because there were none her size. Instead, she had iron chains wrapped around her neck, wrists and ankles. The chains, while not binding her, were locked in place and couldn't be removed. I realized now why they couldn't get any answers from her. They were draining her constantly, so she couldn't use her telepathy even if she wanted to.

The Wolves had really done a job on Alia. Her long hair was a tangled mess, and there were dark, muddy stains all over her gown. I wondered if perhaps they had held her underwater. There was blood caked on her lower lip and bruises on both of her arms. Her left cheek was swollen deep purple. But worst of all were her eyes, unfocused and unmoving as she sat there staring out at nothing. Her lips were quivering almost imperceptibly, but no sound came out.

"Ali?" I said softly. "Ali, it's me, Addy."

Sitting next to her on the bed, I held her as closely as I dared considering how injured she was. I knew she couldn't speak, but when I let go, I realized in horror that she hadn't moved at all. Alia was so completely gone that she didn't even know I was there. She sat on the bed lost in her own little world that she had no doubt fled to when the Wolves had questioned her. I gently stroked her back, feeling the crisscrossing old scars through her thin gown, and remembered the words Cindy spoke to me on my first day at her house: "You'd be surprised at what Alia has survived."

Was this how she had been when Cindy first brought her back from the forest? How had Cindy taken care of her? I wished Cindy was here now. I almost wished the Wolves would catch her, so that she could come here and take care of Alia. I didn't know what to do. All I could do was hold Alia's hand, and for how long I don't know, but we just sat together, two filthy kids, one terrified, the other lost. I barely even noticed it when the metal rods in my control bands touched me again, and the steel door opened.

"Time to go," said a soldier, pressing a small pistol-like device against my right arm. It made a muffled popping noise, and I remember very little from then on.

12. END OF THE LINE

All I have are vague images, feelings, and fragments of thoughts and dreams: Bright lights. Motion. Dizziness. Darkness. A giant room. The sound of an engine. *"Addy."* Thin gray clouds. A man with a clipboard. "Sign here, please." Cold. A sunset over a barren field. Descending. Sliding doors. Nightmare. A white corridor. Warmth.

I squinted in the painfully bright light. As my eyes slowly adjusted, I saw that I was lying on a hard bed in a medium-size white hospital room. There was a giant rectangular mirror covering most of one wall, and some computer-like equipment along another.

"Good morning, Adrian," said a man's voice. It was calm and friendly, but there was no one in the room with me. "My name is Dr. Otis," continued the disembodied voice, "and I am the head researcher of the facility that you are now our guest at."

"Where are you?" I yawned, sitting up on the bed and stretching.

"I will see you in person presently. However, please understand that at our first meeting, your powers will be restrained."

I looked down at myself. I had been cleaned up and dressed in a white short-sleeve shirt and long white pants which I guessed might be made of cotton. My somewhat loose-fitting clothes matched the decor well. In fact, aside from the giant mirror, there was hardly anything in the room that wasn't white.

I also noticed that I still had a pair of control bands on me. They were different from the ones I was tortured in. These were slightly smaller and fit more snugly around my wrists. I noticed some markings on the casings and examined one closer. "P-47" was stenciled across it in black ink.

I looked at the mirror, suspecting that this Dr. Otis was behind it, and asked, "What is this place?"

"This is the Psionic Research Center," answered the voice of Dr. Otis. "I am here with Dr. Kellogg, and it is our job today to explain to you the conditions of your stay with us."

"Where is Alia?" I asked the mirror.

"If you cooperate, you will see her very soon."

"What do you want me to do?"

"We are going to restrain your psionic powers and then enter the room. Please remain seated on the bed."

I felt the little motors spin in my control bands, and the dull and heavy sensation of draining washed over me. A door slid open automatically, and in walked two men. The older of the two looked to be about sixty and was dressed in white doctors' garb and a lab coat. The other man, who I guessed was in his mid-thirties, looked a bit like Mark, with a shaggy beard and round glasses. He was wearing a tattered brown suit. They stood a few feet away from me.

"This is Dr. Kellogg," said the man in the lab coat, "who is our resident psychologist. I am Dr. Reuben Otis, and, as I said over the speaker a moment ago, I am the head researcher at this facility."

"Hello, Adrian," said the brown-suited man that Dr. Otis had introduced as Dr. Kellogg.

"Hi," I said, trying not to show how nervous I was.

Dr. Kellogg smiled warmly.

Dr. Otis continued, "We understand that the loss of your powers causes you physical discomfort, and I apologize that we must do it this way. I will try to keep this short. Firstly, we are not responsible for the way you were treated before you arrived here. Here, you will live under our care, and as long as you behave, you will not be harmed."

"Under your care?" I repeated.

Dr. Otis nodded. "Life as you knew it, whatever that may have been for you, is over now. You have been involuntarily committed to this facility. That means you cannot leave here. You will cooperate with our experiments, and, in return, you will be permitted to live in relative comfort."

"I'm a prisoner?"

"You are a research subject," Dr. Otis contradicted smilingly. "Many great minds wish to know how psionic power works, and why certain people have it. You can move things without touching them, and the girl you came in with can rapidly heal wounds. If we could discover how such talents work and recreate them in a controlled environment, it would greatly advance our knowledge of science and medicine."

I stared at him. "I don't have a choice?"

"You have two choices," replied Dr. Otis, his voice remaining quiet and businesslike. "You can make the best of things and learn to live here. Or, you can be uncooperative and suffer the consequences."

"What happens if I don't cooperate?" I asked, trying to keep my tone casual.

"Many of the tests can be done without your cooperation, though they could be considerably less comfortable for you," said Dr. Otis, looking me in the eye and no longer smiling. "I do not condone violence myself, but this facility is run by the military, and there are people here who believe that the research subjects should be motivated to cooperate through, uh... forceful persuasion."

I gulped.

Dr. Otis continued calmly, "Please make no mistake about this: In the sixty-some years since this facility has been occupied, no one has ever escaped. It would be in your best interests to remain in our good books."

"And Alia?" I asked.

Dr. Otis nodded. "She will stay with us too."

"I want to see her."

"You *want* to see her?" Dr. Otis repeated sharply, raising his eyebrows.

"Please," I said as humbly as I could. "Please may I see her now?"

Dr. Otis glanced at Dr. Kellogg, who nodded. Then Dr. Otis asked me in a kinder tone, "Can you walk in your condition?"

"A little," I answered. "But my balance is really bad."

Dr. Otis smiled understandingly and said, "We'll get a wheelchair."

They wheeled me down a spotless white corridor. There were doors lining both sides, as well as identical white passages leading off in other directions. It looked like the inside of a big hospital, but there were ceiling-mounted cameras every few yards, and the few people who were walking along the corridors either wore lab coats and carried clipboards, or wore military uniforms and carried machineguns.

We arrived at a silver metal door that had no knob or handle.

Dr. Otis turned to me, saying, "Dr. Kellogg wishes you to see Alia alone, so we will not enter with you. Your control rods will be retracted once you are inside. But just remember, Adrian, that this facility is under 24-hour monitoring. There are cameras and microphones in every room. We are ten stories underground, and the entire facility is encased in thick, multilayered metal shielding. Please do not abuse our trust."

Dr. Otis pulled out a blue plastic card from his pocket and held it up against a small scanner-like device mounted on the wall next to the doorframe. The metal door slid open, and Dr. Otis pushed my wheelchair into a short and narrow space no bigger than a closet. There was another identical metal door in front of me, and I realized that I was in an airlock. Dr. Otis exited back into the corridor, and the outer door closed between us. I felt the control rods retract in my bracelets, and stood up as the door in front of me slid open automatically.

It was a cozy one-room apartment. There was a small but comfortable-looking bed in one corner, and a wooden writing desk with a cushioned stool in another. There was also a dining table that was not much bigger than the desk and only had one dining chair. An empty bookshelf stood against the wall opposite the bed. There was another door on the other side of the room. It had a plastic doorknob and I assumed that it led to the bath and toilet.

Alia was sitting on the floor next to the bed. Her chains had been removed and she was dressed in a white cotton shirt and pants just like mine. Her back was to me, and she didn't turn around. As I stepped into the room, the airlock's inner door quietly slid shut behind me.

"Ali?" I whispered. "Alia?"

Alia slowly stood up and looked at me.

"Addy..." I heard her voice faintly in my head.

I knelt in front of her and peered into her face. The bruise on her left cheek was gone, as were her other injuries. Her eyes, however, were still slightly vacant.

"Ali, come here," I said quietly.

Alia slumped into my arms, weeping softly with her face pressed onto my chest. I held her gently, more relieved than I ever remember feeling. Alia crying was Alia with human emotions. Anything was better than the silent, hollow Alia I had seen after the Wolves' interrogation. I realized that I was crying too. I didn't care if anyone was watching us through a camera.

I waited until Alia cried herself out, and then I picked her up and sat with her on the bed. For a while, all she did was quietly call my name over and over in my head. I put an arm around her, lightly stroking her long walnut-brown hair. I asked myself what Cindy would do. I could almost hear her voice answering, "Give her time."

"Adrian, may I come in?" asked Dr. Kellogg through a speaker mounted on the ceiling.

I wasn't keen on being drained again, but thought it unwise to refuse, so I answered, "Yes."

The airlock door slid open, and Dr. Kellogg entered the room. Alia drew herself closer to me, rigid with fright. No doubt sensing her fear, Dr. Kellogg politely kept his distance. I realized that my control bands had not extended their rods.

"I'm very happy to see you two getting along," Dr. Kellogg said smilingly. "Quite frankly, I didn't know how to help Alia here. You see, I am a psychologist, but I have very little experience with children. We have never had any children here before. We're not exactly equipped for it."

I looked up at him and said, "I take it you don't usually stand unprotected in a room with people like us."

"That is correct," said Dr. Kellogg, frowning slightly as he sat down on the desk stool. "You would normally be restrained by your control bands, and possibly physically restrained as well."

"But not with me?"

"Dr. Otis thinks I'm being rash, but I believe I can trust you."

"Why?" I asked, and Dr. Kellogg understood that it wasn't a challenge, but a question.

"You are a child—well, a young man, perhaps. And watching you with Alia here convinced me that you would not risk her life."

Alia seemed to relax just a little, though she refused to let go of me as she stared down at Dr. Kellogg's feet. The psychologist had Mark's calm demeanor, and despite all that we had come through and the apparent hopelessness of our current situation, I felt a reluctant liking for him.

I asked, "Would it be okay if I stay with her until she is calmer?"

"But of course," replied Dr. Kellogg. "The testing schedule will not begin until you are properly settled here, so you will have plenty of time to spend with her."

"Thank you."

Dr. Kellogg smiled, and I decided to ask my most pressing question. "Doctor, will Alia have to participate in the testing—the research?"

"Unfortunately, yes. Everyone participates," he said apologetically. "She is our first healer, so no doubt there will be an extensive program for her."

"She's just a kid," I said at once. I thought about telling him Alia's history so that perhaps he would be more sympathetic to her, but I didn't want to go into details in front of Alia.

"We understand," said Dr. Kellogg, "and we will take her age into consideration when planning our experiments."

"Thank you," I said again, though I wasn't particularly grateful to hear that answer.

"Oh yes, I almost forgot," said Dr. Kellogg as he reached into his jacket pocket and pulled out a violet stone on a leather cord. "This is yours, I take it?"

I nodded.

Dr. Kellogg leaned forward on the stool, stretching his arm out, and I took Cat's pendant and put it back around my neck.

"Thank you, Doctor," I said, fingering the smooth stone. "This means a lot to me. Thank you so much."

"Politeness goes a long way, Adrian," Dr. Kellogg said approvingly. "You will soon find out anyway, so I'll tell you that there are presently four other psionics at this facility, and you might even see one or two of them from time to time. However, with the exception of one, their level of cooperation with our research is nearly none. I am hopeful that you will be more willing to work with us."

I sat pondering this for a moment. Dr. Otis had said that the research was for the advancement of science and medicine, but I had a difficult time believing in the merits of such progress. Alia's healing power, perhaps, but what if everyone on the planet had the ability to break things with their minds? Wouldn't that be like giving everyone a loaded gun? Did we really need to make it any easier for people to hurt each other? And what about research on mind control? Who would benefit, and at whose expense? I decided to be honest and tell Dr. Kellogg about my concern.

"You are not the first psionic to say just that," Dr. Kellogg answered gravely. "We have had others who refused to cooperate on moral principles. I sometimes wonder about the logic of it myself. But Adrian, we are currently living in a world where a very select few have psionic power, and some of them are not to be trusted with it."

"I couldn't agree more," I said, thinking of Ralph, "but that still doesn't mean we should hand it out to everyone."

"No, it doesn't," said Dr. Kellogg, nodding. "Unfortunately, scientific progress is like that. Once something is known, there's no way to unlearn it. You can be sure that ours isn't the only country researching psionics. If we don't learn how it works, we may end up being the only ones who don't know."

I thought about that and decided he might have a point, but even so, it just didn't feel like the right thing to do. As if it weren't enough that I was trapped underground with a frightened little girl and facing the looming prospect of being the object of who-knew-what kind of scientific research under the carefully guised threat of torture, I now had to think of the moral side of cooperation with the doctors here.

No, that was really just too much. I had to keep my priorities straight.

"I'll cooperate..." I began slowly.

"Good," said Dr. Kellogg.

"...if you'll let me take care of Alia."

Dr. Kellogg gave me a curious look and asked, "What does that mean?"

"I want to be with her during her experiments," I told him. "I want some say in what you make her do."

"I see," said Dr. Kellogg. "And in return?"

"I'll do anything you ask."

Dr. Kellogg sat stroking his beard for a moment, and then answered carefully, "I can't promise that your requests regarding Alia's testing will always be respected, Adrian, but if you are truly willing to cooperate, then perhaps we can strike a deal. I'll speak to Dr. Otis for you later."

"Thank you, Dr. Kellogg."

Dr. Kellogg smiled. "It'll be my pleasure. It is nearly lunchtime, and I was going to show you your room first, but if you like, you can eat here with Alia and take the tour later. I doubt you are looking forward to being restrained again, but it is a required security protocol in the corridors. Oh, and I am also sorry about the tattoos, but those are military-side protocols as well."

"Tattoos?" I asked.

Dr. Kellogg tapped his upper left arm near the shoulder. I lifted up my left shirtsleeve and found what he was talking about. Just like on my control bands, there was a black stencil-like tattoo that read "P-47." I lifted Alia's sleeve and saw that she had one too.

"P-46," I read, and frowned at Dr. Kellogg.

He shrugged, saying, "Everyone here gets marked, Adrian."

"So what's written on your arm?" I asked dryly.

Dr. Kellogg chuckled. "Touché."

"What do the numbers mean?" I asked, guessing what the "P" stood for.

"It is the order that you arrived here," explained Dr. Kellogg. "You are the forty-seventh psionic to come to this facility."

"Only forty-seven psionics in sixty years?"

"We do not use the same coding system for the ones who come in already deceased. You see, it's the military's job to hunt down psionics, and whenever possible, deliver them alive, but it often is not possible."

I gaped, realizing that the Wolf who had tortured me would never have killed Alia. It had been an empty threat to trick me into giving Cindy away before she could escape, and I had fallen for it. I wondered if she had been killed.

Lunch trays arrived on a plastic cart that had been pushed into the airlock. Switching places with the cart, Dr. Kellogg left Alia and me in the room to eat by ourselves. Our meal turned out to be spaghetti meat sauce, which, though not quite up to Cindy's standards, tasted wonderful after who-knew-how-many intravenous feedings. I sat with Alia at the small dining table. I used the desk stool, which was a bit short for the table, but so was Alia on the dining chair, so we were almost evenly matched.

Alia hardly ever opened her mouth except to eat, so I hadn't noticed it until now, but she was down two additional baby teeth thanks to her time with the Wolf. Both had been coming loose anyway, but seeing the gaping hole in her upper front teeth was a stinging reminder of what Alia had been put through. I wasn't sure who I hated more at the moment, though: the Wolf or my own stupid self.

Alia looked thinner than I remembered, but she ate well enough, and after lunch I played with her until she got sleepy and curled up into a ball on the bed for her afternoon nap. Having nothing to do and not being in the mood for meditation, I sat on the side of the bed and watched her sleep. Dr. Kellogg returned about half an hour later, quietly slipping in and tapping me on my shoulder.

I obediently followed him into the airlock, sat in my wheelchair, and felt the control rods touch my wrists as the inner door slid shut. The outer door opened and Dr. Kellogg wheeled me out. He took me down the corridor to another room, a few doors from Alia's. Once through the airlock, my control rods retracted again, and I looked around at my new cell. It was identical to Alia's right down to the location of the bathroom door on the wall opposite the airlock. I looked up at the camera and speaker mounted on the ceiling, and wondered briefly where the microphone was hidden. I sat down on the bed and Dr. Kellogg sat on the stool.

"I spoke to Dr. Otis over lunch about your proposal," began Dr. Kellogg.

I looked hopefully at him. "And?"

"He said he will think about it. Dr. Otis is a cautious man. Most people here are, considering the nature of our work. You will have to convince him of your good intentions yourself."

"How do I do that?" I asked, wondering if Dr. Otis was watching me through the camera right now.

"Well, you said that you will cooperate in any way you can, so perhaps you can start by answering some of my questions," said Dr. Kellogg. When I nodded, he asked, "Firstly, why can't Alia speak?"

"What do you know about her?"

"We know that she's a healer," said Dr. Kellogg, "and that she has numerous scars from what appear to be long-term physical abuse. Aside from that, however, we don't really know anything."

"You don't know that she's also telepathic?"

"I didn't," admitted Dr. Kellogg.

"Well, now you know," I said, and then briefly told Dr. Kellogg about Alia's time in the care of her devil-obsessed keepers. He listened without interruption, and thanked me for telling him.

"Now you understand why I don't want to see Alia hurt anymore," I said.

Dr. Kellogg nodded. "Under the circumstances, I think it would be best to let your testing schedule start first, and delay Alia's until she is more comfortable in her new surroundings. I have a fair amount of say in when and how certain experiments are conducted, even if I don't really understand the theories behind them."

Suddenly I heard Alia's frightened voice in my head saying, *"Addy? Addy, where are you?"*

The ceiling-mounted speaker crackled to life, and I heard a woman's voice say crisply, "Dr. Kellogg, please report to Monitor Room B."

"Alia's awake," I told Dr. Kellogg. "She's scared because I'm not there."

Dr. Kellogg looked up at the camera and said, "Control, is this about number 46?"

"Yes, Doctor," the woman replied. "She's crying again."

"In that case, I'll go directly to her room," said Dr. Kellogg. "Please lock band 47."

I felt the metal rods extend from my control bands as Dr. Kellogg said to me, "You will come too, please."

Dr. Kellogg quickly wheeled me back, and as soon as the inner airlock door opened, Alia jumped onto me. Once she stopped crying, Dr. Kellogg left us there and I spent the rest of the afternoon keeping Alia company.

Dr. Kellogg showed up again just before dinner. But this time, my control rods were extended because he was with a uniformed military guard carrying a black briefcase. The guard opened his briefcase to reveal a pair of small white control bands with "P-46" stenciled across them.

"We finally made some her size," said Dr. Kellogg. "I'm sorry about this, but it is regulation here. At least she can now leave the room... uh, if she wants."

I could see that it was no use to protest this, but Alia shook her head and cowered behind me, refusing to let the guard near her.

"Dr. Kellogg, please hold her down," said the guard.

Alia started to bawl again. Though dizzy from being drained, I got between them, explaining that the problem wasn't the control bands, but rather the man who was scaring her. I asked Dr. Kellogg to teach me how the control bands worked so I could put them on Alia myself.

Taking them from the guard, I examined the insides of Alia's new bracelets. I saw the little holes where the metal rods extended from and where the battery pack went. The control bands were designed to snap into place and not come off unless the correct radio signal was sent either from the facility's Central Control Room or from the little white remote controls that the doctors carried in their pockets.

Dr. Kellogg showed me his remote control. I examined the small buttons on it, which were set into the device so that they wouldn't be pressed by accident. The buttons were marked with numbers zero to nine and the letters E, R, U and I. Dr. Kellogg explained that the letters stood for Extend, Retract, Unlock and Incapacitate, which was their polite word for sending jolts of electricity through your body.

If only for a reason to delay the moment I would have to snap the bands onto Alia's wrists, I asked Dr. Kellogg, "Back in my room, why did you ask the Control Room to drain me if you have this remote control?"

"Oh, well, it's a little tedious to press these little buttons, see? It's easier simply to ask," replied Dr. Kellogg, pocketing the remote control again. "We rarely use the remotes, though we have to carry them everywhere. Just another protocol."

I hated making Alia put out her arms so I could cuff them with a torture device, but it was either me or the big guy. Alia actually took it better than I did, probably because she didn't know what these things could do to her. I prayed she would never find out.

The battery packs made the control bands heavy, but Alia soon got used to it and didn't spill too much of her dinner soup. A woman from the Control Room had brought a taller chair for Alia, so I got the dining chair this time.

Having no access to sunlight, the only source for knowing the time of day was the electronic desk clock. As I watched Alia's bedtime draw nearer, I wondered how I was going to get back to my own room without Alia crying again, but found no answer.

"Addy, don't go!" pleaded Alia, grabbing my arms when I stood up to leave.

"Ali, it's almost bedtime," I said, trying to break free of her. But I could already see that there was no way I was getting out of her room that night, so I called Dr. Kellogg and asked for a mat and a sleeping bag.

He instead brought in a folding army cot along with a pillow and a blanket, which we set up in the small space next to the dining table.

The room didn't have a dresser, but Dr. Kellogg had also brought in a change of clothes for Alia and me. It was another set of white cotton shirts, pants and underwear identical to the ones we were wearing. When I asked, Dr. Kellogg informed me that these facility-issue garments doubled as our sleepwear and would henceforth be delivered twice a day to our rooms along with the morning and evening meals. We weren't even allowed shoes or socks, just a pair of simple plastic slippers. I didn't find this too surprising since we were the equivalent of in-patients at a hospital, but I still wished our clothes weren't so unnaturally white. It made me feel really exposed and vulnerable.

"It's just regulation here, Adrian," said Dr. Kellogg. "I'm sure you'll get used to it soon."

Dr. Kellogg made a quick trip back to my room and returned with my cup and toothbrush before bidding us goodnight. Then our control bands were snapped open by Central Control so that we could bathe before bed.

Alia asked me to bathe with her like Cindy often did, but that's where I drew the line. The last time I had bathed with anyone was when I was seven and Cat was five. After a good deal of teary-eyed tugging at me, Alia finally consented to take her bath alone under the non-negotiable condition that I sat right outside the bathroom door and guarded it with my life.

Though she couldn't swim, Alia was a water-baby, often spending more than an hour splashing around in the tub back at Cindy's house. Here, however, she was in and out in less time than even I usually took.

When she got out, she asked me to help her dry her long hair, and then got all upset when, according to her, I went about it the wrong way. I regretted how little attention I had given to all the things Cindy had been doing for her back at home. Parenting should be taught in school.

I took my bath next, though this caused some difficulty as well. Alia didn't want to be left alone in her room. I conceded to leaving the bathroom door slightly ajar, and Alia hid under her bed.

Dr. Otis had not been kidding when he said that there were cameras in every room. Even the bathroom had a waterproof one attached to the ceiling, and it took a while before I could bring myself to undress, but what choice was there?

I found Alia still hiding under her bed when I got out. Once we had brushed our teeth, I put Alia on her bed and lay down on my cot.

"No, Addy," said Alia, getting out of the bed and tugging at my arm. *"Over here. Please!"*

I sighed heavily, though I couldn't exactly say I wasn't expecting this either. Earlier, when Dr. Kellogg and I were setting up the army cot, Alia had watched apprehensively though without comment. Now I could see that she was on the verge of tears again.

It was a single bed, which made for a bit of a tight squeeze even with a little kid, but Alia insisted I lie between her and the airlock door. She lay down on the wall side of the bed and, snuggling up against my side, went to sleep with her arms wrapped tightly around my body. I lay awake for hours, wishing once again that Cindy was there to help me with her.

13. FIRST IMPRESSIONS

My testing schedule did not start the next day, nor the next. In fact, I soon learned that it wasn't going to start for a week. Apparently, Dr. Kellogg had convinced Dr. Otis to let me take care of Alia's psychology for a while, and no one seemed to be in any real hurry here anyway.

Dr. Kellogg came by right after lunch on our second day at the Psionic Research Center. He brought us a small box full of books and magazines from the research center's library up on what he called "Level 9." I took the opportunity to ask more about the facility.

"We are on Level 10," explained Dr. Kellogg, "which is the deepest habitable part of the research center. The building is large and circular, built into the earth rather than above it. There's really nothing above ground. Of course, I can't tell you much about the other levels, but they include additional living quarters for the doctors and military personnel, our main kitchen, library, as well as various entertainment facilities. Many of the doctors, including myself, live here permanently. There is only one way in or out of Level 10, which is the main elevator. The elevator is guarded by multiple security gates, soldiers, and automated defense systems."

Hearing that, I did believe Dr. Otis's claim that no one had ever managed to escape.

Dr. Kellogg's box contained mostly novels, along with a few difficult puzzle books and several comics, but nothing that would interest Alia. There was also an old tennis ball, a deck of cards and a set of Dominoes that he had brought from one of the recreation rooms, but that was it. Dr. Kellogg was right: the facility really wasn't equipped for children.

"Next time I go to town, I'll pick up some books and toys for her," promised Dr. Kellogg. "Is there anything in particular she might enjoy?"

"Coloring books and storybooks and board games," I replied automatically. "Anything with unicorns in them."

Dr. Kellogg raised an eyebrow. "Unicorns?"

"Alia's got a thing for unicorns," I explained, and told him how a giant stuffed unicorn doll was the only toy Alia had taken from her room when we left Cindy's house.

Dr. Kellogg smiled as he stood up to leave. "I'll see what I can find."

I wanted to go see the library with him, but he told me that I was permanently restricted to Level 10.

"And besides, Adrian," he added with a nod toward Alia, who was hiding behind my back and studying Dr. Kellogg from over my shoulder, "how do you plan to even leave the room?"

With her eighth "birthday" only a month away, Alia was not a baby anymore, but she was certainly acting like one. Growing up in Cindy's house after Mark had moved away, Alia should have been used to being alone. She was alone in the daytime while Cindy was working at the hospital, and she even spent nights alone when Cindy was out looking for me in the city. After I started living at Cindy's house, Alia had lost some of her self-reliance, but she still had very little trouble being left to herself. After all, until Cindy and I managed to coax her into coming to the pond with us, Alia spent those days on her own in the house. But the shock of being separated from Cindy, tortured by the Wolves, and then drugged and sent to this place... Well, I couldn't say I didn't understand how she was feeling. Besides, Cindy's house was familiar ground to her. Mark's place was change enough for her to regularly cling to Cindy at night, and Alia had trusted Mark. How could I possibly hope to get Alia used to a place like this? "Give her time," said Cindy's voice in my head again.

Well, time was the one thing we had in abundance. For the rest of that day, Alia and I sat in the room and played together as if we were back in Cindy's house, stacking Dominoes and throwing around the tennis ball. Alia was calm enough when she was alone with me, but as soon as the airlock door started to slide open, such as at mealtimes, she immediately reverted to baby-mode, retreating behind me or hiding under the bed.

"We'll just give it some time," suggested Dr. Kellogg through the intercom that evening, confirming Cindy's tactic. "I hope you don't mind too much."

"Great!" I replied sarcastically, looking up at the camera and rolling my eyes. "Now I have the bedtime of a seven-year-old."

Actually, I didn't mind the early bedtime nearly as much as how painfully stiff my body had felt in the morning as a result of Alia clinging to me all night. Being unable to move at all was really uncomfortable, but Alia asked me to sleep in her bed the second night too. Again I obliged her, but once she was peacefully snoring, I carefully pried her fingers off my arm and moved over to the cot. The next morning, Alia discovered what I had done and was sullen about it all day. I promised never to leave her side during the night again, and even had Dr. Kellogg remove the army cot, resigning myself to being Alia's new pet unicorn.

Whether playing sentry at the bathroom door while she bathed or lying in bed with her and shielding her from the airlock, I felt silly pretending to be Alia's bodyguard. I knew there was nothing I could do to protect her if the doctors decided to take her away. Nevertheless, I dutifully played the part, reminding myself that it was worth it if only to keep her calm, and since I was the idiot who got her into this mess in the first place, I had little right to complain. Besides, I knew how frightening it was to be at the mercy of powers beyond my control. At least Alia could think she was being protected by someone.

A few days of idleness later, Dr. Kellogg came with two large bags full of new toys and books. As per my request, there were several board games as well as lots of storybooks and coloring books. One of the coloring books was dedicated exclusively to unicorns, and though Alia still kept her distance from Dr. Kellogg, I could tell that she was pretty happy with him.

"I did my best in the unicorn department, but this is all I could find in my limited time," Dr. Kellogg said apologetically.

In addition to the unicorn coloring book, there were a few babyish picture books that featured horses and unicorns. However, many of Dr. Kellogg's selections were pretty common stories that Alia already knew well.

There was *Alice in Wonderland* and *The Wizard of Oz* as well as popular Disney adaptations of Brothers Grimm stuff like *Rapunzel* and *Hansel and Gretel*. But I knew that Alia wouldn't mind repeats because Cindy used to read these stories to her every night. Despite being entirely unicorn-free, *Hansel and Gretel* was one of Alia's all-time favorites. (I never asked, but this was probably because being lost in a forest was something that Alia identified with.)

"Thank you, Doctor," I said, meaning it.

"It is my pleasure," said Dr. Kellogg.

Then he told me that my first experiments would begin the very next day. I somehow managed not to frown.

The following morning, Alia tagged along with me to a place called Lab-C, which was at the far end of Level 10. This was where my telekinetic powers would be tested.

The Lab-C Testing Room was slightly larger than a gymnasium. It looked like one too, except that the floor was made of stone and there were various items such as concrete blocks, metal bars, broken televisions, washing machines, and even an old and busted grand piano there. Mounted on the far end wall was a series of targets made of paper, plastic, and metal, and on the other end was a large and very thick rectangular window. Behind this window was the Lab-C Control Room, which was a smaller room filled with computers and occupied by a handful of lab technicians, researchers, and well-armed military guards.

Dr. Kellogg, who was escorting us, introduced Alia and me to the researchers in the Lab-C Control Room. I won't bother you with their names except for one Dr. Denman who was the only researcher that refused to shake my hand during the greetings. Dr. Denman was almost as old as Dr. Otis, taller, and had thin, gray hair and hawk-like eyes. He scowled at Alia and me, making Alia even more frightened than she already was in the presence of so many unfamiliar faces. Dr. Otis was in Lab-C Control too, so I did my best to "convince him of my good intentions."

Alia, however, did not. That morning had already been a shaky one for her, ever since she had demanded that I stay with her in our room. Not wanting to be left there alone, she had reluctantly accompanied me to Lab-C, but the military guards and researchers here, especially Dr. Denman, really freaked her out. We both had our control rods extended so I couldn't hear Alia's voice in my head, but I could see that she was trembling during the introductions, refusing to shake hands with anyone. Still, the draining effect I myself was experiencing kept me from caring too much.

Dr. Otis asked me to start showing them what I was capable of by going down into the Lab-C Testing Room alone and doing anything I wanted. When Alia had a fit of separation anxiety, Dr. Kellogg talked Dr. Otis into allowing Alia to enter the Testing Room with me.

Our control rods retracted as soon as the heavy door closed behind us, and I immediately heard Alia's telepathic voice frantically begging me to take her back to our room.

"Dr. Kellogg can probably take you back if you really want to go," I said, "but you'll still have to stay there by yourself."

"No, Addy," she whimpered into my head. *"You come with me too."*

"You can't have it both ways," I told her firmly.

Alia looked up at me, her eyes dripping tears.

"I'm sorry, Ali," I said in a softer tone as I crouched down in front of her, "but I can't do anything about this. I wish I could, but I can't. I'm really sorry. Do you want to stay here with me or do you want to stay in your room?"

Wiping her eyes, Alia silently weighed both unacceptable options for a moment before saying miserably, *"I'll stay with you, Addy."*

"Okay," I said, giving her a smile.

I turned my attention back to the Testing Room, knowing that if I was going to convince Dr. Otis to let me be Alia's guardian, I would have to show him that I was at least as worthy a test subject as Alia.

I started by levitating some of the smaller concrete blocks into the air and throwing them one at a time at a metal target. I flew Alia once around the room, and then switched with her, bouncing off the ceiling and hovering upside down near the observation window. I carefully pushed the piano keys one by one from yards away.

Next, I showed them what I could do to the targets without the concrete blocks. I quickly shredded the paper targets with normal telekinetic blasts, and then moved on to cracking the plastic ones with a few well-placed focused shots through my right index finger. Of course, the heavy steel targets were left completely undamaged, but surely they didn't expect me to break those. Deciding to show some initiative, I asked them to dim the lighting so that they could see the streaks of silvery light as I released my blasts in the dark.

"That is very impressive, Adrian," I heard Dr. Otis say over the speaker as the lights came back on. "We've seen telekinesis here before, but nothing of your caliber. Can you fire while in the air?"

I had never tried that before, and I was getting tired. Still, it was a request by the head researcher. I lifted myself up about five feet off the floor and extended both arms toward a plastic target. As soon as I shot my energy at it, however, I lost my focus and fell back onto the hard, stone floor.

Alia came running up to me, and so did Dr. Otis and Dr. Kellogg from the Lab-C Control Room, dutifully followed by the guards.

"You could have just said it wasn't possible," said Dr. Otis.

"I didn't know if I could do it," I replied, holding Alia's hand so she wouldn't start panicking near the guards. Our control rods had extended the moment the doctors entered the Testing Room, and once again I couldn't hear what Alia was saying.

I wasn't hurt too badly, but it was already nearly noon so Dr. Otis ended the session.

After lunch, I was taken to a smaller laboratory to take various physical examinations, so Alia, tagging along, missed her nap. The doctors had a database containing all of my medical records from the day I was born so that they could compare them to my present condition. They drew my blood and took other samples, as well as checked my eyes and ears.

It was mostly routine stuff, but one test really scared me at first. The doctors called it an "electrocardiogram," but I had no clue what that meant. A series of wires called "electrodes" were attached to me, all over my bare body, and you can imagine what I thought was about to happen next. Fortunately, the electrocardiogram was entirely painless, as were most of the other tests.

The only real problem was Alia. Watching my examination from the side, Alia was constantly on edge, and when she saw the fear in my eyes during my electrocardiogram, she completely lost it. It took forever to get her to stop crying, and that night she latched herself onto me so tightly that, as tired as I was, I found it difficult to fall asleep.

The next three days were no better. During the mornings and early afternoons, I was given more physical examinations. I was also interviewed at length about everything that had happened to me since I was in kindergarten. They asked me how I had initially trained my powers. They wanted to know every detail of my two confrontations with Ralph. I even told them about my run-in with the cycling graviton.

My main interviewer, a comparatively young doctor at the facility, was particularly interested in my account of how I seemed to have possessed a touch of uncontrolled telekinetic power for years before I became a full-blown psionic.

"How old were you when you used your power for the first time?" he asked.

"I honestly don't know when it started," I replied. "All my life, things around me sometimes just moved a bit. I always thought that was normal so I didn't think about it. I never suspected that it was me."

"That's quite intriguing!" said the doctor, whose perky personality I instantly disliked. "Psionics usually gain their powers over a much shorter time. Anywhere from a few days to a few months at the very longest. Before that, they have nothing."

The young doctor suggested that perhaps my telekinetic power had been simmering just below the surface of my consciousness for most of my life, and that my abrupt contact with a moving vehicle might have jolted my body into accepting the change. Only after I gained control over my power did it become strong enough for psionic finders to sense my presence from afar.

"Of course, that's just an uneducated guess, Adrian," he added with a chuckle. "We've never heard a story like yours before. This could be quite a mystery to solve! You might be the key to an amazing discovery!"

Irked by the doctor's excitement, I said dryly, "What makes you think I care about your discoveries?"

The doctor frowned, and I instantly regretted my words. I had to be a good boy for Alia's sake. For the rest of the interview, I kept my responses professional and my attitude to myself.

Once the doctors ran out of questions, it was back to Lab-C, where I showed them more aerobatics. Dr. Otis was not there on the second or third day, and Dr. Denman terrified Alia by constantly glaring at her during the sessions.

It must have been only about 5am the next day, but my eyes had opened, probably because Alia had her arms wrapped tightly around my neck and was slowly suffocating me like a boa constrictor.

I heard the intercom crackle, and Dr. Kellogg's voice came on. "Good morning, Adrian. I see you're up early."

"Morning, Dr. Kellogg," I croaked, looking up at the ceiling camera.

"Mind if I come in?"

"Alia's still sleeping."

"I know. I'll try not to wake her."

A few minutes later, the door slid open and Dr. Kellogg entered quietly.

He leaned his back against the wall, looking down at us and remarking in a slightly amused tone, "She really does cling to you, doesn't she?"

"Quite literally," I replied hoarsely, feeling Alia's arms around my neck tighten even more. Alia was giving me a hands-on lesson on what it felt like to be a teddy bear. "Can't blame her, though, Doctor," I said, "considering what she's been through."

"No, I suppose not," agreed Dr. Kellogg. "And how about you?"

"Excuse me?" I said, wondering what I had just missed.

"Well, Alia deals with her insecurity by attaching herself to you. How are you managing yours? Surely you are not feeling much better than she is."

He was, of course, right. I didn't share Alia's phobia of strangers in this place, but my fears were no less serious. Unlike Alia, who would be just as terrified walking into a shopping mall, I understood that the dangers we faced at the Psionic Research Center, despite Dr. Kellogg's kindness, were very real. Here, psionics were not people. We did not share the rights of fellow human beings. The doctors could kill us on a whim with no consequences to themselves. At least one of them, I strongly felt, wanted to. And even if they didn't, how long would the tests last? A month? A year? And would they let us go free when it was all over? Neither Dr. Otis nor Dr. Kellogg had mentioned anything about when we might be released, and I was afraid to ask, especially after Dr. Otis's remark about how life as I knew it was over. If there were only four psionics at this facility aside from Alia and me, P-46 and P-47, what happened to the other forty-one? I feared for Cindy and Mark as well, and often wondered where they were, assuming, that is, they were still alive.

"I'm okay," I lied quietly.

"Well, I'm still no expert on child psychology," said Dr. Kellogg, "but I think that it would probably be best to keep the sleeping arrangements as they are, at least for the time being, if it's alright with you."

I cringed. I was already regretting my decision to return the army cot. It wasn't that I disliked Alia or that I didn't care about her wellbeing. Of course I wanted her to feel secure. But the bed was too small for the two of us, and Alia still slept with her arms around me every night, often all through the night, which meant that I was waking up every morning with a painfully stiff neck and shoulders.

"I noticed Alia's birthday is coming up," said Dr. Kellogg.

It was the first of March, meaning Alia's birthday, or "finding day," was only three weeks away. I realized that we had already been here ten days.

Dr. Kellogg smiled, saying, "Anything we can get for her, within reasonable bounds of course."

"So I guess an elevator pass would be out of the question?" I asked jokingly.

"Unfortunately," said Dr. Kellogg, chuckling.

"How about a double bed?" I suggested.

"Hmm, yes, I think we can arrange that, assuming we could get it through the airlock."

"And some more unicorn stuff, if you can."

"Certainly," said Dr. Kellogg. "And Adrian, I believe Dr. Otis has come to his decision about your offer. You will have the day off today, but I will be around later to collect you and deliver you to his office."

"Any idea what his decision is?" I asked nervously.

"I would hate to spoil the surprise," Dr. Kellogg said simply, and left the room.

I gave the morning up as a bad job and shook Alia awake.

Alia was delighted to discover that we had the whole day to ourselves. At Dr. Kellogg's instruction, the guards who delivered our meals no longer entered our room, but instead simply left the cart in the airlock for us, which meant Alia could spend the entire day without fear of human contact.

That didn't keep her from falling into one of her long silences shortly after breakfast, though. I already knew that sitting silently was Alia's way of steadying and recharging her emotions. When she was in one of her moods, it was always best to just let her be, so I sat beside her and quietly flipped through some of the magazines Dr. Kellogg had brought for me.

After a little over an hour, I suddenly heard Alia's voice in my head say quietly, *"I miss Cindy."*

I looked up from my magazine and noticed that Alia had come out of her spell. I squeezed her hand and said quietly, "I miss her too, Alia."

"Do you think she's okay?"

"I'm sure she is," I lied, touching my forehead to hers, "and you'll see her again soon."

Alia hugged me tightly, and then jumped off the bed, all smiles. She wasn't about to waste any more of her precious day off being upset. We spent the rest of the morning and early afternoon playing with her new toys and cracking each other up with silly jokes and tickles. I was surprised to see Alia acting so normal, but I guessed her silent time had done the trick.

Dr. Kellogg came for me just as Alia had curled up on the bed for her afternoon nap, and I decided to chance it and leave her there.

Dr. Kellogg pushed my wheelchair into a spacious office not far from Lab-C. There was a large oak desk at the far end of the room. In the middle of the office was a wide, rectangular table lined with comfortable-looking chairs on both sides. Unlike most of the facility, the walls here were painted light brown, and had framed pictures hanging on them. There were even some potted plants in two corners. But what surprised me most was that Dr. Otis was not the only one there. The head researcher was sitting at his big desk, but there were also twelve other researchers sitting at the table. Also, curiously, there were no military guards present.

All thirteen heads turned toward me as Dr. Kellogg wheeled me up close to Dr. Otis's desk. Seeing how nervous I was, Dr. Otis stood up and introduced me to the other doctors, telling me their names and fields of study, which included physics, chemistry, genetics and neurobiology, to name a few. I had met many of the doctors already, but I learned that this was the core group of researchers studying psionics here. Dr. Denman, the neurobiologist, was present too, and once again he just glowered at me.

"Now, Adrian," began Dr. Otis once the introductions were over, "Dr. Kellogg has told me of your willingness to cooperate with our study program in exchange for some limited authority over Alia Gifford's treatment at this research center."

"Yes, sir," I said as crisply as I could manage in my drained condition. I chose "sir" over "doctor," hoping it would make me sound even more sincere.

Dr. Otis continued in his businesslike tone, "Dr. Kellogg has assured me that we can trust you, and my impression of your attitude so far has been equally favorable."

"Thank you, sir."

"Some of us," said Dr. Otis, glancing at Dr. Denman, "are against what I am going to do, but I have convinced our military counterpart to waive the control band protocol for you in the corridors, as well as give you limited security clearance within Level 10. Alia will remain, for the time being, your ward, provided you both behave and Dr. Kellogg is sufficiently convinced that it is in Alia's best interests that you continue to be her caregiver. Do you understand these terms?"

"Yes, sir," I said earnestly. Dr. Otis liked his long words, but I understood the general gist of his speech.

"You understand that this is a conditional permission?"

"Yes. Yes I do," I said, and added a moment late, "sir."

"Very well," said Dr. Otis, pulling out his white remote control and pushing some buttons. "I expect to see you at our meetings once Alia's testing begins. Welcome aboard the team, Dr. Howell."

The rods in my control bands retracted, so I stood up from my wheelchair and bowed. Most of the doctors laughed and clapped good-naturedly, and I breathed a sigh of relief as Dr. Otis placed a red plastic card in my hand. It was labeled "PRC-A Level 10 Limited Security Access E: Adrian Howell / P-47."

"Alia's testing will begin in three days," said Dr. Otis. "Dr. Kellogg will teach you how to use the card. Would you like to say anything before we finish?"

"Just th—thank you," I stammered. It wasn't easy speaking to a large group of white-coats, even though they were smiling. They were still my captors, after all. But I did have something to ask for Alia, so I steadied my voice and said, "I'm sorry, Dr. Otis, but there is one thing I'd like to request."

"Already?" asked Dr. Otis, raising an eyebrow.

"It's about Alia," I said carefully. "She's a healer and a telepath. She's not dangerous at all, and without her telepathy she can't even talk."

"Yes, of course," said Dr. Otis, nodding. "I will speak to Central Control about her security protocol, and I'm sure they will agree."

I thanked Dr. Otis again several times before Dr. Kellogg led me out of the office, leaving the wheelchair behind.

"Hold the card up to the scanners next to the doors," explained Dr. Kellogg as we walked back down the corridor. "It will open your living quarters and give you access to all minimum-security areas on Level 10, including the doctors' lounge and dining hall."

"There's no scanner on the inside of the bedroom," I said.

"Yes, but all you have to do is raise your voice and request that the door be opened."

"So I'm still being monitored?"

"Of course," said Dr. Kellogg. "All day, every day."

I frowned, but Dr. Kellogg chuckled and said, "You are one of only a handful of psionics to ever be given a security card here. And in record time, too. Don't worry. They do trust you."

Dr. Kellogg stopped walking and turned to me, saying, "And to prove it, I'm going to leave you here to find your own way back. I have business elsewhere at the moment. You are welcome to go exploring if you wish, but I think you should probably return to your room before Alia wakes up."

Dr. Kellogg headed down another corridor and disappeared. I was a bit curious about the rest of Level 10, but I agreed with Dr. Kellogg's warning about Alia, who might wake at any moment. I didn't want her to cry on her special day off.

I had just started walking back toward Alia's room when I felt a bony hand grab my shoulder from behind. I turned my head, and found myself looking up into Dr. Denman's severe hawk-like eyes. I tried to pull myself free, but for such an old man, Dr. Denman was strong. His grip on my shoulder was firm and he easily pinned me against the corridor wall. I couldn't move at all, and I didn't dare use my power on him. Though no longer draining me, the control bands were still locked around my wrists.

Dr. Denman looked at me with disgust etched all over his wrinkly old face, saying in a harsh, dry voice, "Dr. Kellogg is very impressed with your attitude. As is Dr. Otis."

"I take it you're not?" I asked, trying to sound braver than I felt.

"As far as I'm concerned," he said, bringing his face up close to mine, "you're just another lab rat. Put one toe out of line, and you'll suffer the same fate."

Releasing my shoulder, Dr. Denman drew an imaginary line across his neck with his right index finger. The effect was chilling, but I glared back defiantly, determined not to be fazed by him. After all, Dr. Otis was the head researcher here, not Dr. Denman.

Dr. Denman cuffed me lightly across the face and growled, "You just watch yourself, psionic."

He walked away, and I stood shaking for a moment before remembering to hurry back to Alia.

14. DR. HOWELL

My new security card opened both the outer and inner airlock doors, but only from the outside of each. To get out, I had to call the Central Control Room through the microphone, which I finally discovered was, not surprisingly, mounted on the camera. It would have been even nicer if we didn't have to wear the control bands at all, but at least I was free of the wheelchair.

After two more days of testing, during which I was asked to levitate the same weight in different materials and order them by difficulty, I was told that Alia's tests would begin the following day. This time, I would be the tagalong.

Alia refused to let go of my hand the next morning as we walked to Lab-D, which turned out to be something like a school classroom with desks and chairs in neat rows. There were also some soundproofed cubicles along one wall, each with an airtight door. Most of the cubicles were as small as closets, though one was larger and contained a small bed. One of the doctors explained that this laboratory was used to test telepathy and other remote communication powers such as dreamweaving.

I was told to get Alia to demonstrate her telepathy. Coaxing her into it was a long and arduous process that reminded me of my own first encounter with her. I chose Dr. Kellogg as the recipient, knowing that Alia would be most comfortable with him, and after nearly half an hour of pleading, I finally got her to send some simple messages through the cubicle walls.

The doctors thanked me for my assistance, but I could only mumble a half-hearted, "You're welcome." Alia was visibly upset with me for making her talk to Dr. Kellogg. I had to remind myself that if I hadn't pushed her, someone else would have. And after all, this was exactly the kind of thing I had signed on for when I made the deal with Dr. Otis.

In the afternoon, Alia, being the first healer to come to the Psionic Research Center, had to begin a series of physical examinations that were even more extensive than mine. But Alia was already stressed out from her morning telepathy session, and as we entered the examining room together, I could tell that we were in for an even bumpier ride.

For Alia, even some of the most basic examinations were emotionally unbearable simply because she couldn't stand to be touched by a stranger. When a doctor tried to listen to her heartbeat, Alia was terrified not of the stethoscope but of the woman's hand holding it to her chest, and no amount of reasoning could get her to breathe normally.

Like I had done when Alia got her control bands, I offered to hold the end of the stethoscope for the doctor, who looked a little insulted but agreed. It worked, and I helped out as best I could with Alia's other tests as well, such as applying the electrode wires for her electrocardiogram.

Unfortunately, that tactic didn't work for everything. I couldn't assist the doctors when they wanted to take a sample of Alia's blood. Alia threw a violent fit as they approached her with the hypodermic syringe, and I decided it was time to try out my newfound authority as her guardian. I promised the doctors that Alia would take her blood test in a few days when she was calmer, and they didn't press the issue. I tried my best not to show it on my face, but I was elated that I had succeeded. Some of the doctors joked that Alia was "more scared of the people than the needle." I didn't find it at all amusing (mainly because it was true) but I dutifully laughed with them.

At the end of the day, I accompanied Dr. Kellogg to the doctors' evening meeting. Alia tagged along uninvited, if not at all unexpected. Chaired by Dr. Otis, the evening meetings were for quick summaries of each day, announcements of last-minute changes to the next day's schedule, and for the planning of future tests. I still hadn't met nor heard anything about the four other psionics here, and Alia and I were only admitted to the meeting during the part where they talked about Alia. Dr. Denman complained loudly about the blood test and certain other tests Alia had skipped, scowling at her and insisting that it was a mistake to treat her...

"Like a child?" I asked, unable to contain my temper.

"Silence, psionic!" he shot back savagely. He was the only doctor who never called Alia or me by name, choosing to use our identity codes P-46 and P-47, or refer to us as "the psionics."

Still, Dr. Otis and Dr. Kellogg were on my side, so Dr. Denman had even less authority than I did regarding Alia's treatment here.

Alia went through another three days of tests, starting with a detailed history of her life and powers, which I told as completely as I could. Not surprisingly, they didn't have any past medical information on her.

Once her medical exams were finished, we moved on to more experiments with her telepathy, testing its range and how well it traveled through various substances. Alia could think her way through three yards of solid concrete.

I was told that Alia's healing ability would not be tested until she was more comfortable in the lab, but I also knew that it was her healing that made her so valuable to the research at this facility. They already had telepaths here before.

A basic testing routine was established: There would be three or four days for me, and then two or three for Alia. We might get a day off between our shifts, but that was never promised. The general agreement concerning the actual testing was that Alia would rarely be experimented on without my consent, and certainly not out of my presence.

I knew perfectly well that my authority over Alia's experiments depended on my complete submission to mine. I did everything they asked of me, including a series of painful medical tests that I didn't quite understand the purpose of. I also started working up to moving, levitating, and blasting larger objects in Lab-C. If the doctors ever feared that they were training me to be a more powerful telekinetic, they didn't show it.

Dr. Denman did his utmost best to make our lives miserable. He would corner Alia and me in the corridors and taunt us with threatening remarks, or tell us stories about what happens to psionics who try to escape.

However, I soon found that thanks to the stringent security system that recorded every second of our lives on Level 10, Dr. Denman could not carry out any of his many threats of violence. In fact, he could do little more than sneer at us. I soon got used to it, but Alia remained terrified of him. I complained to Dr. Otis, and for a few comparatively blissful days, Dr. Denman tried to pretend that we didn't exist.

At the evening meetings, the doctors humored me by asking my opinion on the results of various tests, though Dr. Denman was quick to stop me from talking very much, or at all if he could. Some of the doctors even called me "Dr. Howell," which made the veins bulge on Dr. Denman's furious wrinkled face.

I could easily see that Dr. Denman was hated by all of the other researchers as well. They only tolerated him because he was exceptionally smart, being one of the top neurobiologists in the world. Even so, it was hard to know exactly what his medical field really was because he had opinions on everything, and was quick to put down other doctors' ideas. Even when the others agreed that he was right, they clearly disliked his attitude toward them.

I started making special efforts to get on his nerves, mimicking his arrogant tone and making fun of the things he said during the meetings. I could tell that all the other doctors really loved it, even Dr. Otis. They rarely tried to stop me, preferring to watch our heated exchanges with quiet amusement. At times, they did pretend to disapprove of my disrespectful attitude toward Dr. Denman, but none of the doctors were very good actors.

It wasn't all fun and games, though, especially for Alia.

Alia still couldn't handle being touched, and the doctors had refused to yield a second time on her blood test. They held her down, kicking and screaming, and Alia spent the rest of that day in teary-eyed silence. I was horrified to learn that we would have to submit to these blood tests every few days.

I discussed the problem with Dr. Kellogg, and at his suggestion, the doctors agreed to teach me how to use a hypodermic syringe. From then on, I drew Alia's blood myself. It took a lot of practice at first, and it must have been pretty painful for Alia since I kept missing her veins. It was a testament to how much she hated being touched by strangers that Alia didn't complain.

True to his word, Dr. Otis continued having me as Alia's guardian, making sure to get my consent on any experiments they planned for her. I didn't want to push my luck too far, so I kept my overruling to a minimum and even sided with the doctors from time to time, coaxing and bullying Alia into doing certain tests she disliked.

Yes, they could sedate her if it was absolutely necessary for an experiment. No, they couldn't give her any drug I couldn't pronounce, at least until they had tried it on me first. Yes, they could see how her power worked in freezingly low temperatures. No, they couldn't test how well she could heal burns and bruises on her own body. Exactly how were they planning to do that, anyway?!

There were gray areas. I couldn't stop them from testing Alia's healing on mice, guinea pigs, dogs and monkeys. The animals were given anesthetics and tied to an operating table for Alia to heal while the doctors studied the speed of the animals' recovery and recorded Alia's brainwave patterns using sensors attached to her head. I really didn't want Alia exposed to any more blood, but the doctors would not yield. I usually held Alia's free hand, or at least stood by her side while she worked her power. Alia took it as well as I could hope for, silently saving the animals' lives so that the doctors could cut them open again.

And yes, I conceded, they could test on humans, but only so long as Dr. Denman was used as the guinea pig. I got a good laugh at that one during an evening meeting. However, as much as the other doctors probably thought it was a great idea, they overruled my request, so then I offered my own flesh in Dr. Denman's stead. After testing Alia's healing on a soldier volunteer who was, as Dr. Denman reminded me, "more human," Dr. Otis actually did take me up on my offer. It didn't hurt since they shot my left forearm with an anesthetic before slicing it open lengthwise, but I made sure to remind Dr. Denman of his cowardice at every opportunity.

"I'm getting really sick of you, psionic," hissed Dr. Denman one morning, having cornered us on our way to Lab-A, where Alia's test animals were kept.

"Good!" I said as savagely as I dared. "Why don't you do something about it?"

"Now that P-46 has proven how well she can heal other psionics, perhaps in the near future, we'll revisit our plans to experiment on her self-healing."

"I'd like to see you try!"

The doctors already knew from past experiments that psionic powers could be suppressed by various chemicals, including painkillers. Thus, any experiment on Alia's self-healing would require her to be injured without the use of anesthetics, and only Dr. Denman seemed to have no scruples with that.

"Lab rats are only good for one thing, psionic."

"Better a lab rat than a gutter rat like you!" I spat at him. "You've got no chance of convincing Dr. Otis to hurt Alia like that. Everyone knows you're even uglier on the inside than you look on the outside! That's why they didn't cut you open!"

Dr. Denman didn't come with us to Lab-A, nor did I see him at all that day. In the evening, Dr. Kellogg joined us in our room for dinner.

"You sure enjoy getting under Dr. Denman's skin, Adrian," said Dr. Kellogg as we finished our desserts.

"Well, everyone needs a purpose in life," I joked.

Dr. Kellogg didn't smile. "I thought yours was looking after Alia."

"What's that supposed to mean?"

"Just watch yourself."

I didn't know exactly what Dr. Kellogg was afraid might happen, but of all the people at the Psionic Research Center, Dr. Kellogg was the only one who seemed to have our best interests at heart, so I respected him. I didn't want to repeat the mistake I had made with Cindy and Mark. I cut down on taunting Dr. Denman considerably.

Meanwhile, I was still sleep-hovering from time to time, quietly slipping out of Alia's grasp in the middle of the night and painfully falling back onto the floor or dining table the moment my eyes opened. The noise I made crashing usually woke Alia, and getting her back to sleep was no small task. Once, I even fell on top of her. She jumped up screaming and later had a good laugh at my expense. We never got much sleep on such nights.

The Central Control Room got all of this on video, and I was astonished to discover that I would float for nearly an hour before waking up. I still couldn't stay airborne for more than five minutes when I was awake, and that was without trying to move quickly through the air, so I was as baffled as anyone when trying to explain why I could levitate so long in my sleep.

Like Cindy, Dr. Kellogg also recommended that I sleep with a safety line to keep me from drifting away. I again refused, pointing out that since I was already trapped ten stories underground, I wasn't about to willingly accept being any more restrained than I already was. Dr. Kellogg nodded understandingly, and I continued to risk minor injuries in my sleep.

Dr. Denman suggested that I sleep in Lab-C until I sleep-hovered again.

That way, the doctors could get readings on my brainwaves when it happened. But that would mean either leaving Alia alone in our room or taking her to sleep in the not-so-cozy Testing Room for who-knew-how-many nights, and I didn't think she could deal with either situation at the moment. I overrode Dr. Denman's proposal with Dr. Kellogg's support, and Dr. Denman stormed away fuming.

Alia's birthday came sooner than I expected, and though we didn't exactly have a party, Dr. Kellogg brought us some chocolate cake. My request for a double bed had been turned down by Central Control for reasons I never found out, but Dr. Kellogg left Alia with another stack of storybooks (mostly *Winnie the Pooh*) and lots of coloring books. He also brought a big bag of girls' toys and stuffed animal dolls, including two small unicorns. Our room was not nearly the toy shop Alia's old bedroom had been, but it was slowly starting to look lived-in. We had been underground now for a month.

The doctors kept us busy with the experiments, and though Central Control had long since approved my request to overlook Alia's control band protocol, even on our days off, Alia didn't want to leave the room. Considering that all we could really do was visit the Level 10 cafeteria and lounges, I felt she had a point. Our meals continued to be delivered to our room so there was never any reason to go out.

Instead, we spent our free time playing in our room, and in the evenings I read stories to Alia like Cindy used to do. Alia soon discovered that I was no expert at reading aloud myself, often stumbling over the words, but I gradually got better at it. If it was an easy book, Alia would read along with me, and I found that she could read much more smoothly into my mind than I could read aloud with my mouth. I became a little more sympathetic to Alia's lack of interest in mouth-speaking, and though I felt guilty about what Cindy might have said were she here, I stopped trying to get Alia to speak out loud. There didn't seem to be much point in it down here anyway, and besides, I figured that, with the intensive testing schedule, Alia was under enough stress already.

Now that things were, if not normal, at least becoming more predictable, I began to get restless about our situation. How much longer would we be kept here?

Even with Dr. Kellogg's friendly attitude, life at the research center was both dull and stressful at the same time. Alia and I still had to wear our control bands whenever we left our room, and though it had been weeks since the rods were last extended, I was always feeling slightly drained. I suspected it was partly from all the metal shielding around the facility. But much more than that, it was the dreary white corridors, the complete lack of sunlight, and the sheer hopelessness of our situation.

When I couldn't sleep, I would stay up late reading from the library collection Dr. Kellogg had brought me. I read mostly adventure novels at first, dreaming that I was off in some distant jungle or any place far from here. But the people in those stories were having troubles of their own. That was a nice distraction for a while, but as the days wore on, I got tired of reading about other people's problems. Though I felt embarrassed under the watchful camera eye of the Central Control Room, I actually began to enjoy Alia's books better, in which talking bears and oversized bunny rabbits held tea parties and generally just had a good time together. I even started to miss my old, horridly cute wardrobe. The simple white shirts and pants we wore at the facility, though replaced every morning and evening, were always exactly the same.

During all of this time, I certainly had not forgotten about my sister. Cat's amethyst pendant was the only colorful part of my attire, and did, as Mark had once observed, weigh heavily around my neck. I spent a good deal of my free time thinking about Cat: where she was and what she might be doing now. But I soon realized that those were pointless daydreams. I was trapped down here, and my priority had to be survival for Alia and me. Survival first, and then, if at all possible, escape. Finding Cat would have to wait.

Meanwhile, although Alia was slowly getting used to life at the research center, not only did she continue to have fairly frequent spells of silence, she was still wetting the bed every few nights, which was disgusting and awkward for the both of us. I forced myself to tolerate it, and even refused Dr. Kellogg's suggestion to have Alia wear a diaper at night. I didn't want to make a big deal of it so as to avoid further embarrassment to Alia, who was, after all, already eight years old. At Central Control's insistence, I consented to having absorbent sheets placed on our bed so that our mattress wouldn't have to be swapped out every time Alia had an accident, but that was as far as I was willing to go on the matter.

"You're absolutely sure about this?" asked Dr. Kellogg as he helped me replace the sheets after another one of Alia's bad nights.

"I'm the one who has to sleep with her, aren't I?" I replied wryly, and Dr. Kellogg laughed.

I suppose I should be grateful to Alia actually, because without her problem, we might never have met Mr. Koontz.

During our first month at the facility, I had gradually discovered that Alia's bedwetting coincided with some kind of recurring nightmare that she was having. Alia rarely talked about her dreams, but I could pretty much guess what kind of night she had by her mood the next day. I was being plagued by a number of frightening dreams myself, so I knew it wasn't easy for her. Six weeks into our stay, I finally told Dr. Kellogg my theory. He sat silently stroking his shaggy beard for nearly a full minute before getting up and saying that he had an idea. Instead of sharing it with me, however, he left our room and didn't return until the next day.

As the three of us walked together to Lab-A the next morning, Dr. Kellogg asked, "Adrian, have you ever met Mr. Malcolm Koontz?"

"I don't think so," I answered, trying to remember all of the researchers' names.

"Oh, you'd remember if you met him. He's one of our longest guests. He's our dreamweaver."

"I haven't met any of the other psionics yet," I said, which was true. I had felt the presence of another destroyer here, though I was sure it wasn't a telekinetic. Aside from that, I knew nothing about the others. Cindy had once told me that a dreamweaver was a kind of controller, but even so, I felt I wouldn't mind meeting him if only to break the monotony of life at the research center.

Dr. Kellogg said, "I was thinking of what you told me about Alia's dreams, and after talking with Dr. Otis, I thought we might try an off-the-books experiment. Do you know what a dreamweaver is?"

"Sort of…" I said uncertainly. "He can control people's dreams, right? But if you're thinking what I think you're thinking… I don't know how Alia will feel trying to go to sleep with a stranger in the room."

"Oh, there's no problem with that," replied Dr. Kellogg. "Mr. Koontz can work from quite a distance."

Later that evening, we met Mr. Malcolm Koontz in one of the lounges.

He looked like he was still in his mid-forties, but was pale, frail and slightly balding. I tried to get Alia to greet him, but she refused. Even so, we sat with Mr. Koontz for nearly two hours. Quite aside from seeing him as a possible solution to Alia's bedwetting, I just wanted to talk with a fellow psionic and see what kind of life he lived here.

Mr. Koontz was P-31. He had been a Guardian once, but when their master controller, Diana Granados, was killed, Mr. Koontz was caught by the Wolves during the instability that followed. He had been here for nearly fifteen years! Speaking with him, I learned that the other three psionics were...

"A light-foot finder named Janice, a powerful pyroid called William who, by the way, is completely insane, and of course Nightmare, who lives below," said Mr. Koontz.

"Nightmare?" I asked.

"Well, that's what we call him, because we don't know his name. For that matter, we don't exactly know what his power is either. He has to be constantly drained, and even so, when he has nightmares, things happen..." Mr. Koontz's voice trailed off.

"What things?"

"It's hard to describe. It feels like reality starts to twist. It's my job to keep Nightmare peaceful at night so that it doesn't happen. See?" said Mr. Koontz as he showed me his wrists. There were no control bands on them.

"I've been here long enough to be trusted, though I see you have made quite some progress yourself," he said, smiling. "Janice was our newcomer until you two arrived, and she's been here only ten months. She's having a hard time adjusting, but compared to Nightmare and William, well, at least she can talk."

"What's wrong with William?" I asked.

"William was an Angel. He had just been converted when he was caught, and being separated from the Angels so suddenly destroyed his mind. They keep him locked up somewhere on this floor."

Dr. Kellogg was still sitting with us, but seemed entirely unconcerned that Mr. Koontz was sharing this information. In fact, Dr. Kellogg turned to Mr. Koontz and said, "Tell Adrian more about Nightmare."

"Ah, well, let's see..." said Mr. Koontz, resting his chin on his hand. "Nightmare lives in his own little holding block. We call it Level 12, though that's not really accurate. You see, there's a separate elevator that goes down deep under Level 10 to Level 11. That's where the generators and heating systems are, and stairs from Level 11 lead down to Nightmare's cell. I've only been there once. There's a thick sphere of shielding around him. Even so, when he dreams, this whole place can be affected by his power."

I remembered Cindy telling me that using psionic powers during sleep was a kid thing, but perhaps Nightmare was an exception to the rule. After all, Cindy had also said that everyone's power is slightly different and that there were some powers so unique that they didn't even have names.

Mr. Koontz shuddered slightly and continued, "Nightmare was brought here thirteen years ago. I've no idea how they caught him alive, but when they pulled out his control rods in Level 10, he nearly tore this whole place apart. One doctor and several soldiers were killed. They knocked Nightmare out with gas, but then things got really out of hand, because he had a nightmare."

Mr. Koontz paused, and Dr. Kellogg said to me, "This was all before my time. Dr. Otis would know more about it, but Mr. Koontz here saved the facility."

"Well, I subdued Nightmare's nightmare," said Mr. Koontz. "That's why they trust me now. I'm only a dreamweaver, which really isn't much of a controller power, so I can't hurt anyone. True enough, I can cause nightmares as easily as I can remove them, but there'd be no way for me to escape." Mr. Koontz winked at us and added loudly, "Not that I've never considered it!"

Dr. Kellogg laughed good-naturedly.

I asked, "And you can control Nightmare's dreams through all that shielding?"

"Oh yes," replied Mr. Koontz. "Dr. Kellogg has told me that young Alia here is a telepath, but I guarantee that dreamweaving is by far the better for long-distance communication, as long as it's done at night. I can even project my power out of this facility and onto the surface."

"Really?" I said, amazed.

Mr. Koontz nodded. "If it weren't for all the shielding, I'd be able to throw my dreams more than a hundred miles. A few years back, we tried an experiment with some doctors, having them camp out top-side. I had no trouble controlling their dreams from down here, though I couldn't go much farther than that." Mr. Koontz sighed quietly once, and then, with a knowing glance toward Dr. Kellogg, added, "Still, better than poor Jason Witherland."

"Who's he?" I immediately asked.

Mr. Koontz looked like he was about to reply, but Dr. Kellogg interrupted, saying, "Malcolm, I'm not sure we want to tell these two about Jason."

"Oh, come on," laughed Mr. Koontz, "don't you want to show them the futility of trying to escape?"

"That's Dr. Denman's game, not mine," Dr. Kellogg said unsmilingly, but then he shrugged and let Mr. Koontz tell his story.

"Jason Witherland was a teleporter," explained Mr. Koontz. "Now those are exceptionally rare. He was brought in about seven years ago, and I saw him with my own eyes in Lab-C, jumping from one side of the Testing Room to the other, straight through a wall of concrete, and later even through a two-inch sheet of steel shielding. He got better and better at it. So one day, he decided he was going to jump right out of this place."

"What happened?" I asked.

Suddenly I heard the unmistakably harsh voice of Dr. Denman from behind us say, "Are you telling these test subjects the story of P-39?"

Both Alia and I jumped, but Mr. Koontz smiled serenely and answered, "Why, yes I am, Doctor. Would you like to tell these children about Jason yourself?"

"Alright," growled Dr. Denman, glaring at us. "P-39 foolishly thought he could escape by teleporting through our protective shielding."

"He got through, though," Mr. Koontz gently interjected.

Dr. Denman shot him a nasty look. "Oh yes, he got through alright. Not exactly in the same way as he went out, though. There were bits of him all over the ground, and probably some of his bones are still buried in the shields or in the earth between here and the surface."

Then Dr. Denman rounded on me and said callously, "As P-31 has no doubt already told you, the only things that ever escape this place are his dreams."

Mr. Koontz stood up from his chair and said to me, "I'm getting a little tired of this company and I have a long night ahead, so I will retire to my room now. Perhaps we can talk about Alia's dreams tomorrow evening. Goodnight, Adrian, Alia, Dr. Kellogg."

He nodded to each of us in turn, ignoring Dr. Denman as he left the lounge. Dr. Denman continued to glower at us as Dr. Kellogg led us out too.

In the corridor, Dr. Kellogg looked down at Alia, sighing as he said, "No, I don't like him either."

Alia smiled up at him, and I realized that she must have said something unflattering about Dr. Denman. It was the first time Alia had freely chosen to speak to anyone aside from me at the research center.

After spending another day watching Alia's tests, I met Mr. Koontz again in the evening. Alia was still afraid of him, but didn't cower too much. I explained a little about her past, and spoke vaguely about what kind of nightmares she might be having. From what little Alia had told me about her dreams over the past few weeks, my best guess was that many of Alia's nights were spent repeatedly reliving our encounter with Ralph. (It struck me as somewhat odd that, given what the Wolves had done to her, Alia's primary fear was still the crossbow-wielding Guardian, but I wasn't the psychologist here.) Alia knew that she was the topic of the conversation and was listening to us intently, so I didn't want to go into too many details for fear of making her nightmares worse.

Sensing my discomfort, Mr. Koontz said, "Don't worry, Adrian. Once I get a feel for a person, I can control their dreams fairly easily. We'll start tonight. Meanwhile, please tell me more about the world above."

To my surprise, Mr. Koontz was at least as fascinated with me as I was with him. He asked me to tell him of my life and how the world had changed since his capture. He had access to newspapers and could talk with Dr. Kellogg, but he wanted to hear it from me as well. I hadn't yet been born when he was captured so I didn't know what to say about how the world had changed, but in the days that followed, we met regularly just to talk and enjoy the evenings together.

Mr. Koontz lived on a different schedule, sleeping during the mornings and early afternoons, and staying up all night pacifying Nightmare's dreams to prevent whatever it was that they were all afraid of. If necessary, Central Control could shock Nightmare awake at any time, but they preferred to have Mr. Koontz take care of him and prevent anything from happening in the first place. Though Alia never spoke to him, she soon got used to Mr. Koontz enough for me to even invite him into our room sometimes. "It's just so nice to have someone similar to talk with," he once said, and I understood his feelings. Alia could be difficult and demanding, but I don't know how I would have survived my imprisonment had I been alone.

Mr. Koontz worked his powers as promised and, to my great relief, Alia stopped wetting our bed. Freed from her nightmares, Alia's daytime behavior improved, too. Although she was still nervous in the corridors and around most of the researchers, she no longer hid under the bed while I was taking my baths, and she spent much less time staring off into space.

One day, as I looked at the calendar tacked over our desk, I realized that there was only a week left until May. Two months now. It would be springtime outside. I thought about the light-foot, Janice, who had not yet been here a year, and about Mr. Koontz, who had been here fifteen years. Perhaps Jason Witherland had gotten out of this place the only way a psionic could.

I decided it was high time I faced my greatest fear and asked a long-overdue question. That night, after I was sure Alia was fast asleep at my side, I quietly called for Dr. Kellogg through the ceiling-mounted microphone in our room.

"What can I do for you at such a late lour, Adrian?" whispered Dr. Kellogg as he stepped through the airlock several minutes later.

The room lights remained dimmed, and Dr. Kellogg carefully leaned his back against the bookshelf. I wanted to get up out of the bed and greet him properly, but Alia had an arm around my chest and I didn't want to risk waking her. I lay perfectly still and looked up at Dr. Kellogg, saying quietly, "I have a question to ask you."

Alia stirred a bit, but fortunately, her eyes remained closed. I didn't want her to hear Dr. Kellogg's answer to my question, just in case I was right.

"Ask away," Dr. Kellogg said with a curious look.

"I have a question," I repeated, "but before I ask it, I have another."

"As many as you like, Adrian," said Dr. Kellogg, smiling.

I didn't smile back. "My question, Dr. Kellogg, is if I ask you a question that you can't answer, or aren't allowed to answer, will you tell me the truth and say you can't answer it, or will you lie and tell me what I want to hear, or what you think I should hear?"

"That's a difficult question to answer," said Dr. Kellogg, "because even if I promise to be truthful with you, there's no way for me to prove to you that my promise isn't a lie, too."

I thought about that for a moment. "True..."

Dr. Kellogg looked into my eyes and said, "Listen, Adrian. For what it's worth, I believe in truth. If you ask a question that I can't answer, I'll tell you so. I just hope you'll believe me."

I nodded slowly. Alia wasn't a particularly light sleeper but there was no guarantee that she wouldn't wake at any moment. *It is better to know*, I thought to myself. *Just get it over with.*

"So what's your question?" asked Dr. Kellogg.

"I'm sorry, Dr. Kellogg," I said, staring up at the ceiling. "Now that you've promised to tell me the truth, honestly, I'm afraid to ask the question."

I looked at him again and whispered, "I'm afraid of the answer."

"Then I can pretty much guess your question, Adrian." Dr. Kellogg looked down at me with kind pity. "But why don't you ask it anyway? An answer won't change just because you don't ask the question."

I lay there opening and shutting my mouth a few times. *It is better to know*, I told myself furiously. *It is better to know!* Finally, the words formed in my mouth: "Am I going to die here?"

"I certainly hope not," replied Dr. Kellogg.

"But they're never going to let us go, are they?"

Dr. Kellogg paused for a few heartbeats before answering slowly, "No, they won't."

Deep down, I had probably known his answer from the start, but Dr. Kellogg's words nevertheless tore a gaping hole in my heart. I stared up at him, unable to respond.

"I'm sorry, Adrian," said Dr. Kellogg. "I wish it were otherwise."

Dr. Kellogg stood silently, giving me time to find my voice. When I finally did, I asked him, "What happened to the other psionics?"

"As you know, some died trying to escape. Others, after several years of tests, have been transferred out. Honestly, I don't know where to."

"Will Alia or I ever be transferred out?"

"Possibly, but not for many years, I think."

"Years..." I breathed to myself.

Correctly reading my thoughts, Dr. Kellogg said, "They can't stop you from trying to escape, Adrian. But they can stop you from escaping. I hope you'll think carefully about everything you stand to lose before considering that as an option."

I knew Dr. Kellogg meant well with his warning, but it still felt like something Dr. Denman might have said in a nastier way. It took a lot for me to keep from glaring.

"This isn't right, Dr. Kellogg," I whispered, trying hard to keep my voice steady. "You know this isn't right."

Dr. Kellogg sighed. "I know this isn't right."

"But you're a part of it too."

"Yes, Adrian, I am a part of this too. It's times like this that I wish to God that I wasn't," Dr. Kellogg said sadly. "I know you hate this place, and I know you hate the people who keep you here. I won't make any excuse for my part in your confinement. If you want to blame me for what has happened to your life, I would deserve your anger as much as anyone here."

I shook my head. "I don't blame you for this, Dr. Kellogg. Aside from Mr. Koontz, you're our only friend."

"Then I will have to work hard to be worthy of your friendship," said Dr. Kellogg. "But I cannot help you try to escape. Even if I did, we would fail."

An uncomfortable silence followed, broken only by Alia's soft murmuring in my mind. I wondered if Dr. Kellogg could hear it too.

Then Dr. Kellogg said quietly, "Was there anything else you wanted to ask me? I may not be able to help you in the way that you want, but I will always be truthful with you."

"No," I said wretchedly. "Thanks for the offer, Doctor, but I think I've had just about as much truth as I can handle right now."

I turned my head so that I was facing Alia, and a moment later I felt Dr. Kellogg's hand on my shoulder. "Hang in there, Adrian," Dr. Kellogg whispered gently. "You hang in there."

I didn't respond. Dr. Kellogg released my shoulder, and I heard the soft hissing of the airlock door as he let himself out.

15. THE TELEPHONE GAME

Food, water and air. Back in school, my science teacher had listed those on the blackboard, explaining that they were the basic necessities for life. Obvious, really, but you can't truly appreciate that until you are deprived of almost everything else. A society might sing about "unalienable rights" and "God-given freedoms," but in the real world, people decide who is entitled to rights and freedoms. For a few days after my nighttime chat with Dr. Kellogg, I felt the sheer crushing weight of nine heavily shielded floors above me in a way that I had never felt it before. The hopelessness of our future here was so painful that I was certain I would go insane.

But when faced with a lack of options, people can adapt to almost any environment physically capable of sustaining life. Forever, if needs be. And I had little choice but to adapt, if only for Alia's sake, because as Dr. Kellogg had gently reminded me, I hadn't lost everything yet. I forced myself to calm down and accept my status as a research subject. I remained on friendly terms with Dr. Kellogg. If there was any difference in how I behaved, it was simply that I no longer smiled when people called me Dr. Howell.

Alia and I might have lived out our entire lives in captivity if it wasn't for a curious dream that I had one night about two weeks into May.

I found myself standing in a field of tall brown grass under a dark and gloomy sky. Off in the distance, there was a wall made of small black stones extending from horizon to horizon. The wall was only about as high as my chest, and as I walked closer to it, I noticed two small human shapes sitting on it. They were just shadows in the distance. I thought I heard a woman's voice calling my name, and a moment later I woke up.

"I saw Cindy yesterday," said Alia during breakfast.

I looked up at her. "Really?"

"She was sitting on a wall with..." Alia's telepathic voice trailed off.

"With who, Ali?" I asked, wondering about my own dream about a wall, but Alia didn't answer.

I forgot all about it during the day's experiments, but that night I had the same dream again. This time I was much closer to the wall and I could make out the shapes sitting on it. Cindy was there, and next to her, Ralph. They just sat there and looked at me, Cindy watching me sadly and Ralph smiling mockingly. I felt that Cindy was trying to tell me something, but I woke before I could figure it out. Alia didn't mention anything about her dreams the next morning, and I wondered if the previous day had just been a coincidence.

The next night convinced me that it wasn't.

"Addy, Cindy was looking for me," said Alia when she woke. *"She was sad."*

"Did you have another dream?" I asked.

Alia shook her head. *"It wasn't a dream,"* she insisted. *"I saw her."*

It had been a vivid dream for me too. Like the first two, neither Cindy nor Ralph spoke at all, but I could feel their desire to. I thought about asking Mr. Koontz, the dream expert, what it meant, but I didn't see him that day.

The next morning, Alia said to me over breakfast, *"Cindy wants to talk to you, Addy."*

"I know, but I can't hear her," I replied. It was the exact same dream again, and I knew Alia had dreamt it too.

"She says that you have to want to hear her. She says you're blocking her."

I stared at Alia.

During my testing session later that day, I thought again about talking to Mr. Koontz and asking him what these dreams were. But I already had a hunch, or rather, an ever-so-slight hope, and I didn't want to speak openly about it just in case I was right. My hope was that somewhere, someone was dreamweaving to us. I was certain it wasn't Mr. Koontz because, though I had told him about Cindy, I never told him about Ralph. And how could Ralph be there if...

"Adrian?" said Dr. Otis over the intercom. "Focus please."

I fired another telekinetic shot at the scanner-mounted target in the Lab-C Testing Room. And then another, and another. I was sweating profusely by the end of the session. Before leaving, I looked around once at the Testing Room, at the dreary concrete cave where I spent my days dancing to the doctors' every demand. This was where Jason Witherland had jumped from in his desperate bid for freedom, and now, more than ever, I understood why. Despite Dr. Kellogg's warning, I decided that if there was even the slightest chance of escape, I'd take it too. I was never going to live fifteen years down here like Mr. Koontz. One way or another, I wanted out.

I meditated for nearly an hour before bed that night. I hadn't done that ever since arriving at the facility, and Alia did her best to shake me out of it, but I sternly silenced her and went about my breathing exercises. According to Alia, Cindy said I was blocking her, but I didn't know how or why. Meditation seemed to be Cindy's answer to most problems in her life, and as I lay beside Alia in bed that night, I prayed it would work for me.

I was once again standing in the field of brown grass, almost touching the wall. Cindy and Ralph sat there looking down at me. Ralph... What was he doing here, anyway? I felt a chill run through me, and opened my eyes.

The chill, I discovered to my annoyance, was caused by Alia having pulled our blanket off of me as she slept. The luminous clock on the desk showed 2am, and I knew I had little time to re-enter the dream I had woken from. I had to find Cindy and Ralph again. Carefully so as not to wake Alia, I pulled the blanket back so that it was covering us both. Closing my eyes again, I nudged my mind back toward the field of brown grass swaying in the wind. Back to the long wall of little black stones. Back to Cindy and Ralph. Back to sleep...

I felt as if I had been walking for several thousand years, searching, but now I could finally see the black wall off in the distance. As I warily approached the two sitting there, I wondered why it couldn't just be Cindy. Ralph wasn't welcome here. I glared at him furiously, daring him to use his psionics on me, but he just sat there wearing his mocking smile. Cindy was also watching me with the slight frown she often wore when commenting on my lack of power balance. I looked again at Ralph, took a deep breath, and cautiously let down my guard.

I immediately heard Cindy say, "Adrian, we are very close now. We are going to try to get you out of there. Ralph has agreed to help us. He has brought some Guardians."

"We have agreed to try to rescue you and Alia," Ralph said quietly, "but you have to understand that there are no guarantees. We'll give it our best shot, but you're in a real fix."

I noticed that Ralph didn't have his usual accent or attitude. And I knew then that there was someone else hiding behind Cindy and Ralph... or perhaps hiding inside of them.

"Who are you?" I asked. "Who are you really?"

Cindy said, "Keep Alia safe. I love you both very much, and I promise we will do everything we can, but we really don't know much about the research center yet."

"Who are you?" I asked again.

"We are working on a plan," said Ralph, "but it may take a while. You have to be patient, Adrian. If it is possible to rescue you, the Guardians will see it done."

Suddenly the wall vanished along with Cindy and Ralph, and I was standing alone in the field, which became hazy and finally disappeared completely.

"Cindy? Ralph?" I called out into the void. "Where are you?"

I felt a presence behind me, and turning around, I woke.

I was looking into Alia's eyes, which were wide open and staring back at me.

"Addy, did you hear Cindy?" asked Alia.

"Yes, Ali, I did," I whispered.

"I want to see her, Addy."

"Go back to sleep, Alia."

I was certain it was a dreamweave now. What else could it be? Mr. Koontz had said that he could project dreams out of the facility, so certainly someone could project in. Whoever it was knew Cindy and Ralph, and knew how to dreamweave to Alia and me. I had never met a dreamweaver before Mr. Koontz, but he had told me that all he needed was an image of someone in order to control the dreams. It seemed possible for the mystery dreamweaver to just hear about us from Cindy and know enough to send dreams to us.

I thought about what might have been happening outside while we were trapped down here. In order to save us, Cindy had searched out Ralph and somehow got him on her side. Ralph was a former Wolf, so he had probably known where the Psionic Research Center was. And Ralph would have Guardian friends to help him, such as a dreamweaver.

I wondered what Cindy had promised Ralph for his aid. Could it be possible that she had agreed to rejoin the Guardians? I felt horrible thinking about what I must have put her through for my refusal to listen to reason at Mark's house. I knew that even if we managed to escape, things would be very different.

At the moment, however, Alia and I were still trapped down here, and this was our chance for freedom. I would apologize to Cindy later, and I would make it up to her if ever I could, but right now I had to think about how to help them get us out.

Another two dreams later, I was convinced that the Guardian dreamweaver could not hear anything that I was saying in my dreams. The connection just didn't work both ways, so I had no way to return a message or ask any questions.

I had also discovered that dreamweaves, just like normal dreams, fade away quickly once you're awake. I had to make a conscious effort to quickly recall everything I had seen and heard as soon as my eyes opened. It wasn't easy, and I probably lost a fair bit of information, but I learned that Cindy was hidden somewhere near the facility, along with Ralph and about ten other Guardians.

The reason they hadn't stormed the place yet was that none of them knew what kind of defenses the facility had. Even Ralph had never set foot in here before. Cindy, or rather the dreamweaver controlling her likeness, told me that if the odds proved too great and a good plan could not be formed, the Guardians would have no choice but to abandon the attempt and leave us here. I knew that the real Cindy would never say such a thing, but it was a crushing blow to hear it from her mouth.

Three more nights passed, and the Guardians were not any closer to forming a plan. In the most recent dream, Ralph had hinted that they were considering giving up the rescue, and I woke up in a cold sweat.

I desperately wished I could somehow return a message. It was, if anything, even more frustrating knowing what was happening above us and being unable to respond, especially since I knew I could help them get the very information they needed. Were they really going to abandon us? I knew Cindy wouldn't, but alone she couldn't do much. We needed the Guardians' help, and to get it, I had to help them first. But how?

Fortunately, no one but me could hear Alia talking about her dreams, so when she did, I kept quiet or changed the subject. I felt sorry for Alia because she so wanted to talk about Cindy, but I knew it was the only way to keep this a secret.

I racked my brain for an answer to my communication problem. Alia would never be able to reach Cindy, even if Cindy was standing at the entrance to the facility and there was no shielding at all. Ten stories down was just too far. If I could only get Mr. Koontz to dreamweave back to Cindy just like she had used a dreamweaver to send her messages to us...

But that was impossible. Every room, every corridor, even every toilet had surveillance cameras and microphones. There was simply no way to talk to Mr. Koontz without letting Central Control in on our conversation.

Unless... I thought for a moment. Yes, there was a way. It was dangerous, even reckless perhaps, but it just might work. If I failed, I would be lucky just not to be killed, and Alia would lose her only protection here. I knew what was at stake. I did, as Dr. Kellogg had suggested, think very carefully about everything we stood to lose. It was because of my recklessness that Alia and I were trapped down here. Perhaps my solution would prove to be equally disastrous, but the Guardians had already been on site for at least eleven days, and they might not be around much longer if I didn't contact them soon.

That night, as Alia pressed herself up against me and closed her eyes, I turned onto my side and put an arm around her, pulling her even closer. Afraid that the camera would see my mouth move, I turned my head slightly, bringing my face so close to Alia's that I was almost kissing her. I knew from watching my sleep-hovering videos that the surveillance camera could see surprisingly clearly in the dark, but I didn't want to pull the blanket over our heads because it would look too suspicious. When I opened my mouth, I tried to make it look like I was just taking a breath, and I did my best to keep my lips and cheeks from moving as I whispered, "Alia."

Alia opened her eyes. *"Addy?"*

"Keep your eyes closed and listen to me," I said in a whisper of a whisper. I could barely hear my own voice, and I prayed that the microphone wasn't sensitive enough to pick up what I was saying. Alia must have sensed how nervous I was, because her whole body became rigid, but she did as I told her to. I closed my eyes too, but kept one slightly open so that I could be sure Alia was keeping hers shut. For all anyone would know, we were sleeping.

"Ali," I breathed, "you know those dreams about Cindy?"

"Yes, Addy," said Alia. Her voice in my head was much quieter than usual, as if she was afraid her thoughts could be heard on the microphone.

"She's really up there. She's going to come get us."

"I know."

"We have to help her."

"She can't hear me."

"I know, Ali," I whispered. "We're going to ask Mr. Koontz to help us talk to her. Can you speak to Mr. Koontz?"

Alia was silent for a moment, and then answered uneasily, *"I don't know."*

Alia had never spoken to Mr. Koontz, or anyone aside from Dr. Kellogg for that matter.

"Alia, Cindy needs our help."

"I'm scared, Addy."

"I know you are, but I need you to be brave, Ali. You're a big girl now, and I need you to be brave for Cindy."

Silence. Alia didn't open her eyes, but I could tell she was struggling with her emotions.

"Ali, will you talk to Mr. Koontz for me?" I asked in my near-silent voice.

Alia took a moment longer before answering, *"Okay, Addy."*

"Good. I want you to say hello to him. Can you do that?"

I felt incredibly restless but I knew we had to take this slowly. I couldn't push Alia and I didn't want Mr. Koontz to jump in surprise either. When I could no longer bear the tension, I asked, "Did you say hello to him?"

"Yes."

"Good. Now, I want you to tell him that I have a plan to help us escape. I want you to ask him if he will help us."

"Okay."

"Tell him that if he wants to help, he should…"

Should what? Wink at me? Put a thumb up? Every second of our lives was being recorded so I couldn't risk any odd gestures, and I didn't want him to reply in a dream just in case I accidentally blocked it again. There was no telling how much longer the Guardians would stay.

"Addy?"

I whispered, "Tell him that if he wants to help, he should ask when my birthday is the next time we meet."

There was a pause, and then I heard her quiet voice in my head say, *"Okay, Addy. I told him."*

"Good girl, Ali. You're very brave. We're going to be rescued soon. Go to sleep now."

Alia and I met Mr. Koontz the next evening, and we sat together in the lounge for an hour after dinner. I was beginning to think that either he hadn't gotten Alia's message or that he was unwilling to help, but as we stood up to go, he called back to me, "Oh yes, Adrian, I've been meaning to ask when your birthday is. It'd be nice to have a party now and then."

I grinned and said, "It's still a while away, in October."

"What about Alia's?"

"Already over."

"Well, time doesn't mean much down here anyway. Perhaps we'll have a party soon and just pretend it's your birthday!" Mr. Koontz laughed heartily.

From the look in his eyes, I instantly knew that he was game. I wanted to send our first message to Cindy that very night, but like most insane plans, things were much easier said than done.

First off, I wanted Mr. Koontz to send the dream to both Cindy and Ralph so that they would be sure it was a dreamweave and not just a normal one. I figured that since Cindy must have managed to get her dreamweaver to contact Alia and me by just describing us to him, the same would work on our end. However, although I had told Mr. Koontz a little about Cindy, I hadn't described what she looked like or anything. And about Ralph, Mr. Koontz knew nothing.

There was another potential snag as well: Ralph's Guardians would no doubt be inside Cindy's hiding bubble. Could Mr. Koontz dreamweave to them when they were psionically hidden? I believed that he could, since the Guardian dreamweaver managed to reach us deep underground in exactly the kind of place a psionic gathering might be hidden. But there was no way to be sure.

That night, I once again pulled Alia up close to me. She was expecting it, so it probably looked more like she was trying to snuggle closer to me. I hoped it looked that way anyway, since I usually didn't cuddle Alia like this and Central Control might get suspicious.

"Close your eyes. Pretend to be sleeping," I said under my breath. I was still terrified that the microphone would pick up my words, and my heart was pounding louder than my voice. "Ali, I want you to tell Mr. Koontz about Cindy."

"What should I say?" Alia asked in her quietest telepathic voice.

"Tell him that her name is Cynthia Gifford. Tell him what she looks like. Tell him about her hair, and how she smells, and how she walks."

I paused, trying to think what I might say if I were the telepath.

"Tell him how Cindy is quiet and nice and caring," I whispered. "Tell him how much you love her."

I waited until Alia said, *"Okay, Addy, I did."*

"Good, Ali. Now, next I want..."

I hesitated. I really did not want to put Alia through this, but I had no choice if this dream was going to go to Ralph as well.

"Alia, I want you to tell Mr. Koontz about Ralph."

Just as I expected, Alia became extremely tense, and I feared Central Control might see that she wasn't actually asleep. I held her gently, giving her some time to adjust to the idea, before whispering, "Ali?"

She didn't answer.

"Alia, please tell Mr. Koontz about Ralph."

"No, Addy," said Alia.

"Ali..." I pleaded, my voice becoming a little too loud for comfort.

"I don't like Ralph."

"I know, Alia. I don't like him either."

"Ralph is a bad man."

"I know that, Ali."

Holding Alia in my arms, I realized again the precariousness of this faint sliver of a plan that was entirely at the mercy of a frightened little girl. Without Alia, however, there was no plan.

"Alia, please," I whispered. "I know you're scared. But I need you to talk to Mr. Koontz. Ralph is a bad man, but you have to tell Mr. Koontz about him so Cindy can rescue us."

Alia was silent for nearly a full minute before I heard her say nervously into my mind, "Okay..."

I hugged Alia even more tightly as I told her what to say about Ralph P. Henderson. I had her describe his looks, his various powers, his personality and some of the things he had said. Ralph was a soldier, a killer. When Alia had finished talking to Mr. Koontz for me, I could tell she was near tears.

"Good job, Ali. I'm really proud of you. Now, I want you to ask Mr. Koontz if that's enough information to send a dream to Cindy and Ralph. I want you to tell him that they are very close, but they are in a hiding bubble. Ask Mr. Koontz if he can dreamweave to them."

I thought of another password, having Alia tell Mr. Koontz to say that I looked small for my age. The next evening, he did.

Our connection was complete, and I was finally ready to send my first message.

Later in bed that night, I had Alia ask Mr. Koontz to send a dream to Cindy and Ralph, telling them that we had gotten their message, we were well, and that we were ready to help in any way we could. Also, that Mr. Koontz was coming with us, and possibly Janice as well.

Mr. Koontz wouldn't be able to send the message until Cindy and Ralph were asleep, and then they would have to respond through their dreamweaver, so there could be no return message until the next night. The following day was a day off for us, and I waited restlessly with Alia in our room. I didn't want to meet with Mr. Koontz, fearing that we might accidentally say something that could give away our plan.

It took some time getting to sleep that night, partly because I hadn't had any exercise, but mostly because I was so nervous. What if we had just missed them, and the Guardians had already given up and left us? Even assuming they were still camped up there, could Mr. Koontz really get through to Cindy and Ralph? Would they respond tonight? What would they say to me?

I remembered my desperately foolish plan back at Mark's place to catch a random psionic for the minuscule possibility of getting information about Cat. Was our plan here any less hopelessly optimistic? Cindy was the optimist. I had nothing but doubts.

Alia was already sound asleep, and I heard her murmuring incoherently in my mind. Despite the clear advantage of dreamweaving in long-distance communication, I decided that I still preferred straightforward telepathy. The problem with dreams, I thought as I closed my eyes, was that there was no way to know you were in one until after you woke up. That, and the fact that they were so hard to remember...

Staring blankly at the wall made of small black stones, I wondered where Cindy and Ralph were. They weren't sitting there this time. Suddenly the wall rose higher out of the ground, stretching up toward the murky sky until it was towering over me. The little stones started to move around until they formed a giant face on the wall.

It spoke.

"Greetings, Adrian Howell," the face said in a booming voice. "My name is Derrick. Since you obviously know what these dreams are, I see no reason to continue pretending to be Cindy and Ralph for your sake. And in case you are wondering about this face,"—the stone face frowned—"I am the dreamweaver, this is my dream, and I will present myself to you in any which way I please."

I took a step back from the wall, looking up at the massive face. It was so utterly absurd that suddenly, for the first time in my life, I actually realized that I was dreaming. Even as I stood there, gaping up at the face, I knew that my real body was still sleeping beside Alia. It was the strangest feeling, being in two places at once, but somehow I had woken up inside Derrick's dreamweave.

"Your message has been received, and Ralph thanks you," said the giant dream-face. "It is fortunate that you contacted us when you did. We had nearly given up on this attempt, but with your help, there may yet be a chance of getting you and Alia out."

I was all ears now. I forced myself to stay calm, fearing that if I got too excited, I might physically wake up and exit the dream before it finished.

The face grinned manically once, and continued, "Ralph wants you to tell us as much as you can about the inside of this facility. Specifically, we want to know how deep you are, how many floors there are in between, and how strong the military presence here is. We want to know about the security systems, what kind of weapons the guards have, and the general floor plan of the installation. Ralph says that you should start acting your age and help us solve the mess you have made of things. Cindy asks that you assist Ralph only so long as it does not put you or Alia at risk. As much as she appreciates our need for information, she wants you to stay safe and remember your promise to protect Alia. She says that under no circumstance are you to risk your life gathering information for us. She adds that if it becomes too dangerous to continue sending dreams, you should immediately stop doing so and wait patiently for rescue. Message ends."

The stone face grinned again, and then faded away.

I woke up, breathless. Not only had the message come through, but because I had been mentally awake when Derrick gave it to me, I remembered everything he had said. The plan had worked!

I thought back to my past life as a normal kid and the telephone game we used to play in elementary school, where we whispered a message from one ear to the next to see if we could get the message to the end of the line. Now we were playing that game with our lives. Me to Alia to Mr. Koontz to Cindy and Ralph to Derrick the Dreamweaver and back to me.

That day was a testing day for Alia, and since I was just the tagalong, I took the opportunity to ask Dr. Kellogg more about the facility. I didn't want to arouse his suspicion, so I tried my best to keep my questions conversational. I asked about what kind of entertainment facilities were on the other floors. I pretended to be worried about what might happen if the power failed so deep underground. I asked what would happen if someone, such as the crazy pyroid, were to get loose in Level 10. Whenever I could, I deliberately let Dr. Denman overhear me asking these questions. I knew he could never resist an opportunity to get my hopes down by telling me how secure this place was.

I learned that there were primary and secondary power generators, in and below the facility. I learned that the guards worked in three shifts, and since I knew that the only place where guards were really needed was on Level 10, I could get a rough idea of their total strength by multiplying their usual number by three. I learned that the Central Control Room was not on Level 10, but up on Level 2, where it was too far away to be tampered with by psionics down below. Level 2 was where the military commander worked, and also where everything from the surveillance cameras to...

"...the nuclear auto-destruct system is operated from," Dr. Denman said with his usual sneer. "You're actually standing right over the bomb, which is on Level 11. You see, psionic, they may have given you a card to let you in the lounge, but no one gets out of this place alive. They'll turn this place into hot metal soup before they let you escape."

"So long as you're by my side," I retorted. I actually wanted to thank him. News of a nuclear bomb under our feet was not very encouraging, but at least now we knew about it.

I relayed what I learned that night, and the next night I was visited in my sleep by Derrick again, this time in the shape of a giant yellow walrus. Again, I gained consciousness inside the dreamweave. It was easier the second time, not just because of Derrick's crazy disguise, but because I knew it was possible to wake up in a dream now, and I knew that I needed to hear Derrick clearly and remember his words. Derrick told me thanks from Ralph, and requested more information.

In the days that followed, I slowly gathered what I could.

Everything I did was being monitored, so I couldn't exactly sneak into the offices and steal blueprints like a trench-coat-wearing secret agent. Still, I realized that I had two clear advantages. The first was, of course, that I had help from outside. Though they were considerably outnumbered, the Guardians above were powerful psionics who also had the element of surprise. My second advantage was that, in the eyes of the researchers here, I was still just a kid. Powerful... obnoxious, perhaps... but just a kid nevertheless. I doubted even Dr. Kellogg, who treated me like a near-equal, could truly believe that I might be up to the challenge of undermining their security and of plotting an elaborate escape only months into my stay.

I thought that perhaps many psionics had tried to escape within a short time of their capture, but those would have been desperate, frantic attempts without any real planning. The military guards would have been expecting it, and the psionics would have tried it alone. That's why they failed. I did my best to remain patient. I had already been here three months. A few more days wouldn't hurt. I needed to get Ralph all the information I possibly could, so I continued my cautious questioning.

I learned that the guards were armed not only with automatic rifles but also with knockout gas grenades. Many years ago, they had successfully used the gas grenades on Nightmare when he got loose in Level 10, but I doubted they would find gas effective against a windmaster like Ralph. Bullets were a greater concern, and I learned more about the automatic guns mounted in the elevator room and how they would shoot anything that moved if the facility was on security alert.

I discovered that the nuclear auto-destruct system could be operated not only from the Level 2 Central Control Room, but also directly from the bomb's location on Level 11. It was set for a fifteen-minute silent countdown. Once activated, only the top military people and a handful of trusted doctors could shut it off.

I learned that the various security systems were not controlled by a single central computer. Instead, the Level 10 airlocks and security doors, the elevator, the cameras and microphones, the auto-destruct and the control bands were each operated by completely separate computers in the Central Control Room, so as to avoid damage to the other systems if one was disabled.

I already knew from Dr. Kellogg that our control bands could be operated from either the Central Control Room or the little white remote controls that the doctors carried, but I further discovered that the remote controls sent out radio signals independent from the Central Control Room system. This unfortunately meant that even if the Control Room computer was shut down, the doctors could still directly operate our control bands. On the positive side, however, the limited range of the radio transmitters in the remote controls meant that they didn't work through the walls.

All this and more, I learned from carefully prepared conversations with Dr. Kellogg and Dr. Otis during our breaks between experiments and after meetings, as well as from provoking Dr. Denman.

Occasionally, I might get a dreamweave back in the early morning after sending a message the night before, but usually it took two days for one complete communication cycle. Also, I often couldn't get the answers to Ralph's questions in only two days, which meant that many of the dreams we sent to the surface were just pleas for more time. Weeks passed.

I knew that the more information we sent out, the better prepared the Guardians would be, but I was also eager to get out of here, and afraid that, sooner or later, someone would discover what we were doing. My active questioning wouldn't go unnoticed forever.

However, it turned out that I didn't have to do all of the snooping around by myself. Mr. Koontz's fifteen years of experience living in the research center was invaluable to my espionage effort. He had been down below Level 10 when he visited Nightmare once, and he had been above Level 10 several times as well, though hardly ever higher than Level 8 and never to the Central Control Room on Level 2. He had memorized much of the facility's floor plans, so all I had to do was relay the Guardians' questions through Alia and he would pass the necessary information back to the surface.

Once, I even tried having Alia ask Mr. Koontz to properly introduce himself to Cindy, so that Cindy could then describe him to Derrick and establish a direct communication line between the two dreamweavers. In my next dream, however, an annoyed Derrick, taking the shape of a gingerbread man wearing a pink tuxedo, told me that dreamweavers simply couldn't control each other's dreams.

Thus required to stay in the loop, I ended up learning a lot about the floors above me from what Derrick would say when he was passing me further questions about Mr. Koontz's information.

The entire facility was built around the central elevator in the shape of a giant concave cylinder, like a can that had been crushed around the middle. In terms of floor space, Level 10 was the most extensive, though Levels 9 and 8 were pretty large too. Above that, each floor was fairly small until Levels 2 and 1, which were wider.

The middle floors didn't matter too much because the central elevator went from Level 10 all the way up to Level 2. However, the elevator doors were well protected on all levels and, because Level 2 was the primary security gate to the rest of the facility, there was no easy access to Level 1 and the surface above it. If the Guardians could get in, fight their way through Level 1 and take control of Level 2, they would have free access to the whole complex. I took hope in the fact that this facility had been designed mainly to prevent breakouts, not break-ins.

And because the facility had been built so long ago and with such sturdy shielding, very little additional security could be installed in Level 10 since its original construction. Derrick had been worried that there might be some sort of high-tech mechanism to flood the corridors with poison gas or perhaps some kind of sticky foam, but as far as we could tell, no such security traps existed here. Instead, it was entirely up to the security gates, the control bands, the auto-destruct and the military guards to keep escape attempts from succeeding.

The military guards, when not on their shift, rested in Level 9 or slept in their barracks on Level 8. Once Ralph's team took the Central Control Room, both of these floors could be locked out from elevator access, which meant we would only have to deal with the one shift of guards on Level 10. That was still quite a few, but two-thirds less than we had originally feared.

Some of the doctors also lived up on Level 8, but most, including the main research team, had their quarters on Level 10. I worried about that a lot because I didn't want Dr. Kellogg to be hurt during the attack, but there didn't seem to be any way to warn him without giving ourselves away.

I also had two other major concerns at the time.

The first was that, according to Cindy, I talked in my sleep. I didn't dare ask the Central Control Room what I might have been muttering during the nights I slept waiting for Derrick's messages. I started meditating regularly before bedtimes, hoping it might keep me from blabbing in the dark, but there was little else I could do. It was just another risk in a long list of risks, but one I couldn't help now that we were committed to this plan.

The other worry I had was that Alia was acting almost normal these days. The prospect of escape and of being reunited with Cindy had brought about a marked change in Alia's attitude. She still followed me everywhere, but no longer cowered when around other people, even the guards, and she flinched only under the cold gaze of Dr. Denman. When I thought about it, Alia was doing much better around people than back when we were living at Cindy's house just last year, and it had been more than a week since she last needed to take a silent break from reality.

It should have been cause for celebration, but Alia's recovery came with a hidden danger: I felt it was only a matter of time before Dr. Kellogg suggested we stop sharing the bed, which would destroy the communication line we had so painstakingly established. Alia certainly seemed more than ready to sleep alone, so I had long since stopped even pretending to want my own room. I restlessly awaited each new dream exchange, hoping it wouldn't be our last.

"Adrian, may I have a word?" I heard Dr. Kellogg's voice say over the speaker one evening as I sat reading at my desk. Alia, who in recent weeks had resumed her habit of taking annoyingly long baths, was busy splashing around in the tub.

"Come on in, Doctor," I said.

I was still waiting to take my bath so I wasn't wearing my control bands, but I figured Dr. Kellogg probably knew that and didn't care. I closed my book as Dr. Kellogg entered the room and sat down on the edge of the bed.

"What's the matter?" I asked, noticing the concerned expression on his face and inwardly suspecting that I already knew. Dr. Kellogg had carefully timed his visit to coincide with Alia's bath so that he and I could talk in private.

Dr. Kellogg said gravely, "Dr. Denman has informed me of your whispered conversations to Alia over the past few weeks."

"Dr. Denman likes causing trouble for me. You know that," I said in an indignant tone, but I knew Dr. Kellogg wouldn't have come if it was just an empty accusation from someone who clearly hated, and was hated by, everyone. I shifted my weight uneasily on the stool.

"I had some trouble believing it myself," said Dr. Kellogg, "but I must admit that it does look like your mouth is moving. What are you whispering to her?"

Thinking quickly, I replied, "Alia wants me to tell her bedtime stories, but if I read them from a book, she keeps looking at the pictures and never goes to sleep. So I tell her to close her eyes and then I whisper them to her."

"I see," said Dr. Kellogg. Then, stroking his beard, he asked quietly, "Do you know, Adrian, the easiest way to tell if someone is lying?"

"Without psionics?" I deadpanned.

"You look at a person's eyes," said Dr. Kellogg. "People usually don't look directly at you if they are lying. If they are making up a story, they often move their eyes upwards. Where do you think your eyes went when I asked what you were whispering to Alia?"

"I have no idea," I answered, trying to keep myself from fidgeting.

Suddenly Dr. Kellogg laughed merrily. "Why, you were looking directly into my eyes, of course!"

He stood up to leave. I was pretty sure I hadn't been looking at his eyes. Was he just trying to get out of the room so that he could seal us in and get help? As much as I liked Dr. Kellogg, he was, after all, working for the research center. For a split second, I even considered blasting him and taking him hostage, but I knew that would only bring the whole place around me.

Dr. Kellogg turned to me as the airlock's inner door slid open. "I will pass my expert analysis of your sincerity on to Dr. Otis," he said smilingly. "However, Adrian, I advise you not to do anything here that may bring further suspicion upon you, or Dr. Denman may manage to convince Central Control to revoke your control band privileges."

With that, he turned around and left the room.

"Was that Dr. Kellogg?" asked Alia as she emerged from the bathroom a second later.

Feeling myself break out in a cold sweat, I didn't bother answering her as I hurried into the bathroom.

Standing under the steaming hot shower, I looked at the P-47 tattoo on my arm and shuddered as I realized again how dangerous my situation really was at the research facility. Dr. Denman was right: Alia and I really were just lab animals here, and Dr. Kellogg couldn't protect us.

16. LAST-MINUTE SURPRISES

That night, Derrick, taking the form of a talking crescent moon in a purple sky, haughtily demanded more precise information about the location of the remote guns mounted around the central elevator doors on Level 10. Shaken by Dr. Kellogg's visit, however, I didn't dare pass his question on to Mr. Koontz the following evening. I instead whispered a fairytale to Alia, deliberately keeping my voice just barely loud enough to be caught on the microphone.

I hoped that my silence would tell the Guardians that I was no longer able to provide information, and that they'd have to go with what they already had, which was, after all, quite a lot by now. However, the very next day, I learned something that would test my resolve for caution.

It was mid-June, and Alia's day for her regular physical examination. Alia no longer needed me to hold the stethoscope to her chest or even draw her blood. She was quite used to the routine pokes and prods by now, and the doctors were hardly strangers to her anymore. Besides, my skill with a needle, though much improved over the months, was still inferior to an experienced doctor's. I didn't always get Alia's vein on the first try, or even the second, so Alia understandably preferred the hand of a professional.

I sat outside the examining room with Dr. Kellogg, who was chatting with one of the military guards. Even though I was no longer planning to contact Derrick, out of sheer habit I was listening in on their conversation while pretending to read a book. This was something that I had lots of practice at these last few weeks, though it produced very little useful information.

That day, however, I struck pure gold.

"So, Commander Wilkins is finally retiring," said Dr. Kellogg, sighing. "Are you going to be at the party?"

"Actually, I'm on duty then," replied the guard. "It's too bad really. I liked the commander a lot. Have you met his replacement?"

If I were a dog, my ears would have perked up. When was this party? It would be the perfect opportunity for an attack on the facility!

"I haven't seen Commander Cross yet," answered Dr. Kellogg. "I heard he was inspecting the upper floors since last month."

"Oh, he was down in Level 10 just yesterday," said the guard. "He came in with Commander Wilkins and greeted Dr. Otis and a few others. You must have just missed him."

"He came down unannounced?" Dr. Kellogg asked in disbelief.

"Apparently the new commander likes surprises. How about you, Doctor? Are you going to be at Commander Wilkins's send off?"

"I'll try, but just in case I can't make Wednesday evening, I'll stop by his office sometime this weekend."

Thank you, Dr. Kellogg! Today was Thursday, so there was no mistaking it. I would have to get this to Ralph before next Wednesday, and the earlier the better, just in case the Guardians decided to attack sooner.

But how could I contact them? I'd risk using Alia if I had to, but was there any other way? In the evening, I took Alia to see Mr. Koontz in the lounge. Alia hadn't sent him any messages the night before, so no doubt he would have assumed something was wrong. It was a long shot, but I thought perhaps Mr. Koontz might find a way for us to talk privately.

"Hey there, Adrian, Alia. How are you two?" Mr. Koontz greeted us without standing, and we sat at his table.

"As good as things could be," I answered dully, "under the circumstances."

We talked for several minutes, but nothing was coming of it. I felt that perhaps there was no way to get my message to him safely.

"What's getting you down, Adrian?" asked Mr. Koontz, peering into my face.

"Oh, everything," I said heavily. "There's just so little to do here. And I've never gone so long without the sun. It's been four months now. I'm starting to feel like a vampire."

Mr. Koontz laughed. "Well, perhaps we'll have that early birthday party after all. It'll cheer you up. You're young enough to have two birthdays a year and get away with it!"

I decided to throw caution to the winds. "I overheard Dr. Kellogg talking about a party next Wednesday night. Something about the commander retiring…"

"Oh yes?" said Mr. Koontz, raising his eyebrows. "Well, I guess there'd be some kind of ceremony and party. I remember when Wilkins was put in charge nine years ago. He was promoted from the ranks here, so I knew him. I haven't heard anything about his replacement, though."

I hadn't heard much either. All I knew was that the new commander liked surprises. I smirked. Well, at least somebody was going to be amused.

Two nights later, I found myself standing on a house-size cheese cake facing an enormous floating eyeball with bat wings growing out of either side. The black leathery wings beat furiously around my head, and I knew instantly that I was dreaming. Derrick liked to assume a stranger guise with every dream.

"You have done well, Adrian," said the eye. "Ralph is very pleased, and Cindy thanks you too, though I once heard her say that she'll teach you to behave if it's the last thing she does. You are not to risk sending any more dreams to us. Barring any last-minute developments, our attack will take place at 7pm this coming Wednesday. This should allow us to take Mr. Koontz while Nightmare is still awake."

The floating eyeball blinked once and continued, "Cindy demands that you stay in your room until you are rescued. Ralph says so too, and advises you to stay out of our way. That is all."

I woke. The cake had disappeared, but the party was just beginning. I still had five days to go, and over those days I did my very best to stay focused on the tasks I was set to do. If there was going to be fighting, I wanted to be ready for it. I even put a slight mark on one of the heavy steel targets in Lab-C.

Tuesday was a day off for us. Alia's testing schedule would restart from Wednesday, though with any luck, it would be her last day in the lab. I spent the morning playing with Alia in our room, but my mind was all over the place. Suddenly, with our escape only a day and a half away, I couldn't focus on anything.

I had read many books at Cindy's place and many more at the research facility. Far more words total than I would have had I remained in school. Some of those books were war stories about soldiers who spent sleepless nights waiting for combat. The stories described the waiting for a battle as being just as stressful, if not worse, than the actual fighting, but I didn't believe a word of it until now. Waiting was really bad.

Despite all the information we had sent to the Guardians, there were still many things left to chance. For one, I hadn't been able to find out who, exactly, could deactivate the auto-destruct system, though I assumed that the military commander and Dr. Otis would definitely be on the list. Ralph's Guardians were mostly destroyers, and Ralph was the only controller among them. If the auto-destruct got set during the attack, unless Ralph could capture the commander or Dr. Otis alive, there would be little chance of shutting it off. Derrick had once told me that as long as everything else went smoothly, fifteen minutes should be enough time for them to get in and rescue us, but I couldn't be sure if he really meant that or if he was just trying to keep me calm. After all, fifteen minutes seemed like an awfully short time to get clear of a nuclear blast.

This was going to be Mr. Koontz's ticket to freedom too, and I didn't want to let him down. We also wanted to take Janice, but, according to Dr. Otis, she was "uncooperative" and so she was kept under tighter security. If the auto-destruct didn't get set or could be deactivated, the Guardians would try to rescue her as well, but Derrick made no promises.

As for Alia and me, well, I should have been comforted by the fact that we were the main objective of the Guardians' break-in plan, but I was anxious as to how the military guards would react when the attack began. Would they go and defend the elevator, or would they try to take us hostage? Or perhaps they were under orders to shoot us before we got the chance to escape. I might be able to deflect an arrow, but not a bullet, and I already knew what it felt like to be shot. It was not an experience I wanted to repeat.

When I couldn't bear the tension any longer, I stood up and requested the door opened. Central Control made no objection, but asked me where I wanted to go. I told them that I wanted to take a walk and stretch my legs, which was true. Alia wanted to tag along, but I told her to stay in the room.

I half-walked, half-jogged down the spotlessly white corridors of Level 10, not really looking where I was going, taking random turns and doubling back at dead ends. It didn't matter to me where I went as long as I kept moving. The purposeful stride helped soothe my aching nerves.

As I briskly turned yet another corner, I suddenly felt my body being pushed against the wall by a sturdy hand.

"Feeling cooped up?" Dr. Denman asked sardonically.

"I was fine until you showed your ugly face!" I spat back. The confrontation felt good after so much waiting, and I was possessed with a sudden desire to blast him hard. It was a desire I kept in check only with great difficulty.

"I know what you were telling P-46 in bed all this time," Dr. Denman hissed at me.

"Snow White and the Seven Dwarves!"

"Liar!" He pushed me down onto the floor, pinning me with one hand as he shouted, "I checked the video log! This all started after you said, and I quote, 'I can't hear her.' Who couldn't you hear, psionic?!"

"Get off me!"

"Control, lock band 47!"

I felt the metal rods extend from inside my control bands. As they pressed against my wrists, I was instantly plunged into the familiar numb dizziness that came with being drained. I still couldn't separate my power from my body. If anything, I had even less balance than before, or perhaps it had simply been a long time since I was last drained. As I sat slumped down on the floor, I was dimly aware of the guards and doctors rushing up to me.

There was some heated discussion, and then Dr. Denman said, "The new commander can deal with him after the ceremony. Put him in confinement until then. I will speak to Dr. Otis."

The guards picked me up and carried me for a while. I was too weak to see where they were taking me, but soon I heard the soft hissing of a door opening, and the soldiers pulled me through an airlock and put me down on the floor.

My control rods retracted, and I carefully stood up and looked around. I was alone in a small, vault-like cell, much like the one I had been tortured in after being shot by the Wolves, though the walls here were smooth white concrete. There was a thin mat on the floor, a tiny toilet bowl in one corner, and nothing else.

What would happen now? Would they torture me? Would they threaten Alia? Unlike the Wolves, the people here knew she could speak telepathically. If they wanted information from her, they would get it. And what would happen then? There was no way to warn Ralph that the military knew an attack was coming. The Guardians would be walking into a trap! I pounded my fists against the concrete wall. We had been so close! Now, it was only a matter of time before they...

I felt the control rods extend again. Leaning weakly against a wall for support, I looked toward the door, but it didn't open. I felt a touch of horror, believing that the doctors were planning to keep me drained constantly from now on just like Nightmare, but a moment later the metal rods retracted back into my control bands. I barely had time to wonder what that was about before the door slid open.

Dr. Kellogg was standing in the airlock holding a lunch tray of fried chicken and steamed vegetables.

"Sorry about that," Dr. Kellogg said with a wink. "I was having a brief argument with Central Control over security protocols, but it turns out that I am still the master of my own safety."

I stared at him, not knowing what to say.

"And I'm very sorry about this too, Adrian," Dr. Kellogg continued unhappily as he stepped into my cell and looked around once. "Dr. Denman has a tendency to get carried away sometimes. Still, I'm also a bit curious as to what you meant by 'I can't hear her.' Dr. Denman seems to think that you are receiving psionic messages of some kind and having Alia send them back. It doesn't make a whole lot of sense, really, but perhaps you could explain?"

"Dr. Kellogg, I don't even remember saying those words!" I said frantically. I did remember, actually, since those first dreams were very mysterious and I had felt frustrated being unable to hear Cindy. But there was nothing I could make up on the spot to explain what I had said, so I pretended to have forgotten.

Dr. Kellogg gave me a sympathetic grin and said, "Well, I suppose we can't expect you to remember every conversation you have with Alia."

"She talks a lot more than you'd think," I said, trying to smile as innocently as possible.

"I understand," said Dr. Kellogg. "However, Dr. Denman feels this is suspicious enough to keep you here and, in this matter, I have no real authority to overrule him. Dr. Otis will need to be present at your questioning, but he is currently at a higher level attending a rather long and important meeting. You see, the military commander of this facility is changing today. The new commander, Commander Cross, will begin his duties as of tomorrow, and he also wishes to be present at your questioning."

"Dr. Denman is making a mistake! Please, Dr. Kellogg," I begged desperately. "Please don't let him hurt Alia. She probably doesn't remember that conversation either!"

"Whoa there, Adrian!" said Dr. Kellogg, holding his hands up. "Just calm down. No one is going to question Alia until you have been questioned. Nor, do I think, considering your near-spotless record at this facility, are you in any danger of being disbelieved. My presence is required at your questioning as well, and I promise to put in a good word for you. When this is all over, we'll both have a good laugh at Dr. Denman."

Dr. Kellogg laid the lunch tray on the floor next to my mat. "I'll be back at dinnertime with some blankets. I'll also see if we can't get Central Control to let you talk to Alia through the intercom. I don't know if her telepathy will reach you here, but you can at least tell her goodnight."

With that, Dr. Kellogg requested the door opened and left.

I could barely eat anything. Total disaster had been averted, but for how long? Commander Cross and Dr. Otis would question me tomorrow, probably before Commander Wilkins's retirement party. Would I really be able to prevent them from questioning Alia?

There was no clock here so it was impossible to keep track of the time. For all I knew, time had stopped completely. I sat down on the mat with my arms folded around my knees, rocking myself back and forth like Alia had done back in Cindy's house. I thought about my promise to protect her. Despite what Dr. Kellogg had said, I couldn't put it past Dr. Denman to have Alia locked up too. Even tortured. Everything was starting to come apart, and our one chance at escape now hung by a hair.

"Hey, Adrian."

I looked up and saw that Dr. Kellogg had entered the room, carrying my dinner tray in his right hand and a bundle of blankets under his left arm. I wasn't hungry at all, and was surprised that dinnertime had already come. Dr. Kellogg placed everything on the floor and then sat down on the mat next to me.

"Good news and bad news," he said.

"Bad news first, please," I said.

"Okay. The bad news is that I couldn't convince Central Control to allow you to talk with Alia. Have you received any telepathy from her?"

"No," I replied honestly. If it was at all possible, I was certain she would have called to me, but I hadn't heard a peep from her in hours. I hadn't realized how much I had gotten used to hearing Alia's voice in my head until now.

"You are still on Level 10, but this room is considerably better shielded," explained Dr. Kellogg. Then he grinned, saying, "Now for the good news. Dr. Otis and Commander Cross have decided to question you first thing tomorrow morning, at 9am."

My heart sank. That was the good news?!

Dr. Kellogg continued, "Also, I've delayed Alia's testing schedule so that she won't have to go to Lab-A alone tomorrow. Once you are cleared of all charges, you will be able to escort her in person, as you always do."

"Thank you," I said faintly. "That is good news."

"You're a good big brother, Adrian."

I remembered how Mark had once called me Alia's "big brother" too, but that was the day we were caught. I frowned at the floor and shook my head.

"You really are," said Dr. Kellogg. "You brought Alia out of her shell. She would never have survived down here without you."

"She wouldn't even be down here if it weren't for me," I said wretchedly. If I had been a good brother, I might have never even met Alia. I would have jumped out the window with Cat.

"In all honesty," Dr. Kellogg said slowly, "I think neither of you should be here. This research center wasn't designed with people like you in mind. Psionics, yes, but not children. You really don't belong here."

I remained silent. Dr. Kellogg removed his wristwatch, which was a cheap digital with a black rubber watchband.

"Take this," he said, handing me the watch. "Nothing messes with your mind worse than not knowing the hour."

Having experienced berserking and peacemaking firsthand, I didn't entirely agree with Dr. Kellogg's opinion about not knowing the time, but I was grateful nevertheless. I looked at his watch, handling it carefully so as not to touch the few metal parts on it, and thanked him.

"I'll be wanting that back," said Dr. Kellogg.

"Doctor?" I said, placing the watch on the edge of my mat. "Why are you doing this for me?"

"I figured you could use a friend right about now," he replied gently.

I slowly shook my head. "You just said that I don't belong here, but you're the one who doesn't belong."

Dr. Kellogg smiled. "That's a compliment, isn't it?"

"You once promised me truth," I said quietly.

"I remember."

"So what are you doing down here, Doctor? Don't you have a family somewhere?"

Dr. Kellogg gazed at me sadly for a moment, and then said, "I had a family, Adrian. I had a son and a daughter, not much older than you and Alia. But some years ago, they were killed, along with my wife, in an automobile accident."

"I'm sorry."

Dr. Kellogg gave me a slight nod and continued, "For all my studies, for all my training as a psychologist, I couldn't deal with my own emotions. I was living in a house full of memories and hurt and nothing else. I thought I would go insane."

Dr. Kellogg paused, looking up at the ceiling for a moment. Then he sighed softly and turned to me again, saying, "So, when I was offered a position here, I accepted. They didn't tell me what I was getting into. They just told me that it would be important work far from home. That's all I wanted, really. Just to get away from it all." Dr. Kellogg gave me a sympathetic smile. "You know how that feels, Adrian."

I smiled too. "Yeah, I know how that feels."

"So now you know why I'm here," said Dr. Kellogg.

"Well, there had to be a reason."

"Adrian, I don't want you to take this the wrong way, because I know it's a terrible thing to say, but I'm glad that you're here. I'm glad I met you."

I nodded. "I'm sorry about what happened to your family, Dr. Kellogg, but I'm glad you're here too."

"Thank you," said Dr. Kellogg. "That means a lot to me."

We sat together for a minute more, and then Dr. Kellogg gestured toward my dinner tray and said, "You'd better eat before it gets too cold. I have to be going now. Is there anything else you would like?"

"Please, Doctor," I said. "Please watch over Alia for me."

"I will," promised Dr. Kellogg, standing up. "It'll be her first night alone, but I dare say she'll be alright. She's made a lot of progress in the last few weeks."

"Yes, she has," I agreed quietly.

"No doubt thanks to those stories you've been telling her."

The moment our eyes met, I was almost certain that Dr. Kellogg knew much more than he was letting on, but he quickly turned his back to me and requested the door be opened.

Stepping into the airlock, Dr. Kellogg said, "Don't worry too much, Adrian. Enjoy your dinner and try to get a good night's sleep. We'll see you first thing after breakfast and get you out of here before lunch."

As I watched Dr. Kellogg disappear behind the airlock door, the fear that I had managed to suppress during our conversation came rushing back to me in full force. I wondered if I would still be alive at lunch tomorrow.

It took a long time before I could get to sleep that night, and when I finally did, it was one nightmare after another. I dreamt that I was being chased by the Wolves. I saw Alia dead in a pool of blood, which swelled into an ocean and swept me toward a whirlpool of wind and mud. Then I saw the giant black stone wall towering over me before it started to crumble and bury me under a mountain of rock.

I opened my eyes. My cell was almost pitch-black, the only glow coming from the dimmed ceiling light. I stood up, and suddenly I felt a presence in the room with me. I turned around once, but I couldn't see who or what it was. Feeling a tingling in my right hand, I looked down at my palm.

There was a small mouth in the middle of it, which opened to speak. "I'm sorry this dream is incomplete," said the mouth, "but I'm having a little trouble with Nightmare at the moment."

I held my open palm closer to my disbelieving eyes. "Mr. Koontz?!"

"Alia told me in the evening that you didn't return from your walk, and I pretty much guessed what had happened even before I got the details from Dr. Kellogg. I've just sent a dream to your friends above, telling them the situation. I'm sorry, Adrian, but I told them to give up and leave. I knew you wouldn't want to risk your friends. This is the least I can do for you now, and I do hope we meet again."

The mouth on my palm vanished, and I opened my eyes again.

For a moment, I lay there wondering if this was a dream as well, but the hard mat was uncomfortable enough to reassure me that I was awake, so I stood up and stretched my arms. According to Dr. Kellogg's watch, it was still only 2am.

I lay down again and stared up at the ceiling. Despite my surprise in seeing a mouth on the palm of my hand, I hadn't actually woken inside Mr. Koontz's dreamweave like I usually did in Derrick's, and Mr. Koontz's exact words were fading quickly from my mind. But I still remembered his basic message: It was over. The Guardians wouldn't come.

But Mr. Koontz was right to do what he did. The questioning tomorrow would probably lead to Alia being asked similar questions, and there was very little chance that she could keep what we had been doing a secret. I'd be lucky to spend the rest of my life locked away like Nightmare or the insane pyroid, William. At least the Guardians would know not to try to rescue us. At least Cindy would be safe.

I closed my eyes.

"Boo!" said a girl's voice.

I jumped up and found myself face to face with, of all people, Alia.

"Derrick!" I exclaimed, and forgetting that he couldn't hear me, asked, "What are you doing here?!"

"Incompetent boy!" hissed Derrick's Alia. Even though I knew I was dreaming, it still felt very strange to see Alia's mouth move as she said irately, "Ralph is very displeased, and I was afraid you might never go back to sleep. It's past three in the morning now. We are not going to wait for your hearing. We will commence our attack at precisely four o'clock. That's 4am, you hear?! Once we get to the Central Control Room, we will lock the elevator doors on

Levels 3 through 9, and then disable all security doors on Level 10, but you are to remain where you are. We do not want you caught in the crossfire. I am dreamweaving to Alia to stay put as well. Wake up now and get yourself ready. Wake up, Adrian!"

My eyes snapped open. I was breathing rapidly as I looked at Dr. Kellogg's watch. It was 3:45. I stood up, stretched, and leaned against the wall, steadying my nerves. It was about to happen.

I slowly began to focus my telekinetic energy around my wrists, just under my control bands.

3:50... 3:55... 3:59... Four o'clock. I continued to focus my energy around my wrists as I waited. I could hear my heart thumping loudly in the sheer, crushing silence. Still nothing happened. 4:01... 4:03... 4:05...

I felt a slight vibration in my control bands. The rods were extending. A microsecond before they touched my skin, however, I released the two most powerful blasts I could from around each of my wrists. They tore the control bands apart, and the plastic casings splintered against the concrete walls.

An unbearably long minute later, both the inner and outer airlock doors slid open, and I could hear the sound of a klaxon and lots of shouting coming from the brightly lit corridor beyond.

17. THE COUNTDOWN

I ignored Derrick's warning to stay put. I had to find Alia and make sure that she was okay. I jumped out into the corridor, squinting in the sudden light as I tried to get my bearings. Though I knew that I was still on Level 10, I didn't recognize this part of the complex.

A small group of armed guards came running down the corridor toward me. But just as I thought they were going to point their guns at me, they ran past. It was a different shift at this time and, in the confusion, they didn't even bother to look at me. I guessed that their job was to protect the elevator entrance, so I followed them at a distance. I had seen the outer door to the elevator room before, so I knew I could find my way back to Alia's room from there. I didn't care if the cameras saw me. My cell doors had opened, which meant that the Guardians were already in the Level 2 Central Control Room.

Sure enough, I heard the overhead speaker crackle, and what I instantly recognized as Derrick's real voice said, "Adrian, find a place to hide. Ralph's on his way down."

I kept running, following the guards. My plastic slippers were slowing me down, so I kicked them off and went barefoot, which also made me quieter.

After a few twists and turns, I was back in a familiar part of Level 10. I didn't actually want to go to the elevator entrance since all the guards in the complex were probably converging on that location, and bumping into them could be a fatal mistake. Instead, I headed down a different corridor that would take me safely around the imminent battle.

I passed another pair of guards. They shouted something at me, but I wasn't listening. If they were going to shoot, let them! But a moment later, I was alone again, running down the last stretch of corridor that led to Alia's room.

The airlock doors were open here too, and I rushed inside, looking around frantically. Under the bed?! No! In the bathroom?! Empty! Where was she?!

"Alia!" I shouted at the top of my voice. "Ali! Where are you?!"

Why would she leave the room by herself? She had to be here on Level 10 somewhere. I wondered if she had been knocked out or perhaps even killed, but then I remembered the control bands. She was being drained! Even if she could hear me, she wouldn't be able to answer telepathically.

I looked up at the ceiling camera. "Derrick! Check the cameras! Where's Alia?"

"I'm checking, Adrian," replied Derrick through the speaker. "There are a lot of cameras. Give us a moment. We've got other problems too. Just stay there in the room till we come get you."

The klaxons stopped. I could hear gunfire coming from down the corridor, probably near the elevator. Some were individual shots while others were rapid bursts of machinegun fire. I heard some small explosions as well, which I guessed were the gas grenades. Even from inside the room, I could feel a slight breeze blowing through the corridors. Ralph must have been brewing up a storm.

And there was something else I could feel. It was William, the pyroid who had lost his mind when he was separated from the Angels after conversion. I could sense him somewhere nearby. He must have broken free of his control bands too, because now I felt his full strength.

I heard Derrick over the speaker again. "Ralph, I can't disable it! You're down to fourteen minutes again! Get moving!"

I started for the door.

"Where are you going, Adrian?" shouted Derrick. "I told you to stay put!"

"I have to find Alia!"

"No! There's no time," Derrick said in a panicky voice. "The auto-destruct kicked in the moment we entered. I managed to reset the timer once, but I can't shut it off. We're almost down to thirteen minutes now including getaway time."

"Reset it again!" I shouted as I rushed out of the room.

"I can't! If you're going anywhere, go to the elevator. Find Ralph!"

Where was Alia? In our four months here, we had hardly ever left our room if we could help it. Had she gone looking for me, like she did back on Mark's hill? Where would she have looked? Thinking I knew the answer, I sprinted toward the lounge where we used to talk with Mr. Koontz, letting my telekinesis push me from behind. The corridors were empty now. The guards had all gone to the elevator, and the doctors were nowhere in sight.

I burst into the lounge.

It had been demolished. One of the tables was on its side. Some chairs had been thrown about and broken. And a giant piece of the concrete ceiling had come crashing down onto the floor. Amidst the rubble, I could just make out the head and shoulders of a man whose body was pinned under the heavy rock.

"Dr. Kellogg!" I shouted, rushing up to him. What little I could see of his chest was covered in blood. There was some blood around his lips too. He looked dead, and I was about to leave the lounge when...

"Adrian," gasped Dr. Kellogg, opening his eyes. "Where do you think you're going?"

Crouching beside him, I answered quietly, "I'm getting out of here, Doctor. I'm going to find Alia, and then I'm leaving."

"Good for you," said Dr. Kellogg, wincing in pain. "You don't belong here anyway."

"I'll get you out, Doctor," I said, though I knew I could never lift this much solid concrete. "I'll find Alia and come back. I won't let you die here."

"No, Adrian... Get out..." Dr. Kellogg looked at me, more blood trickling from his mouth. He winced again and said weakly, "Too late... for Alia... you... get out now..."

"What do you mean, Doctor?" I asked. "Where is Alia?!"

"Denman..." he said, closing his eyes. "He..."

"Dr. Kellogg!"

I couldn't tell if he was breathing. He was either dead or unconscious. I stood up and looked at the wreckage. What had happened here? Suddenly I didn't care. Dr. Denman must have taken Alia from her room. I had to find them.

The intercom crackled to life again, and Derrick said in an agitated tone, "I'm working on it, Ralph!"

I couldn't hear what Ralph was saying, wherever he was, but it looked like the battle was still raging.

A moment later, Derrick shouted triumphantly, "I got it!"

A mechanical voice that sounded neither male nor female began to speak through the intercom. It said in a monotone, "Auto-destruct sequence silent countdown has been disengaged."

Derrick had managed to turn off the auto-destruct! I nearly jumped for joy. We would have time to find Alia.

But then the voice continued, "Twelve minutes to auto-destruct."

What?! Derrick hadn't turned off the auto-destruct after all. He just turned off the "silent countdown" mode, so that this machine voice could announce how much longer we had left to live! I heard Derrick curse loudly over the speakers as I ran out of the lounge.

Level 10 was much too large to search in one hour, to say nothing of twelve minutes, and considering we had to get out well before that, there was even less time. I thought about going to Dr. Denman's office, but I didn't have a clue where it was.

"Adrian, behind you!" Derrick's voice rang out through the corridor.

I spun around, instinctively ducking at the same time. A jet of bright orange flame shot over my head. About fifteen yards down the corridor stood a pale-skinned man with thin, light brown hair that extended past his shoulders. He was wearing the same white shirt and pants that were issued to all psionics in this place. In my panic over Dr. Kellogg and the auto-destruct system, I had forgotten to keep track of the pyroid.

William was drooling at the mouth, and his feet were unsteady as if he was drunk or hadn't walked in a long time. He let out a low roar and, from his outstretched arms, shot another flame at me. I jumped into the air, levitating myself against the corridor ceiling as the fireball flew under me. Dropping to the floor, I returned a telekinetic blast which knocked him slightly backwards, but I could do little to hurt him at this distance.

Then I noticed his wrists. William was still wearing his control bands! I ducked back into the lounge as another flame shot by. William would be here in a moment. If only I could drain him, there would be no need to fight. But I didn't know his identification number. His bracelets would be stenciled, but too small to read at a distance, and I wasn't about to lift up his sleeve to check his tattoo.

"Derrick!" I yelled hysterically. "Lock the control bands! Lock all of them!"

"I can't!" Derrick shouted back. "All I could get were the doors and elevator. I have no control over the bands, or the destruct, or anything! I'm locked out of half the systems! Adrian, the bands can still be controlled by the remote controls that the doctors carry."

"I don't know his number!"

"It's 37. Be quick, he's coming!"

There was no other way out of the lounge. The only other exit, which led to another corridor, had also caved in. I rushed back to where Dr. Kellogg lay trapped under the concrete slab. He was clearly dead. I looked in the only pocket I could see, which was the front left of his shirt.

It was empty.

I reached into the small crack between Dr. Kellogg's body and the concrete slab, extending my arm as far as it would go. I knew what the remote controls looked like. They were small and white. Dr. Kellogg usually kept his in one of his pants pockets. I couldn't reach that far. I didn't even know which pocket it was in. Derrick said something over the intercom, and the computer voice was speaking again too, but I wasn't listening to either of them. I closed my eyes, knowing that at any second, William would appear in the doorway and set me on fire.

Pull it toward me, I thought desperately. *Just like picking a pocket from a restaurant roof.*

But I couldn't do it. Perhaps Dr. Kellogg didn't have his remote control, or more likely it was smashed or jammed under the concrete.

I turned my head to the doorway. William was standing right there, looking at me. His long hair was whipping about his face as if he was caught in a storm. He stretched out his arms again, ready to burn me alive. I closed my eyes, feeling the wind on my face too. The wind...

"It needs oxygen to burn," said a familiar raspy voice.

I opened my eyes. William was still standing in the doorway. I saw a glint of silver at his chest, but because it was facing me, it took a moment for me to realize that it was the tip of a long blade. William fell forward, revealing the wrinkled, leathery face and fidgeting, gangly form of Ralph P. Henderson. I almost smiled.

"Ten minutes to auto-destruct," said the computer voice.

"Come on, lad," said Ralph, lightly stepping over William's body and into the lounge. "It's time to get you out of here."

"I can't find Alia!" I said frantically, pulling my arm out from under the stone slab and standing up.

Ralph didn't care. "We've got the dreamweaver and the light-foot. They're already going up, lad. You have to come too. Now!"

Ralph grabbed my arm and pulled me out of the lounge. I stumbled after him.

"I can't leave without Alia, Ralph," I said, tugging my arm free but keeping pace with him as we headed down the corridor toward the elevator. "I just can't!"

"You can and you will! I hate to lose a healer too, but it can't be helped. We're out of time!"

We came to the elevator room. Both the outer and inner security gates were open, revealing the elevator doors a bit farther in. There were bodies of soldiers strewn about the place. Some were bleeding, some burned, while others just looked unconscious, probably having been suffocated by Ralph or perhaps knocked out with gas from their own grenades. Three of the dead bodies wore white coats, and I recognized Dr. Otis among them. I didn't particularly dislike Dr. Otis, but nor did I feel sad or anything seeing him lying there. Everything was happening too quickly and none of it felt very real.

There were two grim-faced women standing near the elevator who I had never seen before, but I instantly knew by their out-of-place normal clothes that they were Ralph's Guardians. The rest of the team must have already escorted Mr. Koontz and Janice out of the facility. The elevator doors were closed, but the blinking lights above them showed that the car was coming down to us.

"Nine minutes to auto-destruct," announced the flat computer voice.

Ralph grinned. "It's going to be close, but we'll make it."

Derrick came on the speakers again. He said excitedly, "Ralph, I think I know where she is! The video log shows someone pulling her into the other elevator."

The other elevator? Level 11! That was where the bomb was, and the power generators, and Nightmare's cell down farther below.

I felt my world stop turning.

I looked up at Ralph. All I had to do was follow him into the elevator and I would be free. I had once told Alia that I would protect her. But how could that promise matter now? If there was even the slightest chance to save her, then maybe... But Dr. Kellogg was right: It was too late for her. I had to get out. If I died here, what would happen to Cat?

The elevator doors opened.

I shut my eyes tightly, and suddenly I saw Alia's face as plainly as if she were standing right in front of me. Alia, who had taught me how to block Ralph. Alia, who had saved my life in the forest... who had come running after me all alone when I had gone into town. Every breath I took I owed to her, and even if I didn't... No, I couldn't leave her here, even if all I could do for her now was...

"I'm going after Alia," I said quietly.

Ralph stared at me. "You'll die, lad."

"I know," I replied, surprised at how calm I felt. Ralph wasn't causing it. What he said was true, but it just didn't matter.

Ralph frowned. "Cindy won't be happy, you know."

"She'll understand," I said. "Tell her that I kept my promise. Tell her sorry from me."

Ralph slowly reached out to shake my hand, but I didn't take it. Ralph chuckled, saying, "Smart lad you are, little destroyer."

"Goodbye, Ralph."

I turned and ran back down the corridor.

Mr. Koontz had once shown me where the other elevator room was. It didn't take long to get there. The single security door to the elevator room was left wide open, and I sprinted inside. On the other side of the small room was the elevator to Level 11.

It was a bright red wire cage type, like those at construction sites, but the elevator car itself was not on this floor. I hit the only button next to the door, and the motor shuddered noisily to life. I watched the thick metal cable in the shaft start to move as the computer announced that I now had eight minutes left to live.

I waited impatiently for the cage to arrive. As soon as the door opened, I jumped in and hit the "down" button. I was still barefoot, but fortunately the cage floor was lined with thin rubber padding, so I didn't get drained. The door slid back into place, clanging shut, and the elevator shuddered once more before beginning to descend. A moment later, I could see Level 11 through the cage wall.

It was a cavern. Nearly three stories high, the vast chamber had a roughly paved floor set with what looked like an enormous boiler and a bunch of other large machines, many of which were making loud whirring and hissing noises. There were a few rusted tractor-like vehicles and drilling machines here too: remnants of the research center's construction decades ago.

As the elevator continued its slow descent, I finally began to feel the full weight of what I had come here to do.

"This," I muttered savagely to myself, "is why you should never make promises."

I didn't really mean that, of course, but I found that a little raw anger could go a long way to steadying my nerves. The calm I had felt speaking to Ralph a moment ago had all but vanished, and I could no longer pretend that I wasn't afraid. I decided that I wouldn't mind dying down here so long as it wasn't for nothing. The elevator cage was nearly at the bottom now. I wondered if I really could find Alia in the next...

"Seven minutes to auto-destruct," said the computer.

The cage shuddered to a stop and the door slowly slid open. I stepped out.

Near the elevator were stairs leading even farther down into the darkness. Did they lead to Nightmare's holding chamber? Was Alia on this floor, or below? I decided to ignore the stairs and search Level 11.

I suspected that Alia was still being drained, so I shouted, "Alia! Use your mouth! Say anything! Alia!"

My voice echoed around the colossal room as I walked briskly between the giant whirring machines, calling her name again and again. Had I been thinking clearer, I would have levitated myself up above the machines to quicken my search, but my mounting panic was starting to impair my judgment. There was no sign of Alia or Dr. Denman.

I shouted at the top of my lungs, "Ali, if you can't speak, at least scream something! Please just scream something!"

There was no answer. I kicked one of the machines and roared at the ceiling, cursing in frustration. There was so little time left, and I was going to die here alone.

Just as I was about to double back and head for Level 12, I heard Alia cry out, "A-yi!"

I sensed something move to my left.

"One false move, psionic, and I'll slit her filthy throat."

I slowly turned toward them. Standing between two bulky machines, Dr. Denman was gripping Alia's shoulder with his left hand, and had a surgical knife pressed against her neck with his right.

"Six minutes to auto-destruct," the monotone continued irritatingly.

Suddenly the whole room started to shake like an earthquake. I lost my balance and nearly fell over. The vibration continued for a few seconds and then stopped. Steadying myself, I looked at Dr. Denman and Alia again. There was a thin red line across Alia's neck where the doctor's knife had slipped. Alia whimpered, struggling feebly against his grasp. The cut wasn't deep and there wasn't much blood on her neck, but she still had her control rods extended so she couldn't heal herself.

"Want to know what that is?" Dr. Denman laughed manically. "That, psionic, is Nightmare. He's still asleep. I take it P-31 did a runner, which means it's only a matter of time before Nightmare has another nightmare, and we get to share it too."

"We'll be dead long before that, Doctor," I replied evenly. It was almost worth it to know that he would share our fate.

"Oh, you mean the bomb?" said Dr. Denman, laughing again. "I can disable that from here. As for Nightmare, it's just a short walk down the stairs to his chamber, and then I can use my remote to wake him up."

"Then why don't you?"

"Why don't I?" he repeated mockingly. "Because it'd scare off your freak buddies and leave me in peace, that's why."

"Why did you bring Alia down here?"

"This little brat is more valuable than the lot of you put together," he sneered as he tightened his grip on Alia's shoulder. "Dead or alive, she stays."

"Five minutes to auto-destruct," said the computer.

Dr. Denman smirked. "You want me to disable the auto-destruct? Then here's how. Point that dangerous little finger at yourself, and die!"

"You released William!" I exclaimed.

"Not as dumb as you look, are you, psionic?"

"You don't care who dies, as long as you survive."

"Come on, I don't have all day. Kill yourself now, and I'll take good care of P-46."

"You coward!" I screamed furiously.

"Don't you dare take another step!" Dr. Denman yelled back, pressing the knife harder against Alia's neck. Blood started to trickle slowly out of the cut he made. Some of it dripped down onto Alia's shirt, and some ran down the side of the knife and onto Dr. Denman's right hand. Alia was clenching her teeth, refusing to scream.

The room started to vibrate again, though only a little.

I decided to chance it and kicked off lightly, hovering two feet over the trembling floor as I swiftly stretched my right arm forward with my palm open. I knew I didn't have time for a focused finger shot. All I needed to do was blast Dr. Denman away from Alia. I'd hit or at least graze Alia too, but I figured that as long as I didn't kill her, she could probably heal herself once I removed her control bands and wiped the blood off her skin.

The moment I fired, I saw Alia violently jerk herself away from Dr. Denman's grasp. The surgical knife made another thin line on her neck, but didn't draw much blood as Alia broke free. My blast hit Dr. Denman squarely in the chest, knocking him backwards and throwing the knife from his hands. I was pushed backwards too, but in the last two weeks, I had learned how not to fall out of the air doing this.

The tremor stopped. I landed and telekinetically pulled the knife into my right hand. The metal handle had been wrapped in surgical tape. Before I could lunge at Dr. Denman with it, however, Alia grabbed hold of me, wrapping her arms tightly around my waist.

I heard the computer declare that we were down to our last four minutes.

Dr. Denman had already picked himself up. He was breathing heavily, clutching his chest.

"You think this changes anything?" he leered. "I'm the only one who can shut the bomb off."

"So shut it off!" I shouted.

"Kill yourself and I'll think about it," said Dr. Denman, vigorously wiping his right hand on his pants to remove Alia's blood.

"Never thought a little blood would scare a doctor," I taunted. "But then again, you're not just any doctor."

"You have no idea."

"Oh, but I do," I said, looking deep into his eyes, because I finally did know. "You're a graviton!"

Dr. Denman froze. Then his thin pursed lips curled almost imperceptibly as his hawk-like eyes glared back at me. "Well, well, discovered at last," he said. "That's right, psionic, I am a graviton, and a fair hider too."

"What are you doing here, Doctor?" I asked quietly. "What are you doing at this facility?"

"What am I doing?!" roared Dr. Denman, his wrinkled old face contorting with rage. "I'm trying to find a cure to this insanity! People aren't supposed to be able to do these things!"

"You killed Dr. Kellogg!"

"He was in my way," said Dr. Denman, taking a step forward, "just like you are now. I am going to continue my work. You, psionic, cannot be a part of it anymore."

"Three minutes to auto-destruct," said the computer.

I knew Dr. Denman meant to kill me. There was no way for him to return to his work if I was alive, knowing he was psionic. Alia would have to die too.

I dropped the knife. Alia still had her arms around me, so I pulled her off and forced her down onto the floor. Then I turned to face Dr. Denman.

"You can't win, Doctor," I said as matter-of-factly as I could. "I won't let you touch me this time."

Dr. Denman's eyes glinted maliciously as he replied, "I didn't have to touch the ceiling when I killed Kellogg."

I tried to extend my arms toward him, but suddenly they became so heavy I couldn't lift them at all. My whole body was being pulled downwards. The weight wasn't just on top of me. The weight was in me. It was me. I felt like I was drowning in thick mud, barely able to move.

I had lost. Even if I could concentrate, there was no way to blast him at this distance without stretching my arms toward him, but by now I could barely tell my arms from the rest of my stone-like body. I fell to my knees and my vision started to become hazy.

Something white darted in front of me. I inhaled a huge gulp of air, and my vision cleared instantly. I looked at Dr. Denman, who was struggling with— Alia! He hit her hard across the face, sending her flying. Dr. Denman's face was streaked with Alia's blood where she had wiped it on him.

It wasn't enough to drain him completely. It wasn't enough to drain him much at all.

But it was enough.

Even as he refocused his power on me, I forced both of my arms up and blasted him hard. He was hurled backward, slammed into one of the whirring machines and slid down its side, his body limp. His power was completely broken, and I could stand again.

"A-yi!" Alia cried loudly, and an instant later she was in my arms, hugging me tightly.

"Two minutes to auto-destruct," said the mechanical voice.

I picked Alia up and carried her over to Dr. Denman, who was still faintly breathing. He was just knocked out. For a fleeting instant, I felt like blasting the life out of him, but there was enough of Cindy in me by now not to act on that kind of impulse. Besides, I knew that Dr. Denman, along with Alia and me, would be dead in just under two minutes anyway, and I had something much more important to do.

Setting Alia down, I quickly searched Dr. Denman's pockets and found his little white remote control. It was identical to the one Dr. Kellogg showed me on my first day here. I pushed 4-6-U, and Alia's control bands snapped open, falling to the floor. I threw the remote control into the air and blasted it into tiny pieces.

Then I helped wipe the blood off of Alia's neck and fingers, and the cuts on her neck disappeared before my eyes. I heard her quiet voice in my head say, *"I knew you'd come, Addy."*

I took her hand and led her away from Dr. Denman. We walked back toward the elevator. The cage door was still open, but there was no point in getting on. The computer announced, "One minute to auto-destruct."

Alia squeezed my hand tighter. I looked at her sadly, wondering if there really was an afterlife and whether I would see her there. This would probably have been the moment to say something deeply profound, but nothing came to mind.

"I'm sorry I was so late," I said.

"It's okay," said Alia as she smiled and hugged me again.

I thought about Cindy, and how she'd never see Alia or me again. I thought about Ralph, who had once tried to goad me into killing him, and realized I still hadn't figured that man out. I thought about Cat, who would live out her life as an Angel slave, perhaps someday having psionic powers of her own. I thought about Dr. Kellogg, who had died upstairs. "Get out, Adrian," he had said. "You don't belong here anyway."

But I did belong here. Mark knew it, and so did Cindy. I belonged with Alia. Here and now, that really was everything that mattered, and while that might be a far cry from living happily ever after, it was the very best I could ask for at such short notice.

"Addy, will it hurt us when we die?"

"No," I heard myself say as I held Alia closer, feeling her small heart beating rapidly against mine. "No, Ali, it won't hurt."

I wasn't counting the seconds, but I knew we had less than a handful left. I took one final deep breath, and closed my eyes.

18. NIGHTMARE

"Auto-destruct sequence malfunction. System disconnect," said the flat computer voice.

"Addy?"

I slowly opened my eyes. What had happened?

"Boom," said a cold voice in the distance.

Leaning heavily against the giant boiler, Dr. Denman was eyeing us malevolently.

"First thing I did when I got down here was disconnect the bomb," he said with a smirk. "When you lead a life like mine, you tend not to leave very much to chance."

But even as he said that, I thought I heard a distant howling sound deep below my feet, and the next instant, everything was moving.

It wasn't just vibrating anymore. The whole cavern was starting to twist as if it was made of rubber. All three of us were thrown to the floor. The tremor got worse and worse. I tried levitating myself off the floor, but this time the air was pulsing too, and I was rocked back and forth in midair, quickly losing my concentration. I could hardly believe that the machines and the elevator hadn't broken into a billion pieces, but everything was still intact.

What was this power that Nightmare had? I had destroyed the remote control, which meant Dr. Denman couldn't shock Nightmare awake even if he could somehow get down to the holding chamber below.

It didn't matter. If the elevator still worked, then now was our only chance. Alia and I were far closer to it than Dr. Denman, and he wouldn't be able to focus his power on us.

Stumbling over and over, I half-ran, half-crawled to the elevator, dragging Alia along with me. Alia was no longer just a helpless little girl, though. Sometimes she was pulling me.

We got into the elevator. I couldn't stand up, so I telekinetically pushed the "up" button. The door slid closed, and even though we were vibrating enough to knock a building down, the elevator crawled upwards.

The shaking was lesser on Level 10. We scrambled through the corridors to the main elevator, expecting at any moment to meet more doctors or guards. I froze once when I saw the wall-mounted automatic guns next to the elevator. They had been shut off when I was here earlier, but there was no way to know if it was still safe until we stepped in front of them.

They didn't fire. I pushed the button next to the elevator, and the doors slid open at once. Ralph must have sent the car back down after he had reached Level 2.

The shaking was getting worse here now, and the structure was no longer unaffected by it. The walls bent inwards, then outwards. The whole facility was twisting in on itself.

The elevator doors closed, and we were rising. It might have only been half a minute, but as I watched the elevator walls start to buckle, expecting the cable to break and send us plunging to our deaths at any moment, it was as agonizing as the time I spent being tortured by the Wolf.

The doors finally slid open and we ran out of the elevator. There was an enormous, solid metal gate in front of us, but it was half open and we sprinted through, again feeling the floor start to shake. What was happening below us?

I looked around. There were passages leading every which way. Level 2 was bigger than I expected.

"Addy, this way!"

Alia was tugging on my hand. Had she been awake when she was brought in? There were dead bodies lying around here too, but we took little notice as we ran, Alia pulling me along as fast as she could. Two corridors and a flight of stairs later, we were in what looked a bit like the reception hall of a big hospital. This was Level 1, which was still underground. Where was the exit?

"Over here!" said Alia as she pulled me through a large doorway.

I looked around at the room we had entered. It was a medium-size circular space with no furniture and no other exits.

"This is a dead end, Ali," I said, wondering if perhaps we were going to die here after all.

Alia let go of my hand and pushed one of three small buttons on the wall. I felt the entire room start to rise up like an elevator. A few seconds later, a soft breeze blew in through the doorway from which we had entered, bringing with it the heavenly scent of clean, cool night air.

We stepped out.

Dawn was still a long way off, but the night was clear and the moonlight softly illuminated the grassy field where we found ourselves. It was Derrick's dream field, though the grass here was green and not as tall. There was not a single house, streetlamp, or anything manmade giving off light in any direction as far as the eye could see. The entrance room quietly descended back into the earth, leaving us in the middle of nowhere.

The ground started to quiver slightly. Nightmare was still down there. I grabbed Alia's left hand, hoping to run far from Nightmare's power. The direction didn't matter on an open plain. We just had to get going.

I heard Alia shout in my head, *"Addy! Look!"*

I followed Alia's pointing finger with my eyes, at first mistaking the light in the sky for a bright star. As I looked closer, however, I realized that it was a massive military helicopter. It wasn't a gunship, but I figured a transport like that out here could only mean a pack of Wolves.

"Come on, Ali!" I shouted, frantically tugging on her arm, but she resisted.

"It's Cindy!"

The ground was really starting to shake now, and the soft earth felt like it was liquefying beneath our feet. The helicopter swooped low, bearing down on us at full tilt. I could see the people in the cockpit now too. In addition to two helmeted pilots, there was a figure crouched between them and looking out at us. Even at this distance, I could easily make out her long silvery hair shining in the moonlight.

As the helicopter hovered overhead with its side door open, I levitated Alia aboard, and then propelled myself into the cabin too.

I couldn't make everyone out in the dim cabin light, but there must have been at least a dozen people including Mr. Koontz and Janice, whose white clothes I could easily identify. I saw another familiar face grinning at me: Mark Parnell.

Mark slid the cabin door shut, and I felt the helicopter lurch forward. Ralph, who was piloting the huge transport, flew us in a wide half-circle around the site.

Pressing my nose to the cabin window, I watched in stunned horror as the ground below us quickly became a churning vortex of mud and slime, swirling deeper in on itself until only a dark gaping hole was left in the ground. I half-expected Nightmare to appear out of the abyss, but that didn't happen. To this day, I don't know anything more about Nightmare than I've already said, though I still have nightmares about him sometimes.

Turning my face away from the scene below, I saw Cindy. She was holding Alia and looking at me in the gentle way I had so sorely missed, her eyes quiet and understanding.

I opened my mouth, but the words failed me.

What do you say to someone who risked everything to save your life? "Thank you"? What do you say to someone whose love you rejected in selfish arrogance? "I'm sorry"? What do you say to someone who can forgive your betrayal in a heartbeat? What do you say to someone like Cynthia Gifford?

As I stared down at the cabin floor, unable to put into words all that I felt and all that I wanted to say to her, I felt her arms around me. Cindy may well have been a delver reading my mind, because she whispered softly, "Don't say anything, Adrian. Don't say anything."

19. THE LONG ROAD AHEAD

As dawn broke over the hazy, violet horizon, Ralph set the helicopter down next to our getaway car, which was parked in a little forest clearing near a deserted, backcountry road. Cindy could hide us from other psionics even in the air, but the government would probably notice a stolen military helicopter in the daytime sky. Our getaway car, however, turned out to be a psychedelically patterned bright yellow minibus that reminded me of Cat's crazy pillow. The only way in which it didn't stand out was that it couldn't fly.

Mark drove, and Cindy introduced me to the team that saved us. The Guardians' leader was not Ralph, but a lean and muscular man in his late forties named Travis Baker, and he was a healer like Alia. Once Cindy had finished with the introductions, Mr. Baker nodded to her, and she seemed to know what she was expected to say.

"Adrian, you know I could never have gotten you out of there by myself," Cindy began carefully, and I guessed what this was leading to.

"If you mean that I have to join the Guardians..." I said, but Mr. Baker lifted a hand to stop me.

Shaking his head, the Guardian leader said lightly, "Oh, you don't have to join us, Adrian. Not at all." He threw a side-long glance at Ralph and chuckled. "In fact, I doubt very much we could take you by force even if we wanted to."

Ralph shot me a nasty look, and I returned an equally nasty smirk. Well, at least we weren't trying to kill each other anymore.

"Adrian," continued Cindy, "I'm going to rejoin the Guardians. That's the agreement I made with Travis and Ralph in exchange for their help."

I opened my mouth to protest, but Cindy cut me off, saying, "Please don't feel guilty about it! It was my choice. I'm taking Alia with me, and Mark is coming too, until we can find some way to hide him from the Wolves."

"And don't you go feeling guilty about me either," Mark called back from the driver's seat.

I did feel guilty. I had given the Wolves Cindy's real name. I had told them about her connection to Mark Parnell. I knew that it would be very difficult for Cindy and Mark to safely settle down again. But, as with all of the many mistakes I had made, I knew I couldn't undo what I had done. All I could do was try to make up for it. I didn't even want to hear Cindy ask.

"I'll come with you," I said quickly. "I'll join."

"Excellent!" said Mr. Baker, clasping my shoulder. "Welcome to the Guardians, Adrian. I do hope you won't be disappointed."

"I've been very impressed so far," I said.

Mr. Baker smiled. "Cindy here has told me that you want to save your sister from the Angels. I can't promise you that we'll make it our top priority, but God willing, we may be able to help you get her back."

I gaped at him. Despite what I had once said to Cindy, I never seriously believed that the Guardians would help me retrieve Cat from the Angels. If I had, I might have joined them for that reason alone.

In a way, I was glad I hadn't believed it. Cat was already family, flesh and blood. But Cindy and Alia were family too, and joining the Guardians with them made a lot of sense to me.

"So, Adrian," Cindy said brightly, "we have another long road ahead, and I want to hear all about your adventures over the last few months."

"Right this instant?" I asked, my exhaustion from the previous night finally catching up with me. Alia was already asleep on her seat, leaning against what I recognized with a smile as her old unicorn.

"It can wait," said Cindy. "Give it to me little by little. For now, at least you can tell me what happened in town."

I had to think about that for a moment. What town?

"Oh!" I said, finally remembering. "You mean the mystery graviton."

"So, did you find him?" asked Cindy. "Who was he?"

"He was a she," I replied quietly.

"Ah... And what happened?"

"Nothing..." I muttered.

Cindy raised her eyebrows. "Adrian?"

"Okay! She crashed into me on a bicycle, glued me to the sidewalk, threatened me and went on her merry way. Happy?"

Cindy giggled. I looked away embarrassedly, and she burst out laughing.

"Always a pleasure to amuse," I said, rolling my eyes.

"I'm just glad you're okay, Adrian," said Cindy, extending her hand to me. "Friends?"

I shook it.

This pentalogy will continue right where it left off in

Adrian Howell's

PSIONIC

Book Two

The Tower

About the Author

Born of a Japanese mother and American father, Adrian Howell (pen name) was raised for a time in California and currently lives a quiet life in Japan where he teaches English to small groups of children and adults. Aside from reading and writing fiction, his hobbies include recumbent cycling, skiing, medium-distance trekking, sketching and oversleeping.

Send comments and questions to the author at:
adrianhowellbooks@gmail.com

Adrian Howell's PSIONIC
Book One: Wild-born
First Edition

All characters, places and events in this work are fictitious. Any resemblance to actual events, locations, organizations, real persons, living, dead or yet to be born, is purely coincidental.

Copyright © 2009 by Adrian Howell

All Rights Reserved. No part of this book may be reproduced or transmitted in any form or by any means, electronic, mechanical or psionic, including photocopying, recording, telepathy, dreamweaving, and information storage and retrieval systems without the permission of the author, except in the case of a reviewer, who may quote brief passages embodied in critical articles and reviews.

CPSIA information can be obtained at www.ICGtesting.com
Printed in the USA
LVOW10s1448100315

429950LV00002B/338/P

9 781482 349023

Adrian Howell's
PSIONIC

Book One
Wild-born

WITHDRAWN
5555 S. 77th St.
Ralston, NE 68127

Copyright © 2009 Adrian Howell (LP.141204)

All rights reserved.

Cover Design: Pintado (rogerdespi.8229@gmail.com)

ISBN: **1482349027**
ISBN-13: 978-1482349023

WWAADHTIW
Ralston, NE 68127